THRESHER

MICHAEL COLE

SEVERED PRESS
HOBART TASMANIA

THRESHER

CHAPTER 1

Cracks of thunder pounded the chaotic night sky, scrambled with the endless howling of the hundred-thirty-seven mile per hour wind. The sky was a dark black, and the Atlantic Ocean was an ugly reflective grey. The sea rose, forming monstrous mountains of water, which fell upon themselves and rose again. Lightning zigzagged in every direction, illuminating the black clouds above. Each bolt was in perfect form, as if Zeus himself had crafted each one and angrily hurled them towards the abyss. It was as if the sea and the heavens had declared war on each other.

Hurricane Deckard was inaccurately forecasted to be a Category 2 storm that would lose strength as it neared North America. After forming off the coast of Mauritania near Cape Verde, it moved westward toward Puerto Rico, where it upgraded to a Category 3. Meteorologists forecasted that it would lose strength in that area after making landfall over Cuba, and possibly fall down to a Category 1 by the time it would make landfall into the Gulf of Mexico. However, when the strengthening storm reached the Caribbean, strong winds from the south collided with Deckard. This resulted in the storm hooking north, where it would graze the Florida and Georgia coastline before it would finally make landfall in New England.

From high above, the orange and white U.S. Coast Guard rescue helicopter resembled a tiny dragonfly struggling to hover over a vast pot of boiling water. Beneath it was a white speck of equal size, bobbing in the frantic waves. That white speck was the *Abigail Twain*, a twenty-three-foot sailing yacht bound to Georgia from the Bahamas. The owner and the crew hoped to get out of Marsh Harbor and be close enough to St. Simon's Island off the Georgia Coast, and hopefully only catch the rough edges of the storm. However, like everyone else, they didn't expect the storm to sweep northward. They initially tried to drive through the storm to port, but the current was more than they could handle. To make matters worse, a massive wave caused the Captain to fall and hit his head on the foot of the sail. Unable to manage the rough seas, and still over forty miles from the coast, the remaining crew called out a mayday signal.

Lieutenant Ron Park had successfully landed on the deck of the *Abigail Twain*, despite the intense winds attempting to carry him away like a kite as he descended down the parachute line. His orange rescue jumpsuit stood out heavily against the dark atmosphere. The illumination cast upon him from the chopper's spotlight gave him an angelic appearance as he was lowered. At thirty-five years of age, fifteen of which spent in the Coast Guard, he had done over two hundred rescues at sea, with a total of one hundred-thirty-three rescue drops. High wind descents were always the worst. Usually he would instruct the sailors to put on life vests and jump into the water, that way he could avoid getting tangled in the mast. However, he was uncertain of the severity of the captain's condition, and determined the best course of action would be an attempt to land on deck. Park had successfully strapped the injured captain to a harness, and the rescue team winched him aboard the chopper. After the rescue harness was returned, he had strapped it onto the female crewmember. The last remaining crewmember, Steven, had insisted she go ahead of him.

Park motioned to his spotter on the chopper to begin the hoist by raising his clenched hand and pointing his thumb up. The winch reeled, and the crewmember lifted off the deck. She and her cable were viciously tugged by the wind as she was elevated thirty feet above the yacht. The pilot struggled to keep the chopper steady, but the high winds made that nearly impossible. Park could see the chopper rocking in the air, as if teetering on an invisible fulcrum. His radio unit installed in his helmet squealed with static for a moment.

"Lieutenant! The turbulence is increasing. I can't hold position much longer!" the pilot informed him. His voice was calm and didn't show alarm, but Park had been in the U.S.C.G long enough to know that hidden behind that calm was a man eager to get out of this storm. It was a warranted feeling, and he needed a plan to speed up the process. He looked at Steven, who stood soaking wet and eager for his turn. He was a short man, maybe five-foot-six, and fairly skinny. He was wearing a yellow shirt and cargo shorts, which wouldn't add much weight. Park himself was an average size man, so he knew the hoist should have no problem holding the weight of both of them.

"Listen!" Park had to yell to get his voice heard over the intense howl of the wind. "We're having trouble maintaining position! We don't have a lot of time, so here's what we're gonna have to do..." he paused to make sure Steven could understand him. "We're gonna go up at the same time. I'm gonna clip your harness to mine, and we'll be lifted at once." Steven listened as he struggled against the wind to stay on his feet.

"Okay!" he answered. Park looked back up and saw the passenger safely loaded into the helicopter. He waited for a count of ten, ample time for them to free her of the rescue harness, and signaled for them to lower it back down—holding his closed hand up and pointing his thumb down. The cable began its descent, and already the wind took hold of it. The cable reached out at a forty-five-degree angle, and the pilot had the task of positioning the helicopter to allow the attached harness to be within Park's reach. It took several attempts, but he finally managed to grab hold of it. Immediately he clipped the cable to a ring on his own harness. He looked to Steven.

"Alright, let's go!" The chopper repositioned and shone its bright spotlight upon the lieutenant. With the pilot struggling to keep it steady, the light often would zigzag on and off of them, shining into the rough sea for moments at a time.

****

The enormous beast struggled against the current that carried its massive bulk to a destination unknown to it. Rapid currents assaulted its senses as it attempted to idle its body, only to be pushed along by the chaotic direction of the water it lived in. The fish survived every challenge nature threw its way, and this involved previous storms. But this time it was caught further out from its normal hunting grounds, and now it was stuck in a current that was even mightier than itself. In addition, the shark had no choice but to continue moving, or else suffer the consequence of sinking to its death. Sharks' livers provided aide, but they could not float like bony fish. Fighting to continue keeping water flowing through its five gills required it to spend a lot of energy. Its enormous mass added to the ordeal. The creature didn't care about the hurricane, nor did it care about the destination it would end up. It needed one thing: it needed to feed.

The crashing waves around it played havoc on the sensory organs that made up its lateral line. There was much vibration in the water, but hardly any of it could be perceived as struggling prey. Its sense of smell had trouble picking up anything. Plenty of water made its way through its nostrils, but even the fragment of a scent that could indicate prey was untraceable. Ironically, it was the sense used the least that gave the shark a possible target. Its eyes caught the glimpse of lights flickering in the water above. These lights were unlike the other lights created by the storm, which were random and dim. These lights were much brighter and focused, in a steady stream, and concentrated on one basic area. The shark moved its enormous caudal fin and arched its body upward to point its large black eyes toward the point of interest. The lights brought form to a shape that floated on the surface. The shark was uncertain if the object above was living prey, due to the fact that its other senses were compromised at the moment. It was close enough to see that it was a large object, though a bit smaller than itself. The movements were rigid, as if it was in distress.

Hunger dictated the massive shark's actions. It believed that the object above was food. With several thrusts of its enormous tail, it moved like a homing missile towards the target. Its eyes rolled back, resembling white marbles against its dark green skin. Its jaw opened, bearing three-inch jagged teeth. In a straight line, it struck from beneath.

****

Park had just gotten the harness around Steven's arms and legs, and was about to clip it onto the cable when suddenly a tremendous impact shook the yacht from beneath. Both men fell to their hands and knees, unsure of what just happened. They didn't have time to regain their posture, as a tremendous wave immediately slammed into the portside. Already unstable from the impact from below, the *Abigail Twain* gave in to the rolling mountain of water that rolled it starboard.

Park didn't have time to warn Steven of what was happening, and the action they needed to take. Truthfully, even he was caught off guard by the current predicament. The vessel groaned as it rolled, and finally water filled the deck. Steven wanted to scream but didn't have time. He and Park were quickly under water, being sucked downward by the pressure caused by the vessel as its mast crashed nearby. Water filled the cabin, and remaining sections below deck, causing the boat to sink. Park opened his eyes, and through the sting of the salty water he found Steven sinking a few feet to his left. He grabbed down for him, and grabbed fists full of his shirt to pull him closer. As he did so, their heads banged together, creating a nosebleed from Steven.

Onboard the rescue chopper, Ensign Wells witnessed his superior officer plunge beneath the thrashing water, followed by the mast of the boat coming down on top of them. He grabbed the side of the door to keep from falling out, as the chopper dipped due to the wind pressure. The two passengers were secured by straps in their seats behind him. The captain was still unconscious, but the other passenger helplessly yelled as they dropped uncontrollably. An alarm sounded from the pilot's controls, and the operator gritted his teeth as he struggled to maintain control. The chopper dropped a dozen feet before he regained full control. He quickly put his hand to his microphone.

"Lieutenant, we can't hold position! We have to go!" There was no immediate response, and there was no time to wait. He looked back to Ensign Wells. "Reel him up! We've got to go!"

****

The shark determined that the mysterious object was not nutritious, and quickly regurgitated the substance. However, its Ampullae of Lorenzini suddenly picked up electromagnetic signals of two struggling life forms nearby. The signals were strong enough for the shark to discern from motions caused by the large object it had bitten into. It circled around to create some distance, and positioned itself to face the direction of the target. Its sense of smell picked up a very particular scent. The smell of blood. To the massive shark, it was confirmation that these were fleshy targets. The light shone upon them from above, allowing the shark to see what it was approaching. For it, these were two bite sized prey, but it would be enough to satisfy its bodily needs. It swam forward until it was within range. It would follow its instinctual procedure of stunning before moving in for the kill.

The shark tilted its head slightly upward and tucked its pectoral fins below its stomach. It moved under the thrashing targets, and at lightning speed it whipped the scythe shaped upper lobe of its caudal fin, striking both targets at once.

****

Park didn't know what hit him. He struggled to reach the cable clip to Steven's harness, and nearly made the connection when a horrific streak of pain flooded his nervous system, and almost all physical control was taken away from him. He was still alive, but could not move. He looked at Steven, who also appeared immobile. The flashlight from Park's uniform shone onto the paralyzed sailor, who drifted away from him. His eyes were bulged, and his arms were reached out as if the need to survive still persisted. But the current pulled him out of reach. Park then could feel the tug of his own harness, and recognized the sensation as being hoisted up by the chopper.

His eyes were still fixed on Steven. Park could still see him, but the view dimmed as he lifted toward the surface. There was something else there, something moving in behind Steven like a monstrous shadow. Torpedo shaped, the form covered all of the background behind him. The next thing Park witnessed was Steven, still alive, disappearing into a dark abyss lined with monstrous teeth that reflected his flashlight. And then he was gone.

Park couldn't speak as he was hauled aboard the chopper. He hung on his strap, barely able to move his arms. He couldn't feel his legs. He knew they were there, but it was as if they weren't. Ensign Wells frantically pulled him into the body of the aircraft, and slammed the sliding doors home. The pilot heard that familiar sound, and operated the aircraft to move to the nearby cutter. The passengers protested about leaving Steven behind, but Wells ignored their cries as he tended to Park. Blood seeped out of an enormous laceration along the small of his back. He rolled the lieutenant to his side, and pulled away at the clothing to assess the wound. It ran straight across, inches deep. A wave of anxiety struck Wells, inducing a mild sensation of nausea. The injury was undeniably severe, and it was clear that Park was immobilized.

"He must have been hit by the mast!" Wells yelled to the pilot. "Get us back quick!" He quickly broke out the emergency kit to control the bleeding. Park laid motionless on the steel floor. His mind was not on his critical injury, the likely end of his career in the Coast Guard, or even the chopper's struggle to make it back through the intense storm. His mind was fixated on the image of Steven disappearing into those enormous jaws.

"Shark!" he whispered. Wells didn't pay any attention as he rushed to stop the bleeding.

"Shh, don't talk," he said.

CHAPTER 2

The storm continued its rampage northward, following a path that would bring it to landfall in New England. As it did, the edge of the storm swept along the southern states. For the residents living around the coast of Florida, this was nothing more than just an ordinary nasty storm. Beaches were clear, and residents had taken certain necessary precautions. But there was no storm surge, and no flooding. Winds were strong and the rain was heavy, but it was nothing the region hadn't dealt with before.

For the coastal township of Merit, this was also the case. It was a Sunday night, and people were more concerned about the beginning of the NFL season than wind damage. Merit was a small town consisting of fifty-five square miles, holding a population of slightly over forty-three thousand residents. Like much of Florida, it was a spectacular vacationing area. Merit had newsworthy golden beaches, and was renowned for its fishing and sailing charters. Its main attraction, Merit Beach, stretched for seven beautiful miles, with a large port on the northern side. Businesses lined the upper parts of the shore, and the town itself was a strong business center. Brand new restaurants had opened over the late summer, all set and ready for the next season's bringing known as the autumn crowd. Sadly, among tourists it often went unnoticed. The town didn't completely rely on revenue from tourism, as there were plenty of local customers to keep the economy healthy. However, the township business owners always beseeched their local government to raise tourist awareness for the area, which would increase economic prosperity. But hardly anything was ever done in the past few years. It was believed that distractions brought by physical ailments within the Mayor's family were the root of this.

However, a hot moment of prosperity was approaching for the local business owners within the next week. Merit was about to be put on the map in a special way. The National Association of Sailing declared the Adult National Championship Sailing race to take place off the port of Merit, Florida. This was a championship that would bring all sorts of media attention. This race included over one hundred and fifty participants whose goal would be to set sail from Port Merit all the way to the Bahamas and return. A grand prize would be awarded to the participants in first place, and other prizes awarded to those in second and third place. In addition to those involved in the race, there would be the added population of family members, coaches, media, and other spectators that would stay around Merit as the competitors worked their way back.

The states along the northeast coast were currently bracing for the surprise landfall by Hurricane Deckard. For the residents of Merit, it was a blessing in disguise. For them, this wasn't just another bad storm, it was horrible timing. It was initially predicted that the storm's trajectory would put it into the Gulf of Mexico, and would've engulfed the entire state. The flooding and property damage would likely have delayed, or worse – canceled the big event. Hotels were already booked, as well as beach houses being leased. Those visitors would arrive around the upcoming weekend, and business owners were rushing to prep for the crowds.

One such business was a bar called the Shallow Reef. Built with stretching bond brick and asphalt shingles, the outside shape of the building resembled a large house than a bar. Bright blue letters over the front entrance hung that spelled the words *Shallow Reef.* On the front window was an electric sign spelling OPEN in bright red letters. The lights stood out in the dark stormy evening. Behind the building was a long stretch of beach, and a distant view of a thrashing ocean. The inside of the bar was not a busy site, even for 8:30 P.M. on Sunday night. All of the dining tables were empty. Three individuals were grouped by a pool table, and one man sat alone at the bar counter, drinking whiskey while staring at the weather broadcast on T.V. The owner was taking advantage of the slow hours by inventorying his supplies.

At the pool table, two men were in the middle of a game, while a third bald individual sat at an empty table nearest to them. He was a fairly large man, wearing a black long sleeve shirt under a brown leather vest and blue jeans. His two friends at the pool table chatted about their wives and their jobs. They each had a bottle of beer balancing at the edge of the table. The bald fellow sat by himself, left out, forced to listen to the sound of the balls cracking together. However, it wasn't their game he was eyeballing, rather it was the beverages.

"Hey!" he called out to his friends. His voice was naturally loud. Both the men at the table looked at him.

"You do realize we're only ten feet away from you, right?" one of them said. The bald fellow ignored the complaint.

"What would shut me up is a drink, man!" Both his friends looked up to the ceiling, simultaneously exclaiming "ugh!" All evening he had been pestering them to buy him a beer, or a shot of whiskey, or a scotch—whichever he thought of at that particular moment. He had no job, nor did he have any money. The worst part was he also had no shame. He used to work in construction, until he was fired...for drinking on the job no less. The other two were happy to continue their friendship with him, but they weren't going to indulge him.

"I swear this is the hundredth time you've bugged us about this," one of them said. "Well, this will also feel like the hundredth time I've told you—you want a beer, get a job and buy yourself one. Neither of us will do it." The bald fellow stood up. He wasn't being threatening. He wanted a drink, not a fight. His friends knew that while he was imperfect, he never seemed violent. However, he was damn annoying.

"Just one beer! That's all!"

"No! That's all!" his friends responded. There was an exaggerated moan of displeasure as the bald fellow turned away. He had finally learned there wouldn't be any headway in getting his buddies to subsidize his drinking. He looked around the room, hoping to find another possible sponsor. He saw the owner was back behind the counter at the far end, counting supplies. Obviously, he wasn't the right candidate. The only other person he saw was the fellow sitting at the counter watching the news. *Why not,* he thought. He went and approached the individual and took a seat off to his right, leaving one empty stool between them. He eyeballed the patron and evaluated his chances of the guy being a good sport and buying him a drink. He was an average sized man with a fairly muscular build, wearing blue jeans and a blue denim jacket covering a black shirt, along with black Roper cowboy boots. On the counter in front of him was a fourteen-ounce glass and a bottle of Jim Beam Kentucky Straight, three-fourths empty. He leaned towards him, resting his elbow on the counter.

"Hey buddy?" he called out in a friendly voice. His grin was like a shark tracking down easy prey. However, this didn't turn out to be so easy. The patron did not seem to notice him. The bald man tried again. "Hey pal, could you spare a drink for a pal?"

Leonard Riker took no notice of the large, bald individual sitting to his right. He filled his glass halfway full with bourbon, and began chugging it down as he had done over a dozen times prior. He watched the weather reporter comment on Hurricane Deckard. He couldn't have cared less about the storm's development, but it was something to keep his mind distracted. The bourbon served the same purpose. And it was having an effect, but not to the level he needed it to. A few months prior, he would already be passed out at this point. Like with everything else, the human body builds up a tolerance. The slight feeling of sleepiness that acted like a fog in his active mind was a welcome feeling. He justified it to himself—not that he just needed it, but deserved what he was doing to himself. It certainly helped to block out the squawking voice of the bald idiot nearby- an added bonus. He took another swallow and shut his eyes, embracing the burn down his throat. He then leaned toward the table and rested his chin on his fist. He opened his eyes and watched the television some more. The news channel changed their coverage to football. It was the first week of the NFL season, and the news anchor began going over the wins and losses of the day. Although the T.V. set was only about ten feet away, the anchor's voice sounded as if it were coming from outside. It was the same for the person pestering him. Riker didn't care. He filled his glass again and took in the drink.

"Damn! I gotta hand it to you, buddy! To drink all that and not be passed out on the floor, you've got to have brass balls," the man persisted. Riker tilted his head to glance at him within his peripheral vision, without actually looking right at him. He then redirected his attention to the T.V. and his drink. The bottle was getting close to empty. The next swallow Riker took was deliberately to block out the bald guy's nagging. "Hey man, it's not polite to ignore people," he continued.

"Try a welfare office," Riker mumbled.

"What'd you say?!" the bald man called out. The friends called to him from the pool table, telling him to leave Riker alone. The freeloader turned his attention toward them. Riker ignored them all, barely even taking in the argument that was starting. He instead focused hard on shielding his mind from something deep within. It was a terrible torture, a psychological pain that he tried to drown out, and it was continuously climbing to the surface of his conscience. He kept his eyes on the newscast. After a report on something political, the channel went to commercial break. The first commercial was an advertisement for a new truck. He didn't even pay attention to the brand. He also barely noticed the second commercial, which was for a new restaurant opening in Miami. Then the next commercial came on. The female narration broke through the fogginess he felt in his head with ease: *Marriage is meant to be joyous. We think it's all about happiness and companionship. But sometimes the bond is weakened, and the joy turns into sadness. But rather than explain why marriages fail, we put our efforts into saving them. If you and your spouse are going through a struggle, but are not sure if divorce is the answer, see Katherine at K-Counselors. Located in*

Melbourne." He didn't care what was advertised, but the words he heard tore open the floodgates constructed by alcohol, and the raging river of anger came splashing. As a physical reflex, he squeezed his glass…until cracks lined up and down the sides. He let go before it could explode into a thousand pieces. His blood pressure skyrocketed. His heart rate increased. He grinded his teeth together, and he let go of the neck of the Jim Beam bottle, before he would hurl it and shatter the T.V. screen. This was not the first instance he felt this meltdown billowing within him. And in the past, it caused other problems. Despite his inhibition lowered by both the intense sudden rage, emotional pain, and the heavy intake of alcohol, he barely had enough self-control to leave. He left money on the counter for the drink before standing up. He began walking toward the door, stepping past the bald man.

The bald fellow stopped his conversation with his other buddies when he saw Riker heading for the door. His hotheadedness got the best of him and he stood up from his stool.

"Hey pal! You too good to lend me a few bucks for a beer?" There was no response. He walked after Riker, putting his right hand on his left shoulder to turn him around. "I'm talking to-" he stopped midsentence, caught off guard by the sensation of cracking bones within his fingers. Riker had reached his right hand across, clenched the offender's unwelcome hand, and squeezed. He turned around to face the bald man, who had fallen to his knees at this point. Riker squeezed tighter, and felt his left hand clench into a tight fist. The bald man, already rife with intense pain, noticed this. "Hey, I didn't want trouble! Honest... OW!" He tried to pry Riker's grip off with his other hand, but it was no good.

His two friends saw what was going on, and they approached with cue sticks in hand. But a deathly cold glare from the average sized man who had effortlessly brought their bulky friend to his knees stopped them in their tracks. They saw the large red scar that ran above his left eye down to his jaw. They didn't know who he was, but they weren't messing with him.

"I'm sorry," the man continued, "I just wanted a drink, was all. I wasn't trying to be a bother, I just wanted a drink!" Tears formed in his eyes at this point. Any fight he had in him was gone. Even seeing this, Riker's inner rage demanded he finish him off. Instead, he let go. The bald man exasperated in relief, and clutched his hand with his other. The other two kept their distance. Behind the counter, the owner watched in shock. He'd seen plenty of bar brawls, but he never saw a man of such bulk be overcome so easily and simply. Riker looked at the owner, and dug his wallet out of his jeans pocket. He placed a twenty-dollar bill on the counter top.

"Get him a beer," Riker said before turning around. The door shut behind him, nearly held open by the strong winds blowing in from the sea.

****

The drive from Shallow Reef to Riker's house was only about a half mile. The sound of two trashcans getting smashed by the front of his GMC Terrain signaled his arrival. He stumbled out of his car, not even parked on the pavement of his driveway, and fought against the wind toward his front door. The rain came down in a torrential downpour and lightning flickered throughout the black clouded sky. The ocean was in view past a neighboring property, and the waters were thrashing. But this storm was pale to the one raging within Leonard Riker. He slammed the door open and staggered into the entry hallway. On the first right was the living room, and the end of the hallway led to the kitchen. Supporting himself against the wall, Riker made his way there. His foot bumped into a full cardboard box that had spilled over from a pile at the edge of the living room. He kicked it aside, causing the opening to unfold and its contents to spill. The living room consisted of a large sofa on the side wall, and a seventy-inch flat-screen at the back wall. The rest of the room was jam packed with boxes from the recent move. Despite being at this residence for several days, they remained unpacked.

Riker stepped into the kitchen and went directly for the refrigerator. There were three shelves. The top only had a few slices of cheese, and a pack of lunch meat. There weren't even any bread slices anywhere to go with them. The middle shelf was completely empty. The bottom shelf, however, was loaded with beer. Beer and nothing else. He grabbed a bottle and twisted off the cap. He was already halfway done with it when he went into the living room. He maneuvered around the boxes and fell onto the sofa, nearly planting his face into the cushion. He kept the bottleneck facing up. He repositioned himself to sit normally and took a chug. As he did this, he heard a thud on the carpeted floor from something that had fallen off the sofa. He quickly leaned down, and found the item he knocked over. It was an 8x5 framed picture. In it was a beautiful green summer background. In the middle was a wooden bench, and sitting on one side was a woman. She had black hair that fell to her neck, wore a red flannel shirt and blue jeans. But what stood out the most was her beautiful smile as she looked toward the camera.

Riker gazed at the gorgeous woman. His eyes welled up and the storm within him raged. It was a strange mixture of sadness, regret, and severe anger. He brushed his finger over the beautiful woman's face, as if stroking her hair. And after several minutes, he laid the picture down beside him. He finished off his beer, attempting to shield the pain he was feeling. That pain built up into rage. That kind of anger one feels when something they love is taken away. It was a pain that couldn't be measured. He threw his bottle into the hallway. It bounced off the wall and crashed onto the floor. It divided into several large pieces of glass, which mostly settled around the spilled contents of the open box. Among those contents were a couple of sympathy cards, another picture frame laying facedown, and a folded newspaper. The side facing up revealed a list of obituaries. There were only a few. On the top of the page was the name of Martha Riker. Her obituary was short and standard. Beneath it there was a special note in italics that read: *In lieu of flowers, donations can be made to the American Foundation for Suicide Prevention.*

CHAPTER 3

Monday morning brought better weather. The sea had calmed down after the storm moved northward. The wind was still blowing hard, but not as bad. The sky was still dark and gloomy, but the rain had reduced to a steady drizzle. It was nothing that would keep the residents from starting their work week. There were few reports of property damage and flooding.

Chief Raymond Crawford of the Merit Police Department was grateful for this. The aftermath of a hurricane often resulted in mass looting. It was his third week in this department, and he wanted things to continue running smoothly. With his scrawny build, he didn't look like much. However, at sixty-one years of age and thirty-six of those years on the police force, he had seen it all. He began as a patrol officer and worked his way up through the ranks. Over his career, he led detective divisions, worked with and led S.W.A.T. teams, got promoted to Deputy Chief, and eventually Chief of Police. All of this was in his home city of Alton, Illinois.

Cities such as Detroit, New York, and Los Angeles often got notoriety for being areas of intense crime. The city of Alton was one city that never got the media attention. Criminals owned the streets. Most of the city's police were unnerved by the job. Shootings were everyday occurrences, and underground crime gave organization and political power to the corrupt. Turnover in the local PD was so high that the city had no choice but to recruit new officers and put them through the academy. Crawford had dedicated his life to turning that city around, but each time he put a criminal away two more would appear. Most of the police were good, honest officers, but they didn't share in the vision he had. He came to realize it was a battle he wasn't going to win, and working in Alton had done enough damage to his psyche and health. The time had come where he faced the fact that he didn't want to spend his remaining years in a city that was destroying itself. The passing of his wife was the final straw. She was a woman of strength, and had spent her whole life supporting his mission. From his five years of service in the

U.S. Air Force, through his tenure as Police Chief, she understood and backed his desire to make the world a better place. The cancer never lowered her spirits, but it gave her one desire which she voiced to Crawford: to find happiness. He honored her request, and the first way to accomplish that was to get out of Alton.

Merit lived up to its name. While it had its share of wrongdoers, the overall crime rate was remarkably low. There were no shootings and stabbings occurring on a daily basis. People actually smiled as they walked along the street. Kids seemed to enjoy going to school, and just as remarkably, the teachers appeared to enjoy teaching. It was the peaceful life he had been craving, and it was the kind of place his late wife had dreamed of living in. It was the first time in his long career in law enforcement where he was not burdened by heavy stress. It was a feeling he welcomed, and somewhat regretted not seeking it earlier in life.

Crawford stood in the briefing room of the MPD headquarters. The room was arranged like a college classroom, with tables lined up in rows facing a podium. The time was seven-thirty in the morning, thirty minutes before shift change. The room was currently empty. He held a cup of coffee in his hand, black with two sugars. Normally he arrived a quarter to eight, giving him enough time to communicate concerns with the midnight shift commander. He usually left the briefings to the shift commanders, and only attended ones in which he had information to pass down. As he sipped on his coffee, he saw the door in the back of the room open and the first officer of the shift arrived for duty.

Rookie officers often arrived extra early in their first weeks of duty. Allison Metzler was no exception. Dressed in the black trousers, greenish tan uniform shirt, and black regulation tactical boots, she demonstrated great pride to begin her first day on the job. Her red hair hung straight to her shoulders and her figure was somewhere between petite and athletic. She looked slightly younger than her age of twenty-eight. Metzler had qualifications far beyond the standards of a two-year degree and a police academy completion certificate. Her background included a Bachelor's degree in Forensic Science, a second Bachelor's in Criminal Science, and a Master's Degree in Psychology. She pursued this level of education with the belief she wanted to counsel people in need, with a primary focus on police officers in distress. In order to do so, she would have to continue graduate school and obtain a doctorate degree.

In a sudden change of pace, she joined the police academy; a decision that shocked friends and colleagues. Questions rose regarding her decision to halt her education, to which Metzler would claim that it was a career-based decision; that working a few years herself in law enforcement would increase her job performance in counseling.

In the police academy, she came out at the top of her class, beating out all of her classmates in academics, as well as much of the practical training. Crawford was confident that Metzler would be a fine officer, and he was especially happy about it. The main reason for this was because hiring her on the force was not necessarily his choice. Metzler's hiring was a personal favor for the town mayor, or rather, a return favor. Usually recruits hired under such circumstances proved to be unsatisfactory officers.

"Good morning, Chief Crawford," she greeted him. She approached him and extended her hand. He enjoyed the smile on her young face. Behind that smile was a nervous young woman. He recalled having a similar smile on the first day of his career.

"Good morning, Officer Metzler," he greeted back and shook her hand. "Feel free to help yourself to some coffee while we wait for everyone to arrive. Your trainer should hopefully be here soon, and we can get you two introduced."

"Thank you," she said. While she was a casual coffee drinker, her body couldn't use the additional jitters. She just barely managed to keep her composure so far. This being her first day as a cop was nerve-wracking enough, but there was more to it than that. She was going to be trained by Leonard Riker. This was news that spread across the department. Riker, who had worked under Crawford in Illinois, was a real life Dirty Harry in the police world. A true legend that brought justice to the underground crime organizations that plagued the city of Alton. Police departments across the country knew his name and his endeavor to fight crime. Stories of his investigations and raids were spoken of frequently in Metzler's academy classes. They often involved certain levels of brutality and unorthodox investigations. But he made more progress against the worst of the worst than anyone else. There was the arrest of Savage Sanders, a notorious hitman who worked for the underground kingpin simply known as Viktor. Sanders was a contract killer that no department wanted to go after. Even the FBI was extremely hesitant about going after him, and any other affiliates of Viktor. It was Riker who managed to gather evidence of a series of killings, and took it upon himself to infiltrate the hideout in which Sanders was located. After singlehandedly neutralizing Sanders and his numerous armed associates, Riker had discovered a hit list of law enforcement and political targets. The press labeled him a hero, the department promoted him, the mayor used him to score political points regarding the war on crime, and crime lords like Viktor declared war on him.

After accepting the job, Metzler was informed that Riker was relocating to Merit and would be assigned as her training officer. This was a dream come true. She was going to be trained by the best of the best. It was certainly something that would appear great on a résumé. She took a seat at the front table and waited. Several minutes passed and finally both shifts started filling the room. She turned toward the entrance each time someone came in, excited to meet her trainer. But every time it was either someone from midnights wrapping up their shift or a day shift patroller clocking in.

Crawford noticed that Riker hadn't arrived yet. The room was filling up and he would soon be giving his announcement to the personnel. He had asked Riker to arrive early, and it was now ten minutes to eight with no sign of him. The Commander had arrived and stood next to him at the podium. Crawford informed him that he was stepping out for a few minutes and went outside. Away from prying ears, he pulled out his cell phone and scrolled to Riker's name in contacts. A press of the call button dialed his number instantly.

****

Riker found himself on his living room floor with his neck pressed up against the leg of his couch. His phone rang twice before his mind registered what it was. It was on the floor with him. He picked it up and saw Crawford's name. *The hell do you want?* he thought. He saw the time and immediately knew the answer…and didn't care. He tapped the touch screen to answer.

"I'm on my way," he said.

"Where the hell are you, Leonard?!" It was as if Crawford didn't hear him. Or more likely he did hear him, and knew Riker was full of it. "Damn it! I told you I wanted you here at a quarter to eight today."

"Had to stop for coffee," Riker said. He scooted to an upright seated position and rubbed his head to nurse a headache that was forming. He had slept for nearly ten hours, but it wasn't enough. "You should've seen the little bastard making my cappuccino. He had a loose band-aid on his thumb! I was gonna get an egg and bacon sandwich, but I was afraid that thing would end up in it." He could tell his fibs were not amusing the Chief. But he didn't really care.

"Leonard, shift change is starting and I need you here," Crawford disguised his tone to not sound angry, which would attract the attention of the Sergeant. *"Please hurry up. I can't keep the midnight shift over while we wait for you."*

"Why not? They love the overtime," Riker said. "And why is it so important I be there? You're not making me give a speech."

"*No,*" Crawford said. "*But everyone is eager to meet you, and part of my announcement this morning is introducing you. So, get your ass over here now!*" The screen lit up in Riker's face, indicating the chief had hung up. Riker let his phone drop to the floor as he rubbed his temples. The pain was worst near his facial scar, received from a knife slash during an arrest. It was a deep wound that tore facial muscles. Nerves in the face are some of the strongest in the human body. Headaches often aggravated the nerves in the damaged tissue. It aggravated his mood even worse. He sat on the floor for a few more seconds and finally stood up. He then walked to the end of the hallway and turned left toward the bedroom. He had just walked through the door when he felt as if the room started to spin. It felt as if gravity went in reverse for his insides. A cold sweat came over his brow, and his stomach tightened.

Conveniently, the bathroom was between the bedroom and kitchen. He barely made it in to vomit into the toilet.

****

The time was now ten minutes after eight and there was still no sign of Riker. Crawford did his best to hide his increasing frustration in front of the two shifts of officers that filled the briefing room. The room took on the color of greenish-tan and black. The day shift personnel took up most of the seats, while the midnight officers stood against the wall. They were ready to leave for the day, but most were eager to meet the new additions to the department. Comradery was one thing this department excelled at, which was another reason Crawford was drawn to his new job. The day shift crew took notes as the Sergeant began the briefing. It was nothing out of the ordinary: keep a look out for looters; stick to normal beats; enforce traffic laws; and passing down a report of a break-in overnight.

"—and now, Chief Crawford would like to have a word with you," the Sergeant said before stepping away from the podium. Crawford had asked the Sergeant to drag the briefing out to give Riker more time. However, it was clear that he had run out of things to say, and finally it was time for Crawford to take the stage.

"Good morning," he began. "I'll make this quick, 'cause I know some of you are ready to get the hell out of here." Some small chuckles echoed through the group. "First thing, I'd like to introduce our newest member—Officer Allison Metzler." He gestured his hand towards her in the front row of seats. "Please give her a hand." There was applause from the officers as Metzler stood up and gave a wave to the room. She smiled and embraced the moment before sitting back down. Crawford continued, "In other news, some of you might already know that Mayor Ripefield is away due to personal matters. So right now, our acting mayor is officially Vice Mayor Kathy Bloom until further notice." There were quiet murmurs throughout the room as many of the officers expressed their disapproval. Bloom was not popular within the police department and to most of the town as well. She was the type to gripe to the press about police brutality, more training for the town's officers— specifically sensitivity training, and often complained about race relations. Most people knew Bloom didn't truly care for these issues, except for their value as political talking points.

"Knock it off," Crawford settled the officers down. His commanding voice had a strong effect, bringing silence to the room. "You don't have to like it, but that's the way it is. Hopefully the mayor resolves his personal matters soon." He did express a bit of sympathy for the officers, since he had similar feelings on the matter. "Another note is that we still have the upcoming event next week for the National Sailing Association. Basically, it's a big sailing race and it's beginning here in our home town. So. overtime will be available, especially next week. Bloom won't stop talking about this whole event. It will be very busy around here to say the least. There'll be people from all over the country here, and sometimes the separate cultures don't blend well. So, Bloom wants us to maintain a strong presence around--" the sound of a door opening down the hall caught his attention. He looked down the hall and there was Riker approaching the briefing room. *Finally!* He almost mouthed the word. "Ah! Look who we have here! Everyone, it is my pleasure to introduce…" he stopped after taking another glance at Riker. He was dressed in black tactical gear, instead of the department uniform. His Kevlar vest had several cuffs tucked in pouches, a couple small knives, speed loaders for his sidearm, among other items. His firearm was his Smith & Wesson M&P R8 revolver, which had an eight-shot cylinder that held .357 cartridges, as opposed to the issued Glock 17 the other officers were required to carry. Riker's face was hard and stern, giving him a terminator-like appearance. Crawford shielded himself from the embarrassment he felt and quickly picked up where he left off.

"Ah-hem!" he acted as if he was clearing his throat. "Sorry. Everyone, it's my pleasure to introduce the other new addition to our department, Officer Leonard Riker." The day shift stood up from their seats and applauded. For these officers, it was like meeting a celebrity. Some of them cheered his name as if he was the winner of a sports competition. Crawford smiled at the warm reception taking place. "There is no doubt in anyone's mind that he will be a great addition to our police force. As you all know from what you've read, Riker is a man of great integrity and professionalism…" he heard Riker yawn while he said this. Crawford felt his blood start to boil, but continued the positive image as if he was running for office. "We appreciate you joining our team, Officer Riker. And we're all quite confident we can look to you for guidance and leadership." Crawford glanced back over towards Riker, who had already started leaving down the hallway. Crawford nearly blurted out, "Get your ass back here!" but barely refrained. He looked back toward the officers. "Okay, that's about all I have for everyone. Midnights, go home! Dayshift… get off your asses and get to work you lazy bastards." The group laughed and began filing out the back entrance. He then looked down the hallway and saw Riker about to disappear out the front entrance. "RIKER!" he called after him.

Riker stopped, paused for a moment and then turned around. Crawford knew he took the time to mutter something profane about him. The body language said it all. He motioned for Metzler to follow him into the hallway. She did so, and as she followed the chief she felt the jitters coming again. She tried not to give off a schoolgirl demeanor. Riker's reputation was nerve-wracking enough, but seeing him at the briefing added a whole new level to it. The no-nonsense body language, tough exterior and facial expression, and especially that nasty facial scar—all told her that this was a man who'd seen and done it all in the world of policing. She was so focused on keeping her cool that she didn't immediately notice Chief Crawford's temper starting to boil. And she didn't know Riker enough to understand that his firm expression was from him suppressing his own angry outburst.

"Leonard," Crawford called him by his first name, "So how was that coffee?"

Riker said, "All I can say is it sucks when you order it black and they put cinnamon creamer in it." Crawford wasn't amused. "Now, unless you need anything else, I'll grab a vehicle and patrol around." He turned and started to leave again.

"Hang on!" Crawford stopped him. Riker gave an exasperated sigh. "I'd like to introduce you to Officer Allison Metzler. You missed the briefing, but today is also her first day on the job." Metzler stepped up, ready to greet Riker, but he responded before she could talk.

"Did you give her a welcome basket?" he quipped.

"It's a pleasure to meet you," Metzler interrupted. She extended her hand. Riker looked at it, then at her, and back at her hand. He gave her a half-assed handshake and let go. His whole demeanor expressed his confusion regarding why the chief was introducing him to a rookie.

"You're going to be her training officer," Crawford stated. Riker glared at him once again and promptly let go of the handshake.

"Come again?"

"The two of you are assigned together. She'll shadow you and learn as much as she can," Crawford said.

"You've got to be fucking kidding me!" The words fired from Riker's mouth like machine gun rounds. Metzler's friendly grin disappeared just as quickly, and her enthusiasm was not far behind.

"Do I look like I'm kidding?" Crawford nearly snapped. "I'm not gonna hear any argument from you about this. This is an order. Take it as a compliment, there's no better instructor."

"Except for everyone else who works here," Riker argued. "It's my first day too! Why the hell am I training someone else?"

"We offered to..." Crawford stopped and turned to face Metzler. "Give us one moment. Riker and I are gonna have a word in our office." He barely finished the sentence before marching around the corner at the end of the hallway. Riker went with him, and Metzler heard the door slam from where she was standing. It didn't sound pleasant.

Crawford stood behind his desk. Before he spoke, he reached down and grabbed a blue hand therapy ball and went to work on it. It helped get him through the many rough days back in Alton. Riker crossed his arms and waited for Crawford to have his say.

"First of all, we offered to have you ride around with somebody," the chief began, "but you said, and I quote 'I don't need a lesson in half-assed policing.' So I figured, if you're comfortable going out by yourself, you're ready to train Metzler."

"Why me? Seriously, why wouldn't you stick her with one of those hotshots that just got out of here?" Riker argued. Crawford groaned, wanting to come up with a different excuse. But he realized it would be easier to tell the truth.

"Leonard, damn it... do you realize how hard it was for me to get the Mayor to allow you to be transferred here for the equivalent pay you made up in Illinois? Just for doing typical patrol duties! It wasn't easy, and I had to do a lot of kissing up--"

"Quit with the martyr story and cut to the chase," Riker said.

"It's just that...ugh! She's Mayor Ripefield's niece," he said. "She had just finished the academy and was looking to get hired. He agreed to meet the terms of your employment under the condition that you be partnered with Officer Metzler. He knows you are one of the best, and he wants her to get the best possible training."

"How nice," Riker sarcastically responded. "Except, I didn't set any terms of employment. I only took this job because you gave me no choice!" His voice rose.

"Listen, Leonard, you may not believe me, but what happened in Alton-- I did it for your own good," Crawford argued defensively. "Just give her a chance. She's a very promising employee. She graduated at the top of her class, and with your help she can really go far."

"Top of her class? From where exactly?"

Crawford hesitated before answering the question, knowing beforehand how Riker would respond. "Clayton Community College's Academy." The words came out in a defeated tone. During the past decade, Clayton had become notorious for producing substandard police recruits. In many cases, new hires who graduated from Clayton were often sent back to training. Riker threw his hands in the air.

"Oh LOVELY!" he exclaimed. "Top of her class, eh? Meaning she paid her tuition on time! Or the Mayor did. Either way, not only is she green, she basically knows nothing. Might as well hire one of those lards working at the mall."

"We both have been rookies once," Crawford said.

"I recall earning my place," Riker said. "She's only here because she's related to the mayor. And Clayton? You've got to be kidding me! I've seen better pursuit driving from kids in go-carts!"

"I don't care why she's here," Crawford said. "The fact remains that you two are going to work together. Period. Oh, and I've got to ask: why in God's name are you dressed like you're about to fight ISIS?"

"It's within regulation," Riker said.

"It is, but we're trying to create an image here! We don't want to give the appearance that we're at war! And for Christ sake, don't you own a razor?"

"Ah-ha! You see?" Riker pointed his finger. "Clearly, having a guy like me isn't suitable for training someone as delicate as the mayor's daughter. God forbid we actually look like a police department and not like a bunch of safari guides." There was a long pause between them, but the tension couldn't be more evident.

"She's his niece," Crawford angrily corrected him.

Metzler had approached the office right after they shut the door. She couldn't help but eavesdrop on the conversation, and she wished she hadn't. Her confidence had dropped to an all-time low, and she hadn't even begun her patrol yet. Also, she found herself growing angry at the

22

same time. *How dare he claim I only got this job from being related to Mayor Ripefield!* She thought. *I came out at the top of my class! I excelled at every course; Pursuit driving, firearms, investigative procedures. I even schooled the instructor on the diving course, since I've dived all my life. Hell, I even know this area better than this jackass. He'll probably rely on me half the time!*

"Hell, I even know this area better than this jackass. He'll probably rely on me half the time!" She cupped her mouth, realizing she spoke the last of her thoughts out loud. She scanned the area, but it didn't appear anyone heard. Suddenly the office door opened, and Riker exited the room. They stood opposite each other, like two cowboys ready to draw upon each other. Metzler put on the tough exterior she learned while in the academy. But in the back of her mind she wondered, *Shit, did he hear me?*

"Come on, let's go," he said. He started walking toward the back exit. She stood frozen for a moment.

"I can do this," she whispered to herself and followed her trainer. It was sure to be a long day.

CHAPTER 4

By noon the wind had died down to a breeze as the storm distanced itself. The sky was still gloomy, although more sunlight was cutting through the clouds. However, on the horizon, a new cloud formation was coming. It was a thunderstorm, but nothing as intense as a hurricane. While it lacked the ferocity, it still brought about considerable darkness where the clouds loomed. About three miles from shore, a fifty-foot white vessel cruised within the calm waters. It would be obvious for any viewer even from a distance to see that it was a research vessel. Lights and camera equipment lined the bridge, aimed down toward the water. On the main deck was a fifteen-foot hydraulic crane, equipped with a winch and cable. Electronic monitoring equipment as well as tagging poles were placed neatly on deck. On the upper level deck was something that appeared to be a large open tackle box. However, instead of fishing equipment, it actually contained items such as pliers and first aid materials used to rescue sea life from drift nets. On the side of the hull was the name of the vessel, *The Taurus*, printed in large black letters. Written in smaller letters beneath the name were the words *Stafford Marine Study Institute.*

Dr. Aaron Stafford stood in the cockpit of the large vessel, located in the superstructure. He was watching blips on a monitor displaying a signal from an Argos Platform Transmitter Terminal. He was a slightly short man, standing at five-foot-five. His build was average, and although he was only thirty-six years old, his hairline had receded greatly. He dressed casually in exercise pants and a UNC Marine Sciences sweatshirt, with white tennis shoes. *The Taurus* was originally a fishing vessel, but the marine biologist acquired it from its previous owner when he began his own practice in studying and rescuing marine life. He was able to get it at a bargain price, and it was the best he was able to afford. His budget was considerably small, and there was often little financial profit to be seen from his work. When working out contracts with institutes, he explained his studies were for studying migratory habits of marine life. The hidden truth behind it was he was devoted to rescuing and preserving the endangered creatures within the area. He'd tag each whale and shark after rescuing them from fishing nets, or any other ailment they might have suffered from.

Dr. Stafford once had a prestigious career working for the Scripps Institute of Oceanography after earning his doctorate from there. Prior to that, he had earned a Master's degree from the University of North Carolina and a Bachelor's degree from Rosenstiel School of Marine Atmospheric Science. Each of these degrees was in the study of Marine Biology. At Scripps, he assisted and eventually led research teams on a research vessel called the *Johan Hjort*. The vessel was designed for studying storm dynamics at sea. This was done by studying the atmosphere and taking samples of the water to understand environmental changes that occur. To him, it was a well-paying career, but his passion changed when the vessel came across a Danish whaling vessel that was actively harpooning a juvenile sperm whale. While he and his crew were able to contact Coast Guard authorities on the matter, he was forced to witness the creature be slaughtered in front of him. He'd seen unjustified harm to sea life before, but this one hit home for him. The whaler's crew did not seem to care that they were being watched. It reminded him why he got into the study of Marine Biology; to study and preserve life. He knew it was time for a change. His job with Scripps required him to be out at sea for great lengths of time, which wouldn't allow him to simply pursue his ambition in his spare time. After saving up some initial funds, he respectfully resigned and started the Stafford Marine Study Institute. He eventually settled a deal to receive funding from the University of Miami in exchange for data on migratory patterns on whales and dolphins that passed through the coastline.

He steered the wheel to the right and throttled back slightly. The blip on the monitor was a great white he nicknamed Roy. Roy was a twenty-three-foot long giant whom Stafford rescued when he discovered it tangled in fishing wire with a giant hook lodged in its mouth. His best bet was that it was hooked by some charter fisherman and broke the line. Great whites are illegal to fish for, so the perpetrator fled as soon as the prize was lost. Stafford happened to be nearby when he located Roy on his underwater camera, swimming erratically. Without concern for himself, he dove in with an air breather and pliers. He pried the hook loose and cut the wire, allowing the shark to go free. Of course, he managed to tag it during the rescue.

Roy was about a kilometer ahead of their position. Every so often the blip would disappear from the screen for a few seconds, and then reappear. He believed the transmitter was going bad. His plan for today was to get a new transmitter on Roy before the current one quit entirely. He glanced at the horizon and determined that they still had a little time to get the job done. The forecast had predicted that the storm would come around later into the afternoon, but here it was a couple hours early. The dark clouds cast a giant shadow over the water, like a huge grey curtain. He stepped out of the cockpit and looked down from the superstructure at the main deck. His assistant, Robert Nash, was nowhere to be seen. *He's probably reading some stupid science fiction book down below,* Stafford thought.

"Robert! Hey, Robert!" he called down. *The Taurus* had three staterooms, a small kitchen, and a bathroom. He knew his assistant could hear him from any of those locations. After a few seconds, Nash popped out of the narrow doorway onto the deck. He was in his early-mid thirties, was dressed in khaki shorts and a t-shirt with a picture of Jean-Luc Picard from Star Trek: The Next Generation. He had short red hair, a goatee, and rectangular glasses. He wore a tattoo on the inside of his right arm, which were Japanese characters spelling out 'luck of the Irish'. He shielded his eyes as he looked upward at his boss.

"You summoned me?" he said.

"We're gonna need that tag set up," Dr. Stafford said. "Hopefully this one works properly."

"It's all ready to go, Doc," Nash said. "These things rarely malfunction. But it is technology, and we're at its mercy." Nash, like Dr. Stafford, had gone to Rosenstiel School of Marine Atmospheric Science, where he earned a Bachelor's degree in Marine Biology. He also specialized in Marine Technology, which was something he began learning during his stint in the U.S. Navy. He walked to the starboard railing and looked ahead at the storm clouds forming in the distance. "Okay…I'll just ask the big question. You want us to drop you in the cage, or do we want to try and get Roy close enough to the boat to tag him? I know dropping the cage would be more efficient in getting the tag secure, but it'll take longer to get set up. And I don't want to be out here in that storm."

"It's not bad. Forecast said it should be over by tonight," Stafford said. Nash was right, however. He thought about it for a minute, and decided the best course of action would be to lure Roy to the surface. "Go ahead and start chumming." Already secured at the stern was a large blue plastic tub. Nash wrestled the lid off, revealing several gallons of red fish guts. The smell escaped the container like ash from Mt. Saint Helens. He hated that god-awful smell, and never got used to it. He picked up the plastic scoop, put a handkerchief to his mouth, and started chumming.

****

The great white gently moved its enormous tail from side to side. Its mouth was kept agape to allow an endless stream of water to push through its gills. It didn't travel in a straight line; instead it moved ever so slightly to the right. It patrolled the area in an enormous circle in search for food. A substantial portion of its diet consisted of blackfin tuna and grouper. Sensory organs located at the front of its snout, known as Ampullae of Lorenzini, were on a constant check for electric potentials created by even the most minute contractions of prey. The sensory organs are electroreceptors which are made up of jelly filled pores. A nerve behind these pores relays information from them to the shark's brain. By doing this, in addition to its other senses, the shark would be able to detect an injured fish from over a mile away. Roy didn't need to travel so far to get his food. This area it patrolled provided plenty of nutrition, and therefore its instincts kept it swimming in a specific pattern.

As it gently swam along its path, its sensitive nostrils picked up the enticing scent of blood. The sense of smell was so great, it was capable of picking up a single drop inside of 100 liters of water. This scent was so much more rousing than that. There were gallons of blood, indicating fairly large prey was nearby. The shark turned toward the blood. While it searched for the source, it paid no attention to the large electric impulses originating from a quarter mile behind it. It had detected these other signals before, but they indicated a lifeform larger than itself. Because great whites only attack smaller prey, it had no interest in investigating further.

The Thresher had detected the presence of the white, and had been moving in gradually. Its brain operated differently than its fellow species. It had no qualms about what it approached to attack. The immense beast was establishing territory, and while the white was smaller, it was still determined to be a threat. It also perceived it to be a source of sustenance. While it swam towards the origin of the electromagnetic impulses, it suddenly picked up the scent of blood. Its brain sent off huge signals of hunger throughout its body. Its mouth snapped at empty sea, as if the prey were right in front of it. It pedaled its giant caudal fin and increased speed. The top scythe-shaped fin rippled with each movement like a snake, equaling the length of the beast.

****

Nash continued chumming, creating a trail of guts that expanded to a quarter mile. He looked back at the horizon. The storm clouds were coming in faster than expected. The strengthening wind pushed the chum line further out than they wanted. *Figures!* Dr. Stafford remained at the console and kept an eye on the tracking screen. He got impatient as the blip disappeared again. The tracking device was just about dead, and if they didn't get a new one on today they could completely lose track of the shark. He had to rely on the fish finder. Luckily, the white was within close range. It appeared as a green blob against the blue background of the monitor.

"Stop chumming and get the bait ready on the reel!" he called out. Nash dropped the scoop and rushed to another big container near a cable secured to a crane on the starboard side. The cable was clipped to a leather harness, and was reeled by a winch that was attached to the arm of the crane. The harness was used to hold bait, and the team would use the crane to hold the bait just above the water. If the shark was interested, it would break the surface to grab the food. At that moment, Stafford would secure a new tag on the shark. Nash opened the container. Inside was a large chunk of elephant seal hide. Nash put some gloves on and lifted the fleshy bait from the container. It was a heavy piece—certainly something that should entice a great white. The stench was awful.

"Oh gosh, I always hate this part," he complained to himself as he strapped the bait to the harness. He then winched the cable and lifted it over the side with the crane. The big ball of flesh dangled about five feet over the surface. "Want me to dip it in?" he asked the doctor. Stafford continued watching the monitor. The blip was moving past them, toward the drifting chum line.

"Damn it," he said. "Any other day this would play out perfectly. But it seems the weather forecasters can't accurately predict anything except their next pay period." He looked out into the water to try and see the shark, but it was too deep. "Robert, throw some fresh chum over the side, and then we'll dip the bait." He watched the monitor screen while Nash chummed. It took a minute, but the form on the screen started to close in on the boat. He called out to Nash. "It's working! Roy's coming this way." He stepped out of the cockpit and climbed down to the deck. He grabbed a twenty-foot long pole, at the end of which was a new tracker. "Okay, go ahead and dip it."

"In ranch or barbeque?" Nash quipped and chuckled. He pressed a lever and lowered the bait beneath the surface. Its juicy fluids permeated the water. The big shark would have no problem finding it. Adrenaline started to rush through Stafford's veins. He gripped the pole tighter and waited for Roy to make his appearance.

"Come on. Come get lunch. I'm buying," he pretended to sweet talk the fish. Nash looked at him.

"What about me?" he asked. Stafford laughed.

"I would like to say that, if we pull off this half-assed tagging, lunch is on me. Problem is; I hardly have any money to spare."

"I would add that I would buy lunch under the same circumstances," Nash responded, "but the problem is, you hardly ever pay me." He laughed at his own humor. Stafford stood silent for a moment, staring out into the water, then suddenly he let out a big excited laugh of his own.

Wasn't that good of a joke, Nash thought. Then he saw the big fin out in the water, approaching the bait. "I guess he decided to take your offer!"

Nash lifted the bait slightly above the water and Dr. Stafford awaited the shark's exposure. While the two scientists were focused on their task, they were oblivious to a new reading on the fish finder. A new blinking shape appeared behind the white. It was a much larger shape, and it was heading in the direction of *The Taurus.*

The grey dorsal fin sliced through the water's rippling surface. Its swimming path took the form of an 'S' while it picked off the small chunks of fish guts. Its nostrils picked up the strong scent of the sea lion carcass. The shark could see the large boat behind the meal, but it didn't sense any threat. It curved its path as to not run into the floating apparatus, and lined itself up along the portside at the bow end. The great white gave a mighty thrust to its huge caudal fin and drove itself forward with intense power. Stafford stood poised at the topside, with the pole raised like a lance in a gladiator battle. The white's head rose from the water. Its jaws extended, exposing one-and-a-half inch long serrated teeth attached to pinkish-red gums. The white underside was somewhat exposed. The jaws engulfed the fifty-pound piece of sea lion carcass, and the teeth sliced into the already battered flesh. The bait disappeared after the jaws closed down. While the fish grabbed its meal, Stafford seized the moment and jabbed the pole right near its left pectoral fin. The shark never noticed the red and black tag clip into its skin. It splashed down, dragging the cable along with it. The metal crane groaned from the heavy downward pull. After the shark submerged, the cable went slack. Nash pulled upward on the lever, reeling in the cable until the mangled harness hung weightless along the side of the boat.

"Great!" Dr. Stafford exclaimed. He and Nash gave each other a high five. "I guess he was hungry today. He wasted no time!" A crack of thunder and a flash of lightning caught Nash's attention. The storm was rolling in quick.

"I'd say that was quite convenient," he said. "Maybe it's time we head in." Stafford was already on his way up to the console.

"Just let me check the signal and then we'll head back to the lab," he said. As he reached the cockpit, his eyes immediately went to the fish finder. He saw the white taking its meal deep. And there was another form on the screen. Whatever it was, it was big. It was going straight for the white. "What in the name of— Nash! Get on the monitors and bring up the camera feed!"

****

The enormous dark-skinned fish tracked the bloody scent deeper into the water, where the electric signals were originating. Through the cloudy vision it had, it could see the torpedo shaped body of the great white shark, which had just finished swallowing its recent meal. The White took no interest in the Thresher and continued going along its way. But the Thresher's intense aggressive instincts went into overdrive. It shot forward with a huge burst of speed. It tilted its cone shaped head up, slightly arching its back, and tucked its fins beneath its body. In less than a moment, it slashed its huge tail over its right pectoral fin and struck the great white in the face. The impact barely missed its right eye, and formed a laceration that ran from the center of its head all the way to its snout. The stunning impact sent the shark into a spasm. It twisted and turned almost uncontrollably. Blood seeped from its large open wound, further enticing the advancing predator.

The Thresher seized the opportunity. With a large push of its tail against the water, it closed the distance. Its mouth opened, lining rows of straight pointed teeth. Those teeth sank effortlessly into the white's flesh as the Thresher bit down. Its bottom teeth sank into the white belly, and the upper jaw tore down on the flesh just above the right pectoral fin. The teeth weren't serrated; they were more like nails driving deeper as the beast applied pressure to the bite. It tasted the blood that seeped into its mouth. The enormous dark green shark slightly opened its jaw and closed down right away, sinking its teeth and creating new wounds. It was essentially 'munching' on the White.

The great white felt a flood of pain fire through its body. It didn't have the conscious awareness of pain that mammals possessed, rather its brain contained receptors that detected injuries. And it detected many. It writhed in the jaws of the predator, unable to pry itself from the jagged nail-like teeth. Its flesh tore with each effort, but it didn't stop the white from attempting escape. Finally, it twisted and turned at just the right moment when the Thresher loosened its grip to perform another bite. The wounded shark thrust its body from the grasp, and swung its tail to give itself propulsion. It created distance and began circling back. This great white had never encountered a large challenge by another predator, and its instincts told it to eliminate the threat instead of flee. The Thresher moved in on its prey. Its large eyes granted it better sight than most fish, and it could see that the White was circling back towards it. It registered this action as a sign of aggression.

The great white lined up to face the threat, leaving a trail of blood as it went. It didn't have concern for its injuries, but a sense of self-preservation against this other fish. It increased speed, and like a missile it cruised at the dark creature. It opened its immense jaws, its teeth appearing like pointed pieces of silver in the murky waters. But it was stopped short. The Thresher lashed its tail like an enormous whip, striking the White once again in the face. This impact severed its left eye in two and created a new laceration that ran down to its jaw. Teeth were knocked clear of the gums, and the stunned fish froze motionless. Its head dipped down and it slowly began sinking. It wasn't dead, but momentarily paralyzed. The Thresher quickly moved in for the kill. It bit down hard, sinking its upper teeth over the top of the white's head. Its bottom teeth ravaged the flesh just beneath the gill line. The Thresher bit down several times, weakening the flesh enough to start ripping huge chunks of it off. The great white bled out and the life left its mangled body. The Thresher tore away at the wound, shaking it like a dog to remove more chunks of flesh. Flesh and cartilage tore, and the white's head became completely detached from the rest of its body. A huge cloud of red mist filled the blue water, giving the area a hellish appearance.

****

"Holy Christ, can you see anything?" Stafford asked Nash. Both men were at the monitor located at the stern. There was so much movement in the water it was hard to see the activity. They had to continuously change camera feed as the creatures moved. Plus, the darkening sky began taking away their sunlight. All they could see was a dark shape overtaking the great white they had just retagged.

"There's something down there!" Nash said. His voice was a combination of amazement and fear. "It's too dark, though. I can't make out what it is."

"It has a dark outer appearance," Stafford said. "And whatever it is, it's freaking enormous!"

"It's got to be a killer whale," Nash said. The doctor studied the monitor harder, struggling to make out any images. Thunder cracked overhead, and the sky briefly illuminated with flashes of lightning. Then, as if deliberately to make their work more difficult, the clouds released a torrential downpour on them. "This is just great!" They covered the monitor with a plastic tarp. The electronics could handle some water, but too much would cause them to short out.

"We're not gonna get anymore done in this," Stafford rose his voice to be heard over the pounding rain. "The weather's supposed to be good tomorrow. I want to head out again. I don't suspect our friend's leaving the area anytime soon."

"You think it was an orca?"

"Possibly, but I think it was big even for that! But if it was, I'd like to see it and possibly tag it!" Stafford started up the ladder and worked his way up to the cockpit. He cursed himself when he realized he left the door open, and rainwater had covered the floor. He stepped in and almost immediately slipped on a puddle. As he caught himself, his elbow knocked over the fish-finder monitor and cracked the screen, causing it to switch off. "Damn it!" he yelled. *Just what I need: another damned expense!* Also, he wanted to check it before pulling *The Taurus* away. He didn't waste time examining it. The weather was bad and he knew his assistant really wanted to head back. He shut the door behind him, throttled the boat and turned toward shore. Nash had gone below into the kitchen to save himself from the rain.

As the *Taurus* pulled away, neither of them noticed the explosion of water behind them where the boat was previously resting, as a large creature breached the surface. After killing its first enemy, it had detected something else on the surface, and its killing instincts drove it to attack. But the strange object sped away before the creature could sink its teeth into it. The Thresher's fin cut along the surface as it swam in a tight circle.

The Thresher dove deep, continuing to establish its new territory.

CHAPTER 5

The time was 4:30 P.M. and the storm was still going strong as Allison Metzler parked her Pontiac G6 into the lot. The drive from work to home normally would take fifteen minutes, but the weather slowed traffic down, which added to her intense frustration. She rushed from the parking lot to her front porch. The heavy rain soaked her hair and her uniform while she fumbled to unlock the door to her apartment. She pushed herself inside and slammed the door shut behind her. She leaned back against the door, dripping water onto the floor mat. Her face was red due to her eyes welling up during the drive home. She brushed away wet strands of hair that stuck to her face, and stood in the dark living room. She shut her eyes and fought to lift her wearied spirits.

That morning, she was in great spirits. It was the first day of what promised to be a great career. The location was good; the fellow officers were welcoming; and the Chief seemed to appreciate her background and saw her potential. The part she was most enthusiastic about was to get to train with one of the most renowned officers in Law Enforcement. Right now, she was feeling the polar opposite. She never felt more miserable regarding her new career. She felt alone, humiliated, and very depressed. From the very get-go, Riker made it obvious he despised her very presence. At the beginning, she tried to make small talk in an attempt to break the ice, but these attempts were fruitless. The first couple hours of the shift were spent in almost complete silence inside a patrol car. Aside from a few quick instructions from Riker on how to do certain things, he avoided conversation. His body language and facial expression displayed an underlying anger within him, and he wasn't very subtle about it. It was clear to her that there was some tension going on between him and Chief Crawford. Both served in the city of Alton, and Crawford went through some effort to get Riker transferred to Merit. She was under the impression this was something Riker wanted, and that the chief was doing him a great favor. But it seemed like the former detective carried a lot of hatred for Crawford. Also, it was hard for her to ignore the slight aroma of alcohol on him. However, she didn't have the courage to address it.

There weren't many calls during the morning hours. However, after 10:00 a.m. Riker spent plenty of time performing traffic stops. Metzler wasn't bothered by the idea of keeping busy. He walked her through the first one, doing most of the talking when getting the offender's information and issuing the citation. During the second traffic stop, he allowed her to take charge of interacting with the driver. This was the one moment when she thought things were starting to go well. She handled the job well, which increased her confidence. However, it was after that when things got unpleasant.

Riker flashed the lights and pulled over a third vehicle. The offence: traveling at forty-six miles per hour in a forty-five mile limit. Metzler suddenly became anxious when he instructed her to write up the citation. As she expected, the driver was furious and initially uncooperative. She failed to present a strong presence and allowed herself to appear flustered, opening her to more ridicule from the driver. She remembered glancing back to Riker, hoping he'd step out of the patrol vehicle and provide assistance. Her spirits sank when she noticed him grinning while watching her. Luckily, the driver decided to give up his information, while making a crude remark. The anxiety nearly got the best of her, and she struggled to keep her hand from shaking while writing the ticket. It wasn't just that the driver was rude and angry, but primarily the fact that her training officer was deliberately humiliating her.

She hoped that was the only time he'd pull that stunt. That hope was quickly crushed when he pulled another vehicle for driving one mile over the limit. This time it was a semi-truck driver. This stop nearly turned into a shouting match between her and the driver, who argued he was within the speed limit. As with the previous stop, when she explained why he was stopped, the driver went into a fit. He cursed at her and called her every foul name she thought was possible. He accused her of being a young woman who thought she was tough to be picking on big men. Once again, Riker provided no assistance.

This process continued for the next couple hours, and Metzler had a hard time dealing with the stress. She expected to deal with unruly people and experience tense situations when she took the job. It was all part of being a police officer. But she was being purposely placed in these altercations by her trainer, who prior to this day was a name she greatly admired. To make things worse, she was more than certain she'd have to make a court appearance for each of these tickets. She had heard of the district judge, and was certain she would be chastised for pulling over people for an extremely minor offense. With her name on the tickets, she wouldn't be able to pin it back to Riker.

During the afternoon, things seemed to slow down...literally. Vehicles were hardly going over the speed limit. It was as if word was getting around that a police officer was pulling over vehicles for the slightest moving violation. The thunderstorm had moved in, creating conditions that discouraged speeding. Metzler felt a great sense of relief about this, since it prevented more of these stunts from Riker. Or so she thought. This led to the final and worst occasion. While patrolling the streets, Riker pulled over a pickup truck. It was traveling at the limit, so Metzler asked why they were pulling it over.

"Didn't you notice? The bastard didn't use his turn signal," Riker answered her. She felt as if a cloud of doom was floating over her. She had no choice but to do what Riker instructed as long as it was within the law. And unfortunately, this was. She took her time getting the license plate info, in the hope that Dispatch might call them away for something more important. Rain pounded down on her while she went to speak to the driver. When he heard the reason for the traffic stop, he furiously responded by hurling a barrage of insults at Metzler. He rudely ogled her chest and remarked that she 'must've become a cop to compensate for only having a C-cup'. To make matters worse, he blatantly refused to present ID 'to a man-hating feminist', as he phrased it. Metzler attempted to be more assertive and demanded he produce his license and registration. The only response she got was a middle finger. She grew flustered. All training went out the door. She was lost on what to do. The rain was making it worse. Uncertain of what to do, she went back to the patrol car to seek assistance from Riker.

"Show you have bigger balls than him," was his only advice.

What does that even mean?

She bit her lip and reluctantly went back to the driver. At this point, she was just sick of it. It was a damn turn signal violation. More than that; this was a damn amusement show for Riker. She just wanted the situation over with. She informed the driver she'd let him off with a warning if he'd cooperate. He seemed content with this, and handed her his license and registration. She returned to the vehicle and recorded the information into the computer. No warrants; no felonies issued for this individual. She went out to return the items, but before she could hand them back, Riker suddenly stepped out of the patrol car. "What are you doing? Letting him have a free pass?"

"I don't under--" Riker snatched the ID from her hand and shined a flashlight on it.

"If you paid attention, you'd have seen all that!" He was referring to the laser perforations and fine lines near the photo. "What's your real name, pal?" The driver repeated the name on the license. Riker than asked him about a small cut on the left side of his head, to which the driver cursed at him. Riker ordered him to step out of the vehicle. The individual refused, and quickly regretted it. Before he knew it, he was struggling not to drink muddy water from a puddle after he was put on the pavement and cuffed.

"Riker, what are you doing?" Metzler allowed herself to protest. At the police station, fingerprints revealed that the driver's real name was Paul Wilder, who was on the run after beating his girlfriend nearly to death in Georgia. The name came from an accomplice living in Orlando who sold him his identity. The report of the incident stated that Wilder received a cut on the side of his head during the assault. At shift change, Riker received a round of applause for the arrest. Metzler, however, could not shake off the overwhelming humiliation. It was simply an attempt by Riker to bully her, and it resulted in him looking like a hero and her looking like an idiot. In addition, it crushed her confidence. She ignored the evidence in front of her and nearly allowed a fugitive to remain on the streets.

She opened her eyes and turned on the living room light. She emptied her pockets and tossed her items on the table. Among those items was her smart phone, which she had turned off during her shift. She turned it on and saw she had a missed call and a voicemail. It was from her older sister, Tammy. Metzler never told anyone about her, as she was the ultimate reason she rushed her way into the police academy after college and got a job in Law Enforcement.

She had gone to college to become a therapist, specifically to work with police officers. Her intended career required a doctorate, which she could no longer afford because of the cost of Tammy's care. With her education, and the help of her uncle, Metzler was able to immediately get into the Clayton Police Academy, with assurance she would be hired at Merit PD. As part of her benefits package, she was able to list Tammy as a beneficiary on her health insurance. Treatment for chronic leukemia was an unpleasant and expensive process. Tammy had no spouse, and their parents had no money. Her uncle, the mayor, did what he could as well to help. Being the mayor of a small town, his income was not as substantial as many people thought.

"Hey girl, it's your big sis! Oh my gosh, you're officially a police woman today! I just can't believe it. Listen, just remember: donuts make you fat!" Her voice was delightful to listen to. She was the type to keep good spirits despite how bad her situation seemed. *"Well, Allison, I just*

wanted to tell you I'm proud of you. You're gonna be great at this. And, I want to say thank you for what you've done for me. I think I can honestly say nobody's ever had a better sis. Well, I better get off before I start crying, hahaha! Let me know how it goes!" The message ended, and Metzler debated whether or not to call back. She decided to wait. Her mind was still dwelling on the unpleasant eight hours of work, and on the fact she was going to endure it again tomorrow. She then realized she was stuck with Riker for two months at least. Her spirits sank lower than she had ever experienced. She felt the urge to quit. She couldn't believe that after being so renowned in her academy class that she would struggle so hard her first day on basic police duties. Riker set her up to fail, and forced her to become the opposite of what she hoped to be as an officer. He made her into a bully by fining people over minute offenses.

Not an option, she thought. *I can't do that to Tammy.* She accepted the fact that all she could do was get better. She decided she wanted to call her sister back. But first thing was first; she had to get into some dry clothes.

****

The first thing Riker was interested in after getting home was grabbing a beer from the fridge. He barely twisted the tab off when he pressed the bottle to his lips. In no time, it was half gone. He removed his vest and most of his gear and tossed it on the kitchen table. He put the bottle to his mouth again and pointed the bottom toward the ceiling. In almost a single gulp, he had washed down the remaining half of the bottle. He tossed it like a baseball, landing it in the trashcan.

"Oh! It's out of the stadium!" he mimicked a sports broadcaster voice. He grabbed another beer and took a seat in the living room. He was in the middle of a large gulp when he heard a knock at the door. A thousand bad memories flooded his mind from his service in Alton. Many of his cases dug deep into the city's black underbelly. There were times when he received an unexpected knock on his front door. It was usually gangbangers or certain 'attorneys' who had stopped by to relay a warning. A couple of other occasions it was contract killers. There were several times when he had to replace his door after greeting them with his R8. The .357 rounds would leave large holes in both the door and the unwelcome intruder. These memories caused him to instinctively grab hold of his firearm, still strapped to his leg holster. He opened the door a crack and peeked outside.

"Hi," Crawford said. "Mind if I come in? It's a little wet out here." Riker opened the door the rest of the way. Crawford noticed him holstering the large revolver back to his leg. "Sorry. I guess I've already started to forget the old days. Those were some long investigations." He brushed the water off his suit jacket.

"At least it kept the damned insurance salesmen from dropping by," Riker remarked. He sat back down on the couch and turned on the television. "Want a beer? Help yourself." Crawford gazed at all the unpacked boxes and other assorted mess between the living room and kitchen.

"Don't mind if I do, actually," he said. He was a moderate drinker, and usually didn't partake in quick visits such as this. But this time it sounded good. He helped himself into the kitchen and looked into the fridge. He sighed when he saw hardly anything on the top and middle shelves. The bottom shelf was loaded with beer—and nothing else. "I see you've been shopping," he sarcastically remarked. He walked back into the hallway, noticing the spilled packing box on the floor near a broken beer bottle. He noticed a picture frame had slid out of the opening, lying face down. He knelt down and looked at the picture. It showed a handsome young couple; a beautiful bride in a wedding dress holding hands with her new husband. He was handsome, in his early twenties, clean shaven, and well dressed in a tuxedo. The biggest contrast from the version sitting in the living room was the smile. It displayed pure happiness. His eyes then went to the broken beer bottle. "Do you need help with unpacking?"

"I've got it covered," Riker said. He chugged on his beer while watching a sports channel. Crawford noticed the picture of Martha on the cushion next to him. "Is that why you're visiting?"

"I'm here because I care very much about you," Crawford said. He took a drink of his beer. He knew he was going to need it. "Listen, Leonard, life has thrown both of us a raw deal..." he noticed Riker toss his head back and roll his eyes. He was never a good recipient of advice.

"I'm definitely gonna need another one of these," he mumbled to himself.

"No, you don't," Crawford asserted. "Listen to me, I'm begging you—don't do this to yourself!"

"Do what?"

"Don't play dumb. This!" Crawford took the beer bottle from him and held it up. It was empty, but it made his point. "You think I don't know what you're doing to yourself? You're digging yourself into a grave. You think you're punishing yourself. You don't deserve it!" He realized he didn't want his own beer anymore and set it down on the table. "You and I have probably the worst possible thing in common..."

"The uniform tailor tried to fondle you too?!" Riker quipped.

"We both had to bury our wives," Crawford said. "It's an unbearable pain, but I promise you it gets better."

"Ray, I know you mean well," Riker said, "and with all due respect, it's not quite the same thing. Actually, there's a big difference."

"Don't be angry with her," Crawford said. He understood very well that Riker carried a lot of anger within him. There was the intense heartbreak that he was suffering from, but there was a fury he contained within him. Crawford believed he blamed Martha for leaving this world, and that he hated himself for causing it to happen. "You need to focus on the good memories. You need to be able to smile when you think of her. It's what I had to do, and believe me, it helps."

"What are you talking about?" Riker raised his voice. "You focused on the good things? All you had were good things with your wife. And yet, you still ran away to get away from it all. You came here, and you dragged me here with you!"

"Leonard, I was trying to help you," Crawford said. "Working there would've…"

"Kept the mob under control," Riker cut him off. He stood up. "Do you realize you and I were practically the only people who made a difference back there? Everyone else was too chickenshit to take the fight to people like the Malone Brothers. I didn't want to leave, but you forced me out. Now, the syndicates are celebrating. There's nobody that'll stop them now. We made a vow to make a difference, and get to the heart of the problem. All that work we did, every bit of it…it's all for nothing. And for what? To save cats from trees in paradise?"

"We'd done our part," Crawford said. "It was time to end the fight."

"Maybe for you, but not for me," Riker said. "Now I'm stuck with these losers, wearing uniforms that look like they should be hunting rhinos in Africa. Recruits back home have more experience than the idiots here. Hell, the knucklehead you're making me work with has probably done more today than anyone so far. And that's why you planned this. You want to ride this job until you can retire. Well, you got your wish. We've got a lovely place with no stress and a nice view of the beach. I'm sure the sunset is lovely and romantic. Too bad we're both single." Riker stopped himself. He desired to continue his rant, but he knew he'd said enough. Crawford could feel his own resentment burning. He made himself remember that the real Leonard Riker didn't believe these things, and this was only a shell of the real man. However, he felt he overstayed his welcome.

"If you need me, you know where to find me," he said as he turned to the door. "Thanks for the beer." Riker didn't say anything back.

Crawford stepped out into the rain and walked to his vehicle. The sky was dark and ugly.

I guess this fits the mood, he thought. He got in his truck and drove home.

CHAPTER 6

The following morning brought much better weather. It was the first time in days when the sun could clearly be seen. The 6:30 a.m. dawn gave birth to a beautiful sunrise that sparked a golden glint over the calm coastal waters. The forecasts indicated that there were significant weather developments in the area for the next couple of weeks.

Scott Gerald stepped onto the front patio of the beach home where he spent the night. Dressed only in grey exercise shorts, he looked out to the horizon and enjoyed the glow over the water while sipping on coffee. He was a well-built man, standing at six-foot-one and with the physique of a champion swimmer. His hair was blond, which did well to attract the ladies. Another factor that helped was his income from being the vice president of an electronics retail giant.

Scott was a vacationer from New Jersey. Over the summer, he and his wife had planned a getaway but couldn't find the time with their busy schedules. He was a company vice president and she was a Dean of Human Resources at a university. The last couple years of their five-year marriage had not been pleasant, with his wife suspecting him of infidelity. He pleaded his innocence from each accusation, and the wife didn't have the evidence to prove his guilt. Despite her gut feeling on the matter, she tired of the drama and decided she would try and forget her husband's past shortcomings. They planned a trip to Florida in September to avoid the vast summer crowds. The school season was just starting, so it was very difficult for her to get the time off, but she got it granted. However, problems arose when a board meeting was rescheduled to take place on the day they were to leave. They had a hotel booked and paid for already, so Scott decided to fly down himself and his wife would stay behind to meet her obligations, then join him the next day.

He arrived in bad weather, so going to the beach wasn't an option that night. He went to a bar instead. He spoke to his wife on the phone to check in. As he was saying 'I love you,' he was winking at a young brunette who was gazing at him. He had one of those deep manly voices that drew her in. She knew he was from out of town, which worked for her. She had just gotten out of a crummy relationship, and was relishing the joys of rebound. In her mind, it was just the way to get back at her ex: let another good-looking man put himself on her. She scooted his way, and he quickly got off the phone and ordered her a beer. The foreplay began in conversation about her job; modeling for a sporting company. This increased his interest in her, although her slim figure and seducing blue eyes were doing enough on their own. Of course, he had to emphasize his position with his company, and how he thought he could use someone with her 'talent' for marketing. He then made a smooth one liner, "Babe, I could sell the moon if I advertised it with you standing next to it." With the wife across the country, there was no worrying about her getting home early or him being seen by peers. It was as simple as going to this stranger's beach house and enjoying a sensuous affair.

The first time he committed adultery he spent the next several days feeling guilty about it. He found himself awake at night wondering whether he should confess his unfaithfulness. Now, he didn't think twice about it. He didn't bother to rationalize it outside of the common phrase *you only live once*. It was all a matter of keeping it hidden from his wife; an art he believed he mastered.

While the weather was nice and free of rain, the previous storms left behind a high humidity level. The temperatures were rising again as well, giving the air a soggy sensation. Scott felt himself starting to sweat. He stepped back into the house and checked the bedroom. His sensuous partner was still asleep naked in bed, lying on her left side. Her womanly regions were just barely covered by the bunched-up sheets. He wondered if they'd have another adventure before parting ways. He sat at the edge of the bed and ran his finger along her bare shoulder. The touch of her golden skin was electrifying in itself. She stirred a bit but kept her eyes closed.

"What's up, big guy?" she said, following an 'mmmmm' sound. Scott answered by running his tongue over her lips. She smiled, and kept her eyes closed. "Obviously you're impressed with yourself."

"I'd rather impress you again," he said. She gave a small chuckle.

"Good things come to those who wait," she said. She was still waking up. Scott felt himself grow more excited just by looking at her figure. He initially intended to undress what little he had on and lay in bed until she was ready. However, the humidity made his skin feel moist and sticky. He thought he could use a shower, but his eyes caught the beach again through the bedroom window. A nice swim sounded much better. He got up and went back out onto the porch while his date continued to doze. The water was as still as a plate of glass. Scott could tell it was the perfect temperature for swimming. He removed a watch he was wearing on his right wrist. It was custom engraved on the bottom, *Scott Gerald E&R Vice President*; a gift from his CEO.

He sprinted into the water like a lifeguard going in for the rescue. In no time the water was up to his abdomen. He took a breath and dove beneath the surface and kicked his arms out. The water felt great. It washed the morning grime and sweat right off. The exercise also felt really good. He kicked his legs and stroked his arms. When he surfaced, he was already twenty feet out. Swimming came naturally to Scott. He was a silver medalist in his high school swim team, and made some side money in college as an assistant swimming coach. Initially he only thought he'd take a quick dive, but he was enjoying the swim more than expected. He swam out deeper, imagining himself in a championship swim race. He hadn't competed since his youth, but his abilities never waned. By the time he slowed down to take a quick breather he was already one hundred and fifty feet from shore. He glanced back and was surprised he swam out so far so quickly. He wasn't bothered by this and instead decided he wanted to swim a bit further out.

****

Pings of electromagnetic signals awakened the Thresher from a mindless trance while it moved around its new established territory. Because it had to constantly move in order to push water over its gills, its brain never went into a deep sleep state. Instead, it would go through periods of time where parts of its brain shut down, temporarily ceasing functions such as sensing for prey. Its body would naturally swim in circular patterns, which prevented it from swimming into undesirable locations. The shark had spent the night in this sleep-like state. The previous day it spent large amounts of energy stalking other creatures in the area. Its swelling brain gave it a heightened aggression, and this also gave it a strong sense of territoriality. Other sea life of significant size was seen as a threat, and its natural response was to kill the adversary or drive it away. It had come across a small pod of orcas, who also determined the beast itself to be a danger to them. During the clash, they were unable to get past the whip-like tail, which sliced flesh wherever it made contact. The pod leader was determined to bring the giant predator down, but the Thresher landed a strike on its blowhole. The orca's airway collapsed and filled with blood, and the mammal drowned as the shark bit huge chunks of flesh from its throat. With their leader dead, the rest of the small wounded pod retreated and vacated the area. This effort, along with other vicious encounters, left the shark in a state of exhaustion and it had to recoup its energy.

Its own movements were very small, with just enough tail motion to keep it continuously moving forward. After it was 'awake' it maintained its slow pace while it tracked the new signals traveling in the water. The fish immediately knew that the point of origin was a smaller creature, suitable for food. It did not perceive the presence as a threat. The signals were steadily getting stronger and more frequent, meaning the source was moving towards it. Hunger set in, and the fish decided to investigate. It turned toward the sandy regions, keeping its movements steady and quiet. Its line of sight was much improved due to the illumination in the water. There were no storm clouds above to filter the sun's rays. Its vision was clearer, and with those large bulb shaped eyes it scanned the nearby area for prey. Its nostrils took in water, waiting for the familiar scent of blood. Its lateral line glittered with signals it picked up from the water. The source was close. It was able to determine that it was coming from above. The shark angled upward and saw a shape moving along the surface, contrasting with the sunlight from above. It had rapid muscle contractions and a rapidly increasing heartbeat. The shark swam upward and circled the unsuspecting swimmer, creating a few ripples along the surface as it put itself in position.

****

A strange feeling swept over Scott, causing him to stop swimming outward. He caught his breath, scissoring his legs hard enough to keep him afloat. In the corner of his eye, he noticed a rippling in the water nearly thirty feet away from him. It was then like a sixth sense switched on within him; a bizarre feeling that he wasn't alone in the water. The surface was awfully still, aside from the occasional wave every twenty seconds. The ripples went against the current, which brought him to question why there was a disturbance so far away. He glanced back to shore and suddenly regretted swimming out so far.

Dolphins? He thought to himself. He was no expert, but he figured if dolphins were around, their presence would be more obvious because they traveled in pods. He turned to look around him, seeing if there were any signs of something in the water with him. When he turned to his right, there was another ripple dissipating. It was on the exact opposite side of him from the other disturbance. His curiosity got the better of him. He took a breath and dipped below the surface to look around. The salt water stung his eyes and caused him to squint hard. His vision was limited, and he couldn't make out any shapes. He turned three hundred sixty degrees and did not see anything around him. Finally, he looked down. He wasn't sure what he was looking at, but beneath him was a large black shape. It was absolutely enormous, and he knew it was alive. An electric blast of adrenaline surged through his body. He drew in a panicked breath after surfacing, and he raced for the shore. He swam at the speed of a gold medalist.

****

From high above, the shark's body and tail length would've created a near perfect circle while it circumnavigated, with its prey unknowingly in the middle. It swam just beneath the surface, creating slight disturbances in the surface with its dorsal fin before descending back beneath to perform its attack. When the Thresher was in position, the target detected its presence and began to flee. The huge fish swished its tail against the water and pursued. It was about fifteen feet below and twenty feet behind, within range to attack. Its tail swung overhead like a scorpion's stinger and struck its target.

****

Scott felt an impact from behind him, striking him just below his left hip along his quadriceps. The water erupted around him and he was hurled several feet above the surface. He felt himself hit the water, disoriented. After a few long moments, he forced himself to stroke his arms and kick his legs, despite the intense strain his entire body felt. He broke the surface, but struggled to stay afloat. He felt himself kicking, but he couldn't feel the water's resistance on his left leg. While keeping his eyes on the shoreline, he reached down, fearing the strange incident may have broken a bone in his leg. The reality was far worse; his entire leg was gone beneath the hip, sliced clean off from the impact. He looked at the water around him and saw it was bright red with his blood. He looked up to the heavens and screamed his last breath, unaware of the shape that encompassed him from below. His scream turned to a bloody gurgle when his ribcage crushed in on his lungs while the huge jaws closed upon him. Jagged teeth punctured his flesh. His rib bones, chest plate, and spinal cord splintered under the intense pressure of the Thresher's bite. Scott's throat filled with blood, which was replaced by seawater after he was dragged beneath the surface. The Thresher opened its mouth and bit down again, working its prey down its gullet. It swallowed and left the area in search of more food.

****

The mistress had been lazing in bed for several minutes, expecting her date to return to the room. Surprisingly, he didn't come back. She sat up, covering herself with the sheet. The bedroom door was open, giving her a line of sight into the living room. He didn't appear to be in there. She stood up and put on a robe before stepping out.

"Hey you," she called out in a seductive voice. There was no answer. His clothes were still scattered on the bedroom floor, so she knew he didn't leave. She walked through the whole house, but there was no sign of Scott. She stepped outside, thinking he was out on the patio. No sign of him there either. All she saw was a wristwatch left on the patio chair, and a trail of footprints in the sandy beach leading up to the water. She looked out onto the ocean and saw nothing but blue water. Nobody was swimming.

CHAPTER 7

It was fifteen minutes before shift change while Allison Metzler sat in her parked car in silence. She kept the engine running and blasted the air conditioning. The heat and humidity already caused her to start sweating through her undershirt. The anxiety she was experiencing added to the misery. The previous day was such a miserable experience that she couldn't shake the foreboding feeling of dread that filled her mind. While staring at the entrance through her cracked windshield, she questioned in her mind whether she made a good decision taking this job. Her enthusiasm was still lagging, and her confidence was gone. She repeatedly reminded herself of her sister who desperately needed the financial assistance. The clock on her car radio flashed seven-fifty. She switched off her car and went into the building.

She sat in the same spot at the front table as the previous day. The room was already half full and officers were still coming in. As she went for her seat, several of her fellow officers would ask things such as "How's it like to ride with Riker?", "Holy crap! A felony arrest on your first day!" or "How's it feel to be trained by the best?" She answered most of these with a simple nod or a brief "It's good," said in a passive tenor. So far there was no sign of Riker. She remembered he arrived late previously.

He'll probably arrive after the briefing, she thought. Another young male officer sat in the vacant seat next to her. She remembered his name from the day before, Officer Jim Perry. He was slightly younger than her, and his maturity level was closer to that of a teenager. He was polite enough, but he was easily excitable. The coffee didn't help—she watched him pour at least four packs of sugar into the cup, and there was already creamer in it.

"Here she is; Riker's apprentice," he said, speaking as if she was a *Star Wars* Jedi character. Even his voice sounded like a high schooler's. "That was a hell of a first day. Keep this up, you'll be rising in the ranks faster than anybody here." She gave a small, polite laugh. It was a small and slightly insincere way of saying 'thank you'. All the while, she thought of what he and everyone else had been saying. *"Holy crap! A felony arrest on your first day!"* *"You'll be rising through the ranks!"* She came to realize a certain fact: this department did not see much action. She glanced around the room at all the officers. She studied their faces. They were laughing, smiling, drinking coffee, and having a good time. She determined that, based on what she was seeing along with the things they would say, these officers did not carry much experience. They were amazed by a felony arrest on her first day, like it was a rarity for Merit. True, the crime rate was significantly low, but the atmosphere was so different than what she trained with. During her coursework in college, and also when she attended the police academy, she visited many police departments all over the state. In most places, a quiet uneventful day was considered a gift amongst the officers. In Merit PD, it was the norm. During her studies, she learned a rookie could often encounter anything from responding to an armed robbery to a vicious assault. With each visit, she could see the seriousness, grit, and stress built into the officers. Law Enforcement was no game. Officer Perry spoke again, breaking her train of thought.

"So, I didn't get to ask yesterday. What was it like to work with Leonard Riker?" The way these officers spoke of him, it was clear his reputation was well known. Metzler wanted to tell the truth of her experience, but she couldn't find the right words.

"I certainly learned a lot," she said. "He's not the sort to screw around." There was a pause while she thought of something more to say. "He has his own way of doing things." Of course, Perry had no idea she was referring to Riker bullying trainees.

"Man, I would love to get a chance to work with him," Perry said. "Maybe I can arrange with Crawford or the Sergeant to let me hook up with you guys." Metzler looked at him and forced a small smile. Her tone was matter-of-fact.

"Perry, the thing is this… Riker's the kind of guy…" her voice trailed off. She wasn't quite sure what to say exactly. More than anything, she could tell she was already living under the famous officer's shadow. And she hated it. She hated that she was forced to train with him. The fact that he hadn't arrived yet showed he had no respect for the job. She wondered why he was here to begin with. She'd be far happier to train with any of the inexperienced cops in the room. At least they'd show her the ropes and not make a fool of her.

"The thing is…what?" Perry interrupted her thoughts again. She forgot she trailed off mid-sentence.

"Well, you read how Riker tends to work," she decided to go with a mild answer. "When he worked in Alton, he faced criticism because he preferred to work alone. At least, that's what I've read. I suspect he is still like that, and that he's training me as a kind of favor."

"Oh, I see," Perry said. "That's cool of him, though. He sounds like a nice guy."

Oh God, I hope you don't try and make Detective, Metzler thought. Suddenly the Sergeant emerged from the hallway, followed by Chief Crawford. He was accompanied by a finely dressed woman. She wore an austere expression on her face, especially when she looked into the room of officers. The Sergeant spoke with Crawford for a moment, passing along information before the briefing. "Oh, this is lovely," Perry complained under his voice.

"What's going on? Who is that?" Metzler asked. She followed his example and kept her voice down to avoid being heard.

"You don't know who that is? That's Kathy Bloom, the Vice Mayor," he said. He sighed and shook his head, as if he disapproved of her presence. "Mayor Ripefield is out of service because of some family issue, so she's the acting mayor now. This is just fantastic."

"I'm guessing she's not well liked?" Metzler asked. Perry shook his head, keeping an eye at the front of the room to be sure they weren't heard having this discussion.

"She's got issues," he said. "She's one of those… you know, self-important types. Treats everyone below her like they're worthless. She'll complain about police officers and minority treatment, yada-yada-yada. Personally, I think she hates men." He stopped to sip on his sweetened coffee. "I know she had daddy issues."

"What do you mean?"

"Her father is a United States Senator," Perry answered. "From what I've heard, Bloom thought she was gonna get a free ride to a grand political career. I don't know if they had a falling out or what, but she clearly didn't get what she wanted. Now here she is as a Vice Mayor of a fairly small town…not the most high-profile job when you want to be in Congress or the Senate. The only reason most people here even know her name is because she never held back on her criticism of the department…and police in general."

"Attention everybody!" the midnight shift sergeant called out. The commotion started to settle down. Metzler glanced at the Chief, who stood silent while the briefing took place. It was evidenced in his face that he wasn't in a good mood. Vice Mayor Bloom stood next to him, maintaining her sour facial expression. Metzler had no problem believing everything Perry said was true. Another man stood behind them. He looked as if he didn't want to be there. Metzler guessed he was Bloom's driver.

Crawford subtly gazed across the room. He saw Metzler sitting in the front row, and no sign of Riker. It was only five minutes after eight, and he could feel his blood pressure going up. He spent several minutes before briefing getting chewed out by Bloom because she wanted his officers to take sensitivity training. She was the polar opposite of Mayor Ripefield, who was a much friendlier type. He trusted the people in his community to do their jobs, and didn't express the need to micromanage. He definitely lacked Bloom's superiority complex. *Why he had her as his running mate, I'll never know*, Crawford thought. The Sergeant completed the briefing and stepped away from the podium. Crawford took his place.

"Good morning everyone," he opened. "I know I mentioned this yesterday, but I'm reminding you once again of the sailing competition that'll take place next week. It's a big deal to the community, and I just want to urge everyone to represent this department with the upmost integrity and discipline. Of course, you should be doing that anyway, but it's especially important next week because we'll have people from all over the country here in Merit. Now…" he paused and gestured toward Bloom, "Acting Mayor Bloom wants to have a quick word with you before you head out." He was sure to include the word 'Acting' rather than 'Vice', at Bloom's insistence. He stepped away and allowed her to take center stage. She was a woman of medium height in her mid-forties—although she appeared a bit older. At the podium, she glared into the room as if she was expecting an applause.

"Good morning," she began. The greeting was dry and insincere. "Like your chief said, we have the National Association of Sailing arriving over the weekend." She punctuated each word, almost as if she was indirectly reprimanding Crawford for simply calling it 'the sailing competition.' "I'll be perfectly clear. There'll be a lot of people here. A lot of <u>diverse</u> people!" Crawford tightened his jaw while he listened, and he was certain much of his staff were doing the same. *Maybe Riker being late is actually a good thing,* he thought. He doubted Riker would be able to withhold comments during Bloom's speech. He was having a hard time doing so himself.

"There'll be no harassment of the tourists. I expect you to treat each individual with respect. This event costs a lot of money, and it is bringing a lot of business to the people here in Merit." *And a lot of media attention to you,* Crawford thought. He knew all this was her expressing her authority to the department. "I won't describe how unhappy I'll be if I get reports of persecution based on race, gender, ethnicity, religion preference, you name it. You'll just face the consequences. I'm sure your chief will uphold these standards, and I hope there'll be no problems. That's all." There was no 'good-bye' or 'have a safe shift' or anything like that. She and her driver walked through the room and exited out the back exit. Metzler watched her do this, confused why she went out that way. Perry noticed her puzzled expression.

"She doesn't like to come through the front of the building," he answered her unspoken question. "Apparently, she doesn't want to be near the people that come through the intake area." Metzler let out a small scoffing chuckle, then quickly covered her mouth and pretended she was coughing when she realized it was loud enough to be heard. Nobody seemed to notice, and if they did, they didn't care.

"Thanks, everyone. Briefing's over," Crawford said as he walked into the hallway. His voice was exasperated, and he didn't bother to hide it. The officers all started out the door to begin radioing their beginning shift information, including Perry. Metzler went into the hallway after Crawford. Initially she thought to inform him about Riker's absence, but she realized he probably already knew. Instead, she wanted to plead her case about no longer training with him. Crawford walked past his office and headed for the front of the building, near the intake area.

"Excuse me, sir!" Metzler called out. Crawford slowed down and looked back.

"Officer Metzler," he said. "What can I do for you?" He continued walking and Metzler kept pace with him.

"I want to ask you something about me training with Riker," she said. "I'm grateful to have the opportunity, but perhaps it might be best if I continue training with someone else." Crawford stopped and looked at her. For a moment, she thought he was angry at her. However, she recognized the expression in his eyes as concern.

"Dispatch reported you two had a productive shift," he said. "You've made numerous traffic stops, and during one you two made an arrest for somebody with a warrant out for them. That's a helluva first day." Metzler started to speak, but suddenly she just wasn't sure what to say. She had a whole speech planned in her mind, but instantly it went away. She didn't want to admit she nearly screwed up the arrest. "What did he do?" Crawford suddenly asked.

"Well sir, he, uhhh," she stuttered.

"Come on, kid, spit it out. I want to help you, but I don't have all day," he said. The firmness of his voice conveyed that she needed to get her act straight.

"Did you see any of the tickets we brought in?" she asked. Crawford laughed.

"I'm the chief, kiddo. I handle bigger pieces of paperwork, and don't even get me started on the politics and red tape. Tickets go right into a database, you should know that."

"It's just that he--" a large slamming sound from the entrance cut her off. The entry door opened wide and hit the side of the wall. A stream of sunlight streamed into the lobby, lighting the way as Riker strolled in, dragging a handcuffed suspect by the shirt collar. The individual appeared to be in his early twenties, dressed in a t-shirt and shorts, and covered in piercings. He yelled and complained while Riker took him through the lobby, and pushed him toward the check-in counter where an intake officer took custody of him.

"This little guy made me late," he said to the officer. "I caught him trying to sneak through a broken window with intent to loot. I already dusted for prints and have pictures of the scene." As he began to walk away, he saw Crawford and Metzler standing together. Crawford knew Riker too well. He may have found and arrested the looter, but it was just an excuse to arrive late in hopes of Metzler being assigned to somebody else.

"Just in time," the chief said, "Metzler was wondering where you were. Oh, and you know you could've called that in." He pointed at the suspect being processed. Riker shrugged his shoulders.

"Nah," he said. "I didn't need help taking care of it."

"No, I mean it would've been nice to know what you were doing. It's called procedure." He turned to Metzler and quietly said, "Let me know if he gives you more problems. In the meantime, make the best of it." She nodded. Although she didn't explain to him, it appeared he had an idea of what was going on. However, in her mind she was screaming. *Why is it so important that I have to train with this guy?!* She faked a polite smile at Riker.

"Good morning. Good catch!" Her voice was upbeat. He growled under his breath and moved on. Metzler gritted her teeth and followed him. She knew she was in for another long day.

****

Metzler sat in the passenger seat of the patrol car, with a signed citation in hand. They were on road patrol for about an hour, and Riker was starting in on the misery. This recent routine stop was for a vehicle that ran a red light. The rear bumper was just clearing the intersection when the light went red, and naturally the driver argued with her about it.

He didn't resist signing it, but was intent on challenging it to the judge and threatened to notify her supervising officer.

"You can switch off the lights now," she said. Riker sat in the driver's seat and eyeballed the car they stopped. She followed his eyes and noticed he was looking at the brake light, which was fading. *Oh, hell no*, she thought. Without hesitating she hit the switch to stop the flashing lights, and the vehicle then drove off.

"What the hell are you doing?" Riker said.

"I think we've pissed him off enough," Metzler answered. She was starting to sweat heavily from being out in the heat and humidity. She reached over and turned the air conditioning on full blast.

"Need me to get you a snow cone?" Riker condescendingly remarked.

"Easy for you to judge," Metzler said. "You've been in here the whole time. Although I will say, I don't know how you can stand wearing that black heavy outfit."

"Beats those pansy ass cub scout uniforms," he said, pointing at her shirt. He started driving. There was a bit more awkward silence, such as there was the previous day. As much as she hated working with him, the silent treatment added boredom to the misery. She tried breaking the ice yesterday with no results. In her mind she argued against it, but ultimately decided to try.

"How old were you when you became a cop?" she began. Riker glanced over at her and then back at the road. She could read his mind: *Why do you care?* She expected him to respond with that, or some sarcastic remark, or just not speak at all.

"Twenty-two," he said.

"Oh!" Metzler exclaimed. She failed to hide her astonished reaction from the fact that he gave an intelligent answer.

"*Oh*? Why does that surprise you?" he said. "A lot of guys go in around that age."

"Uh, no, no, I'm not surprised," she stammered. She didn't plan this conversation out in her mind. She fumbled for things to say. "Did you always know you were gonna be a cop, or were there other interests?" Riker sat quietly for a moment while he continued driving.

"I thought of becoming a physical therapist for a while," he eventually answered. "I guess I'm better at breaking people than putting them back together."

"Why did you become a cop?" There was a long delay after this question. He shrugged his shoulders before answering, as if he didn't want to explain.

"I knew someone growing up," he answered vaguely. "I guess I joined because of him."

"Your dad?" Metzler guessed.

"He acts like it sometimes," Riker said. His voice was bleak as he answered. He hated being asked questions, so he decided to turn the tables. "So, what about you? What made you want to want to run around and play Cops and Robbers?" Metzler didn't answer right away, and she knew Riker would read into that. She thought of her sister, but she wasn't too fond of the thought of telling Riker about the situation.

"I just wanted to play a good role in the community and…"

"Oh, don't give me that 'protect and serve' bullshit," Riker interrupted. "I read your file. One doesn't go through seven years of higher education to become a cop in this dinky little town, unless they needed money fast and didn't want to risk going through the more competitive job market. Also, your file showed you began work in pursuing a doctorate, but stopped suddenly and was sponsored into Clayton and accepted into Merit PD."

"There are worse jobs to have," Metzler defensively said.

"It'd fit if you were married or engaged and just wanted to settle down," he continued. "But as far as I know, you're neither of those. And my gut tells me you're not attached. So, something's brought you here."

"I'm just here to do a job," she said. "What difference does it make anyway?"

"It's all about a matter of judgment," Riker said. "Someone who plans for something bigger their whole life, just to suddenly settle for less, is probably someone who hasn't made very good judgment." He glanced at her. She stared back at him and held back every insult her mind was forming. It wouldn't matter anyway; Riker didn't seem the type to be hurt by mere words. "Ah HA!" Riker suddenly exclaimed. He pulled the vehicle off to the side of the road and pointed ahead. "You see that?" Metzler looked to where he was pointing to. Two large men had crossed the road in a non-designated area.

"You've got to be kidding me," she muttered. Riker turned in his seat to face her, leaning on the center console.

"You want me to believe you're seriously here to uphold the law?" he questioned. "Then, go out there and show me." She glared at him. She knew he didn't care why she was here. This was just another way for him to make her miserable. Sadly, this was considered an order from a training officer, and she had to follow it. She opened the door and stepped out. Before she slammed the door shut, Riker called out, "Don't forget the ticket book!" She reached into the inside pocket of the door and pulled out a ticket book for jaywalking. Without saying a word, she slammed the door.

The two men were dressed as bikers. Both had large, round bodies with meaty arms. They wore sunglasses and leather vests with no sleeves. One had a red bandanna on his head, while the other didn't cover his bald head. They appeared to be in conversation with each other until they noticed Metzler approaching.

"Excuse me gentlemen," she called out to them, "I couldn't help but notice what you did just there." They looked as if they were holding back laughter. She knew instantly they were judging her by appearance.

"Did what just when?" one of them squawked. His voice was raspy, indicating he was a heavy smoker. The other one was already starting to chuckle.

"The two of you were jaywalking," Metzler said. She fought to maintain her composure. These two large men were naturally intimidating and already seemed intent on challenging her. It didn't seem to matter that she wore a badge and gun.

"Oh JAYWALKING!" The same one shouted, pretending it was a revelation.

"My! That's bad!" The other one played along. "How do we sleep at night?!"

"We're totally in trouble," the first one said. He looked down at the shorter female officer. "What must we do to atone for this?" He let out a small laugh. Metzler felt herself starting to sweat again.

"Well, uh," she started to stammer, "you can start by presenting your driver's license or state ID." The two of them looked at each other and then burst out into fits of laughter. They laughed hard enough, tremors rippled through their large bellies. It was a very off-putting sight for Metzler. She turned away and looked to the patrol car. Through the windshield, she could see Riker smiling. He knew she was miserable, and he loved it.

That's when she realized something. She thought of Chief Crawford's words to her earlier; *Try to make the best of it.* She figured he was blowing her off, but now she knew otherwise. Riker's entertainment was from seeing her be miserable and uncomfortable. Each time she showed how fed up she was, Riker was more pleased with the situation. So now she vowed to do the opposite. Her expression and body language went from uneasy to steadfast and confident.

"You think this is funny?" she said to the big men, who were still laughing.

"A little bit, lady," one said.

"Well then," she said. She reached along the sides of her duty belt. In one hand she pulled a set of handcuffs. One of the men was preparing to make a crude comment, but stopped when she pulled out an expandable baton with her other hand. With a press of a button, the weapon expanded into a sixteen-inch piece of steel. The laughter came to an immediate stop. Their eyebrows lifted and both men stepped back, alarmed.

"Holy shit!" both yelled.

"What's your problem lady?" the one with the bandanna said while pointing at the baton. "That's going a little bit overboard, don't you think?"

"Refusal to follow police instructions after committing an offense is grounds for arrest," Metzler said. Suddenly, she sounded like a female terminator.

"So...what?" the bald man said. His voice was now the one stuttering. He looked at the baton. "You going to bust us up with that or something?" He tried to play tough, but he was suddenly feeling intimidated by this young female cop who was a third of his size.

"I would like to avoid that," she said. "But to perform an arrest, I am authorized to use any means necessary to do my duty. So, we can do this the easy way, or the hard way." She allowed her words to sink in. "Or there's a third option... just present your IDs, and we can all go about our day." They didn't even think about it. Both men fumbled into their jeans pockets and pulled out their wallets. It was almost as if they were eager to be issued citations. After reviewing their IDs, she collapsed her baton and placed it back in her belt, along with the handcuffs. She politely smiled at the two men. "Thank you for your cooperation. Consider this a verbal warning. Please cross the roads at designated areas for your own safety. Enjoy the rest of your day and be safe." Both men were puzzled and relieved at the same time.

"Oh yes ma'am!" Both of them enthusiastically agreed. "Thank you very much. If you ever need some donuts, I'll be your delivery boy!" They continued with a series of compliments while she walked to the patrol car. She couldn't help but smile...her first feeling of positivity while on the job. She sat in the passenger seat, and noticed Riker glaring at her. He appeared puzzled himself, and trying desperately to hide it.

"You forgot the tickets," he said.

"I let them off with a warning," she said. "Trust me; they won't be jaywalking from now on. And by the way, you said 'don't forget the ticket book'. Nothing about actually writing one. Therefore, I didn't forget. How's that for judgment?" Riker gave no response. An awkward silence consumed the police cruiser for several seconds. Static suddenly buzzed from the radio.

"*Unit One to Unit Eighteen?*" It was Crawford's voice. Riker pressed on the transmitter.

"Yes, Unit One, go ahead."

"*Unit Eighteen, I need you to meet me at Manson Dock as soon as you can,*" Crawford said. Manson Dock was where the police patrol boats were docked. It was devised to keep the police boats separate from civilian fishing vessels in the harbor.

"Is it an urgent matter?"

"*It depends on your definition of urgent. Just get over here please.*" He didn't sound pleased. Riker shared a similar feeling. He turned the patrol car around with a U-turn. Metzler tucked the ticket book away, feeling pleased with herself.

"So, what'd you do before becoming a cop?" she asked. He didn't answer, and she knew he was getting fed up.

I'm getting damn sick of these questions, he thought.

****

Manson Dock was a very small site for the vessels. There were at least a dozen police boats, all lined up near a deck that extended about twenty feet into the water. On shore was a small building that looked like a garage, except on the front was written *Merit Police Department: Harbor Patrol.* In front of the building stood Chief Crawford. Standing next to him was Officer Marley, the officer assigned to the building. He was a short stocky man, who constantly wore a smile on his face. His job was to issue keys to officers assigned to patrol boats. In the police car, Riker had lit a cigar before arriving. Metzler was gagging and coughing from the smoke that clouded within the vehicle. She rolled her window down, but it didn't filter it out completely. After they parked, she was the first one to step out. Riker casually leaned on the car after standing up, and gave a two-finger salute at Crawford.

"What's up, Chief?"

"They could build monuments to your stubbornness!" Crawford said. He acknowledged Metzler with a nod. "How are you doing?"

"I'm surviving," she said. He noticed a hint of cheerfulness in her voice.

"Good," he said before returning his attention to Riker. "Do you seriously know what a pain in the ass you are?"

"No, but something tells me you're gonna tell me," Riker said.

"My office has been swamped all day with phone calls. People bitching about being ticketed for driving one mile over the limit. What the hell have you been doing?"

"Don't know why you're mad at me. My signature wasn't on the tickets," Riker said before puffing on his cigar. Astounded, Metzler's eyes widened and her mouth dropped open. Riker was trying to pin this on her!

"Oh, shut up," Crawford said. Metzler relaxed, realizing he didn't take the bait. "You're her training officer. Everything she does is a reflection on you. Plus, I'm confident she wasn't the one who selected these traffic stops."

"So what?" Riker said. "You're gonna grill me for pulling over people for speeding? Technically that's what they were doing."

"No," Crawford said. "It's what I told the people who complained. You're right, it's definitely the truth, no matter how ridiculous it is. But I know why you're doing this, and it isn't going to work. You can make me as miserable as you want with these games, but I'm going to win in the end. Now come over here please." Metzler walked up and Riker lagged behind. "I'm assigning you guys on Marine Patrol," he said. "You won't be handing out speeding tickets out there."

"Sorry, but I haven't been trained to operate a..." Riker began.

"Don't give me that crap!" Crawford nearly yelled. "These boats are very similar to the ones we had on the lake back in Alton. You know how to operate them. Oh...and I happen to remember you hated it." He laughed. "You want to play games with me? Well, now you see how I play." He started to laugh again, but it turned into a small cough after Riker casually blew a puff of cigar smoke in his face. The building officer backed away, feeling awkward from the whole situation. He went into the building and sat at his desk.

"Need a doctor there, Chief?" Riker remarked.

"I ought to be going over the no-smoking policy with you," Crawford said. "But you're going to be so bored out there, I'll let you have it. Officer Marley will issue you a key." As he walked away, he passed Metzler. "Good luck," he whispered. Riker stood in place, puffing on his cigar. Finally, he stepped inside the building. Seated at the desk, Officer Marley looked up at him and quickly noticed he had the cigar.

"You know you're not supposed to," he paused, seeing Riker's expression growing increasingly livid, "...inhale those!" He stood up and fumbled in a cabinet for a key to a patrol boat. Riker nearly crushed it in his hand after he took it.

CHAPTER 8

Over the previous night, Allison Metzler had lost sleep because of anxiety over patrolling the roads with Riker. Now, she longed heavily for road patrol. Harbor patrol was the most boring assignment in the department. Hardly anyone volunteered for it unless they specifically wanted light duty. Any disturbances out in the water were usually further out and handled by the Coast Guard. However, the previous chief of police managed to get funding for the police force to have their own harbor patrol.

Metzler hated Riker for his previous stunts more than ever now. They had spent a mind-numbing two hours on the twenty-five-foot patrol vessel, and it appeared they were going to be on it for the remainder of the shift. She leaned on the railing at the stern while Riker stood at the cockpit. He had lit up a fresh cigar, and the wind was blowing the smoke right at her, no matter where she moved to. The one nice thing was that the vessel had a cooler loaded with bottled water and cans of soda. She opened a water bottle and continued to scan the horizon. Every once in a while, they'd see a fishing vessel pass by. Other than that, it was empty sea, except the image of a mid-sized fishing trawler in the distance.

"You know, we should probably install a fighting chair and fish for marlin whenever we're out here," she joked. As she predicted, Riker didn't give any reaction. He just puffed his cigar and steered the vessel. For Metzler, the boredom was too much. She grew restless, unable to surrender herself to simply looking at the water all day, no matter how beautiful it was. "Oh God, could this boat have a damn T.V. at least?" she complained.

"This is the life Crawford wanted," Riker said, seemingly to himself, "a life in law enforcement where nothing happens. This place is a damn joke." Metzler now started to regret initiating conversation. She didn't particularly care for what he had to say. Although she was bored, she didn't question the duties assigned to her.

"I wouldn't say that," she said. "This place has an extraordinarily low crime rate. The police here must be doing something right for that to be so." Riker chomped on his cigar and put the boat on autopilot. He grabbed a soda from the cooler and walked to the port side. Once at the rail, he spat a huge wad of saliva into the water. "Charming," Metzler remarked.

"Merit is a relatively small place," Riker said. "It used to be primarily a residential area. It didn't have much of a business growth until sometime in the last decade. It's a high gun ownership area, so home invasions don't typically happen here. There doesn't seem to be much of a drug problem here, except for when tourists smoke weed in their hotels. There never was anything here to make the crime rate high. Plus, the department is a damned disgrace. The knuckleheads working here probably couldn't spot a teenager with a fake ID if their lives depended on it."

"If you think it's so bad, then why did you come here?" Metzler asked. Riker turned away, ignoring the question. She wondered what the answer was, and she thought she knew how to press him for it. She joined him at the port railing. He seemed to be looking at the trawler in the distance, which seemed to drift a bit closer. It was the only thing to look at. She wondered what was on his mind; specifically, why he seemed so unhappy. She wondered if it had anything to do with stress from his service in Alton. There were so many stories about Leonard Riker she couldn't keep count of them all. One of the common beliefs was that he would coin a catchphrase when dispatching a suspect. It sparked a curiosity that she wanted to satisfy. "So, here's a question for you…"

"You seem to have plenty of them," Riker said. He sounded fed up and impatient.

"When you arrested Johnny Quibbs, the Enforcer, did you actually say 'chew on this' before hitting him in the face with a brick?" Quibbs was a notorious mob enforcer who conducted 'jobs' all along the northeast. He was well known for his love of chewing gum. The case ended in a violent physical confrontation, in which Riker reportedly got the upper hand with a rubble stone brick.

"And why do you want to know this?" he asked.

"Well, it's one of the things we learned about you," Metzler answered. "You had more one-liners than Arnold Schwarzenegger. You should've seen our academy class. Everyone was imitating some of your reported quotes."

"Sounds like it was a big game," he grumbled. "Do you believe everything you see on television?"

"This stuff is more prominent on the internet, actually," Metzler sarcastically said. "A lot of your cases were covered in our textbooks, most of it was positive. Also, there are law enforcement websites our instructors encouraged us to visit. One of them had a notification that you were no longer with Alton PD, but it didn't say why. Which brings me back to my other question; why did you transfer here?" Riker stared angrily at her.

"According to you, my whole career is available to read online," he growled. "Why don't you go read about it there and come up with your own conclusions like everyone else?" She thought for a second. It was obvious he was getting fed up by all the questioning she had been doing all day. Deep down, she actually enjoyed getting on his nerves. It beat the awkward silence—and it felt like payback for yesterday's misery.

"The media hit you pretty hard on that kidnapping case you were on," she said. Metzler was referring to the Joan Carter kidnapping. It was without a doubt Riker's most notorious case he had been on. Joan Carter was the six-year-old daughter of the CEO of a wealthy construction company. The kidnappers demanded a ransom that would've forced the CEO to sign over company rights to a rival. Riker tracked the girl down, and discovered that the kidnappers were mercenaries that worked for the owner of that rival company, intent on bringing down the competition. He was able to recover Joan Carter unharmed, but the ensuing chase resulted in a large-scale firefight on a four-lane highway. Several civilians and some police were injured in the process, although there were no fatalities except for some of the suspects. The local media cast the blame on Riker for the massive incident, saying the shootout wouldn't have taken place if he hadn't persisted on the case. However, the department gave him support. It was revealed that the mercenaries were also contracting for a terrorist organization, and their cut of the ransom would supply funding for illegal weaponry.

Riker's facial muscles tensed. He was getting more irritated by the second. It was like this rookie was interrogating him on his background, looking to see if she could create a case of police brutality or something. Metzler found herself enjoying the scenario. Yesterday, Riker was testing her limits, and today she was testing his. The tables had turned in this battle of who-could-make-the-other-more-miserable.

"I bet it was that," she continued. Her voice contained excitement. "You couldn't handle the media pressure, so you resigned and followed Chief Crawford here."

"I couldn't give a duck fart about the fucking reporters," Riker said. "If you ever work a real police job, you'll understand they learn a fact or two, and they'll make up the rest."

"I see," she said. "Perhaps the reason you transferred was…"

"What the hell is this psycho-babble bullshit?" Riker snarled. "Does this seriously work on other people?" *It's working just fine on you*, she thought. "What is up with your need to know why I'm here? What'll it be after that? My bank records?"

"I'm just figuring out who I'm working with," Metzler said.

"I thought you had the internet for that," he said. "Well, I found out who *I'm* working with! A cocky, snot-nosed, naive little girl who only got a job because her uncle's the mayor. She reads shit and assumes it's true. She studies police tactics, but can't apply them practically, and yet she thinks she can make the world a better place."

"I came out the top of my class," Metzler became defensive.

"Oh right, from *Clayton*," Riker smirked. "So much great experience quoting one liners during firearms training? Let me ask you; did they even teach you to disassemble your Glock?"

"Well yes, of course..." Metzler said.

"How 'bout how to remove the firing pin?" he added. Metzler stuttered, finally shrugging her shoulders. "Point proven. That's who I'm working with. Someone who believes she knows how it is, but really doesn't know shit." Metzler grew angry.

"Oh yeah? Well it looks like *I'm* stuck working with a macho cowboy who spends his time bullying people for his own amusement," she shot back. Her blood pressure rose, and she felt herself getting so mad that arguing actually felt good. "I wouldn't be surprised if this attitude of yours is why you're here. I know Crawford pulled some strings to get you here."

"...And stuck me with you!" he said as if completing her sentence. His voice sounded like he was comparing their partnership like a bad relationship. That's how Metzler took it.

"Being stuck with you hasn't been a picnic," she said. "Thank God it's only for eight hours a day. Can't imagine doing it for any longer. God forbid we ever have to work a double-shift. Shit, imagine being married to you. I'd probably kill myself." Almost instantly, Riker's whole demeanor changed. His angry expression was still there, but Metzler could see something in his eyes that was different: something very dark. His unopened coke can exploded in his hand, crushed by a tightening grip intensified by rage. Blackish grey suds foamed over his hand. He spit his cigar into the water. Metzler instantly regretted pushing his limits. She didn't feel physically in danger, but she could tell she made a bad judgment. She felt her face turn red. It seemed today was going better, but now she felt like she made it far worse.

Shit! Well, now I really hope that he demands from Crawford to partner me with someone else, she thought. Yesterday, she felt foolish because she allowed herself to be easily intimidated. Today she felt foolish because she tried to show strength in challenging her trainer.

A shadow in the water took her attention off the tension on deck. Her eyes went to the dim shape. She gasped when she realized it was the watery reflection of the enormous fishing trawler. It was adrift, and it was directly in the path of their patrol boat. Riker saw her reaction and looked behind him to see what she was looking at. The trawler was seventy feet long and its bow was bearing down on them.

"Holy shit!" he yelled. He made a dash for the cockpit and cut the wheel hard to starboard. The patrol vessel cut to the right. Its portside barely cleared the trawler's peak ballast point. He accelerated the throttle and created some distance between the two boats. Water sprayed as the propellers increased rotation speed. Riker quickly glanced behind him at the trawler. He didn't get a good look, but it didn't appear there was anybody on deck. He cut the wheel again to circle back. "Alright," he growled angrily, "who in the hell is steering that damn thing?" Metzler studied the trawler while he steered the vessel. The boat didn't appear to be operating at all. It simply seemed to be moving along with the current. She felt a chill run down her spine when she noticed other strange features on the large boat. The police vessel pointed its bow at the front of the trawler, and Riker reduced speed while they approached it on its starboard side.

"Riker..." Metzler said. He looked ahead, able to get a more stable view.

"What the..." he said. It was like they were staring at a ghost ship. On the starboard side of the hull was an enormous gash that started a few feet from the peak and stretched roughly twenty feet, angling upward. It was as if something had struck the ship in a whipping motion. Up above on the superstructure, they could see that the glass windshield had been shattered, and the forward and port walls had been somewhat dented in. The gantry cables hung freely, and the side of the trawler had several miscellaneous indentations. Along the side, just under the railing were the words *Mary Westward* etched in the steel.

"Oh my God," Metzler said in awe. "What happened here?" Riker looked at the vessel name while he steered the patrol boat to line up with the boarding ladder.

"Well, shit! It's the *Mary Westward*," he said.

"*Mary Westward*?" She was oblivious to the name.

"During the hurricane, the Coast Guard reported it missing. It was supposed to dock in Miami, but it seems the crew got caught off guard when the storm changed course." Suddenly his tone returned to being more hostile. "Wait a minute, why am I explaining this? Didn't you get the memo?"

"No, I don't recall getting one," Metzler said.

"Start checking your work email," he said. "The Coast Guard received a mayday signal from this ship, but they lost contact. They probably would've found it yesterday if we didn't have that second storm roll in." Metzler examined the haunting sight. There was so much damage to the hull, she figured it was lucky not to be taking on water. It was as if a battering ram had repeatedly hit the trawler's underside. The huge laceration above the waterline was a disturbing sight, along with the lack of visible crew.

"Why isn't anyone on deck?" she questioned. "And what the hell happened up there?" She pointed to the ravaged wheelhouse. Riker didn't answer. He wondered these same things. He manipulated the vessel to turn and face in the same direction as the *Mary Westward* and lined up with the boarding ladder that ran down the side.

"Take the wheel," he ordered Metzler. She took his place in the cockpit and he went to the portside, grabbing hold of the steel bars.

"What are you doing?" she asked. Riker got a foothold on the ladder before looking back.

"Whaddya think?" he said. "I'm checking out the site. Since I'm training you, I guess I can say the proper phrasing is 'commencing an investigation'. I also like to call it police-work." Metzler rolled her eyes.

"What am I supposed to do?" she asked.

"You can notify dispatch," he said. He may as well have said 'you should know this already.' "Tell them we found the trawler. They'll want to notify the Coast Guard." He started climbing the ladder. While he ascended, he called down, "Remember to tell them it's the *Mary Westward*," in a condescending tone.

"Fuck yourself," Metzler mumbled under her breath before grabbing the radio.

Riker climbed and stopped when he was about halfway up. A small section of the ladder, roughly two feet of length, had been broken away. He examined the ends of the bars on both sides of the missing section. They were bent inward, pressing into the side of the boat, and there was a slight indentation in the steel. It appeared to be the result of some sort of impact. He was able to reach over the broken portion of ladder and climb over topside. After he pulled himself up on deck, immediately his eyes went to the floor near the ladder. A huge streak of dried blood was crusted on the deck and railing. It had turned brown, indicating it was a couple days old. It also seemed to be partly washed down by the rainstorms. He suspected it was originally a much larger pool of blood, because of the fact there was some remaining despite heavy rain washing it away. He was also certain it was human. Riker scanned his eyes across the deck. It was a mess of fish netting, bait, wiring, nightlights, and other equipment, but there was no body.

Toward the bow was a stairway that led up to the wheelhouse on the superstructure. He started up the stairs and entered the open doorway, which led into a small, dark hall. The hallway light was burnt out, but Riker could see the two doors in the hall. There was one straight ahead which led to the control console, and there was another to the right, which led downstairs. He stepped inward, and stopped to listen. He could hear something coming from the other side of the wheelhouse door. It sounded like radio chatter.

"Once again, this is the U.S. Coast Guard, trying to make contact with the Mary Westward. Captain Torey please come in." It was the type of message that was repeated over again every few minutes. It was standard procedure for missing ships that haven't been officially considered lost at sea. But Riker could also hear something else. Another voice, but spoken much clearer. It was as if someone was speaking from inside the room. But the dialogue was odd.

"I was so wrong. I'm so sorry," the voice said. The voice was female, and definitely not from the radio. Riker slowly grasped the handle of the door with his left hand, and his other hand instinctively clutched the handle of his revolver. Normally, he'd identify himself as a cop before entering the door, but something about this didn't seem right.

He turned the handle and pushed to open the door quickly. However, it only opened part way. Something on the other side was blocking it. He shoved his body against it, opening it further to squeeze through. With some effort, he got it open wide enough. He stepped inside, still clutching his holstered revolver. The room was a huge mess of debris. The windshield was completely gone, and the forward and port side walls were slightly caved in. Glass riddled the floor and controls. The helm was detached from the panel, and laying on the floor next to it was a television set. There was a DVD player hooked up, and the disc had been playing on a loop the whole time. It was some horror movie, and the scene featured a young woman making a confession.

After that, Riker noticed something else right by the television: a pair of boots. He moved past the stuck open door, and saw the person they were attached to, laying mostly flat on his back on the floor. His upper torso was slightly propped up against the wall. His face was completely gone, caved in as it ended up directly absorbing the massive impact of whatever came through the windshield. The eyes, nose, mouth, and cheekbones had disappeared into a blackish red hole. It was a haunting image that Riker was too familiar with. At this moment, the excruciating smell hit him. On the outside, he kept an emotionless, stable expression. On the inside, he felt his heart sink into a deep dark place, just as it had during previous homicide investigations. The radio blared again. He didn't answer it, since Metzler should've been notifying them from the patrol boat. Looking around the room, he didn't see anything indicative of whatever caused the damage. All the debris appeared to have originated from inside the room. Wind and rain couldn't bust the walls in. The anchor was loose outside, but it didn't seem like it was in a position to swing around and cause this. Riker assumed this dead individual was Captain Torey, although he didn't know what Torey looked like... and even if he did, he wasn't sure it'd do much good. He exited the room and went to the other door in the hallway.

He opened it up just a crack and peeked. There was hardly any light, but he could see that it was a stairway. He pulled a flashlight from his vest and illuminated the stairs and entered. They led to the mess hall, where the crew would normally eat and watch programs on a T.V. It was empty. The room appeared in good shape, aside from a few books, videos, and plates having fallen on the floor, most likely because of the boat rocking in the storm. A doorway led to the galley. It reeked of rotten food. The refrigerator and freezer had lost power, which naturally caused the contents to go bad. Once again, there was no sign of any crewmembers. Riker stepped from the dark kitchen into the crew room. It was a small room, only built for the crew to sleep in. Riker had seen prison cells larger than this room. The bunks were two-high, and there were four sets. He shone his light on all eight beds. Six of them personal contents on them. One had notebooks and pens on it, a few others had some novels. One of them had porno magazines.

What went on here? Did you guys abandon ship? Riker thought. The second crew room was slightly larger, and only contained two bunks; one for the captain, and another for the first mate. Not being crammed with so many people was one of the perks of the job. As Riker expected, it was empty too.

A creak from behind him drew his attention. He quickly distinguished the sounds were footsteps, steadily approaching from the mess and kitchen area. Riker's mind went on full alert. He stood behind the door in the officer's room and listened to the footsteps come through the main crew room. The door pushed open. As the individual stepped in, Riker shined a light in the intruder's face. He was about to yell 'freeze' before he realized it was Metzler. It turned out he wouldn't have needed to yell the instruction, because every muscle in her body froze up.

"Jesus!" Riker exclaimed. He took the light off her face and backed up. "Are you a special kind of stupid, or what? I almost shot you." She took a deep breath and recovered from the briefly intense fright.

"I thought I'd follow you up here," she said. "You had been on the ship for a while, and I figured I'd check on you."

"First of all, I already have a mother," Riker said. "Second of all, we have radios, you knucklehead. Use them! Don't sneak up on me." He felt the intense urge for a stiff drink. It was nothing the contents of the cooler in their patrol boat would quench. "Did you notify dispatch?"

"Yes," she said. "We don't have an ETA on when the U.S.G.C. will get here." She glanced around the two rooms. "It's weird. I understand this boat got caught in the hurricane, but I don't understand how everyone seemed to have disappeared."

"If anyone was on board, they'd likely be here," Riker agreed. He saw a stairway that led below. He wasn't an expert on fishing trawlers, but he knew there had to be a processing room and storage area. "I doubt anyone would be downstairs, but it's worth a look." He shined his light down the steps, and Metzler followed him, turning on her own flashlight in the process. There was the preparation room and the processing area. They checked through and found nothing except fish guts and machinery. Metzler saw the head of a swordfish on the floor, completely severed from the body. It felt as if the big circular eye was staring at her. That and the dark silent atmosphere gave her the creeps.

Suddenly, the silence was replaced by a very faint noise coming from a room down the hall. With caution, they went down the hallway and tracked the noise to the storage room. It sounded like incoherent muttering and shivering. They slowly opened the door. Piles of frozen fish thawed all over the floor. Metzler plugged her nose when the repulsive smell flooded the hallway. Huddled in the corner of the room was a man, shivering and clutching himself. Both officers rushed to his side. Riker shone his light on him. His face and hands were pale white and his eyes were droopy.

"Hey, buddy," Riker said. "We are police officers with Merit PD. We found your ship adrift. Are you okay?" The man continued shivering and muttering gibberish. Much of what he mumbled appeared to be an old sailor song. Riker looked at Metzler, who appeared puzzled. "I'm willing to bet he's been hidden in this freezer for a while." Metzler knelt down.

"Sir, can you tell us where the other crewmembers are?" She spoke very slow and concise. He didn't answer. "It seems he's in a catatonic state," she said to Riker.

"Lovely," he said. "Well, it's still cold in here, so I think we should at least move him up to deck." They both reached to help him up when suddenly he squealed and scuttled a few feet back.

"N-no!" he muttered. "No, please...please don't." He then started to whimper, and his face flooded with fright.

"Why is that? Are you hurt?" Riker asked. The man shook his head.

"It's...it's still...o-ou-out there!" he said. Riker and Metzler stared him down.

"What's out there?" she asked. The man whimpered for a few moments.

"S-sh-shark," he moaned. Metzler was clearly the more sympathetic of the two. She asked a few more questions regarding the shark, but the fisherman didn't give any coherent answers. He would consistently repeat, "It's coming back."

"Sir, I can assure you, there's no shark outside," Metzler said. The man just shook his head, refusing to believe her. "Look," she tried to reason with him, "Officer Riker and myself were safe on the water. We found your boat, and we didn't see any shark out there. Please just come up to the deck." Once again, he refused. Riker grew impatient. He shrugged his shoulders in a have-it-your-way vibe, and started walking out. Metzler quickly stood up and rushed toward him. "Where are you going?"

"You heard him," Riker said. "He doesn't want to go anywhere. Let the Coast Guard handle him." Metzler couldn't believe what she was hearing. This could not be the great police officer everyone bragged about. If anything, he was the complete opposite, and it disgusted her.

"We don't know when they'll arrive, and this guy is not well," she said. "We can't just leave him in here! His condition could worsen."

"He's done fine for a couple days, I'm sure another hour or two won't kill him," Riker said. Metzler shot him a deathly glare. Riker rolled his eyes. "Listen, he refuses to move. What exactly do you expect me to do about it?"

"I thought you were the expert," she said. Riker snickered and walked past her towards the fisherman.

"Interesting observation coming from somebody who's been questioning my whole background," he said. He approached the fisherman and knelt to one knee. "Listen pal, first I'll promise that no shark will eat you. Second, and more importantly, you need to come out on deck with us. The sunshine will do you good." The fisherman shook his head again. "Sorry, but no is not an option. We need you warmed up so you can tell us where the rest of your crewmates are. I already found your captain, but he's," he decided not to mention Torey was dead, "...unable to help us."

"NO!" the fisherman shouted. He was starting to get hysterical. His whimpering became more intense and out of control. He started reaching around him, although Riker couldn't figure out what he was grabbing for. Metzler grew more nervous. Although it was talked about in the academy, it wasn't on the forefront of her mind that she'd be dealing with possible mental disorders.

"Now I'm worried he might harm himself," she said. "Damn, I wish we had a sedative."

"Screw you!" the fisherman suddenly shouted. "I'm not going out there! The shark... the shark..."

"I've got something cheaper than a sedative," Riker said. Just as he finished that statement, he clenched his fist and hurled a right hook dead center in the fisherman's face. The blow made a dull sound and sent him reeling backwards into the pile of fish behind him. He was unconscious.

"Good God! What the hell?! Riker!" Metzler yelled. Riker didn't even look at her. He grabbed the fisherman by the shoulders and pulled him from the fish pile. He stood up and lifted him over his shoulder. When he turned, he could see Metzler's burning red face even through the dark room.

"Oh, here we go," he said. "The girl scout is going to lecture about moral compasses." He carried the fisherman out of the room and started his way back towards the deck. Metzler followed him.

"Listen, this is not what we do," she scolded him. "You don't just punch people out. We are supposed to help people!"

"I *am* helping him," Riker said. "I'm *helping* him by getting him out of that damned freezer, just like *you* wanted." Metzler remained quiet as they went through the crew rooms and galley. When they were in the mess area, she remembered something she wanted to ask.

"You said you found the captain?"

"You didn't go in the wheelhouse?" Of course, her question already answered that. *Let's see how she handles this,* he thought. "He's up there. Feel free to go up there and check on him." He moved to allow her to squeeze past him. She hustled up the stairs and he deliberately took his sweet time moving up. After a minute, he could hear some intense gagging followed by running footsteps heading toward the deck. He smiled to himself. He took no amusement in the captain's death, but it served as another *lesson* for this uptight rookie. When he arrived on deck, Metzler was leaning over the portside railing, continuing to retch. He placed the unconscious fisherman on the deck. "I suppose you don't want to radio dispatch to update them?" She looked back with a disgusted expression. Part of the cause was physical disgust and shock from the horror she saw in the wheelhouse. The other part was Riker's appalling behavior.

How am I going to keep working with you?

****

It was early afternoon in Merit, in the middle of the lunch hour traffic. Like in most American societies, most work places seemed to let out at the same time. Adam Wisk wished he considered this fact while he sat in his old Ford Ranger, waiting in line at a fast food drive-through. The line had been long and he was now finally only two cars away from the microphone. Of course, the individual at the microphone didn't know what to order, and was taking an endless time looking over the menu. Being a journalist for *The Canyon Wall* usually meant Wisk had to eat on the go, and he was always on the go because work was becoming scarce. With a dwindling bank account, Wisk was already cranky at the start of each day. *The Canyon Wall* was one of the very few newspaper companies still around in the area, and it appeared that it would be the next to go under. Many of its employees had already been laid off.

Previously he had been a journalist for a national news agency. It was a job that allowed him to meet with politicians, celebrities, judges, mobsters, and military high ranks. The job was good and the money was great. He got paid traveling, luxury hotels, and lots of attention...including female attention, often under the promise he'd cover a story about them. It was usually an aspiring actress or singer. Of course, it eventually got around to his wife that this activity was going on. The result was an expensive divorce, and a large alimony and child support payment that would last the next fifteen years. To top things off, his career took a plunge when he attempted to do a surprise interview with the South Carolina Senator Mike Flynn. He attempted to ask questions regarding his support of a secret oil pipeline being constructed behind public eye, but the Senator didn't want to take questions at this time. Wisk made the mistake of pursuing him, despite warnings from the Secret Service. He thought he was onto a great story about a scandal. After getting too close too many times, the agents tased him. He was slapped with a large fine, and to top it off, it was revealed that there was no scandal. Because of the embarrassing incident, Wisk was let go. The event was as bad as being blacklisted. Nobody wanted to hire him.

It was only out of pity that the CEO, his ex-brother-in-law, took him in as a journalist for *The Canyon Wall*. Since taking the employment, Wisk found himself constantly reminded of why he was there with the phrase "I only have you here because I expect you to pay the damn child support." He rarely referred to Wisk by his name, rather called him by nicknames such as 'dickless', 'dumbass', 'douchebag' and many others. Wisk withstood it because he was unhirable elsewhere. But stories were scarce, and the upcoming sailing event was looking like the only thing keeping the company afloat. Wisk believed he would be looking at unemployment soon again.

He got fed up waiting for the indecisive customer to make his order. Wisk rolled down his window, which would only come down about two-thirds of the way before jamming. He managed to stick his head out and yelled to the customer.

"Hey! Not all of us plan on waiting for Social Security to kick in to order! Let's go!" The only response he got was a middle finger aimed at him. He sat back into his seat and waited, impatiently tapping on the center console. While he waited he peeked into his wallet. There was a five-dollar bill and a few quarters, hopefully enough for a sandwich. It was another reminder that he needed a good break. Just at that moment his suction mount police scanner picked up radio traffic. He picked up chatter all day but it usually didn't amount to anything. However, this time was much different.

"*Dispatch, Coast Guard is taking command of site. Take note that we have one crewmember on scene, and he'll be in their custody.*"

"*10-4. Are you remaining on scene?*"

"*Negative. U.S.C.G. will be towing Mary Westward off site. We'll be en route to Manson Dock shortly.*"

"*Copy that.*"

The key word was *Mary Westward*. Like everyone else, the *Canyon Wall* had received a notification that the vessel went missing during the hurricane. This was a timely opportunity. The likelihood was that no other news agency was currently aware that the vessel was found. If he could break the story, it could make a nice payday for him. He cut the wheel hard and steered his truck onto the outer side of the drive-thru lane. The passenger side wheels rode the curb as he drove out of the lane, nearly clipping the side mirrors of the vehicles in line. As he passed the car at the microphone, he held up his middle finger to the driver.

****

Metzler embraced the cool breeze while she held herself over the guardrail. She and Riker didn't exchange any words during the trip back from the *Mary Westward*. She held strong feelings of contempt for him at the moment, and Riker preferred the lack of interaction. While heading back to shore, he ignored several radio calls from Chief Crawford. The incident with the trawler dictated they write a detailed report of what occurred. He hoped Metzler would be feeling sick enough to take the rest of the day off, although there was only about ninety minutes left of the shift. They stuck around for the Coast Guard investigation and answered questions, as well as taking photos and recording evidence for their own report. After docking the boat, Riker immediately noticed Crawford's car parked near their patrol car. He stepped onto the deck and returned the boat keys, while Metzler lagged behind. Her face was still pale, and she continued to feel queasy. She followed him into the Dock Station, where Crawford stood next to Officer Marley's desk.

"For Christ sakes, Riker, I called you repeatedly now," he said.

"Sorry Chief," Riker said. "I'm a little busy." Crawford couldn't help but notice the ill-looking Metzler sitting next to him.

"Good lord, are you alright?" he asked.

"I'll be fine, sir," she said.

"If you say so," he said and turned his attention back to Riker. "I just wanted to share some information I got from the Coast Guard commander. The vessel is being towed to Miami, where it originally is from. This is at the request of Kathy Bloom."

"And she wanted this...why?" Riker said while signing a key return form.

"With the big event coming up, she didn't want the negative attention drawn from the investigation, especially with a fatality on board. She also wants this to stay out of the media's attention for the same reason."

"I'd ask how she even knows about the whole thing, but I already know you tell her everything," Riker said.

"It's part of my job to keep the powers-that-be informed," Crawford said.

"Oh yeah, then *inform* them to stay out of police matters," Riker said. He started out the door.

"Before you go," Crawford called out, "The Commander mentioned that the survivor suffered a recent blow to the face. I can't help but find this interesting. What was his condition when you found him?"

"Stupid," Riker said. "And clumsy. The guy fell on the floor and landed on his face. I guess being locked in a freezer for a couple days wasn't a great idea." Crawford looked to Metzler and could read from her sickened expression that Riker wasn't telling the truth. Riker didn't wait for a response and was out the door, only to find a voice recorder nearly shoved in his face. Standing in front of him holding that recorder was a man dressed in a Hawaiian shirt and khaki shorts.

"Good afternoon, my name is Adam Wisk for the *Canyon Wall*. I was hoping you'd be willing to comment on the finding of the lost trawler." Riker pushed the recorder from his face, and felt an intense urge to knock the journalist out. He had an intense dislike for paparazzi due to their constant interferences with his past investigations, and also found them to be generally annoying.

"Here's a quote; interview *Acting Mayor* Kathy Bloom. Apparently, she's in charge of all the investigations around here," he said. Crawford heard this from inside the office.

Please God, don't print that!

Metzler reluctantly followed Riker to the police car, ignoring questions from Wisk. She rolled down the window to let fresh air in. Riker paid no attention to her as he drove the patrol car out of the lot. Day two of training was almost over.

CHAPTER 9

"Oh damn, you see that?" Robert Nash exclaimed as he watched a large U.S.C.G Cruiser tow a seventy-foot fishing trawler in the distance. Dr. Stafford was in the water alongside the *Taurus*, having just surfaced from a dive. He took off his goggles and tossed them on board, and removed his regulator. He saw the ravaged features on the trawler and found it peculiar. However, he had more important matters to attend to. They had gone out on the water to the location where they tagged the great white. The tag was still giving out a signal, which allowed them to track down the remains to the exact spot.

When Dr. Stafford dove two hundred feet to the carcass, he found that most of the fish was missing. The head was completely gone, and there were huge chunks of flesh missing from the sides and underbelly. The fins were still intact, and what remained of the body seemed to hold together well. It was important to determine this fact because he wanted to hook the body up to the crane and bring it to the surface for examination. The carcass remains would have to withstand its own weight and hold together.

"Okay, start hoisting it up," he called up to his assistant. Nash turned a lever on the operator, and it reeled the cable in. It briefly screeched as it struggled with the initial strain of lifting the carcass. After a couple of minutes, they could see the silhouette of the ravaged great white under the surface. Nash stopped the winch when the remains emerged, dangling midway out of the water by the tail.

"Oh shit," he said. The previously twenty-three-foot long shark was now reduced to a length of sixteen feet. The neck was still submerged, but he could see well enough to know it was gone. Entrails and other bits of flesh floated from the open wounds. The flesh was mostly drained of blood and had a paler complexion than when it was alive. Stafford swam to it and started examining the wounds. "Don't you want to tow it in first before doing that?"

"I just want to get a brief examination first," Stafford said. He had a hard time seeing on the sea bottom. He checked around the bite marks, running his finger along the edge of each wound. "Damn, this thing bit deep." As he ran his finger along the neck wound, he felt something rigid. He squeezed his fingers around the object, but could not pry it loose. He looked up at Nash. "Let's get this bad boy to the lab." Stafford boarded the *Taurus* and his assistant was already throttling the boat away. The shark had been lifted out of the water, looking like a huge mangled piece of bait. Deep down, Stafford mourned the animal. Rescuing it took quite an effort, and like with all the other creatures he rescued, he embraced tracking its whereabouts. However, he believed there was a discovery to be made.

In the console, Nash put more speed into the engine. The boat was moving, but it appeared to be slower than it should be. At first, he thought it was the added weight from the shark, but quickly considered that they had hauled larger loads before without difficulty. It would be something for him to check on later.

****

Located just south of the main beaches was Dr. Stafford's laboratory, a former bait and tackle shop that went out of business. Fishing hooks, weights, and pieces of wire were often embedded into the lawn and cement driveway. The front of the building was caked with dirt, and most of the plaster had cracked and peeled off over the years, exposing the fiber cement siding. The back of the building had two overhead sliding doors for delivery. Nearby was a dock, where the scientist secured the *Taurus*, and a small speedboat.

The inside of the lab looked more like a warehouse with a few aquatic tanks. All of the former store's aisle setups had been removed, leaving a large open room. It was evident that Stafford was at the mercy of a budget. Much of his equipment was stationed on old desk tables that were either abandoned or sold at a low price. In the southeast corner were tables with water testing equipment and microscopes. Lining up the east wall were small round aquariums that contained tropical fish being treated for fungal infections. In the middle of the lab was a single long rectangular aquarium. It was divided into two sections. One contained a baby hammerhead shark, which Stafford had rescued after its fins had been removed by a fisherman. The other section was empty, previously containing a little skate which did not survive its injury. The aquarium contained a pump that created a flow of water to keep it going through the creature's gills. Amongst other equipment and work areas was the dissection table, where Stafford performed autopsies.

Stafford had loaded the great white carcass onto the flatbed and Nash backed the truck into the lab. He barely had the vehicle in park when Stafford climbed onto the back. He was still in his wetsuit, although mostly dried off. He immediately went for the decapitation injury and felt for the rigid object. He located it and shone a light on it. The object contrasted with the flesh color, and appeared to be condensed calcium. He tried gripping it with his fingers again, but it was too dug in.

"Hey, get me the twenty-four-inch forceps," he said to Nash. After shuffling through some unorganized equipment, Nash found the tool and brought it over. Stafford clamped the foreign object embedded in the wound and pulled. He tugged on it, but it was dug in pretty tight. He tugged repeatedly. "Damn, this...little...bastard...doesn't want to let..." He held on with both hands and pulled back hard "...GO!" It released suddenly, causing Stafford to fall on his back. Nash rushed to the edge of the flatbed to prevent him from rolling off. Stafford pulled himself up to a seated position and observed what he found. "JESUS!" It was a dagger shaped tooth, roughly three-and-a-half inches in length. There was no root, confirming that it was undoubtedly a shark tooth. Nash saw what his boss was holding and excitedly hopped onto the flatbed for a closer look.

"Holy shit! Doc, is that a..."

"Yep, it's a shark tooth," Dr. Stafford said. He was grinning ear to ear. While he was sad to see this great white dead, it was clear it was done by a predator that had not yet been recorded. There were no known sharks in existence to contain teeth of this size. The University had been on his case regarding him not providing sufficient research to warrant their already marginal funding. Now, he felt he might have something significant to offer the Board.

"What friggin' monster shark does that thing belong to?" Nash asked.

"I'm not sure. Look at it. It's not serrated, and it's long and somewhat triangular. We're going to look at our sketches of shark teeth and compare it," Stafford said. "If it's something new, it could be a subspecies."

"Could something that big possibly be a subspecies?" Nash asked.

"Oh absolutely," Stafford said. "Just as *Carcharodon Megalodon* and *Carcharodon Carcharias* are related, this might be an evolved species." It was just a theory, but it was all Stafford had to go on. He stepped off the flatbed with the tooth and went to his desk in the northwest corner, near the front main entrance. It was the one area of the lab that was well-cleaned and organized. He dug through some files in a cabinet until he found a book containing photos of shark teeth from all four-hundred-and-forty known shark species.

****

Dr. Stafford had been going through the book for an exhausting hour. It was considered the old-fashioned way of determining shark species. In any large lab or university, the tooth would be placed into a sophisticated computer scanner, and the CPU would run the image through a database and quickly determine what species of animal it belonged to. Of course, Stafford wasn't equipped with such advanced equipment. While he was looking through images, Nash was busy taking photographs of the mangled carcass and had also been examining the wounds for any more teeth. Afterwards, he went out to the boat. Stafford was too focused on his task to notice.

As much as Stafford loved his work, looking through endless photos of shark teeth was mind-numbing. It was definitely not related to a great white, because it lacked a saw-like edge and wasn't triangular enough. Teeth from the Mako shark were similar, but a bit too needlelike. The hammerhead wasn't an exact shape match either, but bore some similarities. Unfortunately, the same could be said for dozens of other species. It was a frustrating process, but Stafford had to start somewhere. While he loathed scientists' insistent reliance on computer technology, he was longing for one of those special computers. The next page was a nurse shark. Obviously not even close. He yanked the next page over. The shark tooth shown was from the Bigeye Thresher. He gazed at the tooth design, then glanced back at the recovered tooth on his desk. His eyes went back and forth between the page and the tooth.

"Oh shit," he said. The overall shape was an exact match, adjusted for size. "Hey Robert!" He stood up and looked around the lab for his assistant. He went outside and saw Nash coming from the docked boat. "There you are! Listen, I think I might have a line on what might be out there!" Nash's eyes widened in anticipation.

"Am I supposed to guess, or…" he said.

"This thing is an exact match of a Thresher's tooth," Stafford said, holding it up in the air. "Except for its size of course. But Robert, holy crap, I suspect we have a giant Thresher shark out there. But even if it's not, this thing is the biggest living shark currently alive today." Nash felt himself getting delighted.

"Oh man! Wow, for once I'm thinking taking this job was a good thing!" he joked. Stafford stared him down. Nash grinned nervously. "Well, you know… you hardly pay me anything…and you forget to a lot."

"Well, this will change things if I'm right," Stafford said. "First things first; tomorrow we'll have to take the boat out and see if we can find this bad boy." Nash bit his lip. Stafford noticed his sour expression. "What?"

"Well, before you came out, I was actually coming up to deliver some bad news," Nash said. "When we were heading back, I noticed the boat wasn't making enough speed despite what I was putting into the engine. I just checked, and well here you go." He extended his hand and held out a piece of rusted metal. "This is from one of the propellers." Stafford's jaw dropped open in dismay.

"Oh, you've got to be kidding me!" he cursed. He stomped his foot and looked to the heavens as if questioning why he'd been forsaken. "Can it be fixed?"

"It needs to be replaced," Nash said. "And here's the other part I knew you'd love to hear; propellers for a boat like we have are not cheap."

"No shit," Stafford said. He sighed heavily and paced around. The only way to get it replaced was to make a request to the University who sponsored him. He worried they'd look at this as an excuse to cut funding completely. But there was no other choice. "I guess I have some calls to make," he said. They both went into the lab.

"So, boss, when can we get rid of Roy? No offense, but he reeks."

****

The rest of the afternoon was quiet in Merit. The weather was beautiful and the humidity steadily dropped as the day went on. A few tourists came into town to enjoy the beaches and attractions before the crowds arrived for the sailing competition. As evening set in, the popular place for the September tourists were the bars.

It was nearing two o'clock in the morning. In the *Shallow Reef*, the bartender had yelled last call for the lingering patrons. The customers consumed their last beverages and left for the night. One of the last to go was a man sitting at the counter, dressed in blue jeans and a black t-shirt. The bartender waited a few minutes and wiped down the counters while the customer drank a double scotch…his tenth for the night. This was following several other drinks. He emptied the glass, but showed no sign of leaving. The bartender finally lost patience.

"Hey buddy, didn't you hear me?" he snarled. "We're closing. Time to leave."

Riker looked up from his glass and stared at the blurred version of the bartender. It almost appeared as if he had two heads and was standing behind wax paper. He almost didn't hear what he said due to the drunken numbness in his head, but he did understand the bar was closing. Part of him wanted to ignore the bartender and have another drink, but his diminished rational side was loud enough to convince him to leave. He reached in his pocket and laid a wad of cash on the counter before standing up. He didn't bother carrying it in a wallet. The bartender examined the crumpled cash.

"Hey!" he called. His voice was deep and loud like a bouncer. "You put eight dollars here. Your remaining bill was twenty-two!" Riker held on to the counter to remain upright. He dug into his pocket and pulled out more cash from his pocket and slammed it on the counter, again without counting it. The bartender looked it over. "You put eighteen bucks down. You want your change?"

"Keep it," Riker said, followed by a burp. He teetered on his feet, still holding on to the counter for balance while he made his way to the door. The bartender naturally noticed this.

"Hey pal!" He extended his hand. "Let's see those keys!" Riker took no notice and slowly continued toward the door. "Hey buddy!" The bartender said again. He went around the bar to stop Riker. "There's no way you're driving."

"The same will be said to you when the paramedics load you into the ambulance," Riker growled at him. The bartender had dealt with enough people during his time working at the bar, and he usually knew which ones would deliver on their threat. This fellow would certainly be the grand champion. He rose his hands in surrender and backed off to the side. Riker took a deep breath and despite the room seeming as if it was spinning, he made it out the door. He got into his GMC Terrain. After starting the car, he inadvertently leaned his weight on the accelerator, flooring it. The tires kicked up gravel as the GMC sped out of the lot, bouncing over a parking block. It went out into the road, narrowly missing a truck that cruised down the road. The truck's horn blared as it veered slightly off the road to avoid Riker. The bartender cursed from the bar window for failing to get his license plate.

Riker hugged the center of the road as he went home. He pulled into his property, completely missing his driveway. The tires kicked up grass and dirt from his front lawn before he slumped on the brakes. The vehicle had come within inches of ramming through the living room. He managed to put the vehicle in park and stumbled into the house, not realizing he left the engine running. The front door was unlocked, and he shoved it open. He leaned on the wall as he moved through the hallway until finally he collapsed into the bathroom. He stared at the white ceiling, which looked strangely heavenly as he passed out.

CHAPTER 10

There was hardly any moonlight out during the night. Darkness cloaked the water's surface. It brought perfect cover for the pod of killer whales that moved back into the area. Kept afloat by their blubber insulation, the pod rested on the surface close together in a state of rest called unihemispheric. During this process, one hemisphere of the whales' brain would shut down while the other half would control necessary functions such as breathing. Puffs of air and water vapor sprayed above the surface repeatedly like small volcanic eruptions while the 'sleeping' pod of orcas slowly drifted in a tight group. The only ones awake in this pod of five adult orcas were a female and its calf. They were centered in the pod, and the mother was staying awake to keep the two-week old baby afloat. It would be another three weeks before the calf would develop enough blubber to be able to float on its own. At the front of the pod was a male, which took lead after its predecessor was killed. On its left pectoral fin was a blinking tag device, placed after receiving medical treatment for a bullet wound in its side from a South American poacher.

The pod had nearly been driven out of the coastal area after its leader, a bull male, was slaughtered. Out of preservation for the infant and its mother, the rest of the pod retreated. Communicating with each other in small clicks and whistles, they circled back to their territory. During their 'discussion' they determined to locate the beast that killed their member and devour it for sustenance.

The baby splashed its tail, kicking up water while it played its game. The mother continuously dove under to keep the baby on the surface. The baby would stay on the surface, take a breath and flap its tail before going under again. After diving, the mother orca instinctively released a ping of echolocation. It would do that accidently as it tried to communicate with its offspring. The echo bounced back, and suddenly the mother orca went on alert. Its sonar picked up something big approaching from the east.

****

With its dorsal fin cutting along the surface, the Thresher moved toward the multiple vibrations in the water. In its limited mind, the giant fish perceived that these large lifeforms in the water posed a threat to itself and the territory it claimed. Most of the vibrations were very steady, but there was another commotion in the water that produced more rapid muscle movements. Its lateral line absorbed the electrical impulses generated by this other target. The shark believed that this other target was a smaller creature, suitable for a meal. The nutrition it took in several hours before had long worn off, and its enormous body demanded nutrition. Its aggression was also increasing, fueled partially by the fact that it was hungry. However, it also felt an intense instinctual impulse to kill anything else of significant size in nearby waters. The Thresher had established this area as its new territory and hunting ground. Any other creature posed a threat. It swam toward the source of the electrical impulses, ready to kill anything it found.

****

The orca mother sent out a squeal when she realized the Thresher was closing in. The rest of the pod suddenly awoke from their trance-like state and quickly formed a circle around the mother and baby, remaining on the surface of the water to draw breath. They sent out pings of echolocation to determine the location of the large fish, and communicated to each other with clicks and whistles as if strategically planning a defense maneuver. The Thresher was about seventy-five yards straight away from the new leader.

The Thresher bared teeth while it opened its mouth, tasting bits of saliva and waste from the orcas as water passed through its gills. It was close enough to see them and recognized their actions as signs of aggression. Knowing it was outnumbered, it began circling the pod. The group remained tight in favor of protecting the calf. Under normal circumstances they would flank the threat and attack from multiple sides. But killer whales have significant memory, and they recognized the Thresher as the same shark they encountered nearly a day ago. They were aware that attacking it wouldn't be as simple as bringing down a blue whale.

The Thresher maintained a distance of about twenty yards from the pod as it circled. It couldn't find a clear point of attack. However, its instincts dictated that it must drive the orcas out of the area and secure its territory. After circling for several more minutes, the Thresher suddenly dove deep. The orcas maintained their position, and lost sight of the fish as it disappeared into the darkness. Then it ascended, coming up under the pod, straight for the infant. The pod broke formation. The mother pushed the infant away, while two other orcas escorted them. The other three rushed down to engage the Thresher in a triangular formation, with the leader in the center. It increased the rate of motion of its fluke and opened its large jaw, aiming to bite at the enemy's neck. Unfortunately, it wasn't fast enough.

An electrifying shock went through its thirty-foot body like a tremor. The Thresher's tail sliced the right side of its face, momentarily stunning it. Immediately after it struck the leader, the Thresher whipped its head toward the orca coming in on the right and opened its mouth wide. The orca tried to stop but it was too late. Its whole snout was buried within the shark's jaws. Blood seeped as the dagger-shaped teeth sank into the flesh. Writhing in intense pain, the orca shook its body to free itself from the immense jaws. But it was locked in too tight, and with each jerk of its body the jaws sank in deeper. The sounds of pained squeals and violent swishing water traveled for over a mile.

While the struggle persisted, the stunned leader remained motionless, floating in limbo under the surface. The third orca hesitated, unsure of whether to help the leader or the struggling teammate. If the leader wasn't helped to the surface, it would likely run out of breath. It made a decision and swam to the leader, putting its head underneath its belly region. It pushed upward and brought it to the surface. The leader bled profusely from the large tear in its face, but it managed to release a strong exhale followed by a deep breath. It slowly regained its bearing. While the leader recovered, the other orca dove back under. Its teammate was still in the vicious confrontation with the Thresher, not able to free itself from the vicious jaws. Its movements were slowing down. The lack of oxygen was taking a severe toll on the large mammal.

The fish could see the other orca straight ahead just before it charged like a raging steer. The Thresher tilted its head down, dragging the weakened orca with it. It slashed its whip-like tail overhead. The orca veered left to avoid it, only catching a painful strike on its right pectoral fin. It hooked around the side of the shark and charged again. The Thresher released the bleeding teammate and suddenly snapped its jaws to its right. The orca veered again, barely avoiding getting caught in the three-inch teeth. It moved away to circle back, and during this time the fish redirected its attention on the other one.

Free of the Thresher's grasp, the wounded teammate gathered what little strength it had. It needed oxygen badly. Each flap of its fluke was a struggle. As it ascended, it appeared it was going to get away. But an unexpected strike by the Thresher's tail brought it to a sudden stop. The scything impact landed on its tail, slicing through blubber and muscle, and creating a small fracture on its caudal vertebrae. The killer whale found itself unable to move its tail, and it found itself helplessly staring upward toward the ocean surface. The remaining orca saw its teammate again in peril. It propelled itself around the Thresher in an attempt to get to the injured orca and help it to the surface.

The Thresher felt the muscular contractions by the healthy orca, and also smelled some of the blood that leaked from its bleeding pectoral fin. It turned to face it, while ingesting gallons of blood that seeped into the dark water from the injured foe. The orca tried moving in, but it could detect the Thresher as it prepared another strike. It kept out of range of the vicious caudal fin, which unfortunately kept it from reaching its ailing teammate. There was a brief standoff between the two titans. The Thresher started to charge, partly out of a need to keep moving forward to keep water moving over its gills. Knowing it was no match for the much bigger rival, the orca retreated in a circular motion. It still wanted to reach the other.

The Thresher's pursuit was stopped suddenly when it was driven downward by a vicious force from above. The pod leader had recovered its strength, and rushed downward and bit the shark from above. Its teeth dug in near the dorsal fin, but it struggled to keep a grip because of the shark's immense size. The other orca slowed its retreat and turned around, seeing its leader in combat with the leviathan. It took advantage of the opportunity to seek out the wounded teammate. It located it surrounded by a bloody red mist. The orca quickly pushed it upward, almost in desperate need of oxygen itself. The two broke the surface with a big splash. The orca released a large exhale of carbon dioxide, and sucked in a massive breath of air. The teammate, however, floated motionless on the ocean surface. The orca bumped it with its nose, but it didn't gather any response. The teammate's jaw was slack, and its blowhole was not taking in any air. The orca bumped it a few more times before accepting the distressing reality that its teammate suffocated before it could reach it. It released a mournful cry before dipping back down to help its leader.

The leader was unable to keep its grasp. The Thresher was bigger and stronger, and its intense thrashing about shook it loose. The leader let go and attempted a retreat. However, it wasn't able to make enough distance. The Thresher lashed its tail and struck the leader in the belly. The killer whale lurched and flailed while its muscles weakened. It fought to regain control, forcing its fluke to paddle it away. The

Thresher's aggression only increased after tasting and smelling the additional blood that mixed with the saltwater. When it saw the orca continuing to retreat, it thrashed its tail again, this time striking it over the top of the head. The leader felt another intense shock within its entire body. Its stunned body went limp, and the only sensation it could feel was the Thresher's sharp teeth plunging into its soft white belly. It bit into the already open wound, tearing out entrails with a huge bite. The leader bled out, and within several seconds its life slipped away.

The remaining orca stopped when it saw the Thresher rip into its pod leader. For a moment it debated whether to attempt an attack. But its intelligent brain analyzed the scenario, and determined it was no match for the huge shark. It also knew it was a matter of time before the fish would turn on it once again. Hearing the distant cries of the remaining pod, the orca turned and swam away, forced to leave its friends behind.

The coastal waters were now rife with the mournful cries of the diminishing pod of killer whales. Realizing there was no chance they could drive out the new threat, they had no choice but to migrate elsewhere.

CHAPTER 11

To say that Chief Crawford's morning wasn't his best was a grand understatement. As always, he awoke by 6:00 a.m. He hadn't even made it to the bathroom when he found that his dog, a seven-year old German Shepherd, had pulled down his suit jacket from its hanger and slept on it all night. The dog usually had its own bed, but it had to be thrown out when Crawford learned that it had some mold building up in it. The jacket ended up being covered in dog hair and drool stains. His other jackets were already due to arrive at the dry cleaners on his way to work, so he just had to go without it today. It wasn't a big deal, but it was only the start. He got in his vehicle to leave early to make it to the dry cleaners before going to work. On his way there, his tire plunged into a newly formed pothole, completely flattening it. It took him several minutes to put the donut on and get his truck to an auto shop. To top it off, they didn't open until seven. He waited for them to open, and luckily, they were somewhat quick on servicing his truck. While in the lobby, he helped himself to a cup of coffee, which he took with him when he left. A bump in the road spilled his coffee all over his lap. He cursed himself as he delivered his suits into the dry cleaners. His wet crotch gathered some laughs in the brief time he was there. There was no choice to be had, he had to hurry home, change, and get to the police station.

He arrived just before briefing took place. Usually, being a tad late wouldn't be a big deal. However, there was a phone meeting with the 'Acting-Mayor', Fire-Chief, Parks & Recreations Manager, and several others. Normally meetings would take place with all the members together in a room, but this one was expected to be brief. As to be expected, Kathy Bloom gave her usual lecture. Crawford felt his mind wander elsewhere while she spoke of the upcoming event. He had grown tired of the know-it-all attitude she constantly displayed.

"By the way, Mr. Crawford, have you arranged the special training for your staff yet?" The mention of his name brought his attention back.

Shit! he thought. He cleared his throat and replayed the question in his mind before answering.

"No," he said. "To do this the way you want, I have to hire a professional to run classes, and then I have to work with the officers' schedules to arrange the lessons."

"Just arrange a couple classes and mandate them to attend!" she said. *Of course,* Crawford thought, *it's not like my staff don't have lives outside of work.* While mandatory overtime hours were considered a normal part of law enforcement, Crawford was the type to help his employees the best he could by scheduling job training during work hours.

"I'll do what I can, but it'll have to wait until after next week's event. We'll be busy overseeing the extra crowds."

"Alright, fine," she said. Her voice was very sour. He noticed she was a little nicer to the Fire Chief when discussing event safety with him. *She's probably a fan of the damn calendars,* Crawford thought. She continued griping in his ear. *"Also, I noticed there was a police report filed on the incident with the trawler."*

"Yes, of course," he said. "It was our officers who discovered the boat and started the initial investigation. Our department is obligated to have a detailed record of occurrences we encounter." He wanted to say "this is standard for all police" but knew it would only get her fired up. He truly hoped for Mayor Ripefield to get well and return soon.

"As long as that report does not make it into the public's hands," Bloom said. *"You said people were dead on that boat. I don't want tourists being scared off. This town doesn't need that. And with all the media coming down for the competition, we don't need the bad press."*

Crawford rolled his eyes. *It's not like this occurred off of Merit's Beaches.* It was obvious she wanted the media to promote her image, and not be distracted with other things. The *Mary Westward* would certainly do that.

"Yes ma'am," was all he could say.

****

Metzler grew impatient while waiting in the briefing room for Riker to arrive. The shift Sergeant had another matter to attend to and instructed her to just wait for him. The time was nearing 8:30, the latest he'd been so far yet. She had asked the Sergeant if it was better to drive with someone else, but reminded her that it was Crawford's orders she ride with Riker. She felt herself getting increasingly infuriated with the matter. Everyone thought she was getting top notch training, especially with having a felony arrest on her first day and starting a homicide investigation the second day. But she was miserable. To make it worse, her sister had to go back into the hospital during the night. The emotional and financial stress was eating at Metzler, and Riker's demeaning treatment was only making it worse.

It seemed to her there was no sign of her trainer. With the Sergeant out of the building, she went to Crawford's office. She could hear him talking on the phone, so she waited outside his door. After a few minutes she heard him hang up. She knocked on the door.

"Come in," he said. She walked inside. He looked up from his desk to greet her. "Yes, what can I do for..." he stopped. Once he saw Metzler standing there alone, he instantly knew what the problem was. "You've got to be kidding me." He looked at his watch. 8:35 a.m.

"Everyone else has already taken off," Metzler said. "The Sergeant told me to wait."

"You don't have to explain," Crawford said. He snatched his cell phone and went through his contact list. "I'm dealing with it now." The other line rang a few times and went to voicemail. That concerned him a little. Riker may have attitude issues, but rarely did he not answer his phone. He left a stern message on the voicemail and hung up. Metzler could see the combination of frustration and concern in his face. He looked at his watch again, pondering what to do. "Okay, I'm gonna drive to his place," he decided. "You can take a patrol car and follow me..." he stopped and remembered something. "Oh, damn it!"

"What's wrong?" Metzler asked.

"I've got another damn meeting at nine!" he said. "I can't miss it. I'm sorry, this hasn't been my morning so far." Metzler could tell he was feeling a bit scatterbrained. Her instinctual need to help kicked in.

"Well sir, I can head to his place and check on him," Metzler said. The Chief initially wanted to turn down the offer. He didn't feel it was appropriate to send a rookie to check on an officer's private residence. Plus, he could get in trouble for giving out another person's private information. But his concern for Riker was too great.

"You'd be okay with that?"

"Yes sir," she answered. He didn't see much of a choice. He wrote the address on a piece of notebook paper and handed it to her.

"I appreciate it," he said. "Listen, this meeting should also be quick. It'll probably be over by a quarter after nine. Give me a call if you find him, and I'll deal with the matter later on."

"Yes sir," she said. Crawford turned and rushed to another area of the building. Metzler grabbed a set of vehicle keys and found a patrol car. It felt strangely odd to not have Riker there. After radioing in her beginning shift information to dispatch, she drove out of the lot.

****

With the help of GPS, it didn't take Metzler long to locate Riker's neighborhood. Locating his house was even easier. It was hard to miss the GMC Terrain in the middle of the yard, parked right up to the house. Behind it were tire marks in the grass, and skid marks on the road in front of the property. Metzler parked in the driveway, feeling nervous about what she was seeing. She walked up to the front porch. The door was ajar and the lights were off. Metzler felt herself grow nervous and considered radioing another officer for assistance. It almost appeared as if she was walking in on a crime scene. However, she went ahead and knocked on the door.

"Hello?" she called into the dark hallway. There was no answer. She knocked once more and called again with the same result. Her right hand rested on her duty belt while she stepped into the house. "Riker? Are you here?" She felt like that was a stupid question—his car was in the yard. She flicked on a light switch on the wall, illuminating the hallway and living room. She almost gasped at the enormous mess of packed boxes piled everywhere. Empty beer bottles were everywhere, as well as other various garbage. *My lord, how can anyone live like this?* She walked through the hallway into the kitchen. The light was off, but she could see clearly because of the hallway light. "Riker?" Her nervousness caused her to speak softly. She saw the bathroom door was open and the light was on. She went over to it, and looking in she saw Riker passed out on the floor. He was dressed in his jeans and black t-shirt from the previous night. There was a bit of drool that ran down the side of his cheek. Her heartrate accelerated and she nearly went into a panic. "Oh God!" She fumbled for her radio to call dispatch for an ambulance. Her quivering hands accidentally knocked the remote speaker off of her shoulder strap, and it hit the wall as it fell.

Riker woke up to the sound of somebody in his house. He instinctively reached for his hip, intending to grab his firearm. Except he wasn't wearing it. He then relaxed when he realized he recognized Metzler. He looked around and remembered where exactly he was. A nasty headache started throbbing between his temples. He squeezed his eyes shut at the initial pain, then looked up at Metzler, who had caught her breath.

"What the hell are you doing here?" he growled in his usual gravelly tone.

"Crawford sent me to check on you," she said. Riker wiped his eyes and sat up. His hair was a mess, his clothes stank of alcohol, and as she expected, he was still unshaven. The scruff on his face was now several days old and looking even less attractive.

"And why are you checking on me?" He followed this question by spitting into the toilet.

"Ugh," Metzler automatically reacted, looking away from the disgusting sight. She recalled his question, "Well, it's almost nine. You never showed up for duty and you wouldn't answer your phone."

"Nine?" Riker looked at his watch. "Well shit," he said. "Alright, I'll get cleaned up and changed." He started to stand up when he suddenly felt a huge painful knot in his stomach. Metzler cringed as she watched his eyes bulge and he grunted, hunched over as if to vomit. Only a burp came out. Metzler felt as if she was turning pale. She turned away.

"I'll wait then," she said.

"What do you mean 'you'll wait'?" he snarled.

"I brought a patrol car. Crawford wanted me to pick you up and take you to the docks for Harbor Patrol."

"Ugh, fine," he said. She got out of his way as he walked out and went to his bedroom. She went into the hallway, intending to go outside and wait. She heard the bathroom door shut and the shower run. *Wow, that's a surprise. I figured he wouldn't bother.* She decided to be grateful. She had smelled the stench coming from him.

She grabbed her cell phone and dialed Crawford's cell number. She felt almost eager to tell Crawford that Riker had missed briefing due to being passed out drunk. Perhaps this would be the key to getting out of training with him.

Before she sent the call, she noticed something on the floor next to an open box. It was a framed picture. Curious about it, she picked it up to look at it. She almost couldn't believe what she saw. It was Riker, dressed in a tuxedo walking down an aisle with a beautiful woman in a wedding dress. In this photo he was well groomed, clean shaven, and smiling. It was an odd, but strangely wonderful sight, one that she never thought could ever exist. The bride was lovely and was smiling ear-to-ear with her new husband. She predicted the photo to be roughly a decade old. It wasn't the age difference that made Riker almost unrecognizable, nor was it his clean appearance in the picture. It was the happiness he displayed.

She placed the picture down where she found it and noticed a newspaper. It was an obituaries page. She only took notice because her eyes immediately noticed the last name Riker on one of the columns. She picked it up and read the obituary for Martha Riker. It stated she is survived by her husband Leonard. At the end of it read: *In lieu of flowers, donations can be made to the American Foundation for Suicide Prevention.*

She remembered she was about to make a phone call. She hit *send* and waited for Crawford to answer. It went to voicemail, meaning he was still in his meeting. She hesitated after the beep and continued looking at the article. She glanced at the wedding picture once more.

"Yes, Chief Crawford, this is Officer Allison Metzler," she said. "As you've requested, I'm calling to inform you that Officer Riker is alright. There was a slight power outage in his neighborhood overnight which shut his alarm off, so it didn't wake him up. At least he got to sleep in." She faked a chuckle. "He'll be all set shortly and we'll head out to Mason Dock. Have a good day." She hung up and took one more glance at the photo, then at the numerous empty beer bottles that were scattered everywhere. After hearing the shower turn off, she went out to the car and waited.

CHAPTER 12

Robert Nash arrived at the lab at 9:00 a.m., a half hour later than usual. He pondered the odds of whether he would be chewed out by Dr. Stafford. He was an overall good boss and mentor to have, but he could be a stickler for the rules. Nash entered the lab and found Dr. Stafford sitting at his desk talking on the phone. He could only hear the doctor's side of what sounded like an unpleasant conversation.

"So what you're saying is that you guys are more than happy to spend fifty grand on a bone dig, but saving whales is a big waste?......Research data?...I've been providing research data....Listen, tell the Board... Hey! Just tell the Board that I..." It was obvious to Nash that whoever was on the other end of the line was interrupting him. "...Just tell...Will you shut up for a second?! Tell the Board I might have made an extraordinary find. I don't want to discuss what it is until I have more info, but..." he stopped and grimaced. He slammed the phone down. "Little prick hung up on me," he said to Nash. "That was the financial department at University of Miami."

"Certainly sounds like it went well," Nash remarked. "Sounds like we'll be getting thousands!"

"Smart ass," Stafford said. "The Board thinks we haven't been providing sufficient research." He held up fingers like air quotes. "Apparently they've got too much invested in a paleontology dig down in Mexico to give us six grand to pay for new propellers."

"So, what are you going to do?" Nash asked. Stafford stood up and checked his pockets for his wallet and phone.

"We're going to the bank," he answered. "If the damn university doesn't want to sponsor us, then we'll get the job done ourselves."

"Yeah, except in this job, I'm supposed to be making money, not paying it," Nash said, half-kidding.

"Don't worry, it's not coming out of your pocket," Stafford said. Nash followed him out the door. "By the way, you're late."

****

They had to wait a while before the personal banker could meet with them. But because Stafford had fairly good credit, he was able to get the loan. Of course, Stafford was unsure of how he would be able to make the payments on the loan if he didn't produce any findings. This was another reason he deemed it so important to locate the enormous shark they suspected to exist.

While on their way back to the lab, they noticed a gathering of people near the beach area. It was a large gathering of at least fifty people, and more were crossing the street to join them. They seemed focused on something lying on the beach. At first Stafford suspected it to be a bunch of tourists, but some of the people wore business clothing as well. He pulled off to the side of the road and parked.

"What's going on here?" Nash asked. They approached the huddled crowd and made their way through. Laying on the beach was a deceased twenty-three-foot killer whale.

"Oh, good Lord!" Stafford exclaimed. He informed the nearby people that he was a marine biologist and began inspecting the marine mammal. It was rolled onto its side, with its jaw slack. Its snout was smothered in blood, which had bled from a wide row of puncture wounds. There was a line of wounds on the top of the snout, as well as a row on the lower jaw. On the tail, above the caudal fin, was a deep laceration. Stafford noticed a nick in the dorsal fin. "Oh damn, this is Chip!" he said. Chip was one of two orcas that Stafford rescued from gunshot wounds inflicted by a group of poachers called the Trio. The other was a female, which he placed an electronic tracking device on after treating the injury. Since saving them from their injuries, they joined another pod, which also had another member tagged by Stafford. He ran his fingers along the facial wounds.

"Doc, do you think..." Nash started to ask. As if he read his mind, Stafford reached into his shirt pocket. He pulled out the shark tooth, which was inserted in a cardboard casing. He removed the cardboard and carefully slipped the tooth into one of the orca's puncture wounds. It was a perfect fit.

"Yes, I do," he answered Nash's uncompleted question. "Our shark is still in the area, and Chip had an encounter with him." He walked from the jaw to the tail and looked at the gash. It ran down to the vertebrae. He motioned to Nash to kneel down with him. He whispered to avoid being heard by the crowd. "I think we have further evidence that our visitor is a Thresher."

"You might be right," Nash replied. "But here's a question. The shark killed Chip, but Chip seems pretty intact. I'm not as educated as you on this, but sharks aren't normally in the habit of killing prey and not eating it. And did you notice something else?"

"What else?" Stafford asked. Nash led him back to the orca's head and pointed to the blowhole. It was open. Cetaceans have muscles that must contract to open the blowhole. When the blowhole is shut, those muscles remain in a relaxed state. "He was desperate for air. I think he suffocated."

"Doesn't it take a while for these guys to suffocate?" Nash asked. "Even with the injury to the tail, if Chip was underwater, his blubber should've made him float."

"I think the Shark bit him and held him down," Stafford said. He took out a tape measure and checked the bite radius on the orca's head. It measured nine thousand-four hundred-fifty-three millimeters.

"How big do you think he is?" Nash asked.

"I'm guessing, but this guy is probably between thirty-five and forty feet long," Stafford said. He looked down at Chip and thought of Nash's observation that the orca wasn't eaten. "He's intact, so why did the shark attack? Or did the orca attack the shark? What about the rest of the pod?" He took a few quick pictures with his phone. "Let's get back to the lab," he said. "The mayor's office will probably hire a fisherman to haul it out to open sea. We've got work to do."

They walked through the crowd to their vehicle. Stafford's enthusiasm of possibly finding a new species of shark was being replaced by a growing concern the predator was having on the ecosystem. So far, two magnificent sea creatures he had saved had been killed by it. Yesterday he was feeling the thrill of potential fame in the world of Marine Biology. But the thrill was wearing off, and his root as an environmentalist was resurging.

****

When they got back to the lab, Stafford had barely parked the car when he stepped out and rushed to the front door. Nash was a bit slower. The door had already latched shut when he got to it. When he entered the building, Stafford was already on the computer, checking the electronic transmitters for his tagged orcas. One was showing position a couple miles off the coast. The second was very far off, traveling several miles north near the Georgia coastline.

"Why are you two not together?" Stafford said, looking at the blips. Nash leaned in next to him.

"Maybe they had a bad argument," Nash snickered.

"Not funny," Stafford said. "We need to get those propellers and head back out there." Nash gave a nervous laugh.

"Uh, Doc, we got approved for the loan, but the bank needs to send the check," he said. "On top of that, nobody around here sells the parts we need. We'll have to order them, although it shouldn't take long. I know who I can order them from and I can do that today. He doesn't charge until they arrive and by then we'll have the money ready." Stafford looked down at the screen again.

"Alright," he said. "Are you gonna go now to do that?"

"It makes sense. We've got nothing else to do."

"Wrong," Stafford said. "I'm taking the Boston Whaler and heading out to see if our orca is alright. This is uncharacteristic of our killer whales to suddenly split up, especially after another member of their pod was killed." He went into a changing room near the aquariums. Nash noticed he was grabbing a wetsuit.

"You seriously want to go into the water? With that thing out there?"

"Oh, don't be ridiculous," Stafford called from the changing room. "Sharks don't typically attack people, despite what happens in the movies."

"Sharks aren't typically forty feet long and killing orcas," Nash commented. Stafford came out of the dressing room in his black wetsuit.

"I'll make sure I don't look like a seal if I have to swim," he said. He went to the refrigerator and grabbed some bottled water. Nash followed him out the door and down to the dock. The Boston Whaler was a twelve-foot-long boat which Stafford bought off the original fishing store's owner before the building had been renovated to become his lab. It was no science vessel, but Stafford couldn't afford much more. He climbed in and started the engine. He looked at Nash and saw his concerned expression. "Oh relax. I'll bet you twenty bucks I don't encounter the shark."

"I'd make that bet, except it'd go one of two ways; A—You survive getting eaten but can't scrounge up the money to pay me, like half of my paychecks, or B—you get eaten and therefore unable to pay me anyway."

"You're a class act," Stafford snorted. They both chuckled. "I'll see you when I get back." Stafford throttled the boat out of the dock into the open ocean. Nash gave him a farewell wave, and certainly hoped he'd owe Stafford twenty bucks.

****

Riker almost looked green while he stood at the helm. He barely scanned the horizon while he steered. Metzler noticed he mostly kept his eyes down and knew it was because the sun was probably worsening his alcohol-induced migraine. It was another beautiful and bright day. It was a little after eleven, and most of the fishing yachts had already traveled out of the range of Harbor Patrol's route. For the most part, it seemed they had the ocean to themselves. There were no boats in sight, normal for midday in the middle of the week, except for a small vessel a quarter mile to the southeast.

Although he had showered, Riker still smelled of beer and scotch. She also noticed that he didn't seem to eat anything. *Well, some people often skip breakfast*, she thought, but then considered the fact that he didn't appear to eat lunch during their previous shifts. While he didn't appear to be starving himself, there was no doubt he wasn't getting the right kind of nutrition. She couldn't stop thinking of the picture and newspaper she found in his house. She felt a bit at odds with herself. Part of her felt significant pity for Riker and what he seemed to be going through, the other part of her felt more pity for herself. In her mind she replayed the same thought; *First, we've had so many other problems. Now I've got to deal with this. Would he be drinking on the job if I wasn't with him all the time?* She felt as if she did him a big favor lying to the Chief, and it was sincere. But she felt more uncomfortable than ever working with him. To Metzler, Riker was a ticking time bomb.

"Want a water?" she asked, attempting to break the silence while grabbing one for herself.

"No." Riker's tone sounded flat and mechanical.

"Suit yourself, Robocop," she said. He didn't seem to appreciate the humor. Then again, he clearly didn't appreciate anything about her at all. He despised her very existence. She figured she was done with putting up with it. *I think I'm finally going to ask the Chief for a reassignment.* She wasn't sure what she'd say to him at this point, especially since the whole department was enthralled by the fact they'd done so much in a couple of days compared to the rest of the staff. She continued with her thoughts. *I'm just so damn tired of this.* "I'm just so damn tired of this," she spoke her mind out loud, not realizing it for a moment.

"Tired of what?" Riker asked. Metzler tensed for a moment, scrambling in her mind of what to say, and cursing herself in the process.

"Oh, nothing….this boating duty. It's just been a boring day so far," she stuttered. Riker turned and looked at her. He didn't say anything, nor did he have to. Metzler knew Riker may have been many things, but he wasn't dumb. He resumed driving the boat. Metzler dumped some of her water in her hands and splashed it onto her face to wash away the sweat. She leaned against the port railing and stared out into the water.

****

Dr. Stafford checked his portable computer monitor for the distance between his boat and the orca. It appeared to maintain its position, which concerned Stafford further. Killer whales did not often stay in one exact spot for prolonged periods of time. They were always mobile, even during rest. It had taken a while for him to get out to the general location because the Boston Whaler was not particularly fast. Finally, he was closing in. With the ocean being calm and the weather nice and clear, Stafford knew spotting the orca would be easy if it was surfaced. The depth reading on the monitor indicated that the tracking device was not submerged.

The time was past eleven when Stafford reached the location of the device within a hundred yards. He slowed the boat down and scanned the water to locate any sign of the orca. The surface seemed absolutely clear. There didn't appear to be anything in sight, with the exception of a patrolling police vessel a few hundred yards to the northwest. *Don't usually see many of them out here, especially this far out,* he thought to himself. He refocused on the task. The water appeared flat and undisturbed. A few tiny splashes drew his attention directly ahead. As he steered the whaler closer, he noticed the large bulk on the surface. He found his orca, and as he predicted, it was dead. He drove up next to the floating carcass and stopped. He dropped his anchor, which barely reached the sea floor.

"Oh Jesus," he said mournfully as he looked at the orca. It was rolled slightly onto its right side, with its left pectoral fin sticking out of the water, folded over and barely hanging on by a little bit of flesh. He could see the top of its head and the four-foot laceration that was just above its left eye. Even more disturbing was the enormous wound on its belly that led up to its pectoral fin. Its whole underside had gone from its normal white color to being completely red. Much of the skin was missing, and the innards had been spilling out. Small fish were continuously swimming up to it and taking little bits of the open wounds. Despite the additional damage done by the little scavengers, the bite marks on the belly were still clearly visible. Stafford put his goggles on and gently lowered himself into the water. Because he was going to remain on the surface, he didn't bother putting on an air tank. There was about three meters space between the boat and orca.

Stafford first examined the head injuries. He was shocked when he realized there were two gash marks, one also being on the right side. *You really put up a fight*, he thought. He stroked the creature's beautiful head.

"I'm sorry this happened to you," he said softly. He then swam around to the belly injury. He pushed intestines and other bits of flesh out of the way. The innards stank horribly, and it was the one part of Marine Biology that Stafford never cared for. He ran his hands around the big wound. It was mostly soft and fleshy. "Come on, I know you're here," he said as he searched with his fingers. Finally, he felt a rigid edge. It was too shallow to be the whale's bone. He had a fairly good grip, and he pushed his foot against the orca's tail to help give him leverage as he pulled. The object came loose. He held it up above the water. It was a tooth, over three inches long. He put his arm holding the tooth around the orca's tail to hold himself up while he opened a Velcro pocket. He pulled out the other tooth, which he brought with him. It was an identical match. "You're still here," he said, as if speaking telepathically to the shark that once carried these teeth. He put both teeth in the Velcro pocket and started searching the wound for any others.

A loud metallic bang from behind broke his deep focus. He spun around to look behind, nearly losing his grip on the orca. His boat was bobbing in the water as if it was hit by something underneath. Stafford was puzzled, curious as to what bumped into it. A large splash several meters off the bow drew his attention. He only caught a glimpse with the corner of his eye, but it appeared to be some sort of fin. Whatever it was, it had gone under the surface. He quickly slipped his goggles back over his eyes and ducked under the water. Rays of sunlight reached from the surface to the darkening ocean bed, illuminating the surrounding water. Stafford could see the large black shape as it circled in the distance. He only caught a glimpse of its caudal fin as it circled. It was very large and fish-like in nature, and appeared to be several meters away. The orca's carcass blocked his view. In need of air, he surfaced. As he drew a breath, he heard another splash from the other side of the dead orca, followed by the sight of seagulls fluttering into the air. He pulled himself over the orca to look over it. The bulk of the creature was underwater, but its back had briefly emerged, sporting a small sail-like fin. It turned in his direction and submerged.

"What the hell...oh shit!" He lost his grip on the orca and slipped underwater. He shut his eyes tight to protect against the sting of the saltwater. He slipped his goggles back in place and regained his sense of direction. He was almost directly underneath the orca. He looked in the direction of the fish and saw nothing. He looked around and saw nothing and started to assume it swam off. Then something pressed against his right foot. He looked down and the water around him erupted into a sea of bubbles as he let out a terrified scream. He saw the jaws of the creature open beneath him, forming an entrance to an enormous dark tunnel. His right foot happened to be pressed on the rigid edge of the jaw. His other foot was in it entirely. Survival instinct kicked in. Before the jaws closed shut, he pushed his foot against the creature's head with all his might and launched himself upward. He paddled his arms and kicked his legs, quickly grabbing onto the orca carcass. He glanced down and saw the huge open mouth following him upwards. He didn't see any teeth, but he could clearly see the back of the throat. He pulled himself up onto the orca as if it was a lifeboat. The giant fish smacked into the submerged part, causing the carcass to spin like a top. Stafford hugged the dead cetacean, hanging on for dear life. The black fish backed off and attacked from the rear. The orca's tail bumped up, nearly shaking Stafford off. Then for a moment, it seemed to stop. Stafford remained frozen on the carcass for several more seconds. The tension caused his teeth to clench hard, drawing a little blood from his gums. His brow was a mix of seawater and nervous sweat. He lifted his head up and looked around, not seeing the big fish anywhere. He looked to his boat, which was a few meters further than it originally was. The attack had pushed the carcass a bit further away. He scanned the water again to analyze whether the danger had passed. He slowly lowered himself down the side of the carcass, nearly touching the water. He tapped his hand, testing for any response. The enormous head shot out of the water, almost as if it was waiting for him.

Stafford yelled and fought his way back overtop the carcass. The huge jaws were just inches from him. Its webby fins flapped in the air like wings. The bulk of the big fish was resting somewhat on the orca, weighing it down into the water. Realizing he was about to be submerged, Stafford prepared to kick off and swim as fast as he could. He then saw the orca's pectoral flipper, held on only by a little bit of skin and muscle tissue. He grabbed it and pulled as hard as he could. It was still held on tight, and he felt like every muscle in his body was about to burst until he finally separated the four-foot fin from the body. It was a lot heavier than it looked. With all his strength, he heaved it into the fish's open jaw, losing his balance in the process. He fell into the water. He swam as fast as he could for his boat, kicking up water with each stroke. Against his better instinct, he glanced back. The fish was just submerging, but appeared to be busy chomping on the bait.

The few seconds it took him to reach his boat felt like hours. He welcomed the feeling of solid metal as he grabbed a hold of the sides and lifted himself in. His body made a loud thud when he fell to the floor. He rolled on his back and laid there still as a corpse while he caught his breath. His heart raced while his mind tried to comprehend what happened. After a moment, he found himself starting to chuckle. It was an attempt for his psyche to recover from the trauma it endured. He stood up and moved for the helm, believing the worst to be over.

A heavy blow from beneath rocked the boat. Stafford fell to his hands and knees, barely avoiding hitting his head. The big fish splashed along the port side, banging into the boat with its head like a battering ram. Stafford could not find his balance in the midst of the chaos. He managed to climb onto the helm and turn the ignition key. As the engine ignited, the fish started battering the stern, knocking him forward against the wheel. There was the sound of propeller blades hitting flesh, and then there was the sight of blood. The fish swam under. Stafford regained his posture and tried throttling the boat. It wouldn't move.

"Shit!" he yelled. The propeller blades had busted when they hit the fish. He looked around for the black fish, seeing only traces of blood, indicating it had been wounded by the blades. He realized that he needed help, even if the creature had left. Nash wouldn't be able to pick him up because the *Taurus* was currently inoperable. Then he remembered—the patrol boat. He looked around to find it. It was heading west, furthering its distance. He cuffed his hands around his mouth. "HEY!" he yelled at the top of his lungs. He tried a few more times before digging for a box in a glove compartment. He pulled a red flare gun out of the box. He checked the slide, and it was already loaded. "You better look this way!" he said, directing his thoughts to the officers on the boat. He pointed the flare gun to the sky and pulled the trigger. A bright orange sparkling glow shot up into the sky and began arching at four hundred feet.

****

"Um, Riker, do you see this?" Metzler said and pointed at the flickering flare several hundred yards behind them. Riker turned and looked from the helm. He saw the flare and then the boat from where it came from.

"Whoever that is, they're signaling us," he said. He steered the vessel around. Metzler kept her eye on the small boat. She could see the individual on board. He was waving them over. Even from their distance, she could see that he was very anxious.

****

"Oh yes, baby, that's what I want to see," he remarked as he watched the police vessel move in his direction. Even as they moved closer, he couldn't help but continue waving them on. "Come on, get over here and I'll take back every mean thing I've said about the police." After a moment, he stopped waving and took a seat. He barely rested himself when he noticed a ripple in the water off the portside. The tiny swells were moving towards the boat, meaning they originated from something else. His mind barely processed the meaning of this when the port side lifted upwards from another impact. As the boat leveled out, the massive fish lifted its head over the water and opened its jaw wide. It clamped down on the portside, indenting the topside. Fright had Stafford's eyes wide open, as well as his mouth agape, although he couldn't manage to let out a yell. He kicked away from the huge beast and clung to the starboard side, which was tilting upward into the air. As the fish pulled down, the port side was nearly submerging. Water began spilling over the edge. With his heart racing, Stafford began climbing over the starboard side as it tilted further up.

Just at that moment, the creature lost its grip and slipped beneath the surface. The starboard side fell back down with tremendous force, flinging Stafford into the water. He quickly surfaced a couple meters away from the boat and hurriedly swam back toward it. He frantically grabbed for it, but had difficulty getting a grip. He finally got a good hold and started pulling himself up. He calmed down for a moment when he heard the familiar sound of a boat engine.

****

Metzler watched the individual who had alerted them fall into the water when his boat leveled out. When he surfaced, Riker accelerated the boat to his location. He slowed down and pulled up parallel with the Boston Whaler, leaving about ten feet of space between the two boats.

"Are you okay?" Metzler called out to Stafford. He was halfway over the edge of the boat.

"Bring your boat closer!" he yelled. "Hurry! Bring it right alongside!"

"You're in a wetsuit, you can't swim over?" Riker called back.

"No, you don't understand! There's something in the water! Something huge!" Stafford said.

"Oh shit," Riker said after he looked at the whale carcass and saw the huge bite marks. Metzler saw it too.

"Oh my God, there's a shark out here!" she said.

"I don't—no! It's not a shark, but it's some sort of big fish!" Stafford called back. He then realized that factor was beside the point of trying to get away before it came back. "I can't move the boat, it busted the propeller!" Riker didn't waste time and started to reposition the patrol boat.

"Where is it?" Metzler asked. Her question was answered by a large splash off to their bow as the huge fish breached. It slammed into the hull, pushing the boat back. The fiberglass hull crunched inward, but did not breach. The boat shook violently from the hit, nearly knocking Metzler to the deck floor.

"Christ!" Riker snarled. His expression appeared rather angry than surprised. The fish continued ramming the starboard side of the boat. The officers felt like they were riding an earthquake. Riker reached into the cockpit and pulled out a loaded Remington Autoloader shotgun from a rack. He chambered a round and fired several blasts at the black shape under the surface. The sound of each blast was intensely loud and deafening. Metzler felt her ears ringing and cupped her hands over them. The water erupted in red, and suddenly the bombardment ceased when the fish ducked under. Riker checked the ejector on the shotgun and determined he had emptied it. Metzler quickly stood up and looked for the creature. The water was full of its blood, but there was no sign of its body. Her ears were still ringing, unconditioned to firearms in the real world. She was used to having ear protection. She noticed Riker clearly wasn't fazed at all by it.

"I don't see it," she said. Even her own voice sounded muffled to her ears. The sea calmed down. She continued scanning the water. Suddenly some small splashing from the starboard side aft drew her attention. She leaned over the side, ready to draw her Glock. She stopped when she realized the splashing was only caused by a couple of herring fighting over a tiny piece of flesh from the creature. She felt the tension ease away. "Oh jeez," she said in relief.

The water erupted on the portside, as the enormous bloody fish breached and slammed into the boat. The force of the hit rocked the boat heavily to the right. Metzler let out a scream as she tipped over the starboard edge and started to fall into the water. She closed her eyes and braced for the splash, but instead felt herself hit the side of the boat. She opened up and saw that Riker had grabbed her by the shoulder. He was barely holding her up. She was facing outward with her back against the fiberglass. Her legs were already submerged. Riker got a better grip, clasping his fingers on her uniform. Suddenly, she noticed the water beneath her start to darken with fresh red blood. Then beneath her appeared a huge black shape. Through the bloody water she saw the giant mouth open, creating an oval-shaped tunnel. It quickly engulfed her entire abdomen and began to slam shut.

Riker lifted with all his might, heaving Metzler out of the water. Her feet cleared the jaws just as they closed. She fell onto the deck and saw the creature's head rise above the surface. With a fast draw, Riker pulled his revolver from his holster and fired a single shot. The hollow point created a fleshy explosion as it penetrated the center of the fish's head. The black beast writhed in agony, kicking up mountains of water that sprayed the officers. Riker never wavered. He maintained his position, keeping his Smith & Wesson R8 pointed at the dying creature. After several long seconds, the fish's movements slowed, eventually coming to a complete stop. It floated on the surface, drifting toward the Boston Whaler. It was dead. Metzler continued to lay on the deck, taking several shallow breaths before she could manage a calm deep one. Her heart was pounding hard in her chest, and her hands were shaking from adrenaline. She watched Riker holster his revolver into his tactical leg holster before moving toward the helm.

"We're coming to you," he called to Stafford. His voice was calm, as if they barely experienced anything. He steered the boat around the dead fish and lined up with the Boston Whaler. The individual on the boat was staring endlessly at the creature he had just killed.

"Oh, my God. It's a black grouper! How the hell did it get this big?" he said to himself. The fish was eighteen feet long at least. The sides were riddled with shotgun wounds, which would've certainly bled it to death in a matter of time. Scales were peeling off the flesh near the wounds, and the mouth remained slightly open.

"You coming aboard or what?" Riker called to him. Stafford broke his gaze and eagerly climbed aboard. While he did so, Metzler lifted herself to her feet.

"Thank you so much," he said. "Well, let me introduce myself. I'm Dr. Aaron Stafford." He shook hands with Metzler and then Riker. "I'm a marine biologist."

"Oh, you're a marine biologist? So tell me, what the hell is that thing?" Riker pointed at the dead fish. Stafford looked over toward it. His entire demeanor had gone from tense and frightened to eager and excited.

"It's a grouper," he said. "I was out here tracking an orca I tagged and found that," he pointed to the orca carcass. "I went into the water to examine it. That's why I'm wearing a wetsuit. While I was completing my examination, that thing attacked me." Riker looked at the orca carcass, particularly at the belly wound.

"Well Doctor, today's your lucky day," he said. "If that fish could to *that*," he pointed at the orca's injury, "then you would've been a light snack."

"With all due respect, I don't believe that fish did that," Stafford said. His natural urge to explain the scientific facts took over. "The bite marks on the orca are not consistent with a grouper." Riker shrugged his shoulders, completely disinterested.

"Whatever," he said. "You're alive. We can tow your boat to shore." He went to the helm. Stafford quickly followed him.

"Sir, I have a small request," he said. Riker stopped and stared at him. "Let me get a line out on the fish, that way we can tow it in as well." Riker laughed and lit up a cigarette. The initial puff of smoke blew right at Stafford's face.

"You want to go out there with that thing? You sure it's even dead?" Riker had seen plenty of things, and people, take several bullets before finally dying. He didn't find that fish to be an exception to the possibility.

"You don't understand," Stafford said while waving his hand to blow away the smoke. "That is a black grouper. They don't get any bigger than roughly five feet long. That thing is almost twenty feet long. I want to get it to my lab so I can do an examination." Riker laughed again.

"If you want to go out with that thing, then go ahead. We'll even be nice enough to get a tow line on your boat while you do so." Stafford didn't waste any time. He grabbed a piece of rope from his boat and swam out to the dead grouper. Swimming up to the immense jaws that tried to kill him minutes ago was daunting. Reaching his hand inside it to get the rope through the gill slit was worse. While doing this, he certainly hoped for Riker's misgiving to be false. The huge circular eye seemed to stare at him the entire time. He tied a strong knot and swam back to the police vessel. Metzler had already tied a line to the Boston Whaler. She reached out and helped pull him up to the patrol boat's deck.

"Why do you think it's so big?" she asked him. She was clearly more curious than Riker.

"That's what I want to find out," Stafford said. "I'll let you know where my lab is." Without saying anything further, Riker throttled the patrol boat toward shore, pulling the Boston Whaler and the grouper behind it. Metzler leaned on the guardrail while Stafford started to explain some things about what he was studying. Her eyes went toward Riker, who stood at the helm looking dead ahead. She felt water dripping from her brow from when the fish splashed them, and she realized her pants were soaked from nearly falling into the water—almost right into the creature's jaws. The reality suddenly sank in; she almost died at that moment. That fish would've crushed her easily had it gotten a hold of her, but it didn't...all because Riker kept her from falling and pulled her away in time. The man whom she hated working with had saved her life.

She silently embraced the sunshine, the cool summer breeze, and the new respect she found for her trainer.

CHAPTER 13

Adam Wisk dusted some crumbs from his hamburger bun off his shirt while he sat in his Ford Ranger. He was parked in the empty driveway of a resident's home, relying on the possibility of the homeowner being away at work. He held a pair of binoculars to his eyes, looking down at the ocean view. He panned his vision down the road a ways, catching the sight of the former old bait and tackle shop that was now called *Stafford Marine Study Institute*. Coming in from about a quarter of a mile out in the water was the MPD Harbor Patrol vessel, towing a small Boston Whaler. Wisk could see something else towed behind them, but they were too far out for him to know what it was.

Wisk had spent the whole morning looking for anything worth getting a story on. There was no statement from the police regarding the *Mary Westward*, other than it was found intact and taken home by the Coast Guard. Not enough information to put toward a story. Sadly, there was hardly anything else. The only thing that held any sort of interest was the upcoming sailing contest, and all he could do was interview business owners about how they were preparing for the crowds. It was hard times for him and *The Canyon Wall*, and currently the big sporting event was the only thing that would produce even a little revenue. While doing his futile search for news, his police scanner picked up some chatter that sparked his interest.

"Harbor Patrol, Unit Eighteen to Dispatch?"

"This is Dispatch. Go ahead Eighteen."

"We've picked up a gentleman, about two miles off of Rock Reilly. He had a little trouble out there. Some big fish tried to eat his boat. No injuries, although shots were fired to kill the thing. He has a little lab near the shore, and we're towing his boat there." There was a bit of a pause. Wisk thought it was because the dispatcher was puzzled from the information.

"Copy that. Will there be a report written on this?"

"Affirmative. We'll head into the office after we drop this guy off."

"Ten-four."

When Wisk heard this exchange, he knew the lab mentioned had to be Stafford's lab. He had heard of the scientist, particularly of the fact that he was a "save-the-whales" type. However, this was the only truly interesting information he had come across, and he believed it was worth exploring. He watched the police vessel come into the dock. He was far enough away that they would not notice him watching. He could see the officers, and he recognized them as the ones he briefly encountered the day before. *Well, that's a bust. They didn't want to speak to me yesterday, so there's no way they'll say anything about this,* he thought. He saw another individual dressed in a black outfit. Wisk determined that that was Dr. Stafford. He watched as they used a line to pull the Boston Whaler into its place in the dock. What was more interesting was what they pulled up to the dock afterwards. It looked like a huge black fish. It was so big he didn't even need the binoculars to see it.

They attached a cable from the bigger boat in the dock to the big fish and winched it up out of the water. It almost resembled a massive prize catch. Wisk saw a fourth individual drive a flatbed vehicle out of the lab and up to the shore, close enough for them to place the fish on the bed. It appeared that the officers were about to follow the scientist into the lab. *I'll wait for them to leave, and then I'll do some fishing of my own,* he thought.

****

Dr. Stafford had spent the whole ride back talking about his background and goals for future study. He explained his conservation efforts and about what he hoped to achieve. Metzler found everything he had to say quite fascinating. She would respond with questions, which Stafford was happy to answer. Riker couldn't have cared much less. When they approached his lab, Stafford called Nash's cell phone to meet them with the flatbed. They hooked the giant grouper to the winch on the *Taurus* and loaded it onto the truck. Nash drove the vehicle back into the lab.

"Would you like to come inside?" Stafford offered to the officers. Although he asked the question to both officers, it was clearly more directed at Metzler.

"Sure, I would love to," Metzler responded with a smile. She was still a bit frazzled from the incident out in the water. For her, this would be a good way to get her mind off of it. She followed Dr. Stafford to the front door. Riker lingered behind, rolling his eyes.

"Hopeless," he said under his breath. He was aware of what the scientist was trying to do. Personally, he didn't care. He just saw it as a grand waste of time. But then again, it beat floating out in the water doing nothing for hours. He followed them through the doorway and saw the lab. They were immediately greeted by Stafford's assistant.

"Hi!" he said with a loud enthusiastic voice. He was wearing a *Godzilla* t-shirt with Japanese lettering. He reached out and shook Metzler's hand, while Riker kept back. "I'm Robert! Thanks for saving my idiot boss..." he looked at Stafford, "who, by the way, owes me twenty bucks."

"Oh no!" Stafford said. "You specifically said I'd get attacked by the shark! This, my friend," he pointed at the dead grouper, "is no shark. You owe ME twenty dollars!" The banter lasted for about a minute, during which Metzler started looking around at the lab.

"Wow," she said. Her eyes went right for the aquariums, particularly the very long narrow rectangular one in the middle that was circulating water. She walked to it and saw the hammerhead inside. It was missing all of its fins, including its dorsal and caudal. It wiggled its body like a worm, like it was attempting to swim. She looked at Stafford. "What happened to this little guy?" The two scientists broke their chatter and turned towards her.

"That's a hammerhead," Stafford said. "We call him Steve. He was netted by some fishermen. They hauled him aboard their boat and cut off his fins, and then threw him back into the water. Sharks can't swim without their fins, and they can't float like most fish. I happened to be diving nearby when they did this. I just couldn't stand for it. I grabbed the little guy and saved him." He then pointed at the pumps that were circulating water. "See, they have to keep swimming or they'll drown. Because this guy can't swim, this container keeps a flow of water going through his gills."

"Oh my goodness," Metzler said. "How does he eat?"

"I do my best to hand feed him," Stafford answered. He heard Riker scoff from his desk. He turned and saw the cop looking at some marine study articles.

"Sounds like quite the luxurious life sitting in that tank all day," Riker said. Stafford didn't appreciate the tone, but ignored it. This cop did save his life after all.

"I'm working on a solution to that," Stafford said. He looked back to Metzler. She seemed more interested anyway, and appeared to have an appreciation for his work. "Have you ever heard of the dolphin Winter?"

"Isn't that the one with the prosthetic tail?" she asked. Riker kept himself from chuckling. *You actually know this shit?*

"Yes!" Stafford said. "My plan is to do something similar, but a little more complex for this little guy. Basically, I'd like to build a body suit for him, which would provide pectoral fins, a dorsal fin, and of course a tail fin. That way…" he turned to Riker, "this guy won't have to stay cramped up like this."

"What would the fishermen want with his fins?" Metzler wondered aloud.

"Oh, come on!" Riker said. "They make soup out of them. Everybody knows that! I bought a can of it once. It's okay." Stafford felt himself growing frustrated.

"It's barbaric," he said. "They catch the shark, cut off their fins and throw them overboard to drown."

Riker continued going through the magazines on his desk. He picked one up and looked at the cover, which featured three shark hunters holding up a pair of shark jaws. The article referred to them as the Trio. The middle man appeared to be an American in his early-to-mid fifties. To the right was his twenty-five-year-old son, and to the left was an Asian looking woman, whom Riker assumed was the leader's lover. Stafford saw the cover from where he stood, and shook his head in disapproval. He had meant to throw that magazine away. He was familiar with that group and he despised them. The magazine paraded them as hunters of man-eating sharks, but Stafford knew the truth. They were not typical hunters, they were poachers. Slaughterers. They didn't even kill for sport, they killed for joy. They only killed a couple known sharks that truly posed a threat. Stafford had encountered them in the past and tried to call them out on their deeds. It was an occasion that didn't go well.

"So, why don't you think that guy killed your whale?" Riker asked about the grouper.

"Technically, orcas aren't actually whales, they're dolphins. They're called killer whales because…" he realized it was pointless to explain. "Never mind. I have evidence that there's something else out there. Something really big." He stopped, realizing he wanted to keep this discovery to himself. Although he was certain these cops wouldn't pass his findings to other scientists, he figured it was best to keep it to himself. "But of course, I need to do further research to confirm my theory. Which reminds me, I'm gonna do a dissection on our grouper today." Metzler started to ask another question regarding Steve the hammerhead. During this, Riker suddenly felt the need to grab the wall to support himself. He felt as if the blood started draining from his face. The room felt as if it was spinning. He forced himself to regain his composure and looked to Nash.

"Mind if I use your bathroom?" He managed to sound casual.

"Sure," Nash said. "It's over there." He pointed to a hallway, and Riker followed his direction. He was careful to land each step before taking the next. Metzler noticed this while Stafford was talking. She watched in the corner of her eye as Riker made his way to the hallway. He quickened his movements when he thought he was out of sight. He slammed the bathroom door shut behind him and lunged for the toilet. He tried not to be too loud when he vomited. He looked down into the bowl and the bloody water inside it. He rested on the floor for a few moments to catch his breath. He realized some of his blood vomit was on the seat and floor. He grabbed some paper towels and wiped it up as quickly and thoroughly as he could. He then noticed he had some blood on the center of his uniform.

"Just fantastic," he mumbled. He wiped it off as best he could, but some of it was soaked in. Luckily, his uniform was black so it would be easy to miss. He stuffed the dirty paper towels deep into the trashcan, and stuffed some clean ones in on top of them to help conceal the evidence. He stood up and looked around, deeming the room clean enough for nobody to notice—except for the smell. He left the door open on his way out and just hoped nobody would use it for a while. As he walked out, he kept one arm strategically placed over the stain.

"Alright," Metzler said to Stafford when she saw Riker. "I think it's about time we took off."

"Awe, okay," Stafford said. "Listen, I can't thank you guys enough for saving my ass out there. Do you have business cards or anything like that?" Metzler pulled a card out of her pocket and handed it to him. Stafford felt a flood of excitement run through him until he realized it was the non-emergency police number. "Oh!...thanks!" He smiled, hiding his disappointment. Nash turned to conceal his laugh.

"Thanks for the tour," Metzler said. Riker was already out the door. "If you need anything, just give us a call." She hoped it wasn't too obvious she was in a hurry to leave. She loved being at the lab, but there was something clearly wrong with Riker. "Bye!" She waved and exited.

"Bye," Stafford and Nash both said. When the door shut, Nash jabbed his boss in the shoulder and laughed.

"I guess saving baby hammerheads isn't that great of a pickup line," he joked.

"Oh, shut up!" Stafford said. "Come on, we've got work to do. Did you order those propellers?"

"Sure did," Nash said. "The guy said they shouldn't take long to arrive." Stafford grabbed some scalpels, gauze, vials, and some other cutting equipment and took it up to the flatbed.

"Good," he said. "Now we've got some work to do here. I want to know why this guy is so much bigger than he should be." He started by drawing some blood.

****

"About time!" Wisk said out loud when he saw the two officers exit the lab. He watched as they boarded their patrol vessel and steered out of the dock. The sound of a car horn blaring nearby caused him to lower his binoculars. Stopped in the road was a black Chevy Cruz, and in it was an angry woman yelling at him.

"Who the hell are you? Get the hell out of my driveway!" she roared. *Well shit*, he thought. He put his truck in drive and floored the accelerator. He kicked up gravel and dust when he sped out. The woman honked her horn as he passed her. "Asshole!" He didn't hear her, nor did he see her middle finger pointing up in her window. His mind was focused on the desperation to get something to write about. He needed anything, even something small to help keep his position in the *Canyon Wall* going. He pulled up to the lab and parked.

****

"My gosh," Nash said with amazement after climbing onto the flatbed. It was his first close look at the fish. He looked at the mouth and extended the lower jaw. It opened so wide he could've fit his whole body in there. "How did you get away from this sucker?"

"Dumb luck," Stafford said while he prepared to make an incision behind the gill line. "If it weren't for those cops being around, he would've eventually got me. I don't know if you saw the Boston Whaler, but it's toast now." Nash continued staring with amazement at the grouper.

"Do you think it's odd that we have this overgrown guy and evidence of a giant shark out there?" he asked.

"I don't think it's a coincidence," Stafford said. "What's also weird is how aggressive it was. The way it attacked the police boat and mine, it's uncharacteristic. That's why we're cutting into this guy to find some clues. We're gonna cut him as if we're filleting him for dinner." Before he got started, the sight of a small odd looking white object attached to the fish's tail drew his attention. Nash noticed it too and they scooted down to get a closer look. It was living, shaped like a huge white ant clinging to the grouper's skin with huge mandibles. It was a few centimeters long, and its head was wider than its body. Its abdomen was swelled up into an oval shape, red with blood.

"What...the hell...is that?" Nash said, looking freaked. He had an intense fear of bugs, and the little organism looked like the ugliest of them all.

"Oh wow!" Stafford said. "It's *Gnathia marleyi*! It's a Caribbean parasite that clings to fish and sucks their blood. They store it until they're out of the juvenile stage, and they let go and live off it. Actually, their mandibles are smaller when they do this, meaning this guy's actually about ready to detach.

"Oh, hell no!" Nash backed away, nearly stumbling off the flatbed. Stafford laughed and trapped the parasite into a jar he had nearby. He pried it from the skin with the rim and sealed it with a lid. It rested on the jar bottom, its abdomen pulsing. With that taken care of, he moved back to the marked incision line. He took his scalpel and pressed it into the skin, slicing through effortlessly. The skin was thick, but the scalpel was sharp enough to get all the way through. He slid the blade vertically down the gill line. A knock on the door nearly made him jump. "Who the hell...? Nash, could you see who that is?" Nash hopped off the truck and went to the door. He opened it to find a man wearing a white button shirt and khaki shorts.

"Hello there! My name is Adam Wisk for the *Canyon Wall*," he said. Before Nash could say anything, he stepped inside without asking permission. He walked past Nash and looked at the lab. "Wow! This is a nice place you have here!"

"Uh... can we help you?" Nash said. "We're in the middle of a serious project and don't really have time for visitors."

"Dr. Stafford!" Wisk yelled across the lab. Stafford looked up when he heard his name called.

"Yes? I'm sorry, I don't know you," he said.

"No, but I've heard of you," Wisk said as he approached the flatbed. "I wanted to stop by really quick because I noticed you were helped by a couple of police men.... Oh wow, nice eel you have here!" He looked at the injured hammerhead.

"It's a shark," Nash corrected him. "Listen, I don't want to be rude, but..."

"I was just hoping to know what happened out in the water," Wisk interrupted. "I'm aware that you had a run-in with a shark or something and that the cops apparently saved you. I think it'd make an interesting story for the paper..." he stood where he could see the huge grouper. "Holy...! Okay, this'll make a REALLY interesting story!" He pulled out a camera from his pocket and snapped a picture.

"Excuse me!" Stafford nearly snapped. He put his tools down and climbed off the truck, preparing to verbally tear the reporter apart. Then a thought came to his mind. *Perhaps I could use this guy.* "Alright, Mr. Wisk, I don't have much time. What can we do for you?"

"Just tell me what happened out in the water," Wisk said.

"I was doing some research out there. This fish came up and attacked my boat. It attacked the rudder, dented in the sides, and nearly capsized the boat. The officers were nearby and they shot it. We managed to tow it back here."

"That's amazing," Wisk said. "Do these fish normally get this big?" Stafford didn't want to give this person too much info. It was clear he was no expert on Marine Biology, and Stafford didn't want too much info getting out yet before he conducted more research.

"It's a little bigger than normal," he bent the truth. Nash quickly cut in between the two and took the doctor aside.

"Listen Doc, we hardly know anything about this guy," he said, keeping his voice down to not be overheard by Wisk. "Why are you telling him stuff?"

"We've got no funding," Stafford said. "He said his name's Wisk? I know who he is. He used to be a real hotshot reporter until he asked the wrong questions to a senator. I hate to admit it, but this guy might be a blessing in disguise. If we can get some media exposure, then we can get someone to give us the funds to conduct more research. Plus, when we're ready to announce our discovery, we'll need someone like this to get the word out."

"Ever hear of Facebook?" Nash said. "We could do that ourselves."

"No, we can't," Stafford said. "We need real exposure, and this guy is desperate enough to go the extra mile to get our story out." Nash thought about it and considered that Stafford was right. Stafford stepped away to continue speaking with Wisk, who was taking pictures of the grouper.

"I think this guy is more than *a little* bit bigger than usual," he said. Stafford took a deep breath, hoping he wasn't making a bad decision by talking to Wisk.

"You're right," he said. "That's why we're performing a dissection. We want to find out why it's so big and aggressive."

"Hot damn! This sounds like a real good story!" Wisk said. "I saw those cops that brought you in. They've been a busy pair. Did you know they were the ones who found the missing *Mary Westward* trawler?"

"I knew it was found, but not that they were the ones to find it," Stafford said.

"Well Doctor, I think you and I both know that there's something weird happening in these waters. From what I heard, there was only one survivor on the trawler, with everyone else dead or missing. The Coast Guard took it away, and the police were ordered not to discuss it with me."

"Interesting, but I don't see how that concerns me," Stafford said. "Something could've happened in the hurricane. But listen, Mr. Wisk; I think I'll be willing to give you a good story. I just need a little time, but my associate and I believe we're on the verge of a great discovery. If you just leave me a business card, I can..." Wisk already had his card out before the doctor could finish. Stafford accepted it and looked it over. It was crumpled up and half of it was stained with coffee. "Wow, okay then. Listen, I'll be in touch with you. But in the meantime, I really need to get to work. We have a ton to do."

"Sounds like a deal," Wisk said. The two shook hands and Wisk started on his way out. While walking out, he saw the magazine pile on Stafford's desk and noticed the one with the Trio on top. *Interesting. I've actually heard of those guys.* He waved goodbye as he walked out the door.

"Okay then," Stafford said. "Now if we can avoid any more interruptions, let's get back to work. Robert, could you bring me a bone saw? This guy's bones will be a bit thicker than we're used to."

"You got it boss," Nash said. "You sure this reporter thing is gonna work?"

"It's worth a try," Stafford said. "I'm not big on reporters, but I think this guy's desperate enough to work for us." He began cutting along the belly. Simply slicing the giant fish open was going to be a lengthy process.

CHAPTER 14

After they had left Dr. Stafford's lab, Riker continued to get worse. He tried to act as if there was nothing wrong with him, but Metzler noticed his subtle hunching over at the helm. More so, she noticed the bloodstain on the nylon of his uniform. The way Riker was holding onto the helm, it was clear he was using it to support himself. When he steered the patrol boat into port, even Officer Marley noticed something wasn't right. Of course, he was too scared of Riker to point it out. Riker walked in a very careful manner as he walked to the patrol car. Before he got in, Metzler stepped in his way.

"I think I'll drive," she said. To her surprise, Riker didn't give any resistance. He nearly fell into the passenger seat. The world was still spinning and his stomach was knotting up even more. Metzler couldn't help but think of all the empty beer bottles she saw at his house. She knew he vomited in Stafford's bathroom, and she knew the red stain on his uniform wasn't there before then. There was no mistaking it was blood, despite his attempts to hide it. Riker almost appeared to be dozing when she drove the vehicle. Instead of going to the police station, she stopped in his driveway.

"What are we doing here?" Riker asked.

"I think you should take the rest of the day off," she said. "I'll let Crawford know you're under the weather." She highly considered taking him to the hospital, but she knew he'd refuse to go in. Nevertheless, he was in no condition to be on duty.

"I think you've finally had a good idea," he said. He stepped out of the car without saying anything else. There wasn't even a 'goodbye' from him. He stumbled to his front door, spitting into his yard. Metzler wasn't offended. For the first time, she truly had heartfelt concern for the veteran cop. She thought of how her life could've ended today had she fallen off the vessel. She also thought of how she reacted to the creature attacking their boat. It was as if all training disappeared and she didn't know what to do. But Riker, even with being so sick, kept his composure and was able to save her and Stafford from the rampaging fish. She now felt foolish for thinking of her previous encounters on the road as tense. But Riker knew how to handle the scenario, even though it was a very uncommon one for police. For the first time she felt she truly had learned something from her partner.

She drove the patrol car out of his driveway. She needed to conduct a report at the police station. Before doing that, there was one thing she felt she had to do. Hopefully Crawford would be there.

****

She came in through the back entrance as usual. She marched straight for Crawford's office and knocked on the door, unsure if he was in.

"Come in," he called. She opened the door and shut it behind her. He looked up from some paperwork on his desk, surprised to see her by herself. "Metzler? Where's Officer Riker?"

"He'll be out sick for the rest of the day," she said. "It seems like he caught stomach flu." Crawford stared insistently at her. He knew she didn't come in just to tell him this.

"Okay," he said. "Is there anything I can do for you?"

"I'm not playing any more games, Chief," she said. Her tone and demeanor caught him off guard. This was something he rarely saw; a rookie cop about to make demands to a high-ranking officer.

"Excuse me?"

"I want to know the story behind Riker," she said. "There's something seriously wrong going on with him, and I think you know what it is. Why is he here, and why am I partnered up with him?" She spoke as if she was issuing a direct order from the chief.

"I don't think I like your tone, Officer Metzler," he said. "You don't come into my office and make demands from ME. I am the leader of this department, and I will not tolerate this kind of behavior, especially from a brand-new member." Metzler felt herself tense up inside. She was partly unprepared for the backlash, but she kept her composure and didn't show intimidation as he continued. "Unless you're looking for an excuse to get yourself fired, I'd suggest you leave my office. I have no obligation to share anything with you."

"If that's the way you want to play it, I'll just have to go to the Mayor's office and report that you allowed an alcoholic officer to work in the department," Metzler retorted. Crawford started to speak but stopped, realizing she was serious. Doing this gave away his poker face, and Metzler knew he was aware of Riker's problems. Acting Mayor Kathy Bloom would have a field day with Crawford if she found out about Riker's condition. In a way, he was impressed with the rookie's negotiation.

"I see you're gonna go far in this field," Crawford said. It was a sincere compliment. Metzler didn't thank him, although it made her feel good inside. Crawford leaned back in his chair. "What do you want to know?"

"Everything. Including Martha Riker," she said. Crawford stared at her. She knew he was curious at how she knew that name. "I went into his house this morning to check on him. He has a copy of an obituary with that name, and I saw the wedding picture. You know what else I saw?" Crawford didn't respond. "Plenty of empty beer bottles everywhere. And I found him, passed out." Crawford's expression saddened. He stood up and walked to the window, staring out into the sunshine.

"I became a cop when I was twenty-five," he began, "Straight out of the service. I got married around that time, and after a few years we got ourselves a little house in a suburb outside of the city. It made for a longer drive to work, but the area was decent. Better than most places in Alton. Of course, it was costly so I had to work some double shifts to help pay it off. There was one sixteen-hour day I worked when I stopped at a little café for some dinner. I'm sitting at the counter and I see this eight-year-old kid trying to get himself a sandwich. He was a couple dimes short, so they wouldn't give it to him. Keep in mind, what he was trying to get was not expensive to begin with. His family didn't have any money because his father had passed away. I waved to the kid and had him sit next to me. I bought him a meal and we sat together. He told me I made him want to be a cop."

"That was Riker," Metzler said. She didn't realize Riker and Crawford went so far back.

"Yes," he said. "After that I got to see him often. When he was in his teens, he'd often make the drive to visit me and my wife. Of course, I could've busted him for driving without a license, but then again I'd be busting half the kids in Alton. He was still undergoing some anger issues regarding his dad's death. Every kid needs a dad. Whenever I had vacation time, I sometimes tried to include him in it. We'd go fishing, shooting, hunting. His mom was happy with it. Poor lady passed away right after he graduated high school. I think that brought new anger issues. I was the one who arrested him when he got into a street fight. He beat the living hell out of this other guy. That was an awkward drive to the police station. Luckily the other guy didn't press charges, and there were plenty of witnesses who reported that he was actually harassing some girl and Riker intervened. Although, I'm glad we got there before he could've done any more damage." He paused to sip on some water. "He attended college and got some really good grades except for Algebra, which he struggled with. Someone offered to tutor him."

"Martha," Metzler said.

"I've never seen him so happy," Crawford said. "My gosh, they were a good young couple. You saw the picture. It was obvious they were meant to be. He went through the academy, and after his rookie year he married Martha. Riker was a natural in the police department— the best there was. He reached instructor level at marksmanship training, he's a third-degree black belt in Kenpo, and he had a natural instinct for finding clues—clues that sometimes nobody else would see. You already know a lot of the stories. He did so well as a patrol officer, they made him a detective." He sighed. "I wish he didn't accept that promotion. Life got very stressful, and dangerous. Riker was praised in the departments as being one of the few officers to really make a difference. But it came at a cost. He could barely sleep at night, especially after some incidents where intruders made an attempt on his life at his own home. One time he shot one through the door. That guy had a Beretta with a silencer in his hand."

"What happened?" Metzler asked.

"Riker was working all day and sometimes all night. He was seeing the worst of people for a grand period of those work hours. Being shot at doesn't help either. I guess he was becoming very emotionally unavailable at home. I eventually learned that Martha suffered heavily from depression. I guess she tried to reach out to him for help, but he was too busy. I don't believe he was ever harsh with her, but he had too much on his mind. I guess he thought whatever problems she had would go away on their own. Well, one day she," he paused and squeezed his eyes shut, holding back tears. "One day, I guess she lost her job. It was a real tough break. She tried again to reach out to Leonard, but he was unavailable again. She was alone at home, and I guess she opened a bottle of pills and..." his voice trailed off.

"Oh my God," Metzler said to herself. She sank into a chair, taking in the heaviness of the story. Part of her almost regretted asking, but she had to know the rest. "What happened after that?" Her voice was very soft. She could tell Crawford was emotionally impacted by these events as well.

"He took a few months absence, mainly because I ordered it," Crawford continued. "I didn't see much of him during that time, although I tried. When he came back to work, he was still a wreck. His appearance was rugged, he was unfocused, and he was much more aggressive. He became ruthless. He picked up a case almost immediately. It wasn't a good experience. It got to a point to where he found a suspect and nearly beat him to death with his bare hands. The officer partnered with him tried to stop it, and Riker ended up knocking him unconscious. It got worse as the next couple months went on. I came to realize that it was certain he would eventually get himself killed. I was already working on making the transition to move here. One of my final acts as Chief of Alton Police Department was firing Leonard Riker." Metzler was bewildered. "I had to do it to save his life."

"And then you got him a job here," Metzler said. Crawford nodded.

"Naturally he still needed a job, and he would've never got one himself," he said. "So, I pleaded with Mayor Ripefield, your uncle, to bring him aboard our department. Although I left out all the details I just shared with you, and made it sound like it was a simple transfer. He eventually agreed on the condition I'd assign him to train you for a two-month period. He thought it would be a good opportunity for you to learn from the best. But now Riker hates me for it all."

"I see," Metzler said. "However, have you looked at it from his perspective? His wife is buried back there, and you brought him all the way down here. You might've made his situation worse by bringing him here."

"I've thought of that," Crawford said. "But you're wrong. It would've been far worse to leave him there. Whether or not he remained on the department, he was going to get himself and maybe somebody else killed. You should've seen him when he first joined. He was the kind of guy who always did the right thing. But it's like his humanity had been stripped away, and he's now a shell of who he used to be." He stepped around his desk and stood face to face with Metzler. "My wife had two miscarriages. One of those was in the third trimester. We never had any children after that. Leonard is the closest thing to a son I ever had. I lost my wife to cancer about a year-and-a-half ago. It was the hardest thing I've had to go through. I'm not about to lose him too." Metzler listened and took it all in, suppressing a couple tears of her own.

"He saved my life today," she said. Crawford stood silent, unsure of what she was talking about.

"Wha—what happened?"

"We were out on a boat, and we came across this scientist in the water. He was being attacked by this huge…fish." She knew how it sounded when said out loud, and Crawford's confused stare confirmed that. "I'm not kidding. It hit the boat and I almost went in the water. It was right there, about to get me. But Riker grabbed me and pulled me back in, and he killed the thing. I guess I'm telling you this because…that good side of him is still there."

"Thank you," Crawford said after a long pause. Metzler started to leave the office. She remembered she needed to type up the report of the incident. Before she left, Crawford called after her, "What do you mean a big fish?" She stopped for a moment and gave a nervous laugh.

"Wait till you hear this."

****

The next couple of hours were exhausting for Dr. Stafford while he inspected the inside of the humongous grouper. Using various equipment, he was able to remove several large flaps of skin, peeling them back with some large forceps. He used the bone saw to remove the ribs, each of which was over an inch thick. The lab began to smell of fish guts. Nash tried to control the smell with air freshener, but it only had limited effect. When Stafford got a good look at the inside of the fish, he nearly gasped in shock. Throughout the inside were small tumors, about an inch thick each. They were riddled throughout, attaching to the organs and muscle tissue. Stafford wanted to remove the organs, but they were too large for storage, so the best he could do was remove tissue samples. He took a small piece of liver tissue and took it to a nearby microscope.

Under the magnifying lens, the cells had a beige color. He looked and saw what appeared to be tiny green blobs within the cell. He knew those were not natural. He collected other tissue samples from other sections of the fish's body and examined them. He found the same irregularity in each one. He allowed Nash to take a look.

"Jeez," he said while examining the microscope. "First this guy is over three times his maximum size, then we find him just riddled with tumors, and now this stuff in his cells. What's next? We'll find out he's radioactive?"

"That green stuff is reminiscent of somatotropin, a growth hormone," Stafford said. "Whatever the combination is, I think this guy somehow got a dose of a growth supplement."

"You think that's what caused the tumors?" Nash asked.

"I think it's highly possible," he said. "But how the heck did it get into this guy? There's no way some company would inject him with it and release it into the wild. But I think it's definitely human inflicted.

"If someone did this…why would they do it?" Nash asked.

"They've always been experimenting on growing new food for the past century," Stafford said. "There's usually some new project trying to prepare for the crisis of world hunger. God only knows what they're putting into the food we get at the grocery store. They spray the vegetation with all kinds of shit." He walked back to the fish. "There's one more thing I want to check."

"And that is…?"

"It's brain matter." Stafford grabbed a Stryker saw and climbed up on board the flatbed. He examined the gunshot wound to the head and determined that it likely didn't cause direct damage to the brain. He cut through the skin with a freshly sharpened scalpel, and then cut through the bone with the saw. Nash hated the sound it made when cutting bone. He looked the other direction until the sawing was done. He cut in a circular shape on the top of the creature's head. He removed the top of the head as if he was carving a pumpkin and looked into the exposed brain matter. Unlike a human brain, the grouper's brain was shaped like a mushroom. It was heavily enlarged, even more so than the creature's size would indicate. "Damn!" he exclaimed. Nash stayed on the floor. He was okay with looking at the other organs, but for some reason brain matter made him queasy.

"How big?"

"It's not just big, it's swollen!" Stafford said to him. He continued examining it. There was major swelling in the amygdala, causing it to be disproportionate to the rest of the brain, compared to examinations of normal sized groupers. "Good gosh, no wonder this guy was so pissed off." Other parts of the brain were swelled out of proportion as well, including the hippocampus, the part that controls hunger. Stafford got up and stepped down, exhausted from the autopsy. He went for a sink to wash his hands, followed by Nash. "It's believed that the amygdala controls emotions," he explained. "Obviously, fish don't have emotions like we do, in fact they don't have any. But they do have aggression, and with swelling like that, this fish was going around our waters like an escaped mental patient bent on mass murder. Hell, I'm not even convinced he was attacking my boat for food. In his mind, the boats just looked like another large animal and he wanted to eliminate…" he stopped as a thought entered his mind. Without saying a word, he walked to his desk and pulled out the two shark teeth. He looked at their large size, and then he looked across the lab at the grouper. Nash watched him and quickly realized what he was thinking.

"Oh my God," he said. "You think our shark…"

"He's been exposed to the same thing. It makes perfect sense," Stafford said. He thought of the recent occurrences. "Oh my God. The orcas, the great white…the orcas hardly being eaten; he's not killing just for food. This animal is highly aggressive, and when he runs out of natural enemies in the area he'll attack anything."

"Holy shit, you think fishing ships are gonna be in danger?"

"You saw the damage the grouper did to my boat, and it rocked the hell out of the police vessel. Imagine what an overgrown, pissed off Thresher shark can do. Hell, how do we know this shark hasn't killed anyone already?" Stafford inquired. "And where did this growth hormone stuff come from? There are no factories around here near the water that I'm aware of. Of course, God only knows what the government might be sponsoring." Another thought occurred to him. He recalled an incident where a reporter was silenced regarding animal testing in a government-owned facility located somewhere in the Caribbean. He only remembered it because one of the senators that supposedly was behind the project was Mike Flynn, who had a role in getting Wisk fired. He began to wonder.

"If what's out there is a Thresher as big as we believe it to be, how much damage could it cause?" Nash asked. Stafford shrugged his shoulders. Then he remembered something Wisk said about the lost trawler, how he mentioned there was a survivor picked up by Riker and Metzler. He remembered seeing it being towed, and his stomach turned upside down when he recalled the specific damage. The gash in the hull and the denting on the sides.

"I think it's time we put our new friend to use." He was referring to Wisk. He used to be a renowned investigative reporter until his career came crashing down. "But first, I want to see if I can ask one of those officers a question." He looked at the time. It was nearing four in the afternoon. He picked out the card Metzler gave to him and dialed it in his cell phone.

****

Metzler was in the briefing room at shift change, waiting for the minute hand on the clock to hit twelve. Then a voice came from the hallway, calling her name. It was one of the dispatchers.

"Metzler, there's a call specifically for you," the dispatcher said. "You can take it up here." Metzler got up and followed her to a small cubicle behind the dispatcher unit. She picked up the phone and released the call from hold.

"This is Officer Metzler," she said.

"*Good afternoon. This is Dr. Aaron Stafford. We met earlier, through a rather interesting experience.*" Metzler recognized the voice as Stafford said his name.

"Yes Doctor," she chuckled. "What can I do for you?"

"*Listen, uhh...I need your help. I'm trying to figure out something that might be going on in our local waters, and I'm curious...*" he trailed off, sounding as if he was trying to figure out how to phrase what he wanted to ask. "*Sorry, uhh, I'm aware you and the other officer found that missing fishing trawler. I heard there was a survivor.*"

"That investigation has been taken over by the U.S. Coast Guard," Metzler said.

"*Oh, I know. But the fisherman, did he give any indication as to what happened? Did he say anything to you guys before the Coast Guard showed up?*"

"I don't think I'm at liberty to discuss..."

"*Please, Allison,*" he remembered her first name when they first introduced, "*it's a very important matter. If you want to know, it might be related to our fish.*" Metzler sat for a moment, contemplating what to do. It sounded like the doctor was onto something important, and the Vice Mayor would certainly not allow the department to do any digging. She figured somebody should.

"All I can tell you is that he was muttering something about a shark," she said. "That's all he said. *Shark.* He had locked himself in the freezer, and he didn't appear to be in any rational state of mind. He was scared shitless." The silence from the other end of the line almost seemed that Stafford shared the same emotion. "You still there?" Metzler asked after several empty moments.

"*Yes, uhh, thank you,*" he said. "*Listen, until we find out more, it's best we keep this conversation to ourselves. I'll update you when I know more, but I think there's something going on. Thanks... oh wait! One more question... has there been any other unusual occurrences or reports? Anyone missing? Anything at all since the storm?*" Metzler thought for a moment. There wasn't much that went on at all in Merit. This had been a rather busy week compared to usual.

"All I can remember is a report of a Coast Guard rescue diver getting injured during a rescue during the hurricane," she said. "I can't remember much about it, other than that the ship fell rather suddenly, and he suffered a severe back injury. The fisherman he rescued was never found." Metzler found herself starting to grow nervous. "What is this about?"

"*I'm trying to figure out where our friend came from,*" Stafford said, referring to the fish. "*Believe me, when I put the pieces together, I'll let you know. I'll be in touch. I gotta get back to work. I appreciate your help. Bye.*"

"Bye," she hung up the phone.

****

After hanging up the phone with Metzler, Stafford started researching on the internet for any known government-funded projects that took place in the Caribbean area. He spent the next hour searching, and the only thing he could find was something called Bio-Nutriunt. There wasn't much information on it online, other than the fact that it was cancelled. Being a well-educated man, he recognized the word 'nutriunt' as the Latin word for nourish. It was a good lead, and one of the articles listed the names of U.S. Senators that backed the project. One was Florida's very own Senator Travis Roubideaux, the father of Vice Mayor Kathy Bloom.

As he continued to research Bio-Nutriunt, he found another article regarding a cargo ship capsized in the Caribbean by a rogue wave. The government had dispatched the Coast Guard to the area, but reportedly the mission was to recover the cargo that had been lost overboard. The article didn't specify what the cargo was, but once again Stafford was intrigued. He saved these articles to a file and quickly got on his phone. He dialed Wisk's number.

"Hi, Mr. Wisk? This is Dr. Aaron Stafford. Do you have an email, because there's something I was hoping you'd look into? I think you'll be very interested."

CHAPTER 15

As night fell upon the coastal waters, the Thresher ascended to shallower depths. It had spent most of the daylight hours going deep, seeking out any competing predators in the area. Larger forms of sea life had previously been abundant in the area. But with the arrival of the new predator, these other species were forced to seek out other locations to meet their nutritional requirements. With an abundant food source and all natural competition eliminated, the Thresher was now the apex predator in the area.

It glided just under the surface. Its extraordinarily long caudal fin kicked up water along the surface while it swung back and forth. With daylight gone, it relied almost entirely on its sense of smell and Ampullae of Lorenzini to detect prey and competition. After swimming aimlessly for several hours, it picked up some large vibrations in the water. They were originating from the surface, and the heavy signals indicated that whatever was causing them was a large object or lifeform. The Thresher's aggressive instinct automatically kicked in, causing it to direct its course to investigate.

It slowly picked up speed, being cautious as to what it was approaching. The signals got stronger as it got closer, and soon it picked up another strong scent. A trickle of blood seeped into its nostrils, enticing its hunger. After another minute it picked up the scent of more drops of blood in the water. It was a trail leading up to something big. The Thresher's violent instinct demanded it attack the source of the blood. While it required sustenance, the drive was a vicious urge to slaughter all else that dared share the waters with it.

****

The familiar sight of the harbor lights was a welcome one for Gene Diebler, captain of the sword fishing vessel *Heavyweight*. Fully bearded and dressed in a ragged flannel shirt and thin cargo pants, he sat in a chair near the helm in the superstructure, looking forward to sleeping in his own bed. Unfortunately, that would have to wait a few hours more until they finished unloading and weighing their catch. They were hauling in four weeks' worth of catch, thousands of pounds of swordfish and marlin. The *Heavyweight* was a sixty-foot-long boat, consisting of a skeleton crew of three and the Captain. It made for extra work for everybody, but it also made for larger shares. Two of those members were out on deck, ordered by Diebler to clean up before reaching port. One was Joe, the youngest member at twenty-five. At the start of the trip he was clean shaven, but now his face was scruffy despite attempts to shave. Working with him was Piatt, a stocky fellow who had been on numerous trips with Diebler before. He had a strong work ethic, and spoke as if he was a military officer, despite never having served. However, he had attended the police academy, although he never actually served as an officer. They scraped up fish guts from bait and catch, tossing them out into the water. During this time, Piatt barked orders at Joe.

"Come on, boy! We're almost home, and you're not done with this deck!" he said. "What do you think Old Man Joel will think if we don't have this thing cleaned?" He was referring to the owner of the boat. Joe continued pushing fish blood off the deck with the scrub.

"He'll think we gutted a lot of fish," Joe answered sarcastically. He had been the subject of verbal abuse for the whole trip. It was unnerving at first, but now he simply considered it a normal part of his day.

"Very funny!" Piatt said. His voice carried through the night sky. "No, you little dimwit. He'll throw a fit, and he'll blame you! He's uptight about the appearance of his boat, and we always bring it back sparkly clean! Except when we hire a new guy!" Piatt was always the type to be the one on the case of each new seaman. Diebler always counted on him to break in the new hires. He figured if they couldn't handle the stress, then they weren't suited for this line of work anyhow. Piatt would usually let up after the first voyage, deeming the individual worthy of the *Heavyweight* crew. Joe seemed to be handling it fairly well. Piatt figured he'd continue until they docked. He walked to the structure, where three full cans of fuel were loaded. He reached in between them and picked up a fish head. He held it up to Joe's face, "What the hell is this doing on the deck? Are you blind?" He tossed it overboard and continued with the verbal punishment.

The fish head sank, eventually getting drawn into the mouth of a large predator that followed the bloody trail left by the fishermen. Unbeknownst to the crew, it was close enough to see the large boat. The fact that it was larger than its own body size made no difference to the Thresher. It had no fear or anticipation. It only had a drive to slaughter what it perceived to be an unwelcome presence in its newly established territory.

****

The time was 9:13 P.M. as Riker took in his third scotch at the bar in the Shallow Reef. He had spent most of the afternoon dozing in and out, but not getting any solid sleep. He hadn't eaten anything except for a few slices of lunchmeat ham and cheese. For the most part he spent the day laying on his couch, staring at the photo of Martha. The smile she had in the picture seemed so alien to him. His mind flooded with the memories of her sadness, taunting him of the fact he couldn't remember when she last smiled. It was a horror he couldn't escape, knowing she was deep in a hell and that she tried to reach out to him, but he didn't answer her plea. For months, he longed for the impossible wish of going back in time and helping her. Now he just wanted to forget it all. It was a luxury that his tortured mind would not grant him. Instead, it was constant recollection of the warning signs that he ignored. A part of him felt he deserved the mental and physical torment he endured.

When he first entered the bar that night, he was relieved to see it was a different bartender than the previous night. He swallowed his scotch and munched on a few pretzels. The bar was starting to empty out for the night, typical for a Wednesday evening. The only other people around were a group of young college kids huddled at a table. He only noticed because one of the women brushed by him, giving him a wink when he glanced over. He only returned the thinnest of grins, but had no interest in the gesture. He returned to his drink, staring blankly at the television screen. It displayed a hockey game, featuring teams that he wasn't familiar with. But it was something to pay attention to, and help fight off the agonizing memories. He heard someone sit on the barstool next to him. Thinking it was the same college girl that walked by, he looked over. Instead it was Allison Metzler sitting there, looking right at him. He almost didn't recognize her in plain jeans and button shirt.

"Oh, you've got to be kidding me," he exclaimed. Instantly, he downed the rest of his scotch.

"Wow. Don't hold back on how you feel about my presence," she stated with a dry smirk. The bartender walked by and offered to take an order from her. She requested a diet Coke before returning her attention to Riker. "So, I see that you went home early today because you were hung over, and now here you are doing the same thing again."

"What are you, my mother?" he retorted. He clicked his fingers at the bartender for another refill. "What are you doing here anyway? Just felt like having a night cap?"

"I wanted to check on you," she answered. "Besides, I'm surprised there's anything left here to drink since it seems you've been sucking the place dry. Have you even eaten anything?" Riker pointed at the pretzels. "Oh yeah, like that's perfectly healthy for you."

"Oh God," Riker groaned. "Did Crawford put you up to this? How the hell did you even find me here anyway?"

"It wasn't hard," she said. "All I had to do was follow the skid marks from your place to here. Now I'll ask you a question: are you trying to kill yourself?"

"If I knew you were gonna be this annoying outside of work, I'd have let the damn fish eat you," he remarked, evading the question.

"You only have yourself to blame for that one," Metzler joked. She watched him guzzle down his fresh drink. "How many of those are you planning on having?" Riker glared at her. She then remembered his hate for being questioned.

"What is this? Why are you checking on me?" He reached into his pocket and stuffed a cigarette in his mouth and sparked a flame on his lighter. The bartender suddenly rushed over.

"Sorry, there's no smoking in here," he said. Riker held the orange flame an inch away from the cigarette, contemplating lighting it in spite. He put the lighter away and crushed the fresh cigarette into an ash tray on the table.

"If there's no smoking, why the hell do you have these things?" The bartender didn't say anything and moved away. Riker looked again at Metzler. "Let me guess, you're gonna tell me 'those things are bad for you'?"

"Actually, I wouldn't mind one myself," she said. Riker was surprised by this, and there was a moment of silence. He was still holding the cigarette pack. It was clear Metzler wasn't going anywhere and the urge to smoke was irresistible.

"Really?" It was more of a response than a question. He looked at the pack. *Oh, what the hell*, he thought. He held out the pack, pointing the open end at Metzler. She pulled one out and they both stood from their seats. Riker threw some money down on the counter to pay for their beverages before they went out to the front porch.

****

Stafford stood up from his computer and went for the bathroom sink. His eyes were droopy from drowsiness from looking into the screen for several hours. He filled the sink up with cold water and dipped his face in it. The sudden icy chill shocked him awake. He grabbed a paper towel and tapped it along his wet face before going back into the computer. During the afternoon he had removed some of the tumors from the dead grouper and examined them. When he cut them open, he saw that the bundles of cells were loaded with the substance he found in the tissue samples.

He had informed Adam Wisk of his findings, including the grouper and the tooth. He specifically told Wisk about the substance that he believed to be a growth hormone, and asked him if he ever heard of the government project Bio-Nutriunt. Wisk immediately started doing some digging, asking sources connected to the list of names associated with the project. Those who were willing to talk explained the purpose of the project. Wisk summed it up in the form of an article which he forwarded to Stafford via email.

According to Wisk's sources, Bio-Nutriunt was a program funded by the U.S. government to develop an alternative for food production. Growth hormones were already used in commercial meats, but with the increasing population, officials wanted to increase quantities. The testing facility was located in the Caribbean Sea, near the Bahamas. The facility was large and held numerous test animals such as cows, chickens, fish, and pigs. The Bio-Nutriunt hormone was immensely successful in increasing the subject's size. One of Wisk's sources specifically stated that he saw one of the test chickens grow from five pounds to twenty pounds over the course of fifty days. Similar results followed for the other test subjects, and at first it seemed the operation would be a major success.

The first sign of trouble occurred when some of the chickens were allowed into a large pen together. At one moment, all was normal until suddenly one began attacking the other. It bit and clawed at the other subject, which sparked a vicious fight between the two. Over the next several weeks, almost all of the test subjects began inhibiting extremely violent behaviors. They attacked their handlers as well as the other test animals. Stafford felt his heart race as he read the next paragraph of Wisk's email. Reported results of the autopsies of dead specimens revealed that the Bio-Nutriunt specimens developed several small tumors scattered throughout their bodies. The doctors believed that it was a side effect of the massive dose of growth hormone, as well as the heightened aggression.

Another issue arose after another test was complete. Lab rats were given meat from the test subjects. Over the course of time, the rats started to increase in size themselves, indicating that the effect of Bio-Nutriunt could be passed on from the host to the consumer. As a result, the experiment was deemed a failure, and the specimens were ordered to be destroyed. However, another issue spawned during the carrying out of that order. A cargo ship known as *The Flat Rock* had been loaded with many of the test animals to ship them away. While still in the Caribbean, *The Flat Rock* was hit by a massive rogue wave and was capsized. The test subjects ended up in the water and a massive effort was immediately underway to collect each one. It was believed that not all of them were found.

With his face still damp, Stafford stared at his reflection in the mirror while he put together all the information he had. A headache had set in from an overload of critical thinking. He thought of the grouper, particularly the parasite he found attached to it; *Gnathia marleyi*. That species was only found in the Caribbean, meaning that grouper had come from there as well. *The Flat Rock sank in the Caribbean,* he thought to himself. *If the contaminated product had gone overboard and was not recovered...oh God.* He stepped out, appearing as if he was in a trance. Nash stepped into the lab after locking up some gear. It was another late night for him as well. He saw his boss in his zombie-like state coming out of the bathroom.

"You okay there, Doc?"

"It's just... when the product spilled off the *Flat Rock*, I think our grouper ate some of it. Maybe a fish test subject or something. When it ingested the contaminated test subject, the Bio-Nutriunt ended up in its system. If I'm right..."

"Then the same thing happened to our shark!" Nash said. His voice was a combination of awe and fright. Stafford wandered back to his computer and nearly fell into the chair from exhaustion. He figured it was time to call it a night. While he started saving his documents and shutting down the screen, he noticed his phone lighting up on the desk. The screen read that he had a voicemail. He picked it up and realized it was from Wisk. He put the voicemail on speaker and listened to it.

"Hey Doctor Stafford, this is Adam Wisk again. Oh man, you won't believe this! I found a friend of that Coast Guard guy you mentioned. I guess he's in the hospital with a severed spine! Poor guy won't be walking again. Apparently, when they medevac'd him out of there he was babbling about a shark. A big one. He claimed it got the guy he was trying to save. Of course, he was loaded with morphine and the Coast Guard thinks he was injured by the storm. Anyway, I thought you'd be

interested to know." Wisk spoke as if he had been best friends with Stafford for years, even though they just met. Stafford rested in his chair and looked over at his assistant, who also heard the message.

"The storm. The shark and our fish got caught in the damn storm, and it drove them up here."

****

"I didn't figure you for a smoker," Riker said. He was lighting up a second cigarette while Metzler was only midway through hers. "I assumed you were too self-righteous or one of those health freaks."

"Maybe once upon a time," Metzler said with her cigarette loosely clenched in her teeth. She leaned back against the outside wall of the bar. "All those years in college changed things. You develop social groups and pick up their habits, even the bad ones." She drew in a breath of smoke, followed by a small cough. "I guess I never got completely used to it."

"I tend to be more of a cigar guy," Riker said. Once in a while, Metzler would notice him glancing at the bar entrance. It was clear he was aching for another drink. There was a very subtle shake to his hand while he held up his smoke. She thought it was probably due to both his alcoholism and lack of diet. Of course, he noticed she was studying him. "Okay, what are you about to lecture me about this time?"

"Just don't do it," she said.

"Do what?"

"Oh, don't play dumb," she said. "Don't go in there and have another drink. If anything, have a sandwich. And some water."

"What is with this sudden concern for my well-being?" he said.

"Again, don't play dumb," she said. "You honestly think it's not obvious to everyone else you're drinking yourself to death?" She stopped and thought about her own question. Truthfully, only she and Crawford were the only ones to know about his problem. The rest of the staff hardly saw him. "I just want you to know, I get it," she said.

"Get what?"

"You think you're shielding yourself from something, but you're only doing something worse," she said.

"Here we go again with the psycho babble," Riker said. "Don't you have a Master's Degree in that crap? Why aren't you doing that instead of working in this circus?" She knew he was deflecting, and she expected such a response. Still, the remark made her contemplate this stage in her life.

"I just think a scotch or whiskey won't make things better," she said. Instantly she realized she was the one now deflecting. Riker finished his cigarette and stomped it into the gravel.

"You don't know shit about me," he said and walked past her to the doors. She motioned for him to stop but he ignored her.

"I saw the picture!" she blurted just before he could pass through the entrance. He stopped inside the doorway, holding the door slightly open.

"What picture?" Metzler fumbled around in her mind for something to say, but she had already committed to the confession.

"I know about Martha," she said. Her voice trembled with anxiety and she looked down to the ground, unable to make herself look him in the eye. She heard the door shut and for a moment she wasn't sure if he closed it behind him or if he stepped back out. The crunching sound of gravel answered the question. She forced herself to look up at him. His eyes were burning holes deep into her soul. He didn't need to ask how she knew his wife's name. Crawford was the only one who'd tell her.

"It's not any of your business," he said, pointing a finger at her. "Trust me, you DON'T get it."

"I get that you're punishing yourself," she said. "I get that your life had turned upside down and you can't figure out how to make it seem normal again. I get why you don't want to be here, so far away. I also get what it's doing to you. You don't think I saw the blood on your uniform after we left the lab?" Riker stood silent. There was nothing good he wanted to say to her. He started to turn around and leave. "One other thing," Metzler said. Riker stopped and she took a deep breath. "You're right; I only got this job because I'm related to the mayor. I got to breeze through the academy and I thought I was better than I am. Despite how our partnership has been, I have learned something. You are a good man and a good cop, even if you don't think you are." She briefly paused for another anxious breath. "Listen, I know it's painful, but there are good memories. I know there are. You need to focus on the good memories." They stood facing each other, with nothing but silence between them. She realized she was still holding her cigarette, which was almost down to the butt. She took a much-needed draw of the remainder and stomped on it.

****

"Alright, everyone get ready to get your hands dirty once more," Diebler spoke into the two-way radio. He reduced speed as they neared three hundred yards of the dock. Of course, two of his people were already cleaning up on deck, while the other should've been down by the freezer. He watched the harbor lights, making sure no other ships were going to be in their way.

A slight pinging sound from the radar screen caught his attention. He glanced at it, seeing that a large object was near the boat. He looked out the window for any lights indicating another boat. There was nothing but black sea. He dismissed it as a whale, although he did find it strange one would be moving so close to port. However, it moved closer appearing to gain speed. *No way would any whale come up like this. Not to a boat this size,* he thought. It approached the vessel at a high speed, and Diebler reach out for the radio to warn the rest of the crew.

On deck, Joe and Piatt were wrapping up. They each wiped their hands clean as best they could of the fish guts and dirt. They had heard the captain's message regarding entering the harbor, and Piatt griped about how it wasn't necessary. They were outside and fully capable of seeing they were about to dock. Piatt opened the door that led to the hallway compartments below, about to call for Zach. It was at this moment the entire vessel suddenly shook. It was a heavy shake, and it nearly caused the men to lose their balance. Piatt grabbed onto the door to hold himself up while Joe grabbed the ladder that led up to the wheelhouse.

In the wheelhouse, Diebler hugged the helm. He had dropped the radio when the impact rocked the ship. He slowed the vessel to a stop and rushed out the door of the wheelhouse, looking down at Piatt and Joe.

"Holy shit, did you hit something Captain?" Piatt asked.

"Shine the spotlights out," he ordered. "Something hit us." Another impact caught them off guard. Diebler grabbed the structure's railing, keeping himself from falling down to the deck. Piatt fell on his hands and knees while Joe managed to get to port. He grabbed a spotlight and beamed it into the water. It seemed to glimmer wherever he shined the light, however he could not see anything but sea. "Christ!" Diebler said. "Piatt! Check the starboard side." He turned toward the rookie. "Joe! Anything?"

"No, sir!" the rookie answered. He continued scanning the light. After a few moments, Diebler decided it wasn't worth figuring out. They were already really close to shore, which meant safety from whatever was ramming them. He turned on the lights in the wheelhouse when he went in. He grabbed the throttle to push the boat forward. He was going to put it at full throttle. It wasn't the safest thing to do when entering port, but he wanted to get away from whatever was attacking them.

"Hey, Captain!" Joe called. He looked up at the wheelhouse and saw that the door had just shut when the captain went in. He called again, trying to be loud enough to be heard from inside, "Captain!" Piatt put his spotlight down and rushed over to Joe.

"What? Did you see something?"

"I don't know what it was," Joe said with a trembling voice. "But it was huge! I lost it, but it was going ahead of the bow." He shined the light toward the front of the boat's path, but couldn't see anything. A ripple in the water nearby caught their attention. It was as if a snake was slithering in the water. It had gone below the surface before they could identify it. Joe and Piatt looked at each other, both as puzzled as the next. Behind them, a tall, skinny man in a black shirt and jeans ran up to deck.

"What's going on?" Zach asked. Piatt turned toward him.

"There's something in the water."

Before Diebler could throttle the boat, another bump stopped him. This one wasn't as severe of an impact, but clearly came from the hull at the bow. He leaned up to the front window, trying hard to see anything in the water. At first, there was nothing but black sea. It was calm and still, aside from the subtle waves. In an instant, it all changed. The water exploded upward, and Diebler's eyes could not comprehend the massive snake-like caudal fin as it swung upward from the surface. Glass exploded inward as the huge tail struck the wheelhouse. It breached the windshield effortlessly, striking Diebler in the face in the same impact. The whole right side of his face was gone, replaced by a fleshy hole. Glass embedded in his chest like shrapnel, cutting into his lungs and heart. The blow knocked him unconscious, saving him from the experience of going into cardiac arrest. His lifeless body dropped to the floor, next to the detached helm. The control console and radio unit also took a blow from the enormous impact.

The crew saw the tail retract into the water like an enormous whip. Piatt rushed to the wheelhouse, only to nearly pass out at the sight of the dead captain. The body twitched on the floor, covered by glass and other debris.

"Oh Jesus!" Piatt said. Seeing a mutilated corpse was horrifying on its own, but knowing it was Diebler was worse. He went for the radio to call for help, but the smoke billowing out of the unit made it clear it was busted. He threw it down in a combination of frustration and panic and went for the controls. Glass was everywhere, the wheel was busted, and some of the electronics were smoking. It looked as if a cruise missile had hit the wheelhouse. Another solid impact rocked the boat from beneath, nearly face planting him into the controls. A weak yellow light flashed from overhead, indicating a hull breach. A huge splash to the right drew his attention, and he watched the huge scythe-like object whip from the water and belt the side of the boat.

The huge tail came inches from Zach, who fell to the deck. The railing crumbled under the beating while the boat rocked side to side. Two of the spare fuel cans fell over, leaking gasoline onto the deck. As he tried to get up, he realized he suddenly become entangled with fishing line, along with the hooks. They had pierced his skin, and the line had wrapped around him when he rolled on the deck. He fought frantically to get free, screaming in pain while he pulled the barbed hooks from his flesh. Joe ran over to him to assist. He pulled some pliers he had handy and began cutting the wire. Zach looked ahead toward shore, estimating they were still a couple hundred yards out. The engine rumbled as Piatt attempted to restart it, but it kept dying. As Joe cut the last of the wire, he looked past Zach's shoulder. He saw the enormous black dorsal fin cutting through the water, coming right at them. Several feet behind it was the rippling long tail, trailing behind like a sea serpent. He saw the huge cone shaped head, and the black eyes reflected the spotlight beamed over starboard.

Piatt tried relentlessly to restart the engine, but it wouldn't take. He looked toward shore. There seemed to be some activity going on near the beaches. He was confident someone out there would be able to see a distress signal. He tore open a metal cabinet and found the flare box. He pulled out the orange gun and went out the rear door of the wheelhouse. He clutched the superstructure's rail and pointed the gun skyward.

He was unaware of the huge shark torpedoing towards them once more. The Thresher rammed its head into the starboard side, shuttering the whole vessel once more. Startled, Piatt lost his footing, and helplessly fell over the railing onto the deck...just as he pulled the trigger. The huge sparkling burst of flame fired right into the spilled canisters. Piatt didn't even realize what he had accidentally done when the deck erupted in a fiery explosion that consumed him. Zach and Joe were thrown aft from the huge blast. The fire instantly consumed the entire superstructure and most of the deck, billowing thick smoke into the atmosphere. Bits of flaming debris and fuel were launched into the water, creating a hellish ring of fire around the ship.

Disoriented, Joe sat up on the deck. He was in one of the few places the fire hadn't spread. He stood up, still dazed and grabbed Zach, who was lying face down on the deck just inches away from the fire. Joe pulled him away and tapped his face to keep him from slipping into unconsciousness.

"Come on Zach, stay awake!" he yelled. Zach began to stir, waving his hands frantically. He remembered where he was and jumped to his feet.

"Oh God, what's happening?" The heat was intense and both men backed away as far as they could. Leaning against the guardrail, they struggled for air as smoke fogged the entire deck. In the midst of the flame, they saw a human figure rise up. They almost yelled in terror when they recognized it as Piatt, still alive and completely on fire. They watched as he blindly made his way to the edge of the boat, falling over the side.

The Thresher smelled the scent of wounded prey. Moving around the large inorganic object, it followed the smell. Piatt's nerves were fired up from the salt water stinging his charred flesh. That stinging sensation was suddenly replaced by piercing pain all over his body. He was unable to see the enormous jaws consume his entire body. Teeth pierced into his body like three hundred huge scalpels at once. The Thresher swallowed him whole before moving on to the huge sinking vessel, which it still identified as a possible living threat.

****

Riker was about to walk away before he saw the orange and red flash in the ocean. Metzler saw his expression change and turned to see what he was staring at, just as an explosive echo rippled through the sky like a huge crack of thunder. Brakes screeched as vehicles on the road came to a sudden stop and people started gathering outside to see what was happening. Riker didn't waste any time. He made a dash toward the beach, quickly followed by Metzler.

"Out of the way! Look out!" he roared as he made his way past curious bystanders, holding out his badge. Metzler kicked up dirt and sand as she kept up with him. It took about thirty seconds for them to get to the beach, where they could more clearly see the ship ablaze. He noticed Metzler pulling out her phone to call the department. "Don't worry about that," he said. "They've already got a dozen calls coming in by now." Panting hard from the unexpected sprint, Metzler put the phone away. Riker looked around for any available boats. Near the dock, there were a couple of people gathered near a small Boston Whaler, appearing to be getting ready to go out and help. He ran for them, and Metzler followed. The two men were clearly hysterical as they started the engine of the twelve-foot craft. "Whoa! Gentlemen, I'm an officer with the Merit Police. I need to requisition your boat!" He held up his badge.

Luckily, the men didn't argue and quickly vacated the boat. Riker hurried to the console and Metzler took the seat behind him. He glanced at her as if to question her if she was sure she was ready to do this. Instead of asking, he put the boat in full throttle. Water sprayed as the propellers kicked into gear, pushing the small boat toward the inferno.

****

The crow's nest collapsed onto the deck, kicking up more flames. Joe and Zach gagged for breath within the cloud of smoke they were trapped in. They realized there was no choice. They had to jump into the water and take a chance, or else suffocate and burn to death on board. Joe grabbed the railing to hoist himself over the port side, but quickly let go when the hot metal scalded his hands. Sweating and gagging, he stuffed his hands into his sleeve and hoisted himself over the side of the boat. The water even felt warm when he hit it. He quickly brought himself to the surface, finally able to breathe in fresh air. On board the ship, Zach hesitated to jump, fearing the Thresher was nearby.

"Zach!" Joe called to him, spitting out salt water as he struggled to stay afloat. "You got to jump!" Flaming pieces of debris were scattered all around him. Ironically, he felt as if he was swimming in Hell. Heat flared in his face and his skin felt as if it was burning. The smell of burning fuel in the water permeated the air around him. He realized he couldn't wait for Zach and started swimming away from the boat toward shore. The sound of a motor stood out in the chaos. Joe stopped and looked through the flaming water, quickly spotting the Boston Whaler approaching. He kicked hard with his legs to stay afloat, and he frantically waved his hand to get the driver's attention.

"There's one in the water," Riker said as he approached the hellish mayhem. The large flaming fishing boat illuminated the sky in a bright orange, which was reflected by the water. He steered the boat toward the waving man. At this time, he saw Zach standing at the port railing. "There's another on the boat! He looks like he's about to jump." He slowed the boat down near Joe, who struggled to stay afloat while he reached for them. On the *Heavyweight*, Zach saw the boat and determined it was time to make a swim for it. He jumped clear over the guardrails and crashed down into the water. As soon as he made contact he started paddling, ignoring the stinging pain throughout his body from the injuries he took from the fishhooks, which continued to bleed.

The huge Thresher instantly picked up the scent of fresh blood, quickly pushing itself towards its source. The electromagnetic signals from distressed prey rippled through its nerves. There were two organic lifeforms in the water, and a third larger object on the surface. It swam up from beneath the nearest one, which the blood trail had originated from. The shark positioned its body in striking formation, and lashed out its enormous tail.

Riker and Metzler reached down for Joe when the ocean seemingly exploded a dozen yards away. They saw Zach launched into the air with blood spraying from the midsection of his body, illuminated by the nearby fires. He was not waving his arms or kicking his legs. He was limp in the air, and crashed back down into the water. It was then they saw the black fin cut the surface. The top of the enormous head emerged, and the snout lifted as if the huge beast was opening its jaws. It closed down on Zach's body and dove back under the surface. Metzler almost screamed, and even Riker appeared in shock from what he just witnessed. He shot back into action, grabbing Joe by the forearm. Metzler did the same, and although in a bit of a panic herself, she maintained her composure and helped Riker.

"Come on!" Riker yelled. Joe's arms were covered in oil that clung to his skin, making it difficult to get a good grasp on him. "Come on, get in here!" They glanced behind him, and saw the fin briefly appear and turn towards them. It then dipped back below, just as Joe looked back and saw it. He went into a severe panic and began clawing at the whaler.

"Pull me up! PULL ME UP!" he screamed. Water breached beneath them, and the creature's tail collided with the bow of the Boston Whaler, nearly launching the boat into the air. Riker and Metzler held on tight while the bow reeled upward, nearly teetering on the stern. It pivoted and crashed back down, knocking them both to the floor. The tip of the bow was smashed, but the engine remained functional. Slightly dazed, Riker stood up and began looking around to find Joe again. He was a few feet off the starboard side aft, swimming toward him. The gigantic mouth opened from beneath him, lined with hundreds of deadly teeth. The huge fish leapt from the water with Joe impaled within its jaws. He was in the mouth up to his upper torso, just beneath the shoulders. His arms were still reaching for them as the shark crashed back down, its forty-foot body mass creating an intense splash.

"Fuck!" Riker said. He went to throttle the boat, but realized the blow had killed the engine. He turned the ignition, but the engine would not fire. He tried again with the same results. Metzler's heart raced as she saw some ripples in the nearby water, likely caused by the shark's long tail. It was obvious it was coming for them.

"Riker! It's coming!" she yelled. The water beneath them began to swirl, caused by a disturbance beneath them. Metzler looked down, seeing the open mouth just below. "RIKER!" Riker turned the key once more. Finally, the engine came to life. He forced it into full throttle, and the boat whooshed from its place like a rocket. They had just moved when the Thresher breached the water where they were at, just missing them.

"Holy Christ!" Riker exclaimed when he looked back. He refocused his vision forward, realizing the boat was on a collision course for the blazing ship. He cut the wheel to turn left. He gritted his teeth as they cleared the bow by less than a foot. He steered the small vessel toward shore and pushed it as hard as he could. Metzler rested herself on a seat, looking to see if the shark was trailing them. While doing this she noticed a small metal boat with a motor installed speeding toward the wreckage. On board were two men clearly on their way to see if they could help. They were regularly dressed and likely not first responders.

"Oh my God," she said. "Riker, we have to stop those guys over there!" Riker saw them and steered the boat to port, blowing a horn to get their attention.

"HEY!" he and Metzler both yelled. The other boat slowed down, and the men on board looked over at them. "Get out of the water! Get back to shore!" It was too late. They watched as the huge tail swung upwards out of the water. For a brief moment, it seemed to point directly up at the black sky. Like a bolt of lightning, it struck down over the middle of the boat with devastating force. A wall of water kicked up as the boat folded in half. Both men were flung into the air, screaming for dear life as they fell helplessly into the water. One ended up landing on the tip of the bow, which impaled his stomach. The other crashed into the water. Riker grabbed the controls to attempt a rescue, but realized it was too late. They saw the fin cutting through the water from the right. His head and shoulders quickly emerged as the shark's head broke the surface, speeding in a straight line toward him. They saw the jaws open, and heard the blood curdling screams of the helpless good Samaritan as he was pierced by the teeth before being forced under. Metzler collapsed onto her seat in pure shock, and Riker steered the boat back to shore.

"Son of a bitch!" he cursed the monster. Within a minute or so, they were in shallow waters. They docked the boat and rushed onto land, catching their breath as they watched the flaming *Heavyweight* slowly begin to sink beneath the waves.

CHAPTER 16

Dr. Stafford had just walked out the front door when he noticed the distant orange glow in the north. He could see it was out in the water, flickering non-stop. With his eyes locked on the phenomenon, he walked to the dock to get a better look. He walked out on the deck. He was too far away to clearly see what was going on, but the glow was clearly a huge fire. His eyes looked to the road when the sound of sirens echoed through the night sky. Flashing red and white lights illuminated the street as two firetrucks and an ambulance sped towards the scene. A few seconds after they passed, a police vehicle zoomed by with its red and blue lights flashing. Sirens from all over the area could be heard for miles.

"Oh my God," Stafford said. A horrible thought came to his mind, and instinctively he ran to his vehicle. The engine barely fired up when he floored the pedal, speeding himself out of the driveway. The tires screeched on the pavement as he rushed to the scene, following the distant emergency lights. He hoped to any higher power that his intuition was wrong on this.

****

Flashing emergency lights flickered all over the beach. Crowds gathered to witness the final moments of the smoldering ship before it went under the surface, while first responders communicated to determine the best course of action. Chief Crawford felt a combination of shock and awe when he saw the sixty-foot ship ablaze a few hundred yards from shore. Police cars drove up close to the shore to help manage the crowds. One of those parked only a few yards from him.

"Get your bullhorn and order these people to back up!" he barked at the officer as he stepped out of the patrol car. The officer complied with the order and dug in the trunk for the device. Crawford grabbed his radio to issue orders for the other officers. "This is the Chief. We need caution tape on the beach right now. Cordon off the beach right now." He searched for the Fire Chief within the crowd. Doing so, he saw the familiar faces of Riker and Metzler. She was visibly shaken, and Riker looked a bit more rugged than usual.

"Well, *Chief*," Riker stressed the title, "How's the post-retirement gig going?" Crawford ignored the pun.

"Leonard, what the hell happened?" he asked. "The phone lines are going non-stop in dispatch. We've got people calling in about a huge shark. What the hell's going on?" Before Riker could answer, a skinny teenage boy with dark shaggy hair and a lip piercing ran up to him and Metzler.

"Oh MAN! Dude, what a rush! We all saw you out there kicking up water with that shark behind you! DAMN it was awesome!" Riker gave him a callous glare, ready to verbally tear the kid to pieces.

"Isn't it a school night?" Metzler said before Riker had a chance to make his remark. The boy stuttered for a moment. "Go on, we've cordoned off the area. Go home."

"And get a haircut," Riker grunted as the boy nervously backed away and left. He returned his attention to Crawford. "So boss, nice job giving me this nice easy job where you won't have to fear for my life. Twice today I nearly got eaten by an overgrown fish." Flashing blue lights out in the harbor drew his attention. Harbor patrol boats were heading out to the wreckage. "What the hell are those idiots doing out there?"

"What the hell do you mean *what are they doing out there?*" Crawford said. "They're going out there to see if--" Riker pushed past him and rushed to the police officer with the bullhorn.

"Hey, what the fu--" the officer shouted as Riker snatched it from his hands. He ran to the shore, stepping knee deep into the water as he called out to the boats.

"Bring it in! All harbor units, withdraw from the water now!" His voice echoed throughout the sky. The faces in the crowds displayed the confusion and slight panic that was being felt throughout. Crawford ran to Riker and yanked the bullhorn from him.

"What in the hell are you doing? Are you drunk?!"

"Chief!" Metzler called. Her voice was equally as urgent. "He's right! Don't let those boats go out there! It's not safe!"

"Ray, there's a huge freaking shark out there! We saw it kill four people, and it nearly got us too!" Riker said, pointing out to the water. Crawford felt as if he was talking to a mental patient. He looked at Metzler, and he saw the same urgency in her eyes.

"Officer Metzler, is this correct?"

"Yes, sir," she said. "Sir, I've never seen anything like it."

"I'm no shark expert," Riker said, "but that bastard was bigger than any shark I've ever heard of. It had a tail that it used like a fucking whip! There were a couple guys who went out there on a metal boat, and the thing folded it in two. I'm telling you, if it's still out there, those officers out on those boats are going to die!"

"He's right, Chief!" Metzler said. "It killed the people on the fishing boat as well! There's no one to rescue!" Crawford stood in disbelief. Against his better judgement, he reluctantly picked up his radio to call the units in. Before he could key the transmitter, a deafening explosion rocked the harbor. The sinking *Heavyweight* exploded from within, creating a new fiery atmosphere. A small tremor shook the beach. Screams from the crowd echoed as flames spread over the water. Much of it was extinguished as it hit the surface, except for what was on the floating debris. *The fire probably got to the fuel system*, Crawford thought. Through the radio, he issued an order for the harbor units to stay away. He then saw the crowd. Many people were in tears, others were busy filming the catastrophe on their phones, while some speculated what caused it. The next thing he saw near the crowd was the Vice Mayor rushing down to the beach. *Oh great! Perhaps I should go swim in the fire...should be equally as pleasant*, he thought to himself.

"Chief! What in God's name is going on!" Kathy Bloom barked at him as if the exploding boat was his fault. She pointed at the patrol boats that were maintaining distance. "Why aren't your officers going out there to help?"

"Ma'am, the conditions are unsafe," Crawford said, stepping out of the water with Riker. "Two of my people were already out there, and they confirmed the crew did not survive the ordeal. Also, we have reported information that there's another threat out there. We're currently assessing the situation, but it's believed there's a shark out there that might've killed the crew."

"It's not speculation, we were nearly swallowed by it!" Riker interrupted.

"Leonard!" Crawford raised his voice. Riker kept quiet and crossed his arms, keeping a smirk on his face. Bloom gave an exasperated sigh and looked out at the fire.

"This couldn't have happened at a worse time," she shamelessly mumbled out loud. It was under her breath, but loud enough to be heard. Metzler felt her jaw drop open at the sheer awe of what she heard. *Unbelievable!* Bloom studied the wreckage as best she could from this distance. "How long should it take to clean this up?"

"Why?" Riker asked, preparing to follow up the question with a criticizing phrase about media attention and the sailing race. Crawford's mind instantly went on alert.

"Leonard! Walk away please," he said. In his mind, however, he agreed with what he knew Riker was about to say.

"Didn't realize I was on the clock," Riker said before walking off. He noticed Metzler following him. "You're like a puppy. What, you looking for another smoke?"

"Actually, I think that would be good," she said. *A drink would be good too*, she thought, but she didn't want to voice that thought to someone with a drinking problem. Her adrenaline was finally starting to ease up after the intense night. The shakes were slowly going away. As they walked away from the beach they could hear chatter from a group of teens. Among them was that shaggy haired teenager standing next to a spiked-haired friend with a laptop.

"I got the video! Here's the shark!" the teen yelled. People tried to gather around through the set barriers. Cops swept in to manage the crowds, yelling for everyone to step back. Riker and Metzler stepped in through the crowd, holding up their badges for the other officers. Near the teenagers was a small flight drone with an installed camera. On the laptop screen was an aerial view of the shark breaching the water just before a motor boat with two people got out of the way.

"Nice to know you guys were enjoying the show!" Riker said. He tapped the nearest officer on the shoulder who was managing the crowd. "Hey, Barney Fife! If you're so worried about people getting inside the barriers, why are these bozos just sitting here?" The twenty-five-year-old Officer Perry, who already felt worn from his double shift, looked nervously at Riker.

"They said they have evidence of the scene," he stuttered.

"Oh man!" the shaggy haired kid said. "Spike! These are the cops that outran the shark!"

Well that's an appropriate name, Metzler thought.

"Dang!" Spike said. "Oh wait! Spud! Here's the part where the two other guys that went out...and...BAM!" Riker and Metzler relived the horrific moment when the tail came down on the motor boat. "Oh damn! That guy landed on the boat's, uh, tip thing. Oh, and there's the shark about to eat the other guy!" They were as excited as if they were at a sporting event. Riker felt his blood begin to boil. Instantly, he grabbed Spike by his Green Day t-shirt and lifted him off his folding chair. His feet dangled twelve inches from the ground. The shaggy haired kid, Spud, instinctively started backing away. Officer Perry took a step forward to intervene, but then stepped back. He felt as intimidated as the teens.

"You find that amusing, you little punk?" Riker growled. The kid's eyes were wide with terror. Caught by surprise, he babbled but couldn't manage to form a sentence. "How about we take you out for a swim and you can see how 'cool' it is then!"

"Uh...no!" he squealed. Metzler looked toward the beach and saw that Crawford was making his way towards them. Luckily, Bloom was looking the other direction, unaware of what was going on.

"Leonard," she said. "Put him down. Please, just do it." Still holding the kid up with one arm, he looked over at her.

"What, we're on a first name basis now?" he said. He dropped the kid, who landed on his feet with a thud. Riker eyeballed Crawford as he arrived, expecting to be criticized for his behavior. After giving the former detective a disapproving look, Crawford put his hand on the kid's shoulder.

"Hey, son, could you rewind that for me so I can get a look at it?" he asked in a calm and polite voice. Spike nodded and moved his finger along the touch screen, reeling the footage back to the beginning. Crawford observed the footage, which began minutes after the explosion. He watched the huge shark kill the fishermen and chase his officers. "Good lord, what the hell is that thing?"

"Let me through!" a voice called out from the crowd. The group looked over as a man tried to get past the barrier. Uniformed officers blocked his way, informing him the area was restricted. Metzler was the first to recognize him.

"Dr. Stafford?" she called. "Let him through!" The officers stood aside and let him through. Stafford rushed over to the computer, just in time to see the huge tail thrash the motor boat in the computer screen.

"Oh my God, I was right," he said mournfully.

"What are you talking about? What the hell is this thing?" Riker said.

"It's a thresher shark," Stafford said. "They're not like your typical great white or tiger shark. They use their tail like a huge whip, stunning their prey before moving in for the kill."

"A thresher shark? I didn't think they got that big," Crawford said.

"They don't," Stafford explained. "Thresher sharks have an average body length of roughly ten feet, and their tail length usually matches their body length. Nor are they usually as aggressive as the one you encountered."

"Wait a minute," Riker interrupted. "You don't sound too surprised to see this thing. Did you know this shark was out here?"

"I haven't seen it," Stafford said. "I've been tracking killer whales, sharks, and other organisms in the area. I've had several of my tagged animals turn up dead in the last few days. First my great white, then some of my orcas. That's what I was examining when we met earlier. I found one of these," he pulled out one of the huge teeth out of his pocket, "out of one of the orcas and the great white." The nearby teens exclaimed loudly at the sight of the tooth.

"That's just great," Riker said. "How big do you think this thing is?"

"I need to see it to say for sure, but comparing this tooth to a normal sized shark, as well as the bite radius on the orcas, I'd estimate this guy has a body length of forty feet."

"That means its tail is just as long," Metzler added.

"Whoa, whoa, hang on," Crawford said, holding up his hands and shaking his head. "This makes no sense. How in the hell can this thing be so big? And why is it attacking boats?"

"I have a theory," Stafford said. "I believe it's been exposed to an experimental growth hormone called Bio-Nutriunt. It was a government project, approved by one of our own senators." The three officers stared at him, waiting for him to continue. "I had somebody looking into it all evening. The project was designed for food production, but backfired due to side effects, such as violent behavior in the test subjects. Also, the hormone passes from the host to the consumer, generating the same side effects. Also, anything that ingests the hormone generates large tumors through its body that are loaded with this shit. This project took place in the Caribbean. When it was defunded, a cargo ship took the test subjects off the facility to take them to some undisclosed location, but it was hit by a rogue wave. I believe this shark ate some of the test subjects, which caused it to grow this size."

"Wait a minute," Crawford said. "That would mean this shark came all the way up here from there. Do they normally travel like that? How would you know it came from there?" Stafford motioned to Riker and Metzler.

"You guys remember that black grouper?" he asked. They both snickered.

"How could we not?" Metzler said.

"There was a parasite on him. *Gnathia marleyi*. Don't ask me to spell it. That species is only found in the Caribbean Sea. I think that grouper also got ahold of some of that contaminated product. Then Hurricane Deckard rolled through and swept north. I believe the shark and grouper both got caught in the storm and redirected to our coastal waters. A Coast Guard diver reported seeing a shark about forty miles out during the hurricane. He's now paralyzed from the waist down from a deep laceration injury to his back. I think that fishing trawler ran into him too."

"The *Mary Westward*? Oh Jesus," Crawford said. "Okay Doctor, let's say you're right about everything you've just said; how unsafe are our waters?" Stafford snickered and pointed at the sinking vessel, which had nearly sunk beneath the surface. It made his point.

"Chief, I'm sure you've dealt with all kinds of crazies in your career," he said. "Well, now there's the worst kind; a psycho shark. There's swelling in his brain that's causing him to behave so violently. He'll attack anything he sees out there. That's why he's killed my killer whales and great white, and that's why he's attacked those ships." He took a moment to catch his breath. "Officers, nobody can go out in that water. Have there been any reports of any disappearances in the past couple days? Any missing persons reports?"

"No, I don't believe…oh God," Crawford stopped for a moment and recalled a report received the previous night. "Tuesday night, a woman came in asking for help to locate her husband that came in a night prior. We didn't consider him a missing person just yet because well…he was last seen spending the night at some model's house. Apparently, some of his stuff was seen by the water, and he never showed. We figured he knew he was caught and was hiding from the missus, but now…oh God." He put a hand over his head, feeling the stress building up…the very thing he had come to this town to avoid.

"So, you say this thing was government funded?" Riker asked.

"Yes. Senator Roubideaux was one of those behind it," Stafford said.

"Oh, that's just great," Crawford said. "That's Kathy Bloom's father." Just as he mentioned her name, he saw that she had approached.

"Are you going to tell me what's going on, or am I going to have to guess?" she questioned. The chief walked away with her to brief her on what was certain. He was going to leave out the details on Bio-Nutriunt. As they left, Adam Wisk ran up to them from the road, holding a voice recorder up to Crawford's face.

"Good evening Chief Crawford! There's word going around of giant sharks in the harbor, slaughtering fishermen. What are the police doing about this? Vice Mayor Bloom, what will this do for the National Association of Sailing? Will the event be cancelled because of the danger?" Each question followed the other so quickly there was no time to answer.

"No comment right now! Press conference in the morning!" Crawford said, moving the recorder away from his face. Wisk then rushed away from them and toward the water like an excited child, snapping pictures of the wreckage from the beach. Bloom looked over her shoulder at him. Riker noticed her sour expression. It was clear this story was going to be everywhere by morning, and she was figuring damage control.

"I'm going home," he said. Metzler accompanied him back to the bar's parking lot, leaving Stafford alone at the beach. Riker could hear her footsteps behind him. "You gonna follow me home too?"

"No, I was just..."

"You were making sure I don't go back in that bar for another drink," he said. "I'll tell ya kid, you're more predictable than the dumbest shoplifter."

"I-I...I'm just trying to help you," Metzler said, stuttering. She felt herself beginning to shake. "I'm sorry, I'm just wound up over everything. We almost had that guy on the boat, and that shark just took him...it's just...aren't you bothered?"

"Only by you," he said and kept walking. Metzler slapped her hands to her sides in frustration, leaving him to walk away on his own. She waited for him to take off in his vehicle before making her way to hers. She got into the driver's seat and slammed the door in a fit of resentment. She felt like she had failed to save those poor fishermen. She failed to save those well-meaning civilians who took it upon themselves to help, only to be killed by the Thresher. Then there was Riker, whom she felt she was failing to save from himself. She slammed her hands on the steering wheel and broke down in tears.

Down on the beach, Stafford stared into the ocean. The fires had officially gone out, extinguishing the hellish appearance of the harbor. However, it wasn't a comfort for him, as he knew there was still a devil beneath the waves. Wisk approached him, holding up his voice recorder.

"Doctor Stafford!" he said. "You're the man who discovered this shark! Do you think it will remain in our waters? How big do you think it is?" Stafford ignored the questions, thinking on the statement of him discovering the Thresher.

"I seriously thought I had discovered a new species," he said, more to himself than Wisk. His tone was somber, as was his gaze.. "But with everything that's happened here; everything that's led up to this...I didn't discover a new species. I discovered a monster." He turned and walked away.

CHAPTER 17

The clock had struck midnight minutes before Kathy Bloom arrived home. It was a quiet place, and the only company she usually kept was a housekeeper who cleaned and tidied up during the day. She had no husband or kids, nor did she desire either. The living room was a nice wide area with a U-shaped sofa in the middle, and an electric fireplace at the end. She passed through and went into the kitchen, tossed her keys onto the table and immediately went for the refrigerator. She pulled out a bottle of cranberry wine and a glass from a nearby cabinet. After filling it to the rim, she went to the living room and turned on the fireplace. She brought the bottle along as well. She set it on a small table that was on the inside the opening of the sofa, and leaned back while draining half her glass.

She pondered about what would happen in the next few days until the event was scheduled to begin. She wondered what she would say at the press conference. It was obvious there would be questions regarding whether the event would be moved to another location. She wanted this situation to go away quietly, but how to manage that would be difficult. Bloom knew it had to be done. Her career couldn't handle the negative blow that this incident would inflict. She would only be Acting Mayor for a little longer before Ripefield would return to duty, and she wanted to make it count. As she finished her glass, she felt her cell phone vibrate.

Who the hell is calling this late? she thought. When looking at the contact listing her frustration turned to interest. She answered the call.

"Hello, *Dad*," she said. It was the first time they spoke in several months, and that occasion itself was the first in many months before that.

"*Hi Kathy,*" he said.

"What do I owe the displeasure?" she said, not holding back on her disdain. She heard him sigh.

"Fine, I'll get right to the point," the senator said. *"There's already news of what happened in Merit. That footage of that shark has been leaked onto the internet."* Bloom felt a headache coming along. It was another reminder of the negative media exposure she was bound to be subjected to.

"You're calling in the middle of the night to tell me what I already know?" she grumbled. She leaned forward and refilled her glass, taking a sip from the bottle before replacing the cork.

"I'm calling you because..." he paused, *"...I need your help."* Bloom froze from sheer astonishment, holding her wine glass an inch from her lips. Never in her life had she ever heard him mutter such words to anybody, even when running for office. He was always the 'do-it-yourself' type.

"I'm listening," she said while setting the glass back down.

"I've gotten word tonight of some hotshot reporter calling around for information regarding a project I helped finance. This project was called Bio-Nutriunt. It was meant to help produce food by making animals bigger, but it didn't work as we planned. Too many side effects and...hell, I'm not gonna get into the whole thing. Anyway, the point is that this reporter is from your area. Some hotshot named Adam Wisk. Obviously, you saw how big that freaking shark was."

"I haven't actually looked at the footage," Bloom said. "What exactly do you want?"

"I'll tell you what I DON'T want," Senator Roubideaux's voice suddenly became much more serious. *"This big ass shark just killed a bunch of people, I don't want everyone believing there's a connection between it and Bio-Nutriunt. We don't need the bad press. I want this situation handled as quietly as possible. I don't want a big local media scene regarding this thing. First, get in touch with Wisk and silence this story. Second, get rid of this damn shark as quietly as possible. No Coast Guard—the media and conspiracy theorists will jump all over that. I'll take care of any funding, but the less public knowledge, the better of this whole thing."*

"Sounds like you really need my help," Bloom said. Her voice almost sounded sinister. She saw this as a timely opportunity to rescue herself from the rut the recent incident left her in. "What do I get out of this?" She could easily imagine her father gritting his teeth at the question.

"You want my help with your political career? It first begins with positive media exposure. If we can have this taken care of quietly over the weekend, I'll make sure the press makes you look like a hero. Obviously, I have connections with the mainstream media, who'll be

there anyway soon for that sailing race. It'll appear you can take care of serious business in the mayor's absence. During the next election seasons, I can pull some strings to get you nominated." Bloom remained silent for several moments while containing her smile. This was the request she was hoping for.

"Looks like I have work to do," she said. "I'll start with this Wisk guy, and I think I know how to handle it. That funding might come in handy right away."

"That's fine. Just get it taken care of fast."

"Whatever you say, *Daddy!"* She hung up the phone and downed the glass of wine. This time, it was celebratory.

****

"Okay, this house here should be the address," Bloom's driver said as he pulled up to the driveway of a small two-story house. The houses in this area were more tightly packed than other neighborhoods, giving the impression that the residents were lower income. Sitting in the back seat, Kathy Bloom looked at the house. There were lights on in the living room area.

"Yeah, that has to be him," she said. With him being a reporter, she figured Wisk would be up all night working on writing the story. She exited the vehicle and walked up to the door while the driver waited. He yawned and rubbed his eyes. Being called in at 2:00 a.m. was not particularly pleasant, and he wondered what was so important that she would visit a person's home address at such an hour.

Wisk typed away at his computer, putting all of the information he had gathered into one big article. He was feeling ecstatic, knowing for sure this was front page news. He wasn't aware of the time until he heard the knock on his front door. He checked his watch.

"Who the hell is knocking at 2:00 a.m.?" he said to himself. His past experience with investigative reporting had him nervous. Having spent the day interviewing people on phone and Skype regarding government projects, he naturally wondered if this visit was connected. He opened the door. "Oh!" he said, surprised to see the vice mayor standing in his doorway. "Uh, hell...can I help you?" He really wanted to ask "Why are you here at this time at night?" but held back.

"Mr. Wisk, we need to talk," she stated. He held the door open for her, checking for any other officials while she came in.

"I'm guessing it's not something that can wait 'til morning?" he asked. He implied that it was sleep he wanted, but in reality, he wanted to get back to writing his article.

"No," she bluntly said. She struggled not to grimace at the poor upkeep of the small house. There were papers and wrappers on the floor. Newspapers were stacked, and the kitchen was a complete mess. "Don't think of me so much as the mayor right now, rather as..."

"Actually, I don't. You're the vice-mayor," he remarked. This time she grimaced.

"Right now, I'm more of a representative of Senator Roubideaux."

"Ah, working for Daddy!" he said.

"Phrase it however you want," Bloom said. "I'm assuming you're busy at work with a story on this shark, connecting it to the Bio-Nutriunt project." She pointed at his computer, with the article on screen. "I'll get right to the point: Our government wants to keep a lid on this, and I've been asked for that to happen. Therefore, I'm here to persuade you to not report on Bio-Nutriunt. The public does not need to think this was the result of government meddling with nature."

"Sorry, *Acting*-Mayor," Wisk said. "But it's not my style to withhold information from the public." He quickly went quiet when she pulled a checkbook from her pocket.

"Is that right?" she asked, flipping it open. "First of all, we're going to have this shark killed. We're prepared to specifically give you first hand coverage of it all. It'll be your story, exclusively. I'm gonna need you to report that the situation is being handled swiftly, and when the event begins, you'll need to do a detailed report to tell everyone that the threat is eliminated and the area is safe. Which it will be, of course."

"Can't you get mainstream media to do this?"

"We will, but people are more likely to believe a local inside source," she said. "But there must be no awareness of Bio-Nutriunt." She began writing numbers on the check.

"You think money's gonna buy silence?" Wisk said. His faced suddenly brightened with interest when he leaned forward and read *$200,000* on the check, made out to his name. It was more money than he had in years. Bloom tore it from the book and slid it towards him, keeping her fingers pressed on it.

"Tax free," she said. "But you will comply with what I told you. Or else." Her glare told him enough not to question that last bit. This money was coming from the federal government, after all. He stared at the check, particularly at all the zeros. A small voice inside of him begged him not to sell his integrity, but it was crushed when he picked the check up with his hand.

"I guess I better get to work on a new article," he said. Bloom gave an ominous smile and started toward the door. "So, what's going to happen with the shark? Is the Coast Guard gonna be called?"

"We're gonna avoid that solution because people will interpret the situation as critical. I don't want this event being moved elsewhere. It would be bad for the businesses in our town."

Yeah, I'm sure that's what you're worried about, Wisk thought.

"I'm going to look into an outside source first," she said.

"You know," he said, "I know of someone who can take care of this for you. It's actually three someones…the Trio. They've gone all over the world hunting things as mean as this shark. They're like mercenaries; they take the money and don't ask questions." Bloom allowed her interest to show. Wisk waved his check in the air toward her. "For another fifty grand, I'll not only tell you who, but I can get you in touch with them." She thought about it for a moment, and finally whipped her checkbook out again and slammed it on the table.

"Get in touch with them THIS MORNING!" she barked as she jotted down his desired compensation. As soon as she tore it loose, Wisk snatch it from her hand, barely avoiding ripping it.

"Pleasure doing business," he said. She rolled her eyes and walked out the door. However, as soon as she slipped back into her car, another sinister smile crept onto her face. *Hotshot reporter, huh? He's motivated by money just like the rest of us.* She even chuckled aloud while the driver drove her away.

CHAPTER 18

The following morning, Dr. Stafford sat in his lab after feeding his rescued animals. He looked at his watch, counting the number of minutes Nash was running late as usual. With each passing minute he got more impatient. The press conference was to begin in a half hour, and Stafford wanted to go. A sense of guilt added to his displeasure. Sitting in his desk chair, he stared down at the two recovered Thresher teeth. He questioned if he did a bad thing by not alerting the police about the shark's presence upon immediately learning of its existence. He had known it was hostile, although at the time he had no idea it was so territorial that it would attack ships of greater size. However, the guilt gave no room for logic.

Nash entered the door, planting the morning paper down on Stafford's desk. "Check this out." Stafford picked it up and read the headline. *Tragedy Strikes Merit Harbor.* The front-page picture showed the glimmering flames on the boat. He read through the article, and felt a surge of revulsion seep through his body.

"What the hell? *After the ship caught fire, it is believed the explosion attracted a large great white shark that was in the harbor. According to footage taken from a civilian drone, it appears the shark killed two of the fishermen who jumped off the vessel.*" He slammed the paper down. "Something's not right there," he said. "That is not something Wisk would write. He wanted a big investigative story, and suddenly he's turning his back on all of the evidence?"

"You think someone threatened him?" Nash asked. "Or perhaps he just isn't ready to release the full story yet."

"I think something's going on. I doubt he actually thinks the explosion attracted the Thresher. On top of that, he KNOWS it was a Thresher and no great white," Stafford said. He checked the time on his watch again and sprung up from his chair. "Come on, let's go to that press conference. Let's hear the bull they're gonna sell everybody."

****

It was a crowded event inside the Town Hall building. The room was a massive lobby with an upstairs ring for additional people to watch from the second floor. Both floors were loaded with people. The first floor consisted primarily of reporters, many of which were reporters who had arrived early for the sailing event. A podium was set up in the front, with Crawford already standing next to Kathy Bloom, the fire chief, and a few other officials. Crawford could see the bags under Bloom's eyes. It was obvious she had been up all night.

Many residents had taken off work to attend this meeting. Among them were business owners who had accounted extra stock of their product in anticipation for the event. Several officers were standing guard outside while people crowded into the building. Metzler decided to take post inside the building. Riker was outside, smoking another cigarette. It was his third that morning, and they were only an hour and a half into the shift. This was one of the few mornings where she took the time to apply makeup to her face. She was still red from the crying she had done all night. Nightmares of those enormous jaws rising up beneath them kept her awake. She had awoken earlier that morning to give her sister a brief visit in the hospital. She was in good spirits, but physically looking more ill than ever.

As the attendance started to settle down and take their seats, Metzler noticed two familiar faces come into the building: Dr. Stafford and Robert Nash. She waved and they saw her. She got a much-needed chuckle when she saw that Nash was wearing a t-shirt with a Vulcan salute. When they saw her, they approached.

"Busy day?" Stafford asked rhetorically.

"It's been a busy week," Metzler said. The thudding sound of a gavel hitting the podium drew the attention of the murmuring crowd. For a moment, it seemed as if they were in a court appearance. Chief Crawford stood at the podium and adjusted the microphone. Just as he was about to speak, Riker walked in and stood next to Metzler. His uniform was unkempt, and his face looked drained. She couldn't smell any alcohol on him this time, although the cigarette smoke was ripe.

"Good morning," Crawford began. "I'm going to let you all know the details we're sure of so far. The name of the vessel was the *Heavyweight*, and it carried four personnel. The captain, Gene Diebler was found deceased in the wheelhouse with multiple burn injuries, as well as lacerations in his chest from glass, among other injuries. The other three members are unaccounted for." Riker noticed a piece of paper on the podium that Crawford was clearly relying on. It was common for him to use notes, but he rarely depended on them so. His eyes barely left the paper, and his body language suggested he was not pleased in reporting this information.

"We are still currently in an investigation, but it appears that the fire was triggered by improper use of a flare gun, which created a flame that spread to the remaining fuel drums. Reports of a shark in the area have been confirmed by sightings of two off-duty officers that responded to the scene, and also by aerial footage. We believe the shark to possibly be a large great white, and we are currently making efforts to make sure there is no further danger to the public."

"What the hell is he saying?" Metzler whispered.

"This isn't him," Riker whispered back. "He's being told to say this stuff. Those notes he has…it's a friggin' script. He knows that was no typical shark." Stafford wanted to speak up, but he knew talking to Crawford would be useless in this setting. Various reporters began to ask questions, mostly regarding safety measures along the beaches. One reporter stepped up from the crowd. Stafford instantly recognized Adam Wisk as he began his question.

"How do you think this will affect the National Sailing Competition?" he asked. Before Crawford could answer, Kathy Bloom stepped to the podium. It was as if she didn't trust the chief to give the answer she wanted.

"The event will take place as scheduled," she said. "We don't believe there will be any further danger to the community." Immediately several reporters started bombarding her with questions.

"How can you know that?"

"How is the situation being handled?"

"Are you notifying the Coast Guard?"

"How big was the shark?"

"Why don't you tell them about WHY it was so big?" Stafford finally shouted over the rest of the crowd. The room suddenly went silent. Bloom stared him down. She didn't know who he was, but her blood pressure was already going up. He spoke as if he knew something. "Why don't you tell everyone here the truth? This shark was no great white! I'm certain most people here have seen the video that was uploaded online. That shark was a thresher, and it's big because of something you're covering up." People instantly began to look on their phones for the video footage. Murmurs of confusion began to spread through the room.

"What video?"

"I can't find it."

"A thresher? Ha! They don't get that big!"

"Who is this guy?"

"There's no video."

Hearing some of the discussion, Nash pulled his iPhone and quickly looked on the site where he had seen the footage overnight after Stafford called him about the incident. When he logged into the site, the video had been taken down. He scrolled to a few other sites, but there was no sign of it. He then tried to discreetly whisper to Stafford to get him to stop, but either he wasn't heard or he was ignored. He motioned to Riker and Metzler.

"They took it down," he whispered. Without saying anything, Riker nodded to him. He remembered Stafford explaining it was a government project that caused the shark to get so large. It was clear that there was a cover-up in the works.

"We can assure everyone that what happened was a freak accident," Bloom said. "It is a horrible tragedy, and we pray for the families of the victims. We have operations in place to either kill the shark or at least make sure it leaves the area. Experts have been called in to assist."

"*I* am an expert!" Stafford called out. "I know everything that lives within these waters, and I can tell you—you are lying about what's out there!" He motioned to the crowd. "This is part of one grand operation called..." Suddenly Riker cut in and grabbed Stafford by the arm.

"Okay sir, you're going to have to be removed from the meeting," he said, pulling him toward the exit. Stafford began resisting by pulling back.

"Hey what the hell? Damn you! Get off of me!" he protested. Riker leaned in to speak softly.

"You don't realize how deep you're treading," he said. "Stop this now, because trust me, the people who are behind all this will make you disappear." He began escorting Stafford out, followed by Metzler and Nash. The crowd started applauding the police. Several people shouted terms such as 'conspiracy theorist' and 'fraud'. As Stafford looked back, he noticed Wisk snapping pictures at him being dragged out. *That little shit!* Riker glanced back as well, seeing Crawford watching them. He knew the chief long enough to recognize he was relieved they were removing Stafford, furthering his theory of what was going on behind the scenes.

"I can't believe this! This is horseshit!" Stafford stomped after they were outside. They moved away from the building in order to not be heard by the small gathering outside the doors.

"Sorry, Doctor," Riker said.

"No, you were right. They've would've silenced me somehow," Stafford said, pacing in a circle. "You know what's really stupid about this? From what I understand, Bio-Nutriunt was truly a well-intended project. A lot of people do believe world hunger will be an issue in the future. The shark getting some of the product was truly an accident, it seems. I doubt they were testing the stuff on sharks. But they just don't want the connection to these deaths."

"What are we going to do?" Nash asked.

"I guess we're just gonna have to shut up and keep conducting our research," Stafford said. "Nobody will listen to us. All that's important right now is Bloom's résumé." After several minutes, it appeared as if the event was ending. People started exiting the building and returning to their vehicles. Riker could see a vehicle pull around the building, likely picking up Bloom. He started walking toward the building, believing Crawford was over there. Stafford and Nash decided to follow them. "How much more trouble can we get into?" the doctor joked.

As Riker marched around the building's corner, he saw the limo pull away with Bloom in the backseat. He was relieved to at least not have to see her again. They went to the loading dock area behind the building, as Crawford had exited the back door, cutting off several reporters who were blasting questions at him. He saw Riker approach.

"So Chief," Riker began. "What the hell's going on around here?" Crawford removed his suit jacket, and his button shirt was starting to soak with sweat from the heat. He glanced to make sure nobody was out there listening to them.

"Listen, your marine biologist buddy was right," he said. "There's a lot of heat coming down to make sure there is no news of this Bio-nutrition thing."

"Lovely," Metzler said. Going by the tone, Crawford almost thought Riker was speaking. "So what's going on? Are the beaches closed?"

"Yes," Crawford answered. "Temporarily. Nobody's allowed on the open sea in our jurisdiction. We're bringing in some specialists who don't mind keeping a low profile. They'll be in by later tonight."

"May I ask who you're bringing in?" Stafford said, just as the door behind Crawford swung open.

"I can answer that!" Wisk jumped out, shutting the door behind him. "Thanks to yours truly, this situation should be taken care of relatively soon, and your headache will be over." He opened a can of soda and started downing it.

Like caffeine's what this guy needs, Riker thought.

"You guys might not have heard of them, but I helped Bloom get in touch with a group called the Trio," he said. Stafford's eyes got wide, and he instantly began tensing up.

"The Trio?! You stupid fuck!" he shouted. "What's with that bullshit story you put out in the paper?! I thought you were a dedicated journalist who only cared about the truth! How much did they pay you?" Wisk simply shrugged with a slight smirk. He was still riding the high of having a significantly increased savings balance. Stafford tensed up and clenched his fists. Riker and Metzler quickly got in between them, thinking Stafford was about to lunge at Wisk. He didn't, but every fiber in his being wanted to. "Chief! Please don't tell me you're entertaining this plan of having the Trio hunt this thing!"

"It's not my call. It's what Bloom wants," Crawford said. Stafford turned and kicked some nearby garbage in a fit of anger. A large crumbled ball of old newspaper and some soda cans launched from the concrete like soccer balls. He then stormed off, and Nash followed. While he didn't emotionally show it as clearly, he was also furious about the Trio's upcoming arrival. Crawford watched him leave and then turned to his cops. "Will you guys meet with me over at Mason Dock? I'll let you know when these guys are arriving."

"What's wrong, boss?" Riker said. "You have afternoon shift patrollers. Why can't they meet you there?"

"Well I would rather..." Crawford was looking for an excuse, but realized that Riker would see right through it. "Okay, you're right. These guys in our department, they're good guys but they're inexperienced and naïve. I just want someone I can rely on."

"You have a suspicion about these shark hunters?" Metzler asked.

"Hard to say," Crawford said, "but I have that bad gut feeling." Metzler was interested, and Riker was appearing indifferent. He turned and started to walk off, keeping with his habit of leaving without any parting gesture. "Leonard!" Crawford called after him. Riker stopped and glanced back. "I need to talk to you later today." Riker simply gave a nod and kept walking. Metzler shared the chief's concern before jogging after him to catch up.

****

The rest of the shift had gone quietly. Everyone stayed clear of the water, complying with the order given by the chief. Fishermen were angry and local businesses were nervous. Some of the early arrivals for the sailing race were beginning to trickle in. For the weekend, it was natural for them to expect to go and swim in the beaches. It was a shock for these tourists to find out they were closed, and none of the residents wanted to explain why, in fear of losing customers.

It was nearly 6:00 in the afternoon. Riker was the first to leave at shift change, successfully avoiding Crawford the remainder of the shift. He spent the next hour at home in his bathroom with nausea, although nothing came up this time. Now his body was quivering from having no alcohol in twenty-one hours. He had his phone turned off, prepared with the excuse of battery failure when questioned by it. Instead of going to his normal hangout, Riker decided Crawford would know to track him there if he wanted to find him, so he located a newer bar outside of town called *Bad G. Goodman's*. The place had a classic car vibe, with older Cadillacs, Lincolns, Toyotas, and other models from the fifties lining up the front walkway.

After Riker found a place to park, he considered turning his phone back on, knowing Crawford wanted him to be there while he met with the contractors. However, his stubborn attitude got in the way. The resentment he harbored toward the Chief was still deep-seated, and he kept his phone turned off. Also, he knew Crawford wanted to have another heart-to-heart about Martha and his alcohol abuse, and Riker had no interest in such a conversation.

Before he switched off the ignition, his eyes caught a glimpse of a familiar sight stopped at a red light in a nearby intersection down the road. The crack in the upper right windshield of the Pontiac G6 was unmistakable. It was Metzler's car. In Riker's fragile mind, there was no coincidence that she appeared in this area the same time he arrived at the bar.

"You've got to be kidding me!" he said to himself. His belief that Metzler had followed him to the bar caused his anger to boil. The anger got so intense that it overcame the torturous need for alcohol. He expected her to pull her vehicle into the lot, but instead she kept going. His anger did not subside, however, and he sped his vehicle back onto the road, clenching the wheel tightly as if to strangle it. Metzler's car continued down the road, and there were a few other vehicles between them. He then saw the Pontiac turn left into a hospital parking lot. *Wait, a hospital?* he thought to himself. He wondered if she knew he was following her and followed her into the lot, keeping plenty of distance. He figured that theory was false when he watched her park in a space. Riker drove to another lot and parked. From his GMC, he watched Metzler get out of her car and start walking toward the front door.

For the first time, he suddenly found a feeling he hadn't felt in a long time: concern. He wondered if she was getting herself checked out, especially when he noticed she was carrying what appeared to be documents. Then she stopped and looked at her phone. He watched her answer a call and talk on the phone for a minute. After hanging up, she suddenly returned to her vehicle. The engine started and she drove out of the lot, unaware of his presence. At first, Riker found this strange, but then realized where she was going. He turned his phone back on and saw he had a missed call and a voicemail from Crawford, asking him to come to Mason Dock. The call had only come a few minutes ago, and he believed Metzler was on her way there. He still wanted to avoid Crawford and avoid his lecture on life.

Despite not wanting to go, he went against his own wishes and started driving toward the dock.

****

Nash spent the previous hour working on replacing the fish finder's screen in the wheelhouse of the *Taurus*. It was a way for him to get his mind off the recent stresses in his life, particularly the likeliness of funding being completely depleted. Stafford had a lot of expenses, and Nash's paycheck was one of them. His pay was low enough to begin with. It wasn't a doubt of character; he knew very well that Stafford would pay him more if possible. However, he had no plans to leave the institute. Stafford had a quality about him that many other scientists lacked; a true love for the sea. Nash believed most marine biologists started out with such a love and fascination, but eventually lost it as their careers and personal lives got in the way. Stafford had given up a well-paying career to dedicate himself to preserving wildlife.

This notion was supported when Nash stepped out of the cockpit and saw the doctor above, standing in the crow's nest. Dr. Stafford had been standing patiently up there all afternoon with a bottle of water and a pair of binoculars. He scanned the seas, looking for any sign of the Trio's vessel.

"You know, doc, there's really no point in doing what you're doing," Nash said.

"What do you mean?" Stafford asked without looking away from the water.

"These guys are specifically being employed by the township, whose acting leading official is doing favors on behalf of the Senate," Nash said. "We're little people compared to them. They won't listen to anything we have to say."

"Yeah, but the chief seems to have his head screwed on straight," Stafford said. "Also, there's those two cops. They've done alright by us. If anyone will listen to us it's them." He finally removed the binoculars from his eyes, squinting to adjust from the surge of sunlight. "This shark definitely needs to be taken care of. But the Trio will do more damage than good. They aren't fishermen; they're slaughterers. To say they kill for sport doesn't even describe what they do. I have whales still out there, and these guys will have no problem harpooning them if they come across them."

"What will they do?" Nash asked. "Take their blubber like in the old days? Is there even anyone who'd pay for that?"

"Hell yeah," Stafford said. "There are some countries in the world who'll pay handsomely for it. Plus, there's the black market. You'd be surprised what it'd go for." He put his eyes back into the binoculars. After a quick scan he noticed a large vessel in the distance, closing in towards shore. "There! That's got to be them! Looks like they're heading for the police docking area." He climbed down from the crow's nest and got off the boat. Nash noticed he was going for his truck.

"Wait? You're going over there?" he asked.

"Hell yes I am!" Stafford said. "I'm gonna try and talk some sense into the chief. You don't have to come with me if you don't want." He opened the door and got in.

"Oh, I hate it when you say that," Nash said, reluctantly jogging to the passenger's side.

CHAPTER 19

A bit of cloud cover had accumulated in the late afternoon sky, casting a grayish shadow down on Merit. Riker parked his vehicle near Metzler's car. He took a different route than her in order to not appear as if he was following her. She was standing outside the officer post near Crawford. Kathy Bloom was there as well, maintaining a demeanor as that of a world leader. The large fishing vessel was coming in from a few hundred yards out. Some of the police vessels had been moved to give the boat a place to dock. Before Riker stepped out, he rested in his seat to gather his composure. His hands were shaking from alcohol withdrawal. He silently hoped for this favor to be over quick so he could go home and down some beers.

Bloom could be heard griping to Crawford about something pertaining to the situation. He couldn't hear what specifically, but the Chief's fed-up expression spoke for itself. Metzler kept to herself. She also appeared completely uninterested in being there, glancing at her car several times. Riker recognized the desire to leave, which he found surprising. Metzler was usually the go-getter type who'd be happy for additional work. But this time, she visibly had no interest in this favor. Riker stepped out of his vehicle and stood near the group, watching the large black vessel slowly approach.

"Well boss, if these guys move any slower the shark will die of old age before they kill it," Riker said to Crawford. He gave no reaction, but Bloom suddenly fired up.

"You've asked him to be here too?" she scolded the chief. "I told you; I don't need an audience for this meeting."

"Oh, relax," Crawford barked. "These two were the ones who responded to the incident. They've seen the shark up close." Bloom was shocked by the aggression in his voice. Normally she'd be quick to chastise anyone who raised their voice at her, but she felt it was better not to this time. Riker kept a distance in order for his shakes to be less noticeable. He watched the incoming vessel. Lettering on the hull spelled

Sea Martyr. The outer rim of the bow was lined with all sorts of teeth of different species. They were of all different shapes and sizes. Some were triangular, others were curved, some looked like granite cones. Riker took an interest in the hull, which appeared to have a protective layer of bull-bars, reminding him of bumper guards on police cars. The bars went around the hull and the sides of the ship, and also appeared to provide protection under it. The black paint on the *Sea Martyr* gave it an ominous appearance against the blue ocean. As the boat closed in, a truck suddenly sped into the parking zone. It came to a screeching stop, kicking up dirt and briefly alarming the officers. Riker and Crawford instinctively placed their hands on their sidearms, and Metzler attempted to do the same only to remember she didn't strap it to her jeans. Out of the truck came Stafford and Nash.

"Oh Jesus," Crawford said, winding down from the brief excitement. "Doctor, may I ask what you're doing here?"

"I'm hoping I can convince you to tell these guys to leave," Stafford said. He approached the chief, who met him halfway.

"Doctor, I'm sorry, but it's best if you and your friend leave. We're in the middle of an operation to kill the shark."

"Chief, these guys are not fishermen. I think it's too kind to even call them poachers. They go around the world, simply killing whatever they can. You see the teeth there?" He pointed at the bow. "Those are not all from sharks. That bastard, Bronson, hunts whales and dolphins...including ones I've tagged. I have other animals in the area and I don't trust this guy to not go after them." Crawford sighed and looked back at Bloom, who was watching the boat pull in.

"Listen, Doc, I get it. You care for your animals, but there's a shark out there that you admit yourself is killing them already. With the restrictions put on me put by..." he discreetly tilted his head toward Bloom, "...I'm stuck between a rock and a hard place." Stafford saw the boat come to a stop near the deck.

"Listen, Chief, have you done any sort of check on these guys?" he asked. Crawford shook his head. "If you did, you'd understand. These guys are wanted for serious crimes in multiple areas AROUND THE WORLD, including trade deals with black market companies. There are warrants in the States for him, for crying out loud. Assault, damage to property, killing of endangered species. This guy's a wrecking ball, and it gets worse..."

"Okay, I get it," Crawford said. "I told you, it's not up to me."

"Listen...let me handle it! I'll go out and kill the thing!" Stafford said. "I'll take care of it. I already have an idea how to do it. You do not want these guys doing the job, especially with their methods."

"No, no," Crawford rose his hands up. "Doctor, I appreciate it, but I can't be responsible for you dealing with this thing. You will submit to the same order as everyone else. No boats on the open sea within our jurisdiction." The sound of a door slamming drew his eyes towards the boat. One of the members had emerged from below deck and appeared to be gathering the tie line. Crawford looked back to Stafford. "What kind of animals are you afraid he'll kill?"

"That's a long list," Stafford said. "Mainly I have some humpbacks and greys out there. There are also dolphins out there as well. A lot of them pass through our waters during their migration patterns. I know this guy; if he comes across them he'll kill them for his own enjoyment and use them for bait. I'm telling you! I'm not losing any more..."

"Okay okay!" Crawford interrupted him again. "Listen, I'll figure something out." Stafford appeared to calm down for a moment. Suddenly he pointed his finger at a post on the side of the vessel.

"What is that?!" he yelled. Crawford looked, seeing what appeared to be a severed caudal fin suspending from the post. Strands of flesh and tendons dangled from the severed end of the tail. Stafford realized it was a shark tail; a very large one.

"Sorry we're late! We ran into this guy on our way here!" The individual on deck called out. He slid down the starboard ladder onto the dock. He was twenty-five years of age with straight blond hair combed back. Another individual appeared on deck; a woman of Japanese descent. She didn't come down with the young man, rather she stood on deck with her arms crossed, staring at the group. The younger individual approached Bloom.

"I presume you're Mr. Bronson," she said.

"Well, you're not wrong," the man said and laughed like an immature high-schooler. Bloom was repulsed at the smell of dead fish that reeked from his red flannel shirt and fishing pants. She reluctantly reached out to shake his hand. It was covered with fish grease. She struggled not to wince in disgust.

"What is that supposed to mean?" she asked.

"His name is William," Stafford said. "He's Bronson's son." Bloom immediately retracted her hand.

"Then where is Mr. Bronson?! The captain!" she snapped at William. As if directly answering, the lights in the wheelhouse switched on, casting a shine over the side of the boat. The door on the superstructure opened, and out stepped a man of six feet. His figure was like a silhouette against the grayish sky, with a puff of smoke rising above him from a tobacco pipe he held in his mouth. He stared down at the group for a moment, as if sizing them up, and then finally started down the ladder. Once he was off the boat, they were able to get a better look at him. His age was fifty-five with graceful features. His hair was silver grey, his build was lean, and his eyes were blue as the sea. He took his son's place in front of Bloom and shook her hand. A twelve-inch Bowie knife hung from his right hip, kept in a brown cow-skin sheath.

"Boy, get back to the fish," he said in a very relaxed, yet reserved tone. "My apologies," he looked back at Bloom. "I'm Mr. Bronson. You may call me Beau if you like."

"Thanks for arriving so quickly on such short notice," Bloom said. Crawford noticed she seemed uneasy in Bronson's intimidating presence. Bronson turned his direction to the chief, shaking his hand as well.

"Good to meet you, sir," he said.

"Likewise," Crawford greeted back. However, he didn't feel the same gratitude that he perceived. The chief knew that behind that charm was something precarious in this so-called fisherman. Riker sensed it too and stayed back, intending not to play friendly with Bronson. There was a moment of tense silence as he made eye contact with Dr. Stafford, sparking a sense that there was an inimical history between them.

"Good to see you doing well," Bronson said. "Still playing doctor with the fishes?"

"Son of a bitch!" Stafford made a lunge for him, stopped inches from him by Riker who grabbed him by the back of his shirt and pulled him back. Bronson never flinched. Instead he sparked a small grin, intentionally and successfully getting under Stafford's skin. "Let go of me!" the doctor commanded to Riker, who held him back with one hand.

"I'm not protecting him from you..." Riker said. His eyes were locked on Bronson. His sleeves were rolled up, exposing a tattoo on the inside of his right arm: *Legio Patria Nostra; Honneur et Fidélité.* Stafford relaxed and Riker let go. As Bronson watched the struggle conclude, he detected the little shakes in Riker's hands. There were no scars on his arms indicating drug injections, and no sign of bleeding or dryness in his nostrils that would indicate inhalations of narcotics. Although he knew there were other possibilities, Bronson had seen enough in his life to know Riker was in dire need of booze.

"Judging by the size and color of that tail, and its crescent shape, I'd say you jerks killed a basking shark," Stafford said. "They're not dangerous. They don't even have teeth!"

"You always were a showoff," Bronson said. "Besides, we need bait. Also, their fins go for a hell of a price. There's a hell of a market for that shit. Good soup." He walked back over to Bloom. "Speaking of price, let's get down to business. It's my understanding we're not dealing with some simple great white like you want everyone to believe. From what I've been informed, this is some science experiment gone haywire or something, or a freak of nature...I really don't give a damn. Whatever it is, this creature is a special case, which means I'm going to require a special rate."

"Three hundred thousand is the deal," Bloom said.

"FIVE!" Bronson said, only slightly raising his voice above his steady calm tone. Bloom was about to protest. "Five, or we take off tonight and when the media gets here, the whole country will get to hear how Merit sucks because the lady running it is too cheap to provide safety." Bloom tensed up. He had called her out and she knew it.

"Fine," she said. "You get paid AFTER you kill the thing."

"Excellent," he said. "That concludes our meeting. We'll start out first thing in the morning." He started walking back to his boat.

"Whoa! Not so fast!" Crawford called out after him. Bronson stopped and turned his attention to him. "There's one other condition that you'll need to meet before you do this."

"Condition?"

"If you're going out, then one of my people will accompany you," Crawford said, glancing briefly at Stafford, who gave a nod of appreciation. Bloom angrily stepped up.

"Chief, what the hell are you doing? You do not have a call on..."

"*Acting* Mayor," he said, "these waters are my jurisdiction, granted by the U.S. Coast Guard. For this to be considered official, there needs to be a police official involved." He was lying, and surprisingly Bloom backed down. However, Bronson wasn't pleased. His demeanor stayed the same, mostly. His subtle displeasure could be heard in his voice, however.

"And why exactly do I need one of your guys getting in the way on my boat?"

"There are laws out there that need to be followed. For it to be assured that those laws are followed, you will be supervised," Crawford said. "Case and point. You're going to be monitored. Otherwise, go ahead and take off." Bloom tensed so hard it appeared her eyes would pop out of her head. On the boat, William rushed angrily to the side, overhearing the conversation.

"You can take that *case and point* and shove it up your..."

"William..." Bronson cut him off. Again, his voice was calm, but there was a ferocity within it that sent the message to his son, who backed off. "Again, my apologies," Bronson said to the chief.

"Chief!" Stafford cut in. "Are you sure you really want one of your people on board? May I remind you, this isn't some ordinary shark. It's been subjected to a product that causes extreme aggression. I'm not exaggerating; this is probably the most dangerous creature perhaps in the entire ocean."

"That's why I'm gonna be the one to go," Crawford said. "I'm not subjecting anyone else to the danger out there."

"Ray! You've got to be kidding me," Riker said. He marched in front of his superior and mentor. Crawford was almost amazed to see the genuine concern in his eyes. "Did you hear what he said? You seriously want to go out there? You're no seaman."

"Someone has to go," Crawford said. "I'd rather it be me." The part he omitted was he especially did not want to subject Riker to that risk. Bronson's eyes glanced subtly toward Riker. Knowing there was no way out of having a liaison on board, he devised a plan.

"Fine, Chief," he said, "but the cowboy will be the one coming with us." He pointed at Riker.

"No. I'll be the one to go with you," Crawford said.

"Not happening," Bronson responded. "Him, or no deal." He paused while Crawford cursed him in his mind. "Remember, you'll be pissing off some bad people if I cut bait," he added.

"This is just great," Riker complained. He gritted his teeth in tremendous frustration. He had no interest in going out with these people. However, although he wouldn't admit it, he hated seeing Crawford subjected to the abuse of government officials. The withdrawal only added to the misery. He paced for a moment, and Bronson hid his pleasure at seeing the conflict within—exactly why he wanted Riker specifically. "Fine! What time?" he said with a pained voice.

"We launch at oh-seven hundred," Bronson said. "Be here." He returned to the vessel. "Emi! What's for dinner?" The Japanese woman didn't provide an answer. She marched to the cabin like an imperial trooper responding to an order. On shore, Bloom marched in a more determined fashion to her vehicle where her driver was waiting. Without saying a word to the others, she got in the backseat and they drove off.

Metzler almost seemed oblivious to the whole conversation. Her mind was focused on her sister in the hospital and the treatment options that her doctors were providing. The recommended option was a stem cell transplant, a risky and highly expensive process. Her sister Tammy had reached a chronic stage, and there seemed to be no other choice. Metzler was just arriving at the hospital with the paperwork when she received the call from Crawford. However, she did keep track of the conversation, and assumed she would be meeting Riker here in the morning. After all, she was assigned to be his trainee. Also, being aware of his condition, she worried about him being on the sea alone with them. Riker looked at his watch. It was getting late and he was dying for a drink.

"At least I won't have to wear that damn uniform tomorrow," he remarked and got in his car. Crawford attempted to talk to him, but Riker already began speeding out of the driveway. Nash and Stafford made sure to get out of the way.

"Damn," Nash said. "He must be really mad about going out tomorrow!"

That's not the only thing that's going on, Crawford thought.

****

Riker managed to park decently this time, despite skidding into his driveway. He pulled his key from the ignition so hard it nearly snapped and marched through his front door right for the kitchen. His mind was suffering much stress without the comforting blockage of alcohol. All the miseries in his life flooded his thoughts. All of the shootings, the fights, long hours, the people whose lives were changed for the worst, the people he failed to save…and worst of all, ignoring the warning signs of Martha's condition. The guilt was overwhelming. Before entering the kitchen, the sight of the framed wedding photo on the floor caught his eye. He glanced down at it, seeing the happiness in his wife's eyes. His mind tormented itself on how he stripped that happiness away from her. With a nudge of his boot on the edge of the frame, he flipped it over, unable to look at it. He opened the fridge and reached for the bottom shelf, only to see that his supply was missing. The shelf was entirely empty.

"What the hell?" he said. His mind was in a whirlwind, almost panicking at the thought of not feeding the intense addiction. The nausea swirled in his stomach, and he rushed his way to the bathroom. There wasn't much to cough up. The bile had some blood in it again, though less than the other day. He caught his breath while resting on the bathroom floor. The sound of his door opening made him spring to his feet. His knees were wobbly, and he walked almost like a drunkard. At the hallway he saw Crawford standing inside the doorway.

"What'd you do with it!" He wasted no time calling the chief out.

"I got rid of it," Crawford said. "Son, you don't need it right now."

"Don't tell me what I don't need!" Riker sounded like a madman. "Give it back now!"

"It's been thrown away," Crawford said. "You think I don't know what you're doing? You're poisoning yourself. I know you're spending half your time with a bottle, the other half puking."

"You don't know shit!" Riker marched toward him, barely supporting himself on his shaking legs. Rational thought and reason went away. Like an insane madman, Riker drew back and fired his fist at the chief's face in a fury of anger. His fist was stopped effortlessly inches away, caught like a softball in Crawford's hand.

"It's not worth it," Crawford said. "You're punishing yourself, and it needs to stop. Martha wouldn't want it for you." Riker yanked his hand free and backed off.

"You really think that? You weren't there when she asked me to stay home! You weren't there when I told her to 'get over it', the last damn thing I ever said to her! Your wife…she had your support! Mine, I blew her off." His eyes began welling up. "What was it all for? Catching some criminals who'd just be replaced by others? Trying to save some junky's life? Spending all my time chasing the monsters in that city? Stupid life insurance policy? Fucking one-hundred grand she put on herself? I'm not touching that blood money!" He slammed his fist into the hallway closet door, smashing it off its hinges before collapsing to his knees. On the floor he fully wept; a luxury he never allowed himself. Crawford knelt down with him, embracing the broken man in a fatherly comfort.

****

Night fell and cast a cover of darkness over the sea. Exhausted from hours of the physical labor of gutting the shark, William climbed up the superstructure to the wheelhouse. There was no processing machine suitable for a fish the size of a basking shark, meaning it had to be butchered the old-fashioned way with a saw. He opened the back door to the wheelhouse, seeing his father leaning back in his chair, smoking his pipe. It was a large room, allowing Bronson to have a couple chairs inside as well as a storage closet. In his hand was a miniature harpoon for a Greener MK II harpoon rifle. The weapon itself was disassembled in its box on a nearby table. William shut the door behind him as Bronson strapped a small device on the stem of the harpoon. Once finished, he set it down next to several other harpoons with the same type of black object strapped to them.

"Don't get grease on the door handle," he scolded his son. William looked at his hands and wiped them on a handkerchief. "Did you keep the fins intact?"

"Yes," William answered in a complaining tone. "The net is all set and ready to go too. Emi's down below getting the buoy."

"Perfect," Bronson said. He stood up from his chair. "Let's get going then and set it out." He noticed that William was bleeding from his left hand. "I warned you to be careful installing the blades on the net. Do you want me to show you how again?"

"No, Dad," the grouchy twenty-five-year-old said. "I just slipped up and got myself. It's not bad."

"Attaboy." Bronson turned around and started up the boat, drawing on his pipe. "Alright, time to go. We've got ourselves a big day tomorrow. Don't forget to spray the deck. We'll have our guest in the morning."

"If I may ask; why did you want that one cop coming with us?" William asked.

"First of all, he was less annoying than the chief," Bronson said. "Second; I believe he'll give us less trouble if we play our cards right. The chief is catering to Dr. Stafford, but I don't get the impression that cowboy holds the same values." He glanced at a nearby fridge, which was loaded with whiskey and beer. "I think there's something we can do to manipulate him if we need to." He slowly accelerated the boat out of the dock.

CHAPTER 20

The early streaks of sunlight piercing the windows into Riker's living room didn't help with the drowsy strain of waking up. Riker awoke at 5:45, laying in bed for the first ten minutes before gathering the strength to get up. He took a brief shower and then dressed in blue jeans and a black t-shirt, strapping his holster to his right thigh. There was a chill that early morning, especially with some minor wind coming off the ocean, so Riker put on his denim jacket.

He had been up much of the previous night. Crawford stayed with him and left around midnight. He insistently reminded Riker that he did not have to go out with the Trio, even offering him time off. Riker refused it, and as much as he wasn't thrilled with going out with the shark hunters, there was a part of him that felt like he needed to do this. His whole life he had been chasing after monsters. Mob bosses, assassins, drug dealers, gang leaders. Now he found himself chasing after a literal monster, which would undoubtedly kill more innocent people unless stopped.

On his way to the door from the kitchen, his eyes looked down at the picture frame, lying face-down on the floor. He stopped and began to reach down to pick it up. He stopped midway, haunted by the flood of regrets that swirled in his mind. Looking at the pictures of their wedding day simply reminded him of the happiness his wife ultimately lost. He gave up the effort and went for the door.

****

"Right on time," Bronson said as he watched Riker drive up to the dock. He stood on the deck next to Emi, who stood silent as a statue with her arms crossed. He dusted flakes of tobacco leaves off his red shirt and then climbed down to meet their police supervision. Riker stepped out of the GMC with a cigarette already lit in his mouth. He saw the captain approach and took quick notice of the military style tactical pants he wore. It was a curious sight, as he didn't think that was typical fishing gear. A twelve-inch bowie knife swung inside its leather sheath, dangling from Bronson's right hip. Another curious sight was the Japanese woman. Her eyes were sharper than the point on a machete, and they seemed to pierce right into Riker. William was currently below deck out of sight.

"Good morning, Cowboy," Bronson said and extended his hand to Riker. He looked at it for a moment before shaking. He made sure to give a firm shake in order to hide the jitteriness he was experiencing. His body was screaming for a drink.

"Captain," he acknowledged him.

"I must apologize, we didn't get formally introduced last night," Bronson said. "I am aware that you encountered our shark already."

"It was a big bastard," Riker said. "It already tried to eat me, and I'm pissed. So how 'bout we go out and kill the big bastard?" Bronson smiled.

"That's exactly what I like to hear," he said and started leading Riker to the *Sea Martyr*. "You see Officer, this is exactly why I wanted you instead of the Chief, with all due respect. Now I know you're not a shark expert, but are you able to tell me something; is this thing a big Thresher like I was told?"

"It had that big ass tail," Riker answered.

"That would constitute a Thresher," Bronson said. Riker stepped in front of him and stopped.

"Listen, you and Dr. Stafford might not get along, but he's right about this fish. It's big and it's a vicious sonofabitch!" he growled. "Frankly, I don't know much about you, and nor do I care. I don't even care why the government wants this handled so quietly. What I do care about is that you kill that thing, so that it doesn't kill anyone else." Bronson nodded, and again he smiled.

"Like I said; exactly why I wanted you along," he said. "Now, before we get started, are there any questions?"

Riker didn't hesitate. "What exactly do you know about me?"

Bronson looked him square in the eye.

"Born on March 18th, 1984; Graduated High School in summer 2001; Sworn in as a cop in 2005; Made detective two years later; I could go over all the cases, but that would take all day. The media covered you very well over the years. Although, I'd say the one that intrigued me the most: the Worton case. Yeah, the cop killer who had killed two state troopers and shot one in your department. I think it was some military dropout or something. But you tracked him down, and the two of you got up close and personal. He pulled a knife, and voila... he made you pretty in the process." He pointed to the large scar over Riker's eye. "But you got him. Nearly killed him, which I can't blame you for." Riker stared back at his eyes. They were crystal blue as pure water, but he could see the darkness behind them.

"Anything else?"

"I know it stays in your head," Bronson said. He noticed the minor shakes in Riker's fingers, which made his point. As they were about to walk to the boat, the sound of tires on gravel caught their attention. Riker gritted his teeth when he saw the obvious crack on the windshield. The engine switched off and Metzler stepped out. Dressed in a grey button shirt over a black tank top with blue jeans, even Riker thought she was stunning to look at. On her right hip was her Glock, strapped straight to her belt rather than a duty belt. The feature Riker noticed were the brown western boots, which were almost identical to the kind Martha wore.

"Sorry I'm late," she said. She grabbed a small bag and started toward them. Riker didn't hesitate to march toward her.

"No. No. NO!" he exclaimed. She refused to stop. "This isn't happening. Go to Crawford and he'll assign you to somebody else."

"I already spoke to him," she said. "I told him I was coming along."

"And he said 'Yes'?" Riker asked. Metzler nodded. "What the hell? You've been dying to get another trainer, and now you have your chance."

"I've decided I don't need that," she said. "Listen, we're partners. And we're in this together."

"Look, you're NOT going, Allison!"

"We're on a first name basis?" she said, more as a remark than a question. "Let me ask you this? Why don't you want me to come along? Be honest." Riker stumbled over his words for a moment, something that rarely happened to him.

"Listen, we can BOTH be killed out there," he finally said. She dropped her bag and stood toe to toe with him, as if to present a challenge. Her face was very serious looking as she stared him in the eye, but not showing anger.

"You're telling me not to come. Is this out of personal concern? Or are you just interested in relieving yourself of training me?" she asked. For a moment, there was no answer. She put her hands on her hips and tapped her foot, getting impatient. A day or so ago, Riker wouldn't have hesitated for a moment to tell her he couldn't care less about her. But this time, he couldn't seem to do it. He wasn't sure if it was even true. With a prolonged defeated sigh, he stood out of her way and motioned toward the black *Sea Martyr*. She picked up her bag and proceeded.

Bronson realized he was getting another passenger. His initial instincts were to insist she didn't come, but he noticed how she stood up to Riker. It was clear keeping her off the boat would be a useless effort.

At least we'll have some nice scenery, he thought to himself while admiring her trim figure. *Something about a woman with a gun...* He broke away from his thoughts and extended his hand, greeting Metzler with his normal charming smile.

"I see you'll be joining us, Officer...?"

"Metzler," she answered. She admired the enormous vessel. The previous evening, she had too much on her mind to take notice of it. It was a unique looking vessel, both beautiful and haunting at once. Bronson could see in her expression that she was impressed.

"She's a beauty, ain't she?" he questioned. He wanted to follow up with a remark such as *kind of like yourself.* However, he refrained, unsure how Riker would react to it. *They certainly bicker like a couple.*

"She is impressive," Metzler said. "If you don't mind me asking; why the protective bars all along the sides and bottom of the boat?" On the *Sea Martyr*, several black bars lined the sides like black rails. They also ran under the boat from bow to stern. They were composed of compressed steel.

"It's the same idea as your police vehicles," Bronson said. "They slow us down a little, but they help deflect attacks from large animals. You can see where we had an encounter with a sperm whale." He pointed at a section of bar that was dented inward near the stern. The sight gave Metzler a feeling of apprehension.

"Sperm whale? Why were you encountering a sperm whale? Unless, you were..."

"Leave it alone," Riker said.

"There are countries in the world where it's legal, and blubber is on the market," Bronson answered. His tone exhibited a lack of moral uncertainty on the issue. Metzler's jaw dropped at his blatant response. She was under the impression that whaling was illegal throughout the world, and it was her belief that it was a despicable act. Bronson could read her thoughts. "I have to make a living like the rest of you. I'm not bowing down to whiny college brats with cardboard signs, claiming they're for conservation." He climbed up on deck, followed by the officers. The large deck of the ship was a dark brown, almost having a red satanic appearance. The Japanese woman stood in place like an imperial guard. She was about Metzler's size, wearing a sleeveless Haori jacket, reminiscent of samurai warriors, over a black shirt. Riker and Metzler took notice of a large red scar on her neck. Near the scar was a triangular tattoo of a shark tooth.

"Let's get underway," Bronson said. Emi nodded and removed the tie off line. Riker and Metzler followed him to the superstructure. Before going up to the wheelhouse, the door opened that led to the lower segments of the ship. William stepped out, dressed in unkempt cargo pants and an untucked shirt. The handle of a sheathed knife stuck out from his shirt along the small of his back. In both hands were white chum buckets filled to the rim. Bits of blood oozed from the lids, running down the sides.

"Alright, are we going out today or...HELLO!" he exclaimed when he saw Metzler. "Damn! You are fine!" Metzler gave him no reaction and climbed the short distance to the wheelhouse. Once inside, she immediately noticed the teeth that lined the upper edge of the wall, circling around the room. They were different kinds of teeth from all sorts of different sea creatures, most of which were sharks. In addition, there were the cone shaped teeth from sperm whales and orcas. In the center of the front wall was a bizarre black object that resembled a huge parrot beak.

"What the hell is that?" Riker asked.

"That's a beak I removed from Architeuthis Dux," Bronson answered. "We were hired by a small government in the Indonesian Sea. Apparently, they overfished the area, which took out its food supply, which in turn drove it to munch on local fishermen." Metzler recognized the scientific term for the giant squid.

"How did this go unreported?" Metzler asked. "It's rare that those things ever turn up alive."

"We got paid our fee, and that was all that matters to me," Bronson said. He fired up the engine, which rumbled with three heavy vibrating shakes when he throttled it forward. "The same goes for this shark." As Riker turned to go back outside, he examined a black and white picture on the wall. It was from the 1920's, and displayed an image of a damaged diving bell. Written beneath it was a small article, listing the names of the two sailors who lost their lives when it was rammed by a bull sperm whale. The name that stood out was Bronson, Tyler. Riker felt best not to ask any questions about it. He embraced the sunshine while he stood at the railing, looking down to the deck below. A few moments later, Metzler joined him and leaned forward on the metal railing. They both knew they were in for a long trip.

****

The time was a little after 8:30 a.m. as Nash drove to the lab. He was just down the road, a straight shot with no bends or anything obstructing his vision. Because of this, he was able to see a large white van pull out of the driveway as he approached. He and the van passed each other, and he was able to catch a glimpse of the logo, recognizing the sketch of a boat indicative of the business he purchased the propellers from. Pulling into the driveway, he saw Dr. Stafford loading supplies into the *Taurus* from the lab. The doctor stopped when he saw his assistant arrive, as if caught doing something he shouldn't have. He looked down at his watch.

"You're early," he said. *The one time I'm counting on you to be late as usual...* Nash slammed his door shut. He saw the additional barrels of fuel on the deck as well as a full cooler, monitoring equipment, and a long rod for attaching tracking devices.

"What are you doing?" Nash asked. Stafford didn't answer. Nash looked at all of the equipment again and also took notice of Stafford's rain and fishing overalls. "Oh, you've got to be kidding me! You're not seriously..."

"I don't trust those psychos out there!" Stafford said, pointing his finger at Nash as if it somehow made his point. "You know the tactics they use. Explosives! They can do all sorts of damage to the ecosystem, and I'm not sure Riker will be able to stop them."

"I suppose there's no point in telling you that you're breaking the law by doing this," Nash said. He took a deep breath, followed by a heavy sigh. In his mind he was not surprised that Stafford was doing this, rather he was surprised he doubted he would actually attempt it. It was the very thing that brought him to admire the marine biologist, and there was no way he was going to let him go alone. "Alright then. How are we going to do this?" he asked and started walking toward the boat.

"What?"

"How are we going to kill the Thresher?" Nash clarified. Stafford nearly dropped the bucket he was carrying. He set it down hard and held his hand out, signaling to stop.

"Oh no! There's no 'we,' Robert!" he insisted. Nash didn't let that stop him from gathering supplies to load onto the *Taurus.*

"Look Doc, I know there's no use in trying to talk you out of doing this. But it'll be a cold day in Hell before I let you go out there alone against this thing." He picked up a full bucket, which Stafford snatched and dropped to the ground, popping a side of the lid off.

"As your boss, I'm telling you you're not going," he said. He rarely pulled rank, and when he did, it meant he was serious. Nash didn't budge.

"Firstly, you haven't paid me a dime in weeks. So the boss card isn't gonna work this time," Nash responded. "And listen; you'll need someone to watch the fish finder. Someone has to chum—which is what

I'm assuming is in that." He pointed at the bucket, as a glob of fish blood ran down the side from the opening.

"Listen Robert, I appreciate it," Stafford said, "but I can't put you at risk out there. This is my choice."

"And this is mine," Nash said. "If you go out there alone, I'll inform the police and just hope they bring your ass in before that thing gets a hold of you. You might fire me as a result, but heck! I'm practically unemployed right now anyway." Stafford realized he had just lost the argument. There was no question Nash would make good on his promise. Instead of getting angry, Stafford felt a strong sense of gratitude. He smiled and waved his hand at the bucket, motioning for Nash to pick it back up. The assistant did so, grinning victoriously. "So, how are we going to kill it? Got any air tanks to blow it up with?"

"Actually, that wouldn't have worked in real life," Stafford laughed. "No, we're going to use our grouper." Nash stopped midway to the boat. He almost looked green.

"I thought you got rid of that thing," he said. "That thing's gonna stink up the whole deck!"

"I've spent my remaining credit card balance on ice bags," Stafford said. "It seemed to slow the decomposition rate down. When we're on board, I'm going to load up the fish with anabasine, a toxic pesticide. We'll use the chum line to attract the shark and when it's near, we're gonna lower the grouper into the water. I'm going to have a cable attached to it to send an electric charge through its body, which will give muscular reactions. The Thresher will think it's alive, and whether out of hunger or simply its violent aggression, it'll attack the grouper. It'll swallow it, and subsequently the poison which should take effect rather quickly." Nash pondered the plan.

"That...actually might work," he said. "Once the shark attacks the fish, we better lose the cable and haul ass because it'll still have enough time to take a crack at us... so to speak." He remembered he was talking about a thresher shark and chuckled nervously.

Within the next fifteen minutes they had the gear stowed away on the *Taurus*. Afterwards, they spent several minutes loading the grouper onto the deck. Stafford had spent some time stitching up the autopsy incisions in order to keep the innards from spilling out. Using the crane on the *Taurus*, they managed to lay it out on the deck and covered it with some blue tarps. After that, Stafford fired up the engine. Nash watched the water kick up as the newly installed propellers pushed them out to sea. His eyes looked down at the heavenly blue sheet of ocean that seemed to stretch out forever, knowing that somewhere that blissful sea was a devil worse than anything they had known.

There was certainly a feeling of anxiety in them both.

CHAPTER 21

From a high view, the ocean resembled a flat glistening blue mirror that seemed to stretch forever. On its shiny surface, a black speck appeared, followed by a thin red line that stretched for a long mile.

The hull of the *Sea Martyr* sliced effortlessly through the calm ocean surface, splashing up small jets of water as it journeyed east. The dry exhaust puffed out fumes of ghostly white-grey while the engine shuttered ripples of reverberation deep into the sea. On deck, Emi was busy chumming chunks of fish and blood over the transom, stretching a chum line behind the vessel. Standing in the crow's nest high above the structure was Bronson, who scanned the waters with his binoculars. On a clear day such as this, the dark skin of a Thresher shark would stand out easily in the clear blue water. Riker leaned on the portside coaming on deck near the structure, puffing on a cigar. He had finished eating half a turkey sandwich, which was all he could summon an appetite for. Metzler was sitting on a chair near the structure, looking over some papers on a clipboard. It had been several hours since they had cast off, and the trip had been mostly uneventful. For a while after leaving, Bronson told stories of sharks he had killed, which consisted of adventures all over the world's oceans. He explained his first shark kill, at age fifteen, when he shot a tiger shark with a Browning Auto 5 shotgun while fishing off the Grand Banks. His first contractual job was for the owner of a private coastal resort in Nova Scotia, who lost a customer supposedly to a shortfin Mako attack. He spoke of shooting at least two sharks up there with his bolt action Remington rifle, which was secured on a rack in the wheelhouse beneath the trophy squid beak.

The door on the deck level structure opened and William stepped outside, wiping bits of mustard from his chin. Emi turned toward him and pinched her finger and thumb into her mouth and blew a loud whistle. It meant it was time for him to take over chumming. As it was his most hated assignment, he blew a frustrated sigh.

"Knock it off and get to it," Bronson called down from his post. Emi moved away from the stern to the washdown hose. William took her place and dug the scoop into the red goo inside the large bucket. As he chucked it into the water, he looked maliciously toward Riker and Metzler, who were both biding time.

"So, when are they going to take a turn?" William called out. Riker glared at him with fierce eyes.

"Well, when I'm making five-hundred grand for a single job, I'll be happy to take over," he replied. It was the nicest thing he could conjure.

"What he really means is you'll get an ass kicking if you don't shut up and get to work," Bronson said. Riker felt as if his thoughts were read. Planting his cigar in his mouth, he went to the ladder to climb up to the wheelhouse deck. He walked past Metzler and caught a glimpse of her documents. On the top header read *St. Peter's Hospital*-- the same one he tracked her to the day prior. It was a billing sheet, which she spent a while filling out. He decided not to interrupt her and proceeded up to the structure. Once up there, he leaned on the handrail and tried to enjoy the view. A few moments after he climbed up, Emi climbed up the ladder and quietly went into the wheelhouse. As the door shut, Bronson climbed down and joined Riker on the upper level deck.

"If that shark of yours is out here, it's probably run deep," he said.

"It's not mine," Riker said. He glanced back to make sure the door was shut behind him. "Tell me, what's the story with the T-1000?"

"Oh, Emi," Bronson said. "She's mute, as a result of a shark attack when she was a teen. A tooth went right into her vocal cords."

"How in the hell did she survive that?"

"She's a fighter," Bronson said with a proud laugh. "She's a descendant of Fujiwara imperial clan. Samurai blood runs through her veins."

"How'd she end up with you?" Riker asked. He knew it wasn't simply a casual relationship between the two.

"You could say she was looking for a fresh start," Bronson said. "I don't suppose you're concerned about laws in a foreign country."

"No more than you guys seem to be," he said. His mind had been on the subject of laws and these individuals he was floating with. Bronson was in slight disbelief about the shark, so Riker was certain he wasn't fully aware of its vicious capabilities. He figured in Bronson's mind, this was just a fish. With that in mind, five hundred thousand dollars seemed awfully much to simply kill a fish. In Riker's experience, those who demand such high fees either are simply planning to enjoy a nice retirement, or owe some debts to someone. He didn't know which, and didn't try to think on it too much.

"So where is this big bad Thresher?!" William called, interrupting Riker's thoughts. The younger fisherman clearly didn't have a great deal of experience like his father, and suffered from impatience and a generally bad attitude. Riker could also see that William was quick to get antagonistic and also determined that he was the type to get into fights. The side of the twenty-five-year-old fisherman's face contained several tiny red and grayish marks. Riker believed these to be little scars possibly from having a glass bottle broken over his head. During his years as a cop, he had seen several of these injuries inflicted, sometimes leaving similar marks. Riker felt uneasy with this individual. Aggressive, stupid, and self-centered; not a good combination.

"In the water," Riker remarked sarcastically. William burst an exaggerated laugh before flipping the middle finger. This time, Bronson wasn't cutting in. He leaned back against the wheelhouse, almost as if he wanted to see what was going to take place. *You're about to have a new piece of bait here in a moment,* Riker threatened in his mind.

"Hey Dad! I'm not sure this shark even exists!" William called. He spoke in a manner clearly designed to get under Riker's skin. "I thought this thing was insanely aggressive and attacked everything in the sea. I don't see any super big shark attacking us. I'm starting to wonder if these cops are full of shit!" Riker tilted his head to discretely look at Bronson within his peripheral vision. The captain was smiling, as if he was enjoying the banter—a strange contrast to his behavior prior. This left Riker unsure of how he would respond if he cursed out William, and he felt it would be best to take the abuse. His eyes went to Metzler, who shot out of her chair.

"Why don't you go for a swim and find out, you little fish turd!" she barked. Even Riker swallowed hard at the unexpected aggression she revealed. *She really has been training with me,* he thought. William was surprised as well, looking at her with great big eyes and his mouth gaped, unsure of what to say. He was expecting a reaction from Riker, not from her. A laugh from Bronson somewhat eased Riker's nerves, showing the exchange was amusing him more than anything. Riker could tell there was clearly another side behind that charming smile and blue eyes. The type of company he kept was indicative of that, even if one was his offspring. He stood away from the wall and went into the wheelhouse. Riker puffed on his cigar another couple of times and decided to go back down to the main deck. William had gone back to chumming and Metzler stood at the starboard side and leaned on the coaming. She was clearly disgruntled, and he didn't think it was simply because of William's cocky attitude.

"Need a smoke?" he inquired half-jokingly.

"If you don't mind," she answered. He dug into his back pocket and pulled out his cigarette pack and lighter. A puff of smoke erupted from her cigarette as she lit one up, and she resumed resting against the upper exterior of the deck. She looked out to the far reaches of the horizon, where the ocean seemed to stretch on forever.

"That isn't casual smoking, that's stress smoking," Riker said. She rolled her eyes and took another draw of it. The hot sun added to the tension within her. She clenched the cigarette in her teeth and removed her buttoned shirt from over her black tank top. Riker couldn't help but notice the muscular tone in her arms. She had been going to the gym heavily during the past several days as a way of relieving herself from the stress at work. He looked up to the wheelhouse after hearing the door open up. Bronson stepped out, holding several cans of beer in his arms.

"Now it's a real fishing trip!" he said. He tossed one to William who opened it as soon as he caught it, spraying suds all over his face. "How 'bout you, Officer?" Bronson said to Riker, tossing down a can before he could even answer. Riker unflinchingly snatched it out of midair. Bronson looked to Metzler, about to toss one her way.

"Oh, no thanks, I…" she couldn't finish as he tossed it anyway. She flinched and barely caught it, accidentally dropping her cigarette over the side. "Damn!" she muttered. Riker handed her another and she lit it up, putting her beer down to the deck. He looked at his. It was some sort of German beer he didn't recognize, but his mind didn't care. The intense urge to fulfill his alcoholic needs began screaming at first sight of it. It was almost an unconscious, automatic action to pry the lid open. He held it to his lips, stopped only by the vicious glare from Metzler. "What are you doing?"

"What?" he said. "Smoking is alright, but drinking is taboo?" He felt like he was arguing with a lecturing girlfriend.

"We're on the job!" she exclaimed.

"We're not driving a patrol car," he said. "We're babysitting these guys." She stared at him judgingly, but also somewhat sympathetically.

"You've managed to keep it out of work, as least as far as I've seen," she said. "You're telling me you're really at rock bottom that you'll drink while on duty?" He shrugged and took a drink, signaling his concurrence. She looked down at his left hand. He still wore his wedding ring. She reminded herself of the pain he was trying to hide from with the alcohol. "Remember, there are good memories. I know it's hard, but try to embrace them rather than run away from the regrets."

"Here we go again," Riker said. "You know, you ought to be a counselor or therapist or something. You're in the wrong career."

"I AM in the wrong career!" she snapped. Immediately she put her hand over her mouth, surprised at her own reaction. William looked up from chumming, muttering "damn" before resuming his duties. She drew on the cigarette and looked to the relaxing blue sea. Riker put the beer down, but not before taking a quick sip to try and satisfy his urges. "Sorry," she said.

"You don't need to be sorry," Riker said. It was probably the gentlest thing she heard him say. He glanced back at the stack of bills still on her clipboard. Whatever they were for, it was major. He assumed it wasn't for her, as each new officer undergoes a physical before being offered employment. "Is the insurance not good enough?"

"What?" Metzler asked. Riker motioned at the bills. She sighed and resumed looking at the sea.

"They're regarding my sister," she said. *She's the one in the hospital,* Riker thought. "I wasn't aiming to be a cop," she continued explaining. "I was hoping to work with police to be a counseling therapist. That's what I have my Master's Degree in, and I studied Criminal Science before that so I could fit into the criminal justice field. However, I still need my doctorate, which is expensive. But my sister got chronic leukemia. Our family had spent what money they had to put us through school, so they couldn't pay for treatment. The doctors believe they have a treatment plan, but it costs a lot of money, obviously. That's why I put everything aside and got this job, with my uncle's help of course." She drew on her cigarette, nearly burning it down to the base. "I figured it'd still be good for my résumé down the road, since I wanted to work with police. But with everything that's going on, it looks like I'll be paying this debt off forever." Riker didn't say anything as he took it all in. He had thought his partner to be some hotshot rookie who thought she knew it all. As it turns out, she was going through her own misery.

"WE GOT A FIN!" William called out, pointing port side aft. Riker and Metzler broke from their thoughts and turned to look. Bronson shot out of the wheelhouse with binoculars already lifted to his eyes. "It's a big fin," William said with excitement. "I think that's our fish!" The officers went over to the other side of the boat for a better look. They could see the big fin several yards out. It didn't seem to be following the chum line, which they thought was odd. The big fish seemed to glide in the water nearby, appearing uninterested in the chum and the boat.

"I don't think this is it," Riker said. He squinted as he looked harder. The color of the fin appeared more blue than black. "Captain, I'm not so sure that's our shark!"

"It's not," Bronson said, lowering the glasses. "It's a whale shark." He disappeared into the wheelhouse. For Metzler, the brief moment of tension and anxiety turned into wonder. She had never seen a live whale shark before, except on television. She climbed up the ladder to the second level deck for a better view. Inside the wheelhouse, Emi steered the *Sea Martyr* to port. The boat got closer to the large bluish-grey fish and lined up parallel with it, giving everyone on board a better view. Metzler smiled when she saw its wide flat head, which was only a foot or so beneath the clear surface. Its mouth was partially open to allow water to filter through its gills. Its jaws looked like they were layered with white sandpaper. Metzler knew those specks in its mouth were tiny teeth the size of a raisin. She recalled reading that despite the fact that the whale shark was the largest fish in the ocean, it was a filter feeder. It was an angelic sight watching the huge gentle fish gently sway with each turn of its tail, keeping pace with the boat. Even Riker felt a sense of fascination. For both of them, there was a sense of relief that came from watching the great fish.

A slam of the cabin door drew their attention away from the shark. Bronson marched out, holding a brown Greener MK II harpoon rifle by the handle. He kept the weapon pointed safely toward the sky as he positioned himself at the handrails. It was already put together, with the harpoon clenched in Bronson's other hand. Riker quickly took notice of a black square item strapped to the twelve-inch barbed harpoon. His eyes then went to a black radio remote clipped to the captain's belt, which wasn't there before. Bronson loaded the harpoon onto the barrel of the gun.

"Whoa, whoa!" Riker called out. "What the hell are you doing?"

"What is that?" Metzler asked, pointing to the harpoon gun. Bronson held up the weapon by the barrel.

"This is a demonstration of how we'll kill the shark if it's out there," he said. "We'll stick it with a miniature harpoon, which will be strapped with an explosive charge." He pointed at the black object strapped to the metal barb. "We need to be a somewhat close distance because it weighs down the harpoon. But once it's in, we can explode the bastard."

"If we have to be close to the shark to hit it, wouldn't we also be close to the explosion?" Metzler asked.

"It doesn't explode on impact. After we stick it, we make some distance, after which I detonate the charge with this." He pointed to the radio remote on his belt. "With a press of the red button here," he moved his thumb over it, "the shark will officially be soup." Suddenly a large smile creased his face. "Allow me to demonstrate!" As soon as he spoke he reached for the explosive charge and turned a tiny knob, tuning it to the frequency of the radio control. He turned toward the shark, with the rifle raised to his shoulder. He took a brief moment to adjust his aim, and before Metzler could protest, he fired off a shot. There was a shutter of recoil from the rifle, along with a loud *whoosh* noise as the harpoon launched. It punched its barb into the side of the shark near the fin. The fish barely felt it pierce its thick skin. Sensing the presence of the large boat nearby, it decided to move away. The whale shark made a large splash with its tail as it suddenly veered to its left and began swimming off.

"Good God, what's wrong with you?!" Metzler roared. She saw Bronson about to reach for the remote on his belt. Furious, she lunged forward and snatched it off before he could grab it.

"Hey!" he yelled as she chucked it toward the stern. William grabbed for it, missing it by inches as it went past him. It hit the transom, and William quickly went for it again. Before he could reach it, it fell over the side and hit the water. William flung himself over the top of the transom, nearly upside down as he quickly reached for the device. With his thighs on the panel, he managed to grip the tip of the antenna with his fingers just before it sank out of reach. He remained suspended upside down over the stern, without a good grip to pull himself up. Bronson rushed over to him and pulled him back onto the deck, snatching the wet device from his hand. He shook the water out and pressed down on the red button, now out of concern for testing the device function. Nothing occurred. He knew they were still in range of the shark, meaning the water fried the circuits. His face tensed with anger and he looked up to Metzler.

"You little runt!" he snarled. "This equipment is not cheap, and not easy to come by!"

"There's no need to kill that shark!" she called back and climbed down the ladder. "Whale sharks eat plankton! They're not even dangerous!"

"Is your name Mrs. Stafford, by any chance?" he remarked. "Their fins sell for quite the price on the market."

"You're already making five-hundred grand," Riker cut in. Bronson gave him a dreadful look, and for a moment there appeared to be a brief standoff. Finally, Bronson looked again at the device and started walking back to the wheelhouse.

"Obviously these things are not water friendly," he said, now in a more relaxed voice. "Luckily for you," he looked at Metzler, "I have a spare. Don't be chucking that one anywhere." He brushed past her and climbed up to the wheelhouse.

"Hey Dad!" William called after him. "Do you think it ended up in the net?"

"It's a possibility," Bronson said. "That's where we're gonna go."

"Net? What net?" Riker asked. Bronson didn't answer and slammed the door behind him. William disappeared below deck, leaving Riker and Metzler alone in silence.

"I see he likes you," he said to her. He dug in his pocket for another cigar. Metzler was quiet for a moment, and then finally cracked a smile at the small joke. He went over and leaned against the portside and continued to stare at the peaceful sight of the ocean. Metzler joined beside him and did the same.

****

Water splashed against the *Taurus'* chipped white hull as it slowly coasted forward. Stafford was up in the cockpit, with his eyes on his newly restored multifunction fish finder. The screen was split into two functions; on the right was sonar scanning around the boat, and on the left was a display of the fish finder readings beneath the vessel. He watched the sonar display on the monitor, anxiously waiting for the sight of a large object in their proximity. The back door was open, allowing him to clearly see the deck whenever he looked back.

Nash was busy laying a chum trail, while struggling to listen to a Japanese animation program on his iPhone. He would grumble every few minutes due to the faulty signal. It had been several quiet hours since they had departed the lab, and his phone was the only thing keeping his mind entertained at this point. Half the deck was taken up by the mass of the huge grouper they intended to use for bait. Even though it had been iced down and covered with tarps, the smell still permeated the air. Nash was happy the Dramamine was working perfectly, because the smell would've certainly put him over the edge. He leaned on the transom to take a quick break and looked out to stern at the long trail of chum behind them, which seemed to stretch out as far as the ocean's reaches. He began to wonder where the Thresher might be and whether the Trio may have encountered it. Suddenly the background noise from his phone stopped again. He looked down at his phone, seeing the digital loading circle animation spinning on the screen.

"Holy mother of ass!" he cursed. Stafford stepped out of the cockpit, looking down at his assistant as he picked up the phone and tapped on the screen.

"Everything good?"

"Yeah, I just have no friggin signal!" Nash said. He gave up and put his phone back in his pocket. "You'd think we'd have found the thing by now? I wonder if it left the area. Or maybe the Trio already encountered it."

"As long as it's the only thing they've killed," Stafford said. He looked out to the vast open sea. For him, it was the most beautiful sight ever to exist, and it saddened him to know that hidden beneath that beauty was a vicious killer. "I think it's still here, probably undergoing a period of rest. It's spent quite a bit of energy lately." Nash tossed out a few more scoops of chum before going to the cooler. His foot bumped part of the grouper's fin, which protruded from the tarp.

"Agh!" He bounced on his feet, nearly tripping. He grabbed a bottle of water and looked down at the huge piece of bait. Stafford had already loaded it up with the poison, and the crane cable was already attached to its tail. "So, what's gonna happen if we do manage to kill this shark? Maybe we could take its jaws and put them on our wall." He laughed at his own joke. Stafford cracked a smile.

"Sorry, we're not poachers," he said. "I'd like to get it to the lab for an autopsy."

"We could chop him up. Think of all the food we'd have saved up for Steve the hammerhead. We'd save a lot of money there," Nash said.

"No, I don't have a tank big enough for a forty-foot finless shark," Stafford said.

"You think there'd be enough Bio-Nutriunt product in his system for that to happen?"

"Absolutely," Stafford said. "Especially with the number of tumors the Thresher probably has riddled throughout its body. That thing's probably a cesspool of growth hormone." Nash scratched his head in confusion.

"Wait, tumors? In a shark? I thought they're immune from cancer," he pointed out. Stafford chuckled.

"That's a myth," he said. "Sharks do have a much stronger resistance to cancer and tumors, but they are not immune. Around Australia, off the coast of the Neptune Islands, there was a great white found with a twelve-inch tumor in its mouth. And that was a natural tumor. God only knows what other effects Bio-Nutriunt has had on the Thresher's system." Nash was surprised with the new information he had learned. In his mind, he figured Hollywood was probably responsible for pushing the myth regarding shark's immunity to cancer. Another thought burst into his mind, triggering another question.

"Hey Doc, what if there's something else out there? If this shark got so big from eating the test subjects that were lost in the water, do you think there could be anything else out there that got a hold of this stuff?" Stafford analyzed the question in his mind. It was a haunting thought that the Thresher could possibly be just one out of numerous enormous creatures out there as a result of Bio-Nutriunt.

"I certainly hope not," he said. "We've seen what just one of these things can do. Can you imagine the ramifications of multiple sea creatures exposed to this growth hormone? All this--" He pointed out to the vast ocean around them, "this would become savage waters." Nash considered the possibility of such a foreboding threat, which quickly became stressful. He rid his mind of such thoughts and went back to chumming, while attempting to get his phone to work again. Stafford leaned against the wall in the cockpit, also disturbed by the thought of other creatures exposed to Bio-Nutriunt. He looked out the door at the blanket of water beneath them, knowing that beneath it were secrets he may never discover.

In the corner of his eye, he caught a glimpse of a new blip in the sonar screen. He brought himself back into reality and hurried to the monitor. There was something large in the water, approaching from the southeast.

"Nash!" he yelled. "I think our friend has arrived for dinner!" Nash dropped the scoop and went for one of the monitors linked to the underwater camera feed.

"Where's it coming from?" he asked.

"Out to starboard," Stafford called down. "Get the wire ready and prepare to lower our fish into the water." Nash checked the cable to make sure it was secured tight onto the grouper's tail. He also double-checked the electric wire that was inserted into its thick skin to give out an impulse. After he was finished, he went to the control circuit, ready to lift the fish off the deck at Stafford's command. Stafford waited anxiously for the creature to get closer. It appeared to be heading in a northern direction, and its path paralleled theirs by a few hundred yards. As it continued moving, it slightly changed its direction to northeast.

"Wait. What the hell? It's moving away from us," he said. Nash took his hand off the lever.

"Huh? Could it be something else?" he asked.

"I don't know," Stafford said. "I suppose it's a good possibility. But the Thresher's been attacking everything in the area. I don't know if..." the sight of a white object in the distance caught his eye. He grabbed a set of binoculars and ran out on the second-level deck, lifting them up to his eyes. He focused his enhanced vision on the object. White sails lifted around a tall mast overtop a twenty-foot sailing boat. He went back into the cockpit and looked at the large object in the monitor. Its path had aligned right with the sailboat. "Oh shit! Nash hang on!"

"What's happening?" He grabbed the hand rail to keep himself from falling over as the *Taurus* launched forward. He looked around the superstructure and could see the sailboat in the distance, realizing the urgency. "Oh crap!"

****

As he stared out to the water, Riker could feel the tension in his body, and his eyes frequently went to the can of beer still on the deck. Metzler stood between him and it, pretending not to notice the struggle going on beside her. Unfortunately, it was becoming obvious. He had begun to break a sweat, and the hot sun beating down on them wasn't helping. The cool breeze coming off of the water wasn't easing the struggle.

"It's why he wanted you here," she said, keeping her voice barely above a whisper. William was back to chumming on deck, and she didn't want him overhearing. "And it's why he brought those out." She tilted her head toward the beer. Riker nodded. He was well aware Bronson was trying to manipulate him. The worst part was he didn't care. The only reason he wasn't drinking the beer was because of Metzler's interference. She understood this as well. "If I may say so, are you aware of why you are so greatly admired within the police community?"

"They like hearing about gunfights," he remarked.

"They saw you as someone who did the right thing, even when all odds were against you," she said.

"That kind of person is a storybook fantasy," he grumbled. "That guy doesn't exist anymore. Doing the 'right thing'," he held up air quotes, "didn't fare well for me. And it's pointless."

"I don't think so," Metzler said. "I think deep down you're still that guy. And it's definitely not pointless." Riker wanted to make a snide remark such as *keep dreaming,* but managed to keep it to himself. The sight of William standing up and pointing was a timely distraction.

"There's the buoy!" he called up to the wheelhouse. The buoy looked like a black bowling ball bobbing on the surface. The top of the net could be seen forming a long squiggly line in the water's surface which seemed to stretch for a mile. There was no response from the wheelhouse so William called again. "Hey, DAD! We've found the buoy!" Still no response. "You're gonna go past it!" Fed up with listening to William yell, Riker marched to the ladder and climbed to the wheelhouse. When he opened the door, Emi was standing at the helm while Bronson was pacing around the room with a satellite phone pressed to his ear. Instantly upon entering, Riker saw the sour expression in the captain's face.

"Tendré el dinero para ti pronto!" he spoke into the phone. Riker recognized the Spanish language. He didn't speak the language, but recognized certain words in the sentence such as dinero and pronto (money and soon). Bronson saw Riker in the doorway. "Hablaremos otra vez cuando el trabajo esté hecho. Adiós." He pressed a button to end the call and tossed the phone on the console. He could hear William calling again from the deck. "Apparently, it's too much effort for him to just come up here," Bronson remarked and walked out of the door. Emi steered the *Sea Martyr* near the buoy. William was already reaching for it with a pole, hooking the tip under a column of net. Joined by Bronson, he lifted it up onto deck and attached it to a winch. With a flip of a switch, the winch started slowly reeling the net in.

Standing on the second level, Riker saw the net emerging from the water. To his shock, he saw that the net was covered with hooks and spikes which were secured to the line with wire. As the net was reeled in, Bronson and William removed the spikes carefully, placing the sharp objects into a couple of large bins. Several tuna and other fish started rising up with the net. Some were tangled within the line; others had been pierced by the hooks or spikes. Most were already dead when brought up on deck, while others flopped weakly. As more of the net started coming in, so did more species. Hammerhead and blue sharks were hooked on the net, with pieces of bait still clenched in their jaws. Most of them were already dead.

"Alright!" Bronson exclaimed. He removed his bowie knife and with clean strokes of his blade, he sliced off the fins of the sharks before throwing the bodies overboard. Metzler looked away in disgust when an eight-foot hammerhead rose with the net, still alive and struggling to free itself. Hooks had pierced its gill line and abdomen. William stopped the winch, allowing Bronson to slice off the shark's fins. Once they were removed, the shark resembled a large grey tadpole. Bronson pried the hooks from it and the finless shark splashed down into the water. William gave a sadistic grin as he watched the shark wiggle like a worm as it attempted to swim, before sinking into the dark bottom of the sea to drown. Even Riker was disgusted by the act. They continued reeling in the net. More fish hit the deck, the live ones flopping about on their sides.

"Hey look! We've found our shark!" William yelled with excitement. Metzler turned around to look. Caught on the hook was a baby thresher shark, about three feet in body length. It was still alive, and its tail whipped in the air as it struggled to free itself from the net.

Bronson grabbed the caudal fin to prevent it from accidentally striking him. He looked at Metzler.

"Is this the shark that attacked you?" he said with a laugh. He proceeded to slice off the creature's fins, including the long tailfin before dropping the shark to meet the same fate as the hammerhead.

"You do realize what you're doing is illegal here?" Metzler said to him. "This is why we're on this boat. You can't be doing this kind of thing. You're killing species that are protected..."

"Oh, don't give me that crap," Bronson interrupted her.

"When did you put this net out?" Riker asked from the structure.

"Last night, after we secured the deal," Bronson said. "You may not like it, but we've been hired to catch a big shark. And I will use any means necessary to get him if he's out there. You told me yourself you didn't care how." William activated the winch again, and they continued removing the hooks and spikes. Metzler turned away again as she watched a dead dolphin come up with the net. Its jaw was slack, giving it a horrified expression that came with its drowning. "Well that's unfortunate," Bronson said.

"I'm reporting this," Metzler said. Bronson dropped the dolphin into the water and looked her way. While Metzler was looking away, she knew his eyes were burning holes in the back of her head. "Yeah, you heard me." Bronson didn't venture a response. Her threats meant nothing to him, and he was well aware that his client—the government—would have no interest in the matter as long as the shark was dead.

"Whoa!" William said. Bronson's eyes went back to the net. There was a large rip in it, and several of the hooks were bent. A tiny piece of flesh dangled from one of them. It didn't appear very old.

"We had something big in here, and it broke free not long ago," he said. He looked around at the surrounding sea. "Hell, it might even still be nearby." He examined the gash in the net. "It was pretty damn big. We loaded this net with bits of the basking shark we caught yesterday. Maybe your fish tried to get a snack."

"Maybe," Riker said. He started to understand Dr. Stafford's reaction to this group being hired. In addition, he started to believe Bronson would undergo more ruthless efforts to catch the shark and retrieve his bounty. He was certainly eager to catch the fish, but not out of an ambition to catch the best prey but for the pay. Riker thought to the phone conversation he walked in on. It appeared Bronson owed money to someone, and Riker couldn't help but assume that it wasn't anyone good. This mission was his way out of whatever hole he was dug into.

****

Stafford's heart raced as he throttled the *Taurus* at top speed toward the twenty-foot sailboat. He blew the horn, trying to get the operator's attention. On deck, Nash was looking over the side, cupping his hands over his mouth as he yelled at the sailor. His voice could barely be heard over the boat's engine. Stafford looked to the blip on the monitor. It appeared to be right beside the sailboat. Looking back to the white vessel which read *Great Mason* on the bow, there didn't appear to be any disturbance. He eased down the speed as they neared. The operator could be seen standing at the port. He was a man of thirty, dressed in red shorts and a blue shirt. Stafford could see that he was looking down at something in the water.

He brought the *Taurus* to a stop about twenty-five feet away from the *Great Mason,* which it towered over. He got out and looked down at the water between them. A gray whale had surfaced right beside the sailboat, and the person on board was reaching down to touch it. The huge mammal rested on the surface, its head covered in gray and brown barnacles, admiring the humans that it visited. A flood of relief swept over Stafford and Nash, and both of them fell into a fit of laughter. The sailor aboard the *Great Mason* waved to them. He wore a big smile on his face, fascinated by the whale that had swum up to be admired.

"You see this?" he called over, laughing with joy. He stroked the whale's enormous head. Looking down from the superstructure, Stafford could see its fluke gently flopping in the surface, estimating the creature to be roughly forty-five feet in length. He hurried down the ladder and joined Nash at the port side. The whale's other eye seemed to look right at him. As the sailor stroked its eyebrow like a pet dog, it turned slightly and brought its broad flipper up over the water. Stafford felt as if the whale was waving to him, and for fun he waved back. Nash did the same. He could see the instant love in Stafford's eyes for the creature.

"Well, hello there, sir," Stafford said to the whale. All at once, it seemed like all the problems in the world had gone away. He was lost in this fascination; a perfect peace that he wished would last for an eternity. It was moments like this that reminded him why he became a marine biologist. His love for the ocean and all of its creatures couldn't be more apparent than when meeting face to face with them. The enormous forty-four ton mammal sprayed some mist from its two blowholes, and splashed its flipper into the water. As it did this, Stafford noticed something odd. Along its hide were several small lacerations. They appeared like knife cuts, and they were fresh as a couple were still bleeding. They were small, but too long to be considered bite marks. "What the hell?" he said. Nash could see the wounds as well.

In the blink of an eye, the whale broke from its calm state, going into an abrupt panic. It slapped its fluke into the water, kicking up a large splash as it dunked its head beneath the surface. Large swells rocked both vessels, nearly knocking the *Great Mason*'s owner onto his back. Stafford managed to watch the whale as it shot away underwater, passing beneath the sailboat as it disappeared into the distance.

"What the hell was that?" Nash asked, grabbing the hand rail on the edge to keep himself standing. Stafford shook his head, as he was shocked by the whale's sudden departure.

"I don't know," he said. "It was like it was running away from something…" As soon as he spoke, a thought flashed in his mind. He quickly pushed past Nash and rushed to the monitor for the underwater cameras. A button on the side of the monitor changed the camera feed. The first feed was from the port side, which displayed nothing but ocean. He switched the feed to a camera under the stern, seeing the same thing. He clicked the button again to check a feed from the starboard camera. The screen image flipped as the feeds changed, just in time for Stafford to see the open mouth, lined with rows of dagger-like teeth, speeding directly into the camera like a missile.

CHAPTER 22

For the past several hours, the Thresher had cruised deep in a sleep-like state. Its brain maintained control over its basic needs, such as moving its tail side to side to keep itself going forward. Each gentle stroke of its tail still generated several hundred pounds of force, which was minimally needed to keep the enormous fish from sinking. After several hours of pacing under the sea in this restful state, it was 'awoken' by multiple triggering of its senses. First, its nostrils picked up the enticing smell of blood in the water, leading it to follow the trail. As it did so, its Ampullae of Lorenzini detected the muscular movements of a large animal in the water nearby. Its aggressive territorial instincts instantly were triggered, prompting the enormous Thresher to track down the source. Its brain didn't have the capability to identify it as a gray whale; it just knew it was something that must be destroyed. The blood in the water, as well as the slightly rapid heartbeat of the whale it tracked suggested it was injured.

It tracked the large prey down, only to find it had joined with two other large objects on the surface. The vibrations coming from the engines were interpreted as heartbeats and muscular contractions. The whale had departed once it detected the shark's presence. The mindless killer made a split-second decision between the choices of pursuing the whale or attacking the vessels afloat. The larger vessel was larger than the shark's body size, but it made no difference to the shark's killing instinct. With a huge stroke of its tail, it propelled itself upward with jaws wide open toward the large floating target.

****

Stafford didn't have the chance to react to the image on the monitor when a massive tremor shook the *Taurus*. A loud bang originated from the keel along the starboard side. The Thresher rammed the starboard side bow and continued to press forward. Both men on board hit the deck while the vessel began to spin like a top on the water. As it spun, the stern missed the *Great Mason* only by mere inches. Alarmed by the chaotic event that was suddenly taking place in front of him, the man on board broke into a panic. The *Taurus* tilted slightly to port, and he could see the huge Thresher's head and dorsal fin as it pushed the larger vessel. It finally ceased the attack and dipped back under the waves. Seeing the huge black shark sent the *Great Mason*'s owner into a sudden panic, and he immediately started up the engine on his boat. It had barely started firing up when he began throttling the boat away.

The noise and motion alerted the Thresher that one of its targets was attempting escape. With teeth bared, it went for the vessel like a torpedo. It quickly closed the distance, and its killing instinct took control. It tucked its fins under its body and slightly arched its head upward.

On the deck of the *Taurus*, Stafford pulled himself onto his hands and knees when he saw the huge splash. Like an enormous black whip, the tail swung at a long slightly upward angle over the surface. Metal and fiberglass crunched as it slashed into the sailboat's side, hooking over the grabrail onto the hatch. The sailboat rolled violently to the side, barely keeping from capsizing. The impact indented the hull, creating a breach below the waterline. Saltwater instantly flooded the engine, which immediately began billowing large amounts of smoke. The Thresher circled the boat halfway and thrashed its tail once more, striking directly under the vessel, busting the keel. The propellers quit spinning and the boat stopped. The sailor's heart pounded in his chest and a warm sweat trickled down his face as he desperately tried to restart the engine. The sound of creaking metal reverberated through the boat as the added weight of water began pulling it downward. He dashed out of the companionway onto the deck.

His mind could barely comprehend what was happening. At one moment, he was just a man sailing to Georgia during a peaceful day and had stopped to see a beautiful whale. Now he was fighting for dear life. Stafford sprung to his feet and climbed up the ladder to the cockpit. The *Taurus* was now pointing away from the *Great Mason*. He throttled the engine and turned the wheel to turn the boat to port. On deck, Nash was calling to the sailor.

"Just hang on!" he yelled. "We're coming to get you! Just remain…" Another huge eruption of water nearly knocked him back down in shock. The Thresher breached, and as it was nearly out of the water, it shot its tail at the sinking *Great Mason* a third time. It was as if a bomb had been dropped on the vessel. The mast was shattered in half, toppling the sail into the water. The boom collapsed, the backstay line shot like a spring from its secure post, the hatch caved in, and water began pouring over the transom. The impact launched the sailor off his feet, splashing him roughly three meters out into the water. For a moment, he was disoriented. He started to take a breath through his mouth, but stopped when he felt the seawater flood in, accidentally swallowing some. He got control of his bearings and swam up to the surface, emerging with his hands raised in the air. He was facing the approaching vessel and could see Nash looking over the side toward him. He waved at Nash but stopped, realizing that he didn't appear to be looking right at him, rather past him. He saw the sheer terror in Nash's eyes, and against his better judgment, he turned around.

The massive black shark was just over twenty feet away, moving at him like a horrific submarine. The big black eyes were expressionless; however, he could still feel they were focused on him. As soon as he saw the Thresher, he witnessed it dip its head slightly beneath the water as it arched its back. An instant later, it was as if he was hit by a bolt of lightning. The Thresher struck him in the abdomen. The stunning force left him instantly paralyzed and with a large laceration in his belly. Although he was still awake, he had a numb feeling throughout his body, and was unaware that his intestines had begun spilling from his abdomen. The shark dipped under and came up from underneath, closing its jaws around him, much to the horror to those on the *Taurus.*

"Oh Jesus!" Nash cried out. He saw the huge teeth rip into the man's midsection, just above the laceration. His head and shoulders were still outside the huge jaws. As if to further punish its prey, the shark violently thrashed its head from side to side like a dog with a chew toy. Water splashed and turned dark red all around it as it ravaged the sailor. Stafford watched the horrific sight as well, feeling paralyzed with fear. It was as if the shark had gone mad. Finally, it swallowed the sailor and dipped beneath the surface. Stafford took several rapid breaths and regained his composure. He ran outside and called down to Nash.

"Robert! Get to the crane! We can still kill this thing!" He expected Nash to respond with a plea to go back to port. To his surprise, his assistant went for the operational controls to the crane. Stafford looked at the water, unsure of where the Thresher had gone. His eyes went to the fish finder. The monitor displayed a large green image to starboard... only a few meters away! He barely saw the black image of the monster before its tail slashed upward. The cockpit's starboard wall smashed inward, knocking the doctor to the floor. The helm detached, cabinets spilled their contents, and the ceiling lights burst. The Thresher dipped again and began attacking from beneath. With another huge strike of its tail, it busted the keel and quickly bit at the sinking chunk of metal. After realizing it was not organic, it spat it out and redirected its mindless instincts to the *Taurus.*

"Doc! You all right?" Nash yelled after seeing the tail hit the structure. He had nearly fallen to his knees from the impact, but he managed to stay standing. Dr. Stafford crawled from the opening.

"I'm okay!" he answered. "Get the fish in the water and start the electric flow!" With a press of a lever, Nash started lifting the fish with the crane. The tail had barely started elevating off the deck as the boat shook from another hit from the stern. Stafford went back into the cockpit to assess the damage to the controls. With all his might, he pushed the collapsed wall outward, managing to wedge it into its frame enough to hold it up. The helm was busted from the wall falling on it. The throttle appeared to be intact and working fine. He attempted to reattach the wheel when he felt the boat shake again. A huge splash of water sprayed the deck as the fish hit the stern again. He turned around and saw the Thresher's head breach the water with a piece of the boat in its mouth. "Oh my God," he yelled, his voice full of terror and fascination. The Thresher's bullet shaped head was the size of his truck. As it was briefly suspended above the waterline, its huge left eye opened. It appeared to gaze at him as the shark crashed back down.

"Doc!" Nash yelled. "The rudder's busted! We won't be able to get out of here!" He yelled in terror and fell to the deck as the black tail lashed out the water, hooking onto the deck. A portion of handrails crunched and deck wood splintered as the tail thrashed the boat, missing Nash by only a few inches. After it hit, it whipped around as the shark retracted, viciously slicing its tail back into the water. As it did, it lashed the crane down by its supporting structure. The mechanical supports buckled under its weight, as well as the added weight of the grouper. Metal groaned as the huge arm collapsed. Nash sprung to his feet and ran to the stern, barely getting out of the way. It smashed the deck and the side of the superstructure.

Dr. Stafford looked to see that his assistant was okay. He saw Nash standing unharmed at the stern, and then looked upon the damage. The severity of the situation suddenly became real. There was no longer any hope in them killing the shark. It was clear it would not stop attacking the *Taurus* until it had 'killed' it. Stafford realized their only hope was the group he despised. He grabbed the radio remote speaker, and switched it to a broadband frequency, hoping the *Sea Martyr* would pick up the transmission.

"Mayday, mayday," he said. "This is Dr. Aaron Stafford on board the *Taurus*. We have encountered the Thresher and have sustained heavy damage. Officer Riker, if you can hear me, please acknowledge this transmission!"

****

Standing at the second level deck, Riker could hear the mayday call coming from inside the wheelhouse. The audio was loud enough to be heard from the main deck, drawing attention from the fishermen and Metzler. Riker pushed through the door and grabbed the speaker.

"Dr. Stafford? What's going on? Where are you?" he enquired, not wasting time with asking why he was out on the ocean against the chief's orders.

"*We're about along the tip of Rubio Reef,*" Stafford said through the radio. "*The Thresher came out of nowhere, and it's already killed somebody else. We've sustained heavy damage, and it won't seem to let up.*" Bronson had entered at the start of the transmission.

"I know where that is," he said. "It's close." He took control of the helm and turned the ignition switch. The engine thudded three times as it fired up, and Bronson throttled the vessel at top speed.

"Stay dry, Doc. We're coming to get you," Riker said. He hung the speaker up and went outside, grabbing Bronson's binoculars. On the deck, William had finished cutting the remaining net clear with his blade, which he placed back in the sheath on the back of his pants. Metzler joined Riker at the second level as he scanned the waters. He could see a white speck on the horizon. "That's them!" he said.

****

The waters seemed to calm down and a silence engulfed the *Taurus*. Stafford and Nash were not fooled. The dark shape of the Thresher was clearly visible under the surface roughly thirty yards out, appearing like a storm cloud. With its tail trailing its enormous body, it had an overall length of eighty feet. Its body formed a dark crescent shape as it circled the vessel. The way it moved, it appeared as if it was strategically planning its next attack. Dr. Stafford knew better. The shark was simply replenishing energy.

"There!" Nash pointed out to starboard. The black *Sea Martyr* looked like a black peppercorn in the distance. Its deep engine sound could be heard from the *Taurus*. Stafford never thought he'd be happy to see that ship. Nash felt the same. "Hurry up!" he implored the distant vessel. Up on the superstructure, Stafford looked back into the surrounding water. The dark shape had disappeared.

"Where'd it go?"

The huge beast had determined that the large object was inedible. But it had seen the life forms on board, which spurred its killing instinct to continue the attack. It circled the vessel for a few more laps, oxygenating its blood by allowing water to flow over its gills. Ready for another attack, it dove deep and hooked its body upward. Once in position, it shot vertically towards the boat's underside.

The fact that Stafford wasn't sure of the Thresher's location sparked an idea. He slid down the ladder in one clean motion and quickly lifted the hatch door, slipping down into the cargo hold. Equipment had been spilled all over the floor from the bombardment. Tool buckets rolled over the floor, spilling pliers and small knives used for cutting nets. A glass aquarium had smashed on the floor, layering clear amorphous shrapnel throughout the room. Stafford hurriedly moved away various equipment that formed a small pile until he found a GPS tracking tag. He grabbed it as well as a large pole. Before he could climb back on deck, the boat shook violently from a huge blow underneath. The earthquake motion caused Stafford to lose his balance, and he tripped over a big red diver propulsion device. He fumbled to his feet, keeping his items in hand and climbed up to the deck. As he emerged, the Thresher's tail thrashed on the port side, slashing the hull. It had not breached, but a large crease had formed, weakening the structure. Stafford applied the tracking device onto the twelve-foot pole.

"What do you think you're gonna do?" Nash yelled at him. "Are you insane?"

"We need to be able to track this bastard!" Stafford said back. He placed the pole down and ran to stern, hopping over bits of metal from the collapsed crane. After grabbing the sealed bucket of chum, he rushed back to the midsection. He removed the lid and tilted the bucket over the side, spilling gallons of fish guts into the water.

The scent hit the Thresher's nostrils instantly. It was already swimming upward to ram the vessel again. It slightly altered its course, shooting into the bloodstream like a rocket. Its huge eyes saw through the red cloud, over the surface, where the prey was hunched over the side of the inedible object. With a sweep of its tail, it shot upward like a rocket. Its jaws hyperextended as it launched through the bloody surface. A seizure of sudden fright electrified Stafford.

"Mary mother of CHRIST!" he yelled as he fell back. The Thresher's jaws just missed him, and its neck came down on the coaming, busting right through the handrail. Its tail whipped, slicing air in a wild motion. The jaws snapped for anything they could grab, catching nothing but air until it clamped down on the fallen crane. Stafford looked to his right and grabbed the pole that lay next to him. He remained on his back and rammed the barb into the 'armpit' of the shark's left pectoral fin. The device took hold. The Thresher didn't feel the prick, continuing to clench on the arm of the crane. Stafford scurried away from the huge beast, while Nash hugged the port side railing. Looking past the shark, he suddenly began waving his arms at the approaching *Sea Martyr.*

"Good God!" Metzler exclaimed in horror, seeing the shark hanging over the side of the *Taurus.* Its weight was slowly tilting the boat to starboard. Riker joined her on deck, and adrenaline began to flood his veins. It was a sight none of them ever thought they'd witness. Bronson stopped the boat, creating a distance of no less than a hundred feet between the vessels. He stepped out onto the upper deck with Emi, fascinated at the sight of his new opponent. A smile creased his face.

"You guys weren't kidding," he said. With a fresh harpoon in hand and the spare radio remote clipped to his belt, he climbed down to the main deck where he had left his harpoon rifle. He snatched it up and loaded the harpoon, strapped with a black C-4 explosive. He pressed the butt of the weapon to his shoulder, putting the shark in his sights. Before he could focus his aim, the crane gave in to the shark's weight. Metal groaned as the remaining bolts gave way, and the metallic arm collapsed into the water with the Thresher. Relieved of the enormous weight, the vessel rocked to port and back until its buoyancy normalized. "Shit!" Bronson lowered his weapon. The black fin emerged in front of the *Taurus'* bow, circling around to port. Bronson waited as it circled around the stern, hoping for a good opportunity to harpoon it.

Stafford climbed to his feet after the boat leveled out. The huge black fin was about thirty feet out to port. Both he and Nash backed away to starboard, in case the huge caudal fin was to whip up at them. As the shark circled around the stern, it seemed to make a straight line toward the *Sea Martyr.*

"That's right, you bastard fish!" Bronson taunted the Thresher. "Come to me! That's right!" He aimed the harpoon rifle, hoping to stick the barb into the creature's jaw. With it swimming right at them, it should have been an easy shot. He focused the sights on the shark's head. The shark inched closer to the surface, making its shape more perceptible. Riker noticed something in addition to the beast's cone shaped head. The shark's snout began to lift from the water, and Bronson squeezed the trigger. The harpoon hissed from the barrel, hooking down directly toward the soft flesh of the beast's mouth. A metallic clang could be heard, and they could see the barb bounce away.

"What the—shit!!" Bronson cursed. The Thresher still had a portion of the crane in its jaws, which deflected the harpoon. Bronson grabbed his remote and squeezed the button, hoping the shark would be close enough to the blast. The harpoon had sunk about fifteen feet below the surface when it detonated, erupting in a fiery blast, which was quickly extinguished by the surrounding water. The concussion of the blast, however, sent a shockwave out in all directions. The Thresher had already moved out of range, but was startled by the sudden loud vibration. It shot forward as a means of fleeing. As it did so, it rammed into the protected bow of the *Sea Martyr*. The hull was protected by the bull-bars, but the sheer force of the impact put the vessel into a heavy spin. William and Bronson both fell to the deck. On the second level, Emi fell to her knees, grabbing hold of the railing. Riker knelt down and hugged the flat surface of the coaming to keep from faceplanting on it. Metzler, driven by the forward momentum of the tailspin, fell forward onto the edge. Her eyes went wide as she found herself looking directly downward at the splashing water, and she felt her weight pulling her down toward it. With a pinching sensation on her back, her descent stopped. Riker grabbed the back of her tank top and heaved her back onto the deck before she could fall over the side.

"You seem to make a habit of falling off boats," he said. She managed to crack a smile at the remark, also serving as a thank you. It was short lived, as another impact rocked the boat. The Thresher's tail slapped the underside of the vessel, which was again blocked by the solid bull bars. The Thresher gave up and went for the easier target. The dorsal fin cut through the surface as it sped toward the *Taurus*. Emi tossed down a fresh harpoon to Bronson, who caught it as he stood up. He hurriedly loaded the weapon as he stood up and lifted the sights to his eyes. Although a large target, the Thresher had already made considerable distance, and the weight of the explosive weighed down the harpoon. He didn't have a clean shot. He took his best aim and quickly squeezed the trigger. The harpoon shot away and hooked down, impacting down on the Thresher's back. The barb did not embed all the way in, partially blocked by the Thresher's thick skin.

"Gotcha!" Bronson called out. Just as he did, they watched the stern of the *Taurus* suddenly heave out of the water. The Thresher bit on one of the propellers, and was now taking the vessel on another spin as it tried to sink it. Stafford and Nash ran to the structure. The doctor opened the door to the cabin area, sprinting through the small hallway until he reached one of the staterooms. He snatched up a laptop, which was linked to the satellite feed that monitored the tracking device. The vicious rocking of the boat knocked him to his knees, but he continued checking the signal. The laptop switched on as soon as he opened it, as he designed it to, and immediately it showed the signal. The tracker was working. He grabbed a watertight case out of a nearby cabinet and sealed the laptop within.

"We need to do something!" Metzler yelled, watching the water thrash as the shark brutalized the other vessel. Bronson didn't show the same compassion as she did. Stafford was always a thorn in his side when it came to his hunting. With the way the shark was attacking the boat, he figured they were as good as dead. Rather, that was his justification for reaching for his remote to detonate the explosive. Riker noticed his hand grab the black device. As Bronson's thumb moved over the red button, he sprinted the short distance between them, and with a single downward chopping motion, he knocked the device free from Bronson's grasp. The remote hit the deck and skidded to the edge of the superstructure.

"What the hell are you doing?" Bronson yelled.

"What the hell are *you* doing?" Riker yelled back. "You blow that thing, you'll kill Dr. Stafford and Robert Nash!"

"This is our chance to kill that thing!" Bronson snarled. "They weren't supposed to be out here, and if you haven't noticed, they're as good as dead anyway." He started moving toward the device, but he saw Riker's posture, ready to stop him.

"Don't even think about it!" Riker said. He and Bronson locked threatening gazes toward each other in the standoff. In the corner of his eye, Riker saw William standing off to his left, almost behind him. The son's hand slowly started to reach behind his beltline, and Riker knew he was creeping toward his knife. He pointed his finger at him, "I hope you're reaching for a granola bar, because you're gonna have to eat it!" His voice and threatening glare was enough to cause William to reconsider. His hand moved away, and the three remained in the standoff.

With another vicious wrench, the propeller busted away. The Thresher spat it out and went for another dive. As it swept under the boat, its skin brushed against the underside. The barb was pried loose, lodging into the remaining portion of keel. The shark emerged in front of the bow, generating an enormous upsurge of water.

The breach drew all eyes on the main deck of the *Sea Martyr*, pausing the standoff between Riker, Bronson, and William. With Riker's attention diverted, Emi jumped down onto the main deck from the superstructure. Landing in a squatting position, she immediately grabbed the radio and squeezed the button without hesitation.

A fiery explosion engulfed the *Taurus* from underneath. Bits of metal, wood, and fiberglass shot in all directions as the stern burst upward. Protected by the bow, the Thresher swam deep, driven away from the piercing vibration. The blast launched Nash into the door to the common area, hitting it hard enough to knock it off the hinges. Stafford hit the floor of the stateroom. He looked down the hall and saw Nash on the floor, and water spilling onto the deck. The bow started lifting upward as water drove the stern down. Water immediately started flooding over the deck and into the hallway. Stafford ran out of the stateroom and tripped over a piece of debris. The watertight case flung from his hand and skidded into one of the other rooms. Stafford rushed to his feet and turned to chase it, stopped by a grab on his shoulder by Nash.

"Doc! There's no time! We've gotta go!" his assistant yelled. Water was already above their knees, and the deck was already completely flooded. Stafford realized he was right, and both men squeezed through the doorway. When they got to the deck, they were already swimming.

"Hurry! Go for the boat! Don't stop!" he yelled. Both men swam like Olympic competitors, making each stroke count.

"Oh Jesus!" Riker said as he saw the two men emerge from the wreckage. He shoved Bronson and Emi out of the way and climbed up into the wheelhouse. He took control of the helm and brought the *Sea Martyr* toward the scientists to help close the distance. "Metzler! Be ready to pull them up!" he yelled through the open doorway. Metzler stood at the ladder. The boat pulled up alongside the two men. Stafford was the first to grab the ladder. Clenching each bar for dear life, he hauled himself out of the water. As he cleared the surface, Nash began his ascent. He hoisted himself up, bringing his waistline out of the waterline. Suddenly there was another huge spray of water about twenty feet behind them. The huge tail whipped horizontally, skimming the surface before its tip struck Nash in the small of his back. Every nerve in his body lit up like a Christmas tree. He lost his grip, and began to fall.

"NO!" Stafford yelled. With his left hand gripping the ladder, he reached down with his other arm, grabbing Nash by the wrist. Bent down, he managed to keep him from falling back completely into the water. Nash's eyes were bulging, and his teeth were clenched together. Before Stafford could summon the strength to pull him up, the black shape emerged from directly underneath. The jaws hyperextended, and the Thresher's head emerged. The jaws engulfed Nash completely, and the jaws slammed shut...right onto Stafford's arm. Teeth shredded the bicep muscle and tendons, and the sheer weight of the Thresher snapped the bone as it fell back beneath, taking his arm completely off. Stafford gave a blood curdling scream and started to fall off the ladder from immeasurable pain. Metzler grabbed him by his shirt and with all her might she pulled him onto the deck.

Stafford collapsed on his back, and blood instantly seeped from the arm. Riker scuttled down to the deck to join her. Stafford's face was already turning white. With shaking hands, Metzler attempted to put a handkerchief onto the stub of the arm, but the blood immediately soaked through. Stafford's body spasmed from intense pain and shock. Blood covered Metzler's hands and waist. Her mind went haywire as she slipped into a panic. Tears streamed down her face and her body trembled nearly out of control.

"Oh Jesus! Oh God, Riker! I can't do this! I don't know how to do this! He's dying!" Riker grabbed her by the shoulders with both hands, bringing her face directly in front of his. She saw the seriousness in his eyes.

"Listen!" he said. "Pull yourself together! You are a cop! This is the kind of thing we do! This is the kind of thing we deal with! You may not have wanted to be a cop, but it doesn't matter. You ARE one! Now help me save this guy!"

He let her go and snatched up her button shirt that she removed earlier. He tore away at the jacket and tied it along the remaining stub of arm. Metzler took the remaining bit of shirt and pressed it hard into the wound, telling Stafford to stay awake. He shook on the deck and fought to maintain consciousness. His lips trembled as he attempted to speak.

"Don't talk!" Metzler said. She was still shaking herself, but managed the strength to keep going. "You'll be okay, Aaron! Just stay awake and don't talk."

"Track—track…tracking device. Monitor…blue case…boat…" he struggled to get the words out. Riker didn't bother listening and rushed back up to the wheelhouse. He got on the radio, transmitting an emergency mayday to AirSea Rescue. He cut the wheel to turn to shore, pushing the throttle to its maximum speed. On deck, Bronson overheard the words Stafford muttered with interest. He knew they had to give up for the moment, but as soon as Stafford was dropped off he planned on tracking the Thresher down. Nothing was getting in the way of his payday.

As the *Sea Martyr* sped away, the tip of the *Taurus'* bow dipped beneath the surface. A solemn echo could be heard as it hit the sea bottom.

CHAPTER 23

The grey and white AirSea Rescue helicopter hovered like a dragonfly about thirty feet over the *Sea Martyr*. Strapped to a red stretcher, Stafford was hoisted by cable along with a paramedic who rode up along with him from the main deck. As they cleared the superstructure, the helicopter immediately whizzed inland while reeling up their patient. Riker watched them depart, silently wishing Stafford the best of luck. He turned and saw the deck drenched in human blood. Metzler stood at the stern, leaning back against the side with her arms crossed. She was still recovering mentally from the frightening sight of the immense shark swallowing Nash whole and of Stafford losing his arm trying to save his friend.

Using a coiled wash-down hose, William sprayed the deck with water, directing the blood toward a drain near the stern. Riker saw that he had some blood on his black shirt, already drying up in the hot sun. He found his denim jacket and put it on, covering up the red stain. He walked around William to Metzler. She stood quietly, staring off into the horizon. The beautiful ocean provided some good therapy, despite the horror that reaped beneath it.

"You did good," Riker told her. A fresh tear rolled down her cheek. She thought of the words he told her as they tried to save Stafford. She realized helping people came in many forms, but she never considered the personal toll it could take on a person.

Riker looked up at the superstructure, where Bronson was on the deck speaking to Emi. At that moment, he decided the Trio wasn't up for the job. He marched past William and climbed up the ladder. Before he could enter the wheelhouse, Bronson slapped his arm against the frame of the open doorway, blocking him.

"May I ask what you're doing, Officer?" he said.

"Oh, I bet you'd like to know," Riker said. He viciously shoved Bronson out of the way with a palm to his chest, knocking him back several steps. Bronson clenched his fists, but retained his composure, offering a smile instead. But it didn't signify friendliness. Riker glanced back at Emi, making sure she stayed at bay. "I'm calling the Coast Guard. It'll be their show now. And believe me, they'll be interested to know what I have to say about you." He went into the wheelhouse and grabbed the microphone speaker. "Coast Guard-Coast Guard, this is the *Sea Martyr*. Over?" There was no response. There wasn't even static. Riker tried again. "Coast Guard-Coast Guard, this is the *Sea Martyr*. Over?" Again, there was no response. Bronson walked in. He held up his hand, displaying a small green wire.

"Doesn't work very well without this," he said. Riker replaced the speaker, realizing Bronson had disabled it in anticipation of this action. "This is *my* bounty. Understand, you're not gonna get in the way of that?"

"I think I understand too well," Riker said. "This isn't about you getting the best trophy for your collection here." He pointed to the line of teeth along the wall. "It just seems you're awfully anxious to get this shark and collect your reward. This is clearly about the money—but not getting rich. Tell me this; who do you owe money to?" Bronson recalled Riker entering during his phone conversation.

"Nobody who concerns you," he said.

"Oh yeah?" Riker said. "Then let me take a quick guess. A group like you; this boat is clearly your livelihood; I'm guessing you were shipping product for somebody by sea. Coast Guard or somebody came by, so you dumped the cargo. The client didn't take well to you doing that, and now you're trying to pay him-or-her back." Bronson gave another grin. He was genuinely impressed.

"I'll give you this; I saw the trembles in your hands and I thought you were past your prime. I guess I was wrong." He crossed his arms and drew a deep breath. "Now's not the time to worry about that. I have a new idea how to catch this bastard." Riker reluctantly followed him down to the main deck, making sure to keep his distance. He determined the best course of action now would be to kill the Thresher and get back to shore.

"What's the plan, Dad?" William said as he put away the hose.

"Get our net off the hauler and put the hooks back on it," Bronson said. He picked up one of his harpoons that had fallen on the deck. "The bastard's skin is too thick. The only way I can get it is with a precise shot either in the mouth or in his fins, which are pure cartilage. Unfortunately, it's hard to pull off such a shot even with a shark that big. It's a fast son-of-a-bitch and very mean. Meanest one I've ever seen."

"So, your idea is what?" Metzler cut in.

"We've seen he likes to duck under the boat while he attacks. When he does, we'll drop our net on him. I'll install weights on it for it to sink at a precise rate, and if we time it right the sucker will get snagged."

"What if it rips through?" Riker said. "We saw before that something managed to rip your net earlier."

"I'm not waiting for him to drown," Bronson said. "After we snag him, I'll hook the boat around. Once we're over the top of him, I'll drop a depth charge on his ass! Blow him to smithereens." He noticed the sour expression on Metzler's face as she stared off into the water, deliberately avoiding eye contact with him. "I see you don't approve."

"Do you always use explosives?" she asked. "Do you realize the sheer concussion of the blast can travel to great distances and kill other things?"

"Metzler," Riker cut her off. It wasn't that he disagreed with her, rather he was fully aware Bronson was going to do as he pleased, no matter what. Also, he knew the Thresher posed as much of a threat if not more to the local sea life than Bronson's explosives, as well as human life. It had to be eliminated. "So how are we gonna find it? Chum again and hope he comes around?"

"We're going back to the wreck," Bronson said. "I'm sure you heard the doc as he was speaking."

"We were a little busy trying to keep him alive. Especially since they ended up in the water because of YOU," Metzler said. Now she made eye contact. Bronson ignored the statement.

"Well anyway, he said he put a tracking device on the shark. The monitor is in a blue case, and went down with the boat. If we can retrieve it, then we can track the fish down." Riker gave a condescending laugh.

"And how do you plan on doing that?" he enquired while putting a fresh cigarette to his mouth. William brushed by him to collect the tub of hooks and spikes. As he did, he turned to his father.

"Not me," he said. Bronson then looked up to the structure at Emi. Her stare was blank as usual, but Bronson knew her well enough to read her thoughts. It was a 'no'.

"Not you, what?" Riker got frustrated. "What are you talking about?"

"Someone's gonna have to dive and get that thing," Bronson said. "Otherwise, we may be out here forever trying to find the Thresher."

"Somehow I doubt that," Riker said. "Besides, it doesn't look like any of your crew is enthusiastic on taking a dip." Bronson eyeballed Riker. He came from inland, so the likeliness that he had diving experience was unlikely. Then he glanced at Metzler, who lived along the coast as far as he understood.

"What about you?" he said. "You're Emi's size. You should be able to fit into her gear. How 'bout it? You a diver?" Metzler wanted to lie and say she had no clue. She certainly had no ambition to go down into the water. Her lack of response gave Bronson his answer. "You are! Perfect! All you need to do is go down there and get the case. Easy job. Whaddya say?" Metzler said nothing for another moment and then finally stood off the side where she leaned.

"Where's the gear?"

"Second stateroom on the left," Bronson said and pointed. She passed by and entered the door, followed swiftly by Riker.

"Metzler? What—are you insane? You can't be seriously going down there," he said.

"I am," she said. "If we can track it, we can kill it. And finally be rid of these psychos as well." She proceeded into the room. Riker stood in the doorway.

"Metzler! I don't think you realize. If that shark shows up, I think he'll use you as bait. He'll drop a charge down right on top of you to kill that thing." He kept his voice down to not be heard from outside.

"That's why I need you up here to watch my back," she said. "We're partners, remember?"

"Metzler, listen…Allison," Riker fumbled over his words. She pulled out all of the scuba gear and turned toward him.

"If you don't mind," she said and started to lift her tank top to change, exposing her abdomen. Riker exhaled a defeated sigh and shut the door. He walked out to the sunlit deck. Bronson was back in the wheelhouse with Emi, and William was slowly approaching the door to the common area. He had a little grin on his face. "Don't you fucking think about it!" Riker snapped at him. William actually jumped at the sudden threat.

"Tease," he remarked, and went back to installing the hooks on the net. Riker stood at the door, keeping guard against any perverted actions from the fisherman toward Metzler.

CHAPTER 24

It was not difficult for the Trio to locate the wreckage. Bits of wood, fiberglass, unused lifejackets, amongst other debris floated on the surface, slowly spreading out from the point of origin. Bronson centered the *Sea Martyr* in the debris and dropped the anchor. It extended through the three-hundred-foot depth before hitting the bottom, nearly maxing out its chain length. He went down to the main deck.

Metzler was fully dressed in the black foam neoprene wetsuit. It hugged her body tightly, causing slight discomfort. It was designed for Emi, who was slightly skinnier than she was. She strapped on the large white rebreather, hunching as Riker helped put it over her shoulders. It weighed at least sixty pounds. In her hands, she held the full-face mask which was equipped with comms. She would wait until right before going in to put it on. Her anxiety had already begun to spike. This was a much deeper dive than what she ever trained for. The deepest she ever had gone was sixty-five feet, and this was almost five times that depth. Riker wanted to remind her that she didn't have to go down there, but he already knew it would be a wasted effort. On his belt was a two-way radio, set on the frequency to the mask radio. Bronson emerged from a hatch leading to the cargo hold, carrying a large yellow float bag.

"I'm guessing you've never used one of these?" he asked.

"No," Metzler said. "I've never found myself doing deep sea recovery."

"It's easy," he said. "When you find the case, put this strap around the handle." The strap looked like a belt, even including a buckle for it to be secured. "Then take this red cord here," he pointed at it, "and give it a yank. Be careful because the tank fills the thing pretty quick. It's almost as fast as an airbag in a car, so don't let it knock you out." He handed it to Metzler. She spit into the goggles, which was a single circular frame. She put the mask on and installed the rebreather hose. Once everything was strapped on and sealed, Riker took his radio and clicked the transmitter.

"You hear that okay?"

"Loud and clear," she said and gave a thumbs up. Riker could hear her voice in person, and simultaneously over the radio. Bronson climbed up to the wheelhouse with Emi to monitor. Before he entered he turned to look at Metzler.

"Keep in mind, we're over the edge of a reef," he said. "This is a shallow region. We're close to a dropoff. Keep that in mind when you swim down there. Don't step into a moray eel's cave." He chuckled and went into the wheelhouse. Naturally, Metzler failed to see the humor, as did Riker. She stepped over the ladder and began to climb down. Riker helped her over the edge, especially with the heavy tank keeping her unbalanced.

"It does bother me," he said. Metzler stopped, looking at him with a confused expression.

"I'm sorry?"

"The other night, when the Thresher attacked the fishermen, you asked me if it ever bothered me that we couldn't save them." He paused for a moment and took a deep breath. "It always bothers me when I can't save someone. Sometimes greatly." She understood what he was saying, and she also knew the underlying meaning. She knew he had her back. She lowered herself into the water. Once on the surface, she checked her balance before dipping underneath. She switched on a light installed on her shoulder and slowly swam under the boat until she found the anchor chain. She grabbed it and slowly worked her descent. With five pulls of the chain, she was at twenty feet of depth. Within a few seconds she was at thirty-nine feet.

Riker stood at the ladder, seeing the air bubbles from Metzler's rebreather bursting along the surface. He kept an eye to the whereabouts of the Trio. Bronson had come down from the wheelhouse to the cargo hold. A big yellow barrel was sitting on deck, loaded with dynamite. Bronson emerged back on deck with the depth trigger. He placed it into an opening on top of the depth charge. At the stern was the net, folded strategically to keep the hooks from snagging on itself. Two large weights were tied to the two bottom corners, and on the two upper corners were small buoys. They were lighter than the weights, but they would keep the net level; that way it could snag the shark. William stood by the net, chewing on some tobacco. It seemed he expected the shark to show up and wanted to be ready to drop the net on it. Riker needed to get the thought out of his mind. He lifted the radio to his lips.

"How's it going down there?"

Metzler paused her descent when she heard his voice on the radio. "I'm about a hundred feet down." she said. "There's still a lot of sunlight."

"Good, you're a third of the way there," he said. *"I'd like to tell you to take your time, but you'll want to be pretty quick down there. It'll be pretty cold."*

"It's already getting a little chilly," she said. It was true. At this depth, the water temperature was about ten degrees colder than on the surface. It was still warm, but her body could feel the difference. She hung on tightly to the chain, feeling the water current pulling at her. Going further downward, the golden streaks of sunlight darkened into a bronze-like color, cutting downward through the aqua blue ocean. The water itself began to darken a bit as well.

Metzler was about a hundred and fifty feet down when she started to feel somewhat drowsy. She was having symptoms of nitrogen narcosis, a lethargic state caused by inhaling oxygen under elevated pressure. She looked straight ahead, working to overcome the lightheadedness. While doing so she groaned.

"Everything alright?" Riker's voice came through her earphones.

"I'm good," she said. In truth, she hadn't felt that way since graduation night when she got her bachelors. Friends dragged her along to a local bar. After the fourth martini, she was feeling then as she was feeling now. It took her a minute to descend the rest of the way down, although it felt a lot longer to her. The sea floor was much darker than up above. It wasn't pitch black, rather a dark blue. There was enough light however to support plant life. Sea grass stretched upward at heights of three feet. Along the reef were multiple lumps of coral. Although appearing like rocks, Metzler remembered coral is an animal. *Must be a boring life.* She avoided the batches of yellow and red coral to avoid getting cut on their razor-sharp edges. Various small fish swam around her, curious about her light and the gas bubbles that spat from her regulator as she exhaled. Most of these fish were no bigger than one or two feet, unharmed by the Thresher's presence in the area.

She looked for a few minutes, seeing only a few pieces of scattered debris in various areas on the reef. It was when she reached the edge of the reef that she saw the haunting sight of the sunken *Taurus*. Several particles of earth were floating around it, forming a cloud created by the impact. She noticed the dark background beyond the boat. As she approached, she cursed to herself. The boat was teetering on the edge of the drop off. It was lying flat, belly down, and the stern was completely blown away from the explosion. The bow of the vessel was extended over the edge of the three-hundred-foot cliff. The crow's nest was completely busted, and the windshield of the cockpit was shattered.

"*Allison? You okay?*" Riker's voice came through the comms again.

"Should I start calling you Leonard now?" she joked. Her chuckle was short lived, as she struggled to fight the nitrogen narcosis. "I found the boat."

"*Alright. Keep an eye out for that Thresher,*" Riker said.

"I'll do my best," she said.

She proceeded to the vessel, hovering a few feet over it to determine that it was safe to investigate. Seeing that only a third of the vessel was over the edge, she deemed it should be secure enough for her to check. She began her search for the case.

Checking the bow deck was easy; there was nothing there except broken bits of boat. Metzler swam up to the cockpit and peeked through the doorway. The door had been busted off, and the wall had caved in. The wheel and other controls were busted up, but no case could be seen. She descended down to the deck, guiding herself with the ladder. She almost gasped at the sight of the grouper, which had landed a few yards away from the boat. A long cord ran from it, leading to a black metallic box. She shined a light on the box, and despite her dizziness she was able to read the label. *Was he going to electrocute the shark?* She decided to waste no more time and continued searching. The mess area door was already ajar. She pulled it all the way open, revealing a black hallway. She got herself into a standing position and took a step inside. Just then, a fish darted out from the blackness.

"Jesus!" Metzler shrieked, nearly falling backward as the blue stripped grunt whizzed past her. "I'm good," she said into the comm. She shined the light inside and proceeded inward. She checked the first stateroom. It was a very small room, filled with books, comics, and torn pages, all undoubtedly belonging to Robert Nash. She checked the next one, which was almost completely empty. She began to worry that the case had fallen out of the boat when it sank. As she checked the next stateroom, a loud metallic groan echoed through the boat. Metzler froze, gripping the wall. She shut her eyes, praying that the current wasn't pushing the boat further out into the drop off. The groaning stopped. Metzler felt a sense of relief and continued her search.

Instead of going into the next stateroom, she checked the mess area instead. It was as if gravity didn't exist in there. Objects of all different shapes and sizes floated about without direction. Cabinet doors were busted, and their contents spilled. She brushed away some floating trash and wreckage as she stepped in. The water was so cloudy in this room, she could barely see even with the light. The dizziness and overall exhaustion was starting to wear on her. She gave up and turned to exit. While doing so, her foot hit something, tripping her. She fell to her knees and her eyes went toward the object on the floor. It was solid and rectangular. Being up close to it, she ran her hand along its surface, eventually feeling the handle.

"I found it!" she said. She got out of the boat, dragging the thirty-pound case with her.

"*Alright, good news*," Riker responded. "*Just hook the thing up and get yourself topside.*"

"You don't have to tell me," Metzler said. She buckled the strap around the blue watertight case. Holding it away, she yanked on the red cord. The canister quickly inflated the yellow bag with air, and immediately it began lifting to the surface. She looked up, seeing the dark outline of the *Sea Martyr* surrounded by glistening sunlight.

****

"There it is," Bronson called out, pointing out to port. The bag surfaced about twenty feet away, generating a large splash. William grabbed a large pole and began reaching for it. The tip splashed the water around the bag, just barely out of range. He propped up on the coaming and leaned out as far as he could, holding the pole by the very end. He was able to get the tip over the top of the bag. There was enough pressure between the pole and the water that he was able to tug it closer to the boat. After doing so, he jabbed the pull around a loop in the bag and heaved it over the side. Bronson snatched the case from him and set it on a chair. He popped the clutches and lifted the side open. The laptop was inside, dry and undamaged.

"Hopefully we won't need a password for this," Riker said.

"Let's find out," said Bronson.

He opened up the laptop monitor, and the screen flashed on. The screen showed a blue radar background, and a red blinking dot marked the location of the Thresher. Both men blew a sigh of relief. However, that relief went away quickly when they noticed the position of that blinking dot. The center of the screen showed their location, and the blip was only about two hundred yards to the north, and closing.

"Oh God!" Riker said. He grabbed the radio and squeezed the transmitter button. "Allison! Hurry on up! It's coming your way!"

****

Allison Metzler was about to start her ascent when Riker's warning came through the comm. Immediately, she turned around and looked in all directions. There was nothing to be seen except the vast reaches of blue ocean.

"I don't see..." she stopped as a monstrous shadow suddenly cast over her. Her heart pounded with near panic as she forced herself to look up, shining her light toward the surface. The light reflected the open mouth lined with three-and-a-half inch knife-like teeth. She screamed and pushed herself backward, into the hallway entrance. Just as she passed through the open doorway, the deck erupted from a vicious strike from the Thresher's tail that barely missed her.

****

"Allison!" Riker yelled into the radio. The monitor showed the Thresher down at the sea bottom, at the location of the wreckage. "Allison!" He heard another shriek of terror. He saw Bronson crank a lever, reeling in the anchor. "What are you doing?" he said.

"She's not going to be able to climb up the chain. Not with that Thresher after her," Bronson said. "She'd have to make several safety stops while coming up. She'll never get up here without killing herself with decompression sickness!" The chain rattled as the winch rapidly hauled it up.

"Then what are you going to do?" Riker asked. Bronson didn't say anything. He marched over to the barrel and yelled up to Emi.

"You know what to do!" The engine pounded like a drum as the *Sea Martyr* began to circle around to position over the wreckage. William joined his father at the large yellow barrel and helped him haul it to the transom. Bronson then started making adjustments to a device below the opening.

"What are you doing?" Riker said.

"I don't think you realize the situation," Bronson said. "There's no way out for your friend, I'm sorry. I'm adjusting the charge to detonate at three hundred feet."

"Like hell you are!" Riker said. He shoved Bronson back, and turned to William, who already backed away. He stood off to Riker's right, staying about four feet away. Riker's eyes went toward William as he noticed his hand again starting to reach for the knife behind him. "Do we have to go over this again?" Riker said to him.

****

The Thresher slashed its tail multiple times at the entryway, while Metzler hugged the wall. The shark then rammed its head into the structure, desperate to get at her. Chunks of wood and fiberglass snapped off with each vicious motion. Foam stirred up as the Thresher viciously attacked the boat to get to the prey within. Its huge nose pried bits of debris away, widening the opening as it pressed inward. With a thrash of its body, it wiggled itself free and began circling around.

Metzler started moving toward the opening to try and determine the Thresher's location. At first, it looked like it had swum away. The ocean suddenly calmed and the froth disintegrated. Suddenly, its tail lashed the structure again, breaking off a large piece of the door panel. Metzler fell backward from the burst of water that came with the impact. Her head hit the wall, just as Riker was trying to communicate to her.

"Allison! Just hang…" his voice disappeared in a haze of static. The comm unit was malfunctioning. Dazed, she struggled to pull herself upright. The doorframe had broken away, turning into a large oval shaped entrance with ragged edges. Like a missile, the shark slammed its head into the widening entrance. Its snout extended further in, and even its jaws managed to squeeze inside, snapping wildly at Metzler who stood out of range. Its eyes were closed to protect them from injury while it attacked. Once the shark reached inward, they opened. Even though they were black and emotionless, they seemed to look directly at her. She let out a terrified scream, muffled by the mask and water, creating a flurry of air bubbles around her.

****

"Metzler!" Riker grabbed the radio off his belt. There was no response, only static.

"I'm sorry Riker, but I'm afraid she's dead," Bronson said. He made another move toward the barrel. Riker repeatedly called Metzler's name over the radio with no results. Seeing Bronson attempting to move the depth charge, he clipped it to his belt and swiftly moved in front of it.

"You're not dropping that thing down on her!" he yelled. Bronson's gaze at him took on a more sinister look. William started to take a step toward him, and Riker instinctively put his hand over the handle of his revolver. "Don't…" he warned him. The metallic sound of the slide of a semi-automatic chambering a round brought his attention back to Bronson. He realized he was looking down the barrel of Metzler's Glock. Bronson had picked it out of the stateroom earlier while Riker was distracted and hid it under his jacket. Now it was in his right hand, aimed at Riker's forehead, with Bronson's finger on the trigger. Riker moved his hand away from his revolver.

"So, this is what?" he asked. "You're gonna shoot me?"

"Like I said, Officer," Bronson said, "nobody's getting in the way of me killing this fish. Not you, her, nobody! I'm getting this bounty!" His voice was calm, and even sounded polite. But Riker understood the meaning behind his words.

"Oh right, you've got that debt," Riker said. "Exactly how do you plan to explain this when you get back to collect your *bounty*?" Bronson smirked.

"It's a big ocean," he said. "And this is obviously a vicious shark. It won't be that hard for people to understand." He was about to squeeze the trigger, but paused for a moment. "You know, I gotta say; too bad you didn't train her to take this thing apart when she left it. See here? Bullets loaded into the magazine, firearm still assembled…shame she wasn't more cautious, for your sake. Oh well." He squeezed the trigger. The Glock clicked, without any discharge. Bronson's eyes widened with surprise. He squeezed the trigger again, with the same result. He clenched his teeth in anger, realizing that the firing pin had been removed. "What the—"

"Looks like I trained her rather well," Riker snarled. To his right, William unsheathed his knife and thrust it toward him. Riker turned clockwise, causing him to miss. Riker grabbed his extended arm with his right hand and twisted it around his back. William screamed in pain as his wrist bent, dislodging the knife from his grip. Riker grabbed a handful of his hair with his left hand and thrust downward, slamming William's face into the edge of the transom. He collapsed to the deck, with a bleeding cut over his forehead.

Bronson dashed forward, throwing an angry right-handed haymaker. Riker arched backward, feeling a brush of air as the swing missed his face by less than an inch. He shuffled his feet forward and with full force he slammed his right elbow into Bronson's nose. He immediately followed with a left punch, hitting Bronson in the solar plexus, knocking the wind out of him. Bronson's airway briefly closed up and he staggered backward. Riker looked up past him at the wheelhouse, where Emi was emerging from the door chambering a round into the bolt action Remington rifle. With swift motion, Riker drew his eight-shot revolver. With the hammer locked back, he pointed it at Bronson's face. Emi halted before she could aim the rifle, seeing that Riker had positioned Bronson in front of him.

Bronson hadn't looked down the barrel of a gun in a long time. With the hammer locked back, he knew it only would take a light touch to fire off the weapon. He realized there was no chance of disarming the officer. Riker's eyes were locked on Bronson's bloody face.

"I would suggest you put that rifle down," Riker said to Emi. "If not, I'll assure you the next chum you'll be tossing into the water will be made of your hubby's face!" Anger creased Emi's face; a rare display of emotion. She unloaded the weapon and tossed it down.

****

The shark had been wedged into the hallway entrance, snapping its jaws relentlessly at Metzler for several minutes. Its brain lit up at a lack of oxygen intake through its gills. Unable to swim backwards, it tried to wiggle away, but was stuck in the entrance. It thrashed its entire body about, as if in a panic. Metzler felt the vessel groaning from the strain. She gasped, realizing the shark was accidentally starting to push the vessel forward—over the drop-off. The shark snapped its jaws, not to grab at her but as if it was trying to suck water in over its gills. With a twist of its body, a portion of the wall broke away and the Thresher freed itself. The superstructure was creaking, as if it was about to collapse downward onto her. She realized she had to get out. She watched the Thresher's tail whip by as it swum off, giving her clear view to the deck. There was nowhere else to go, so she moved outward. The vessel was now almost halfway off the ledge. As she swam, she saw the huge dark shape circling about, coming again at her.

"Can I get a break?!" she cursed. Just then, she saw the hole in the deck leading to the cargo storage. She swam through the meter-wide breach, just before the Thresher's tail slashed the deck. Again, the shark rammed the deck, shredding up wood and metal. Another mechanical groan echoed, and Metzler could feel the vessel starting to teeter. Realizing she had no choice but to try to make an escape, she shone her light around to look for anything she could use as a weapon. As she scanned through the room, she saw the diver propulsion vehicle. She examined it, seeing that it was functional. The boat shook as the Thresher hit it again and then finally moved off to circulate water over its gills. She watched the shark through the large hole in the deck, waiting for it to turn back in her direction. She started up the vehicle, feeling the force behind the propeller. She removed her watch and put it around the clutch, locking down the accelerator. She lifted the large device and pointed it outward. She released it, and it zipped out of her hands through the opening. It shot upward toward the surface, whizzing past the Thresher. Thinking it was a living organism, it turned to chase the device.

Another large metallic groan echoed through the sea floor. Metzler could feel the remains of the stern lifting upward as the boat started skidding over the ledge. She stroked her arms as fast as she could, exiting the cargo hold. She had just cleared the deck as the *Taurus* fell down the drop off, crashing into the ocean bed below. She looked up and saw the Thresher was chasing the propulsion vehicle to the surface. She swam over to the reef, eventually finding a large wall of coral to hide behind. She tapped on her mask, trying to get her comm. unit to work.

****

"Riker! It's coming up!" Metzler's voice sounded from the radio. With his revolver still pointed at Bronson, Riker snatched the radio with his other hand.

"Are you all right?" he asked.

"I'm fine," she said.

On the deck, William groaned as he pulled himself together. Riker kicked his knife out of reach. He looked Bronson in the eye, keeping his revolver pointed at him.

"You gonna do it?" Bronson said.

"Only if you make me," Riker said. "But I'd rather we kill this bastard fish! It's up to you!"

****

The Thresher ascended rapidly as it chased the diver propulsion device. As it did so, it heard the loud thumping sounds from the *Sea Martyr's* engine. Its eyes caught sight of the large vessel floating above. Baring teeth, the Thresher abandoned its pursuit of the small device and fired upward at the large vessel. It collided from below, biting down on a set of the bull-bars.

****

The sudden massive quake of the vessel knocked everyone off their feet. The sea sprayed in all directions around them as the shark tried to rip off the bars. Unable to get a good grip, it let go, snapping off some teeth in the process. It thrashed its tail into the hull, but each lash was blocked by the bull-bars. The Thresher briefly circled away, creating a little distance. With a sudden burst of speed, it rammed the boat on the port side aft, causing it to spin counter-clockwise. Emi clung to the railing to keep from topping overboard, while Bronson and William hugged the deck.

"God DAMN! This bastard is strong!" Bronson called out.

Riker pulled himself to his feet, despite the intense shaking of the vessel, and aimed his revolver down over the side. He squeezed the trigger, firing off several deafening rounds that hit the shark near the dorsal fin. The water around it turned dark red. The fish's nervous system detected an injury, and it dove down. Bronson pulled himself to his feet in time to see the bloody dorsal fin cutting through the water away from them.

"It's gonna circle back around," he said. He climbed up the ladder to the wheelhouse. "Emi, go down at the net. Wait for my signal." She followed his instructions and joined William at the transom. He was still dazed, but coherent enough to follow his father's instructions. Bronson cut the wheel, pointing the *Sea Martyr* toward the huge black fish. He saw the large fin in the distance turn in their direction. Bronson accelerated the vessel, placing them on a collision course. "Come on, you ugly demon!" he taunted the fish. The Thresher increased speed as well, as if meeting the challenge. "Come on!" Bronson yelled as they closed the distance. Just before they could collide, the Thresher dove beneath the vessel. Bronson quickly turned to his mates on the deck. "NOW!" They dropped the net overboard. The weights dragged the bottom down, while the buoys kept it stretched out.

Without having any time to react, the Thresher swam right into the middle of the razor lined net, which immediately encompassed its body. Hooks and blades sunk deep into its flesh, drawing blood. The Thresher quickly found itself entangled in the net. It twisted and turned, suspended in the water and unable to swim off. Blood seeped from its wounds as the razor blades sliced through its thick skin. It started to sink.

Riker kept an eye on the tracking monitor as Bronson turned the boat around. He snatched his radio off of his belt. "Allison, take cover! You're gonna feel a shockwave."

"*Way ahead of ya,*" she said. The *Sea Martyr*'s engine rumbled as it circled around. With Riker watching the monitor and giving direction, Bronson lined the course over the Thresher's position. Finally, they passed over it.

Emi and William heaved the large barrel over the transom, generating an enormous splash as it hit the water. Bronson throttled the vessel at its top speed to gather distance from the blast.

The Thresher had sunk to a hundred feet, the depth that Bronson set the charge to detonate. It twisted violently, but the hooks were still dug in deep. The need to circulate water over its gills became critical. The

Thresher arched its entire body, nearly bending its body at a complete perpendicular angle. Finally, portions of the net ripped away, and some of the hooks tore loose, taking chunks of its flesh along with them. Finally free of the net, it swung its tail hard to dive.

As it did, it saw the bright yellow barrel descending upon it. The shark's mind was unable to comprehend the brief orange and red flash, as well as the enormous concussion of force that shook the ocean.

The sea erupted upward with volcanic force. The sound of the explosion echoed through the water. Hidden behind the dense coral wall, Metzler pressed her hands over her ears. She felt the downward shockwave as the blast rippled through the seafloor.

Standing outside, Bronson, Riker, and the crew watched the ocean surface turn dark red with bloody froth and flesh debris. Immediately, the Trio broke into fits of laughter. William began jumping up and down, pounding his fist into the air.

"Ha ha!" Bronson yelled. "I got you, motherfucker!" While they continued their celebration, Riker took a seat to catch his breath. He looked at the monitor, which showed no transmission of the shark. He looked at the bloody surface as seagulls quickly started swooping down to collect the fleshy bits. He clicked the transmitter on his radio.

"Metzler, you okay?"

"*I'm a bit dazed. I felt the blast. But I'm okay,*" she said.

"If you feel safe, just come on up," he said. "Take it slow." He put the radio down and blew a sigh of relief, all while keeping a watchful eye over the Trio. They continued celebrating. *You'd think they didn't just try to kill us.*

CHAPTER 25

Metzler ripped off her scuba mask as soon as she broke the surface, taking a gasp of fresh air. The ascent up was an exhausting one, with her having to take stops every twenty feet or so. She was still feeling the drowsy effects of the nitrogen narcosis, and the energy spent while evading the shark made it even worse. Her vision was blurry, but she could easily see the *Sea Martyr,* since the sixty-foot-long black vessel was impossible to miss. Her lungs were aching, as well as every muscle in her body. Everything within her protested as she paddled toward the boat.

Riker saw her approaching off the starboard bow. He snatched up a ring buoy with a life line tied to it and tossed it out to her. It splashed down about ten feet from her. Metzler swam the short distance to it and wrapped her arms through the donut hole, hugging the side of the buoy. Riker pulled her the rest of the way over to the vessel. She climbed up the ladder and collapsed onto the deck. She laid on her back, staring up into the clear blue sky while catching her breath. Riker knelt down at her side.

"You gonna make it?" he asked, half-jokingly.

"Thank God it's Friday," she joked back. Her pained laughter was joined by the laughs from the Trio. They were crowded at the stern, prodding the water with a dip net. The ocean was red with the Thresher's blood. Bits of barrel floated everywhere, scattering along the waterline.

"There's the tracking device," Bronson said, pointing to the busted equipment floating in the water. Riker glanced over at the celebrating Trio, still wary of them. He looked down at Metzler again.

"Did you see it on your way up?" he asked. She laid there silent for a moment, rubbing her eyes and forehead.

"I had a hard time seeing anything," she answered. "I saw a red cloud. I didn't see the shark."

"Oh, look at this!" Bronson's voice rang out excitedly. Riker turned around. Metzler, curious as well, sat herself up. Bronson leaned over the transom, extending the dip net out as far as he could. William stood next to him.

"Is that what I think it is?" he asked.

"It's one of its eyes!" Bronson called out excitedly. He lifted the net back onto the deck and burst into a fit of victorious laughter. "We blew its eye right out of its head!" The eye looked like a large black beach ball, with a red stringy cord attached to the back. Amazingly, it was entirely intact. Bronson slapped hands with Emi and William, and then picked up the large organ and lifted it above his head victoriously. Meanwhile, Riker and Metzler stayed back, watching the bizarre ritual.

"I guess we've killed it," Metzler said. She cracked a smile. Riker didn't smile, however. His expression was as serious as ever. Part of the reason was that Metzler wasn't aware the Trio used her as bait. He did not feel secure on this vessel with the group. Bronson didn't even flinch when he pulled the trigger to her pistol. To Riker, this indicated that he was not the first person Bronson double-crossed. He had a strong desire to get off the vessel.

The blaring sound of a boat horn felt like a timely answer to a prayer. He looked westward over the bow. Two police vessels approached with flickering emergency lights. Riker stood up and waved to them. As they neared, he recognized Chief Crawford at the helm of the nearest one. The chief carefully pulled the smaller cruiser along the starboard side of the *Sea Martyr*.

"I say you have a unique sense of timing, Chief," Riker said. Crawford didn't look very amused. He wiped beads of sweat off his forehead with his handkerchief.

"You wanna talk to me about timing?" he remarked. "I was in the middle of leading a seminar for the security staff at St. Peter's Hospital when we were interrupted by doctors and nurses rushing to the ER, saying a man had his arm bitten off. Then I found out that man was Doctor Stafford. There were mumblings of his assistant being killed. I tried radioing you guys, but nobody answered. After we started rolling out to find you, we thought we heard some huge explosion. What the hell's been going on out here?"

"I have that answer for you, Chief!" Bronson said. He lifted the eyeball again like a trophy. At first, Crawford thought it was a bowling ball until he grimaced at the red stringy blood vessels on the back of it.

"Oh, good lord," he said, feeling the blood draining from his face. He held his hand up to block the disgusting sight. He cleared his throat. "So, you killed it?"

"Better than that! We blew it to bits!" William said.

"Couldn't have done it without these two," Bronson said, putting his slimy hand on Riker's shoulder. The two made eye contact. Bronson's smile quickly faded when he saw Riker's livid face. Crawford even noticed the tension from where he was standing. Riker counted the officers on the police boats. There was one with Crawford and three on the other one.

"Hey boss, you were asking about what happened to Stafford?" he said. Crawford was about to respond, but instead called out "holy shit, Leonard" when Riker drew his revolver toward Bronson, who stepped back with his hands raised. Metzler gasped in shock as well.

"Riker! What are you doing?" she said.

"Whoa, buddy," the Captain said. "Look, there's no hard feelings about…"

"Oh, knock it off," Riker interrupted him. "You really think I was gonna let this slide? The three of you are under arrest. Put your hands on the edge of the boat, and keep them there." At first the Trio stood still, as if testing his patience. It was certainly tested, demonstrated by the cocking back of the revolver hammer. They slowly turned and faced the stern of the boat, placing their hands carefully on the transom.

"You really think you're going to make anything stick?" Bronson asked. Riker noticed he was still wearing that aggravating smile. Metzler stood up and put her hand on Riker's shoulder.

"What are you doing?" she asked.

"What's going on here?" Crawford's question concurred with Metzler's.

"Let's see," Riker began. "We have illegal possession and neglectful use of explosives. Hunting and killing of protected species…you know…the drift net. You blew up Stafford's boat and got Nash killed. Maybe the doc too. You nearly dropped a depth charge on my partner here. Oh! Let's not forget the best part when you pulled her gun on me while I was trying to stop you!"

"What are you talking about?" Metzler asked. Riker pointed toward the deck at her Glock. Metzler's mouth gaped in shock.

"Yeah, attempted murder," he finished. Crawford's shock and confusion was replaced with extreme anger toward the Trio. There was no doubt in his mind that Riker was telling the truth. He whistled to the nearby officers on the other boat.

"Alright guys, you know what to do," he said. The inexperienced officers looked at each other, appearing confused before finally anchoring next to the *Sea Martyr*. Riker watched as they boarded the vessel and placed the Trio in cuffs.

"Ow! God Damn, have you ever done this before?" William cursed at the officer handcuffing him. Riker suspected it may have truthfully been the case for the officer. They sat each of the suspects down on the deck and started sweeping the vessel for evidence. Crawford crossed over to the *Sea Martyr*. As he did, Bronson burned holes into Riker with his devilish eyes.

"You do realize, none of this is going to stick, right?" he remarked.

"You're going to learn a whole new meaning to the word 'stick'," Riker responded. He turned his attention to the Chief.

"Looks like you did good, son," Crawford said.

"We need divers, or somebody with a submersible to go down there," Riker said. "We need to be one hundred percent sure that thing is dead. Dredge the sea floor, whatever it takes." Crawford looked down at the disgusting eyeball down on the deck.

"You're thinking it's not dead?" he asked.

"I just want to be sure," Riker said. "That thing is so damn aggressive, and freakishly strong. It goes after anything and everything. We hit it with a big blast, but I just want confirmation."

"You have that!" Bronson called out, gesturing toward the eyeball.

"I want to see a body. We can't run the risk of that thing possibly being alive," he said to Crawford. He took a breath and started to cross over to the police cruiser. *More than that, I want a beer.* Metzler followed him over, still in her wetsuit. She had to leave her Glock behind, as it was evidence for the arrest. Over the next hour, the officers went through the fishing vessel, bagging evidence and taking pictures. After everything was done, they took the *Sea Martyr* and the suspects to the harbor.

As the adrenaline subsided, Riker could feel the shakes return. Worse than that, he thought of Stafford and Nash. They had come so close to saving them, but yet failed. He felt a strong sense of failure and regret, and also a sense of doubt. The water was filled with the shark's blood, but yet something didn't feel right. He hoped for quick confirmation of its body. He prayed for it, and praying was something he seldom did.

During the drive back, Riker took control of the helm. Crawford and Metzler easily took notice of the vessel's speed to port, but said nothing. Riker didn't say anything as well, focused entirely on shielding himself from his memories.

CHAPTER 26

The weekend was a busy and prosperous one for Merit. Per his deal with Kathy Bloom, Adam Wisk released an in-depth report declaring that the beaches were safe, and that the disaster with the sunken *Heavyweight* was an accident caused by negligence from a crewmember. The news report included details on the rumors of a shark being in the waters. He was sure to describe the fish as a great white, with no mention of Bio-Nutriunt. Also, there was no mention of Dr. Stafford's near fatal injury, as well as the death of Robert Nash. Wisk was sure to report that a team of specialists were successful in hunting and killing the shark, thus rendering the area safe. Wisk also reported the contractors would receive an honorable mention in Kathy Bloom's speech at the start of the event, set to begin at 11:00 a.m.

The first contestants began arriving late Friday night, with the majority of them piling into Merit during Saturday. With them came family members and friends, hoping to enjoy a late summer vacation. Trucks towing sailboats were parked all over town, with many of those boats already being stored in the harbor. Hotels and house rentals nearly maxed out, giving Merit an economic boost that it rarely saw. Bars were packed each night, and stores were making good use of their extra stock. In addition to the contestants and spectators, several news agencies were arriving into town. For the first time, Merit found itself on major channels, such as *ESPN*, *CNN*, and *FOX*. As per Senator Roubideaux's promise to his daughter, many of the major news agencies knew to mention Vice Mayor Kathy Bloom. Reports and articles were released, describing how she took charge during a potentially hazardous situation and managed to provide a safe and economically prosperous environment for the people of Merit. For the first time, her name was mentioned on a national level, and discussions were being made on whether she could handle higher office.

However, during the weekend there were still some questions regarding safety. Most of these concerns stemmed from the sight of a police officer patrolling the waters just outside of the swimming areas.

People would see the scarred-faced officer, riding the patrol boat with a loaded shotgun. Swimmers grew anxious from the sight, and there were a few that even stayed away from the water. Talk began to spread that a shark was out there. Bloom was quick to address these concerns, stating that the shark was confirmed dead, and there had been no recorded shark attacks in Merit Beach in over thirty-eight years. Reporters didn't press too harshly on the issue and it didn't cost the town any economic gain.

Both Saturday and Sunday, Riker kept out on the boat from 8:00 in the morning to 9:00 at night. He kept his hand on the shotgun the entire time, and his eyes never left the water. He had strongly pressed for a search for the Thresher's body, but Bloom blocked any attempt from Crawford to get the Coast Guard to do a search of the area. She believed the animal to be dead, and wanted the word out pronto to get the competitors and media into town. Riker didn't feel right about this. Something inside him felt there was still a danger. Overtime was abundant, so he had free rein to work as much as he wanted. The one up-side was that it kept his mind occupied from the misery that still plagued him.

****

The time was 9:24 on Monday morning when the shaggy-haired Spud rode his bike up the driveway to his friend Spike's house. Dressed in exercise shorts and a white t-shirt, he got off his bike and wheeled it around the back of the two-story beach house, where his spiky-haired friend was waiting. Spike stood on a dock near his father's twenty foot fishing boat, holding his drone. It was small, only about a foot-and-a-half long. Neither of their parents knew the kids had skipped high school, and Spike's father was even less aware that they planned to take out his boat.

"I was wondering if you were gonna show up?" Spike said as he watched Spud park his bike.

"Sorry, dude. I had to hide out until Ma left," Spud said. He walked onto the dock, pulling up his sagging shorts. "You sure your dad isn't gonna know about us taking the boat out? I just think he'd really flip out if..."

"Dude, quit worrying!" Spike said. "Trust me, he's got some big corporate meeting today. He was complaining about it all weekend."

"Alright, sorry," Spud said. He looked at the drone. "You sure we'll get some good overhead footage of the sailing?"

"With this new battery, hell yeah," Spike said. He stepped onto the deck of the boat with the drone. "At least as long as no stupid cops take my footage. Grab the tablet, will ya?"

"Wait, the cops came to your house?"

"Not the Merit Police. It was the State Police, claiming I had evidence of that crazy thing last week. I told them I uploaded it, but the video was taken down. Anyways, who cares now?" Spud said. Spike picked up the black tablet and stepped onto the boat. Spud stepped to the helm as Spike watched nervously.

"You do know how to drive this thing, right?"

"Oh my God, just relax!" Spud said. He started up the boat and slowly steered it out to sea.

****

It was a painful sight for both Riker and Metzler as they saw Dr. Stafford in his hospital bed. Since being admitted, he underwent three surgical hours as physicians sealed the wound, removed infected tissue, and prepared blood transfusions. Stafford remained in critical condition throughout Friday night and all of Saturday, reduced to serious on Sunday.

He was conscious when they entered his room. Metzler placed flowers at his side table. Stafford went to remove his oxygen mask, naturally trying to reach with his right arm. It took a few tries before he remembered it wasn't there anymore. He removed it with his remaining arm, pulling on the IV line. He still looked a bit pale and very exhausted. The officers could clearly see that he was emotionally distraught as well. He could still feel Robert Nash's hand in his grip, which created intense guilt. He regretted going out to kill the shark, knowing that if he hadn't his friend would still be alive.

"It's good to see you guys," he said. His voice was very weak, and his eyes were drooping.

"We're glad to see you're doing better," Metzler said.

"It's gonna be a while before I feel that way," Stafford said. "It's my fault. I had this coming."

"Oh no," Riker said. "Listen Doc, you were right about the Trio. You were right about the shark. You were right about everything." Stafford quietly gazed down at his missing appendage.

"You don't think it's dead, don't you?" he said. Riker didn't say anything. Stafford looked back at him. "I saw you on the news. It was you out in the water, guarding the swimmers."

"They wouldn't retrieve a body," Riker said. "I don't like having even an ounce of uncertainty." Stafford started to sit up. Metzler started to help him.

"Doctor, you shouldn't strain yourself," she said. Stafford ignored her concerns.

"You guys have to be sure that thing is dead," he said. "Those sailors...they can't go out if that shark is still alive." He went back down as a nurse entered the room to change his dressings and take readings. Metzler and Riker knew it was time to leave. "Remember," Stafford said to them as they exited. Both officers took one last look at him.

"We'll do what we can," Metzler said. After they left, Riker started making his way for the front exit. "Wait," Metzler said to him. "Can I make another quick visit for just a minute?" Riker nodded and she started going down a long grey hallway. He decided to follow her. To his surprise, she was heading to a completely different area of the hospital. She weaved through several intersecting hallways, until finally coming to a set of grey double doors. It was the cancer center. She pushed her way through and waved to a nurse who waved back, likely meaning they'd seen each other numerous times. He watched through the door window as she stepped into one of the patient rooms, leaving the door cracked. He entered the check-in lobby. The nurses in the center saw him and appeared a little confused, but didn't say anything. He figured they assumed he was with Metzler.

He peeked into the open doorway, seeing Metzler sitting next to the patient. He remembered she had told him about her sister, who was in for chronic leukemia. One of the nurses came up to Riker.

"It's a real nice thing that girl is doing for Tammy," she said.

"I beg your pardon?" Riker said. The nurse looked surprised he didn't catch on.

"That she took the police job to take over the bills," she said.

"Oh, yes it is," Riker said with a nod. His eyes went back to Metzler and her sister. She had a skinny build, still had her hair, and had a weak appearance. But there was optimism in her eyes. "How much does the treatment cost?" he asked the nurse.

"Oh, it can be expensive," she said. "Insurance will help her a bit, but she'll be in debt at least ninety-grand. Poor thing. Stem cell treatments are not a cheap commodity."

"They certainly aren't," Riker said. He continued to watch Metzler until she got up to leave. At that moment he moved away from the door to act as if he wasn't eavesdropping.

"Oh!" she said when she saw him standing there. She had thought he had been waiting in the main lobby. "Sorry about that. I'm all set." They both walked through the hospital back to the front exit. Riker wanted to go to the beach, having convinced Crawford that heavy harbor patrol presence was needed.

Once in the main lobby, Metzler went straight for the front entrance. Before she went out the door, she realized Riker wasn't at her side. She stopped and turned around, seeing him back in the lobby. He was staring at one of the television monitors. His expression was a mix of shock, confusion, and anger. She walked back to see what he was watching. The television had the local broadcast of the sailing event. Reporters had spent all morning interviewing contestants, judges, and some local spectators. Currently on the screen, they were interviewing Kathy Bloom. However, Riker wasn't watching her, rather he was looking at who was behind her. Beau Bronson stood with his arms crossed while Bloom answered some generic questions. Standing behind him were Emi and William, who had a smug look on his face, clearly eyeballing the female reporter's cleavage. Bloom started answering a question regarding safety.

"Thanks to dedicated honest fishermen like this group here, we can assure one-hundred-percent safety in this event," she said.

"What the hell is this?" Riker said through gritted teeth. He started storming out the lobby door. "Who the hell let them out?" Metzler almost had to sprint to catch up with him.

"Do you think Crawford knows about this?" she asked. They entered their patrol vehicle. She barely shut her door when Riker started speeding out the hospital drive.

"He's the chief," Riker said. "Of course he knows. Unfortunately, I suspect it wasn't his choice." He flashed the lights and floored the pedal. Metzler gripped her seat as he whizzed past several vehicles as he made his way to the beach.

"Riker, you might want to reconsider this," she said. "I don't want you getting yourself in any trouble." He considered her advice, but kept the pedal floored.

****

The beach was heavily crowded with spectators, vendors, judges, and competitors preparing for their race. White sails crowded the harbor like a flock of seagulls. News cameras and reporters could be seen in every corner of the beach. In every direction, there were vendor setups selling cotton candy, hot dogs, popcorn, and merchandise. It almost appeared more like a carnival than a sporting event. Crawford was supervising a command center, which was simply a large white tent with a picnic table in it to set up radio supplies. In front of his tent was a large poster that read *Police*. It wasn't necessarily the most high-tech setup, but it was the best he could do. About thirty feet away, Bloom was finishing up another interview. He did his best to avoid her throughout the pre-race agendas. She had already chastised him regarding the heavy police presence and ordered him to send some of his force elsewhere.

He kept a careful eye on the Trio. He didn't think they would cause any trouble for the event, but he didn't trust them. Per orders he had received from higher office, he released them from jail the previous day. He was instructed to have all charges dropped, and all evidence returned. Bloom offered them a bit more money to stick around for the cameras, that way she could exploit them and further sell the message that the reported killer shark was dead. Once the event began in under an hour, she would present a speech from a boat to the competitors. During which, she would grant a special 'thank you' to the Trio for the services provided. Afterwards, their real services would then be no longer required and they would be on their way.

Crawford began to notice something strange with the crowd. Many people began looking inland, as if watching some spectacular event. Crawford could then see the red and blue flashes of squad car lights reflecting off people's glassware. He stepped out of his tent to see Riker and Metzler exiting the vehicle. Metzler reached in and shut off the flashers before catching up with her partner, who made a straight line for the chief.

"Oh Jesus," he complained. He knew exactly what Riker was angry about. "Leonard! Come in the tent, and I'll explain everything."

"Oh, you certainly will!" Riker said. He had no problem letting himself be heard. "What are those guys doing free?"

"God, Leonard! Keep it down," Crawford said.

"Chief, those assholes tried to kill me when I was diving, and they tried to shoot him with my gun," Metzler said. Crawford felt double teamed.

"I know! I know!" he said. "Believe me, I know! I tried to fight it, but I can only take it so far." He took a breath, and Riker and Metzler waited for him to explain further. "I got a personal visit from a representative of Senator Roubideaux... you know...HER daddy." He swiftly pointed in Bloom's direction. "They ordered the Trio released. Apparently, they didn't want to risk them talking about the truth of the Thresher to get out of jail. They apparently have a history of keeping their mouths shut if paid to." Riker nodded, knowing that Crawford had no choice in the matter.

"I see," he said. He looked into the crowd, and also looked out into the water. He was surprised to see there weren't any harbor patrol vessels out there. "Have you assigned people to be out patrolling the water?" Crawford didn't care for Riker talking to him like a subordinate, but knew where his concerns lay.

"There were some out there, but Bloom ordered they come in," he said. "She didn't want to give the appearance that there was any danger." Riker felt his temper starting to boil.

"You've got to be kidding me," he said.

"Apparently, she cares more about appearances than actual safety," Metzler said.

"She cares about how she looks on camera!" Riker said. Just as he finished speaking, Bloom stomped into the tent. She was so livid, the creases in her face made her appear truly witchlike.

"What is all of this?" she said. Her voice was just below the point of screaming. "What's with you driving up in here with your lights on? We've got reporters here! I was in the middle of an interview when they saw your flashers shining up my background!" Riker had no problem stepping up toe-to-toe with her. Crawford's heart leapt in his chest.

"Riker!" he called. It was ignored.

"What's with you telling everyone these waters are safe?" Riker said to Bloom. She backed away from him, naturally intimidated by his hostile nature. Her anger never wavered.

"Are you an idiot? These waters ARE safe! The Trio killed the shark! You should know! You were the one who went with them," she said.

"I was also there when they tried to kill ME! When they tried to kill HER!" Riker pointed to Metzler. "I was there when they killed legally protected species out there, like dolphins. I was there when they blew up Dr. Stafford's boat! And I was the one who said we needed the Coast Guard to retrieve a body and confirm the damn thing is dead!"

"Listen you shit," Bloom said. "We don't need the Coast Guard here to tell us what we already know. We don't need to give people a false sense of danger out there!"

"It might not be so false!" Riker yelled. "But you don't care about that! You're in such an uproar about appearances, interviews, media, blah blah blah. I know what you're doing! Everyone does! You're trying to make yourself look like the grand savior of Merit, and you're willing to set these people up as a smorgasbord to do it!" Crawford felt himself tense yet again, but there was also a sense of satisfaction hearing somebody confront Bloom with the truth.

"Goddamnit," she cursed him. "It's bad enough you were out there all weekend, scaring people by boating out there with a shotgun in your lap! But luckily, your being here is a mistake that doesn't have to continue. As of right now, you're no longer employed." Both Metzler and Crawford stepped forward, both expressing their protest.

"What? You can't do that!" Metzler said. Unfortunately, Bloom did hold the authority as acting mayor to give this order to any public employee of Merit.

"I sure as hell can!" Bloom said. "Keep it up, you'll be gone with him."

"You can be sure I'll be speaking with Ripefield about this," Crawford said.

"Good! And I'll tell him how it was reported that this man consumed alcohol on the job!" Bloom fired back.

"What the hell are you talking about, you crazy bitch?" Riker said.

"Mr. Bronson reported it," she said. "He also reported assault, constant interference with hunting the shark. He said you even drew your gun on him!"

"Are you kidding me!" Metzler said, just before Riker could cuss her out. "You're willing to ignore all the evidence of wrongdoing by them, but you're gonna just take them at their word for this?!"

"Kathy, this is insane!" Crawford argued.

"*Acting-Mayor*," she reminded him of her title.

"You're not *acting* like a *mayor*!" he said. "You're acting like a lunatic! You're willing to put everyone in jeopardy just to look good in front of a camera. Let me assure you, you won't be seeing much of a career in the senate!"

"Ray," Riker said, gently pulling Crawford back. He was almost in Bloom's face. "Don't get yourself fired too," he whispered. Crawford remained tense, locking his eyes on Bloom like he was marking her.

"That's enough of this," Bloom said. "I don't want to see much police presence out in the water! That's final! And you," she pointed to Riker, "get out of here!" She turned and walked away. Metzler kicked the table hard on the bench seat. She walked in front of the chief.

"Sir! You're not seriously gonna let her do this, are you?" Crawford threw his hands over his head. He felt at a loss for words.

"I...I...I don't have a choice," he said. Just then, Riker extended his arm out over to him. In his hand was his badge, relieving Crawford of the difficult task of asking for it. He reluctantly accepted it. "Leonard...I'm sorry. I don't have any choice."

"Stop apologizing," Riker said. He took a breath. "Well, my problems here are over." He walked out of the tent. Metzler followed him.

"You're done? Just like that?" she asked.

"Not my call," Riker said. He strutted through the crowd, and Metzler carefully avoided bumping into tourists as she struggled to keep up with him. "I've risked my neck for this town, and yet they still don't want to see the danger. It's not my problem anymore."

"It's not the town! It's her!" Metzler argued. "Why are you giving up so easily? This isn't you!"

"What are you talking about?" Riker said. "Didn't you hear? I'm not a cop anymore. Therefore, it's no longer my problem." Metzler was appalled. She didn't think he'd accept defeat so easily. She then considered how worn down he looked when they first teamed up that morning. He had been working all weekend by himself with nobody to talk to. It was clear he was still suffering from the effects of alcohol withdrawal. The shakes in his hands were minor, but only because he was suppressing them. It became clear to her what Riker was planning to do.

"Just don't do it!" she implored him. Riker stopped and looked back at her.

"Do what?" he asked.

"You're a good man!" she said. Her eyes looked as if they were going to start welling up. "You're a man who believes in doing the right thing! Everything you've done in the past few days; it proved that! Don't go back to a drinking frenzy! The chief doesn't want this for you. *I* don't want this for you. I know your wife wouldn't want this for you."

"For Christ sake!" Riker said. He looked as if he was going to be angry. "As I've asked before; what do you know? About anything?"

"I know by hunting the Thresher, worrying about whether it's still alive…it all helped suppress your regrets. Now that you're done, you think you need to go back to previous methods to do that." She approached him. "Please, focus on the good memories." Riker didn't say anything for several seconds. Finally, he turned and continued walking away.

"Good luck with the career," he said. Metzler didn't chase after him this time. She watched him leave until he disappeared into the crowd. She looked down to the ground in defeat and finally started back to the police tent to find Crawford.

CHAPTER 27

An hour ago, the coastal water was a clear blue surface, void of any disturbances. The tide had created normal swells of water, the sky was nearly cloudless, and a gentle breeze was brushing in from the south. It was perfect weather for the event, which was on the verge of beginning. The gentle blue surface had become covered in a huge collection of white sails. Sailing yachts had spread all over the harbor, collecting four hundred yards from shore. The mast of each twenty-foot-long sailing yacht had a number posted to it for judgment purposes. There were two contestants for each yacht. Cheers of joy echoed through the air as enthusiastic sailors were ready to set out for their big race. They had a long journey ahead of them to Bermuda, where they would check in with judges who waited there, and then circle back to Merit.

Ahead of the large group of sailboats was a red Fire Rescue vessel. On it was a crewman who operated the controls, along with the Fire Chief who stood on deck beside Kathy Bloom. She was wearing black slacks with a blue button jacket over a white dress shirt, holding a megaphone in her hands. She was completely prepared for her big moment of coverage. Most of the contestants even felt it was a bit unconventional for her to have her speech out in the water. It was hard for them all to anchor in such tight quarters, and some of the boats didn't even have anchors. However, Bloom had promised a quick speech before allowing the event to commence.

Behind her vessel was the towering black *Sea Martyr*. The sixty-foot fishing boat dwarfed all the sailing yachts and Fire Rescue boat. Many of the sailors were unnerved by the very sinister appearance of the vessel, especially the teeth of various sea creatures that lined its bow. On deck, Bronson leaned on the starboard side while looking out into the large group of boats. His black tactical pants and flannel jacket were a much-suited improvement over the blue jumpsuit he wore in the jail. His bowie knife hung at his right side, one of many items returned to him the previous day after they were released. The deck was cluttered with various items confiscated from the Merit Police Department, including a second depth charge that was propped near the ladder to the structure. Bronson checked his watch, waiting patiently for Bloom to give her speech. Looking down at her on the Fire Rescue boat, she looked like she was going to give a campaign speech rather than a commencement sendoff. He had no real interest in the event or being recognized, but she did pay him extra to use him as a tool to promote her image as Merit's Great Savior. So he stayed, only until after his credit in the speech.

Drifting several yards away of the event were two Police Harbor Patrol Vessels. Chief Crawford stood at the helm of one of them, keeping it parallel with the other which carried Metzler along with the young Officer Perry. He was his normal enthusiastic self, happy to be teamed up with Metzler. He was given no knowledge of Riker's termination, and he assumed it was simply his turn to have the trainee shadow him. He stood at the control console, uncertain why Metzler and Crawford were keeping such a watchful eye over the event.

Despite Kathy Bloom's instructions for no obvious police presence for this specific event, Crawford insisted to Metzler that they go out. He had no clue whether the Thresher was alive or not, but he trusted Riker's gut. He would face Bloom's wrath later.

"God knows she loves the firemen," he said as he watched the red vessel rock in the water in front of the yachts. He had nothing against firemen, but her double standard of treatment couldn't be more obvious.

"You gonna catch shit for this, boss?" Perry asked in his naturally giddy way. Crawford could see Bloom on the Fire Rescue deck. For him, the contempt in her face whenever she'd glance their direction was obvious.

"No doubt," he said. Perry noticed how Metzler was cautiously looking at the water.

"You guys seem nervous," he said. "I get that sharks can be scary, but I don't think there's that much to worry about."

"Clearly you haven't seen this one," Metzler said. Perry responded with a chuckle, which quickly ended when he saw her staring at him with a furious look. It became apparent to him that this was a serious matter.

"Testing, testing," Bloom's voice echoed through the sky, boosted from the microphone. All eyes went to her as she readied to commence her speech. "Thank you all for participating in this grand race…"

****

"Okay, this is a good spot," Spike said, slowing his father's fishing boat to a stop. He didn't bother dropping the anchor, figuring they wouldn't be out for too long. They could see the event way off to the south, a bit over a mile away. The yachts looked like little white snowflakes at this distance. Spud brushed his shaggy hair back as he knelt down to examine his friend's drone. It was a DJI Mavic Pro. Grey in color, it had four flight blades to travel at speeds up to forty kilometers per hour. It had 4k quality video that would deliver a live feed to Spike's tablet.

"Dude, don't ever brush your hair that way again," Spike said. "I swear you looked just like a girl when you did that."

"Up yours," Spud said. He held the camera up to his eye. "We're quite a way out. Can this thing even fly that far?"

"Oh jeez," Spike said. "First of all, yes it can. Second…give me that!" He snatched it away. "Dude, you smeared the lens." He started wiping it away with his shirt. "Turn on the tablet, will ya?" Spud picked up the device and sat back into the fisherman's chair.

"Uh, I need the passcode," he said.

"Two-eight-three-eight-four-eight," Spike said. Spud punched in the digits and the tablet lit up. Immediately, the feed from the drone's camera was projecting onto the screen.

"Alright," Spike said. "Time to test it out. Don't drop that!" Spud shrugged. *What did I do?* Spike picked up the controller, which resembled that of a video game console. He hit a switch on the drone and began moving the thumbsticks on the controller. The four little propeller blades started rotating at high speeds, creating a buzzing sound. The drone lifted off the deck, and Spike elevated it nearly twenty feet higher. "How's the feed look?"

"Looks good to me," Spud said.

"Alright, I'm gonna move this thing higher so it's not seen too easily," Spike said, elevating the drone much higher. It was high enough to the point where it looked like a large insect hovering in the sky. "I think that'll be good. This'll give us a nice aerial shot. It should be looking right down at us. How does it look now?" Spud didn't answer. Spike took his eyes off the drone and looked his way. "Hey! How's it looking?" He saw that Spud appeared perplexed while looking at the screen. Spike walked over to him and looked at the screen. "Dude! What's so freaking…" he stopped after realizing what his friend was seeing. Their boat appeared on the screen, about the size of an acorn. Roughly thirty meters off the bow, there was something just under the surface of the water. On the screen, it resembled an enormous black torpedo, with a long snake-like tail trailing behind it. Both teenagers felt a striking chill run down their spines when they realized it was coming right toward them.

****

Riker slammed his door shut after arriving home. In his hand was a brown bag. The glass neck of a large whiskey bottle stuck out from its opening, and the brown alcoholic fluid bounced as he marched through the hallway. At the beach area, he was able to flag a cab, which drove him to the department. The driver thought it was strange that someone dressed as a cop was taking a cab ride to a police station, but didn't ask any questions. From there, he was able to commandeer his GMC and take off. The local bars didn't open until early afternoon, so Riker had stopped at a liquor store on his way home. He removed the large bottle of Jim Beam and set it down hard on the kitchen table. Before opening it, he went into his bedroom, tearing his uniform off and changing into his already worn blue jeans and black t-shirt.

His boots stomped the floor on his way back. He went right for the kitchen cabinet above the stove. He reached in to grab his personal scotch glass, but stopped as he realized it wasn't there. He scowled as he realized it was still in one of his many unpacked boxes in the living room. He felt the shakes beginning to overcome his suppression, as if they were deliberately taunting him. He hurried into the living room and began tearing open many of the boxes. Packed items started spilling onto the floor as fragments of cardboard tore from each package. With each fresh box he scooped out the contents, getting more frustrated with each failed attempt. Finally, he heard the familiar clanging sound of glass. He opened the box, pulling out a large scotch glass. He kicked various belongings out of the way as he stepped into the hallway. He marched into the kitchen and felt the solid impact of his boot against something on the floor which skidded under the table. He didn't bother looking to see what it was and slammed his glass onto the table. He popped the lid off of the bottle and poured a fifth of whiskey into his glass. He held it up to drink it, but stopped to look at it.

"Hell with it," he said. He poured more into the glass, filling it up to the rim. His unsteady hands caused a few drops to spill from the glass, trickling down onto the floor. Riker lifted his glass to drink. He stopped just before the rim reached his lips. His eyes went to the floor, seeing the silver frame of the wedding picture. He realized it was the object he kicked while walking back from the hallway. The back of it was nearly busted outward, exposing the back of the picture. A flood of guilt suddenly ran through Riker. He reached down and grabbed it, hoping he didn't damage the photo.

He turned it over, seeing the perfectly intact photo of his younger self with Martha as they walked down the aisle. Both were smiling as if the world was perfect. That day it was. He found himself staring at the picture and his mind recalled that special day. The vows, the dance, the kiss, the joy, all came flooding back to him.

"I love you so dearly. I love that you're a man who does the right thing, no matter what. Please, keep being that man." The memory of her words to him were still fresh in his mind as though they were said that morning. Gazing into the photo, Riker sparked a smile. For the first time since her passing, he embraced a good memory. He didn't even notice that the shakes had disappeared.

He set the glass down on the table, still as full as when he poured it.

He restored the back of the picture frame and placed it on his bed. He looked out the bedroom window toward the water. He knew the shark was still out there. He couldn't prove it, but he could certainly feel it. His gut never failed him in the past. No longer being an official police officer meant nothing to him. He strapped his firearm back on, grabbed his denim jacket, and marched to the door.

Before doing so, he took one last look at the glass. He emptied it into the sink and then snatched up the bottle. He marched out the front door and tossed it into the garbage can. The glass bottle shattered when it hit the bottom. Riker got into his GMC and sped out of the driveway.

CHAPTER 28

The short and stocky Officer Marley dozed in and out as he sat at his desk in the Mason Dock Police Building. Being the officer in charge of the Harbor Patrol keys was not a particularly exciting job. He often found himself using the desk computer to check his email multiple times in the same hour. The sound of tires on gravel shook him from his current doze. He sat up off the desk, his face red from the palm print pressed into it. He saw the GMC through the window and Leonard Riker step out of the driver's seat. The door opened and Marley pushed his seat back, naturally intimidated by Riker.

"Listen, Parsley," Riker said.

"It's Marley," he corrected him.

"Sorry," Riker said. "Listen, I need a key to a boat right now." He reached out his hand with the palm facing up. Marley looked down at it, then back at Riker. He shook his head.

"I'm sorry, sir," he said. "I...I can't." His voice displayed his increasing nervousness. "There was a memo released. Your employment has been terminated. I'm not permitted to issue you a key."

"I get that," Riker said. "But you need to do this. I think that shark is still out there and if I'm right, those people are gonna be in trouble." Marley shook his head again.

"I'm sorry, Officer...uh, I mean Mr. Riker. I just can't," he said. Riker leaned over the desk. Marley leaned back away from him. He started to sweat.

"Listen," Riker said, keeping his voice steady and civil. "I'm asking nicely. You do realize it's hard for me to be nice. It's getting harder." There was a slight pause to allow the words to sink in. "Now, GIVE me the keys." He extended his hand again. Marley looked at it again, then smiled nervously.

"Here you go!" He reached back and pulled a key from its hook in the metal cabinet.

"Thanks, Officer," Riker said and quickly left the building. Marley sat by himself, hoping he wouldn't get in trouble for what he had just done.

Riker climbed into the Harbor Patrol vessel marked with the number of the key. After starting the engine, he sped the boat to the open sea.

****

Kathy Bloom was only a couple of minutes into her speech when Bronson began to regret accepting the payment for staying. She spoke about the town of Merit, its many citizens and businesses, and how the National Sailing Association had created an economic boost never before seen in the small town. She also talked of its beautiful beaches and resorts. But the main emphasis was how much of the prosperity would have been lost if it hadn't been for her actions as Acting Mayor. As Bronson predicted, it felt more of a political speech than anything else.

Contestants grew anxious to be sent off. They stood restlessly in their yachts ready to bring in the anchors and sail away. The breeze brushed swiftly against the numerous white sails. Between the yachts and Bloom were a few smaller boats, where news reporters shot pictures with their cameras and held out microphones to record Bloom's speech. In a small twelve-foot motor boat, Adam Wisk was right beside the Fire Rescue boat, snapping away with a brand-new camera. As promised, he got a full insider's scoop that no other reporter in the area would get. His story would be front page again, and his name would once again start to rise in the ranks of journalists. It was as if his career was riding the wave that Bloom's career was creating.

"I know there was concern about the event after there were rumors of a giant shark," Bloom said into the microphone, followed with a chuckle. "I'm happy to tell everyone that what tragically happened to the *Heavyweight* was a simple, terrible accident. The shark was no giant monster. It was simply a great white that happened to be in the area." A hundred yards away, Metzler grimaced at Bloom's lie.

"She'll make an excellent politician," she said. "Who needs the truth when it just gets in the way of your career?" Crawford heard her from the other vessel, nodding in agreement. Bloom continued her speech.

"But for everyone's safety, *I* personally hired these great professionals to ensure the public's safety. On behalf of Merit, I would like to thank these terrific individuals, led by Captain Beau Bronson, for their swift work in tracking down and killing the shark." There was an applause from the contestants. Bronson gave an unenthusiastic wave from the main deck. Down below, Adam Wisk snapped several pictures.

Bronson stopped waving and stepped away from the side. He looked up to the superstructure, where Emi was standing outside of the wheelhouse. William stepped on deck, after hiding in the mess area.

"Are we done here?" he asked.

"Emi, start the engine!" Bronson called up to her. She answered with a respectful nod and stepped through the open doorway. A moment later, the *Sea Martyr*'s engine roared. It pounded the water with its drum like beating sound, sending vibrations through the surrounding sea. The propellers swirled water as the Trio began pulling away.

****

The bow of Riker's police vessel sliced through the water. The wind brushed against his denim jacket as he scanned the horizon for any possible sign of the Thresher. He didn't have any proof that it was still alive. In fact, he couldn't be sure himself, but the feeling was prodding the back of his mind relentlessly.

Hopefully I'm right about this. I essentially stole this police boat, he thought to himself.

The water seemed mostly flat and undisturbed, save for the ripples caused by the breeze. There wasn't any sound to be heard except the distant incoherent echoes of the sailing event.

Finally, a reflective glimmer far off in the distance caught Riker's attention. He squinted as he looked off to the northeast. It was hard to see, but there appeared to be something oddly suspended in the water. From where he was, it almost resembled a white teepee. He increased the throttle and steered the vessel toward the destination. His vessel closed the distance in a matter of minutes.

"Oh Christ," he said to himself. The bow of a fishing boat was pointing upward at a forty-five-degree angle, with the stern mostly submerged into the water. It stopped sinking midway up the deck, possibly held up by an air pocket. Gripping the helm for dear life were two teenage boys. They clung to the console as well as each other, trying to keep from falling into the water. They saw the police vessel pull up alongside theirs. Riker recognized the spiked and shaggy hair on their heads. They were the same kids with the computer footage the night of the attack. He also saw the terror that was in their eyes.

"Hey!" one of them called. "I never thought I'd be so happy to see a cop!" Riker stepped from the console to port.

"What happened? Are you kids all right?"

"There's something in the water!" Spike yelled.

"What was it?" Riker asked.

"It's that shark!" Spike yelled again.

"It attacked us! Started sinking our boat...and then...and then it went away," Spud said.

"Went away? Where? Where did it go?" Riker said. They pointed past him. Riker turned around, seeing the distant view of the huge gathering of boats. "Oh no!" He opened up a cabinet to the cargo. He pulled out a couple of life jackets and tossed them to the boys. Then he grabbed an inflatable raft. With a tug of a cord, it instantly filled up with air from a canister. He pushed it toward them, and they slid down the slope of the deck to get to it. "I'll send someone to help you," he said. The engine hummed as he throttled his police vessel, turning it toward the yachts. He pressed it to go at full speed. He snatched up the radio.

"This is an emergency call for Chief Crawford or Officer Metzler of the Merit Police Department. If either of you can hear me, acknowledge this transmission."

****

Riker's voice on the radio came as a surprise for both Crawford and Metzler. They looked at each other puzzled for a brief moment. Metzler was the first to grab her radio speaker.

"Riker? This is Metzler," she said.

"*Allison! Are you on a boat?*"

"Yes, I'm here. The chief is here too. The race is about to begin."

"I'm here," Crawford said.

"*Chief! Allison! Get them out of the water now! It's coming!*" Both Metzler and Crawford felt their hearts starting to pound in their chests. Perry felt his anxiety increase as well.

"The Thresher?"

"*It's alive! It attacked a boat with some kids on it, and they say it's heading your way!*"

Metzler and Crawford didn't waste any time. They ignited the emergency flashers on their boats and blasted the sirens.

****

The enormous beast stroked its tail hard as it moved toward its target. Its brain no longer registered the many injuries it had suffered from the blast of the depth charge days prior. The flesh on the right side of its face was almost completely gone, including muscle tissue that covered the gums of its upper jaw. Its right eye was completely removed, while its left was still intact. Its hearing was only just beginning to return, as it was completely deaf after the blast. There were still many internal ruptures of blood vessels in its face, causing it to bleed out through its gills. Its forty-foot body was peppered with red scrapes and cuts from the razor-lined net it had been trapped in. Infections had started setting into the wounds, giving some of them a brownish appearance. After being injured, it remained at the sea bottom, with only enough energy to keep moving and keep water flowing through its gills. It didn't feel pain, but it did feel an intense shock from the blast that had tremendously weakened it for a period of time.

Finally, the urge of hunger was settling in again. And with its hunger, the intense aggression it felt went into overdrive. It had found an enemy along the surface, and was in the middle of an assault when its lateral line picked up a familiar vibration. It was a deep rumbling, followed by a drum-like beat that echoed through the water. The shark didn't have a strong memory, but its brain recognized the sound. It recognized it only as a threat; an enemy that it had battled previously. The Thresher abandoned its prey in search of the enemy, following the sounds southward.

As it neared, multiple other vibrations overclouded its senses. Its brain became overloaded with different smells, sounds, and sensations. There was an abundance of prey in the water; amongst them were its enemy. Its aggressive brain sent the beast into overdrive, and it moved in for the kill.

****

Crawford sped his vessel in front of the group of yachts, nearly splashing up water onto Adam Wisk's little boat. He snatched up his bullhorn.

"Listen, everyone! I need you to IMMEDIATELY turn your boats around and head back to shore! There is an emergency situation, and I need you to turn back now!" On the Fire Rescue boat, Bloom's mouth dropped open. Her face lit up with intense anger toward the chief.

"You fucking idiot!" She realized she was still speaking into her bullhorn. She lowered it down. "What the hell are you doing?!" Her voice traveled far, even without the microphone.

"Listen, Kathy! The Thresher is coming this way! We have to get everyone out of here!"

"The shark is dead, Crawford!" she argued. She pinched her thumb and index finger in front of him. "You're about THIS close to finding yourself without a job!"

A series of panicked screams drew everyone's attention to the yachts on the edge of the group. Metzler gasped when she saw the enormous swell of water bulge from the surface. Underneath it was the black bulk of the Thresher emerging with its jaws hyper-extended. It smashed into the nearest yacht, toppling it over its starboard side. The contestants leapt into the water, shrieking in horror as the mast of their vessel barely missed them when it crashed down. An eruption of water swept over them. Metzler saw the enormous face of the beast as it propelled past the sinking vessel. There was no skin on the right side of its face, exposing the inner musculature and jaw line. Its right eye was completely gone, exposing a deep empty eye socket. Its entire body appeared mangled with cuts and lacerations. Thrashing mindlessly, the shark seemed to have gone berserk.

The Thresher smashed inward into the huge collection of boats. Its tail lashed in every direction, slashing through sails and crashing into hulls and decks. Bits of fiberglass, wood, and steel sprayed in every direction with each intense impact. A mixture of debris and carnage instantly covered the water's surface.

The crowd went into a panicked frenzy. Boat engines fired up, and the atmosphere became rife with people cursing their anchors as they slowly reeled up. Several panicked contestants didn't wait for their anchors and throttled their engines to escape. One yacht started speeding away, dragging its anchor along the sea bottom. The anchor then became snagged on a huge rock on the seafloor. The bow plunged viciously into the water and the boat ended up hooking sharply to starboard, where it collided into the portside hull of another yacht. The owner jumped clear of the impact as the tip of the colliding vessel smashed through the bow deck. Bits of wooden deck and metal debris from both engines spat everywhere.

Another team of contestants attempted escape in the same manner, dragging their descended anchor along the bottom. As they passed near other vessels, the chain entangled with the anchor chain of another boat. The chains quickly became taut, resulting in the other vessel capsizing. The escaping yacht dipped so hard into the water that it instantly flooded. Water spilled into its engine, stalling it, leaving its owners to swim for dear life.

"Holy God!" Officer Perry cried out in horror, helplessly watching the carnage. Never in his life had he experienced such devastation and chaos, and he didn't know what to do about it. He could feel himself about to panic as madly as the multiple victims.

Crawford picked up his radio speaker. "This is the Chief! All units, report to Harbor Patrol IMMEDIATELY! This is an emergency! Proceed to Harbor Patrol at once!"

The Thresher continued its relentless, mindless onslaught. It arched its back, thrashing its tail at a nearby yacht. It struck on the stern railing, sending the boat into a crazed spin. The spinning propeller broke free, still spiraling at a high-speed rotation. It twisted and turned in multiple directions in the water, fluttering like a deflating balloon. Its spinning blades hit a large piece of debris, causing it to launch out of the water like a rocket, smashing down into the console of another yacht. The impact caused the throttle to press forward to maximum speed, propelling the vessel forward. The surprised sailors on board fell to the deck as their boat rocketed into the side of another boat, capsizing it immediately. The contestants on that boat let out terrified screams as they fell beneath the waves.

Metzler pushed past Perry, who was paralyzed with shock, and took over the controls. She moved the boat towards the carnage to rescue people from the water. During this time, Adam Wisk snapped pictures of the event, filling up the memory bank of his digital camera with shots of devastation.

The Thresher felt the vibration of the incoming police vessel. With its remaining eye, it saw it approaching from its left. The shark kicked up water as it turned to face it. Metzler saw the familiar arching of its back and realized it was about to strike. She hooked the boat to the left, avoiding a direct hit to the hull. The tail struck on the starboard side, busting off the guardrail. The boat rocked hard, dropping both officers to their knees.

The Thresher didn't pursue. It moved past the stopped police vessel in favor of the other emergency boats directly ahead. It shot forward like a cruise missile. Crawford was able to move his boat out of the way. The Fire Rescue helmsman wasn't so quick to react. The Thresher struck the keel with its tail and then rammed the side hard with its fleshy head. Kathy Bloom shrieked as the boat toppled over to the right. All three people fell off the deck and into the water. The shark circled around, as if looking for a new target. Crawford drove his boat back around the stern of the capsized boat to get to the swimmers. All three emerged in a group. Bloom frantically clung to each of the firemen, babbling for someone to save her. Crawford slowed his boat alongside them, and she made sure to be the first one he grabbed. He hauled her up and she hit the deck, frozen on her hands and knees, ready to vomit. Crawford pulled up the other two men and looked down at her.

"Now there's something you can really take credit for," he said. She looked up at him and said nothing.

On the other boat, Metzler pulled herself to her feet. Perry did the same. In a wild burst of energy, he ran to the controls. He started steering the boat clear of the wreckage, aiming the bow out to open sea.

"What are you doing?" Metzler yelled. She could see the terror in the young, inexperienced officer's eyes.

"I'm getting us the hell out of here!" he yelled. "I can't handle this! There's nothing we can do!" She grabbed him by the back of his uniform and pulled him away from the console. She spun him around and grabbed him by the shoulders.

"Listen!" she said to him. "Pull yourself together! You are a cop! This is the kind of thing we do! This is the kind of thing we deal with! You may not want to be here, but it doesn't matter!" It took a moment, but the shaking officer allowed the words to sink in. Metzler could see him slowly gaining control. "Now, help me save these people!" She took over the controls and spun the vessel around to begin collecting people in the water.

****

"Holy SHIT!" William called out from the stern of the *Sea Martyr*. Bronson turned around, seeing his son staring out towards the event. Bronson saw the Thresher topple the Fire Rescue boat, then watched its dorsal fin cut through the water as it hooked around. He saw Crawford's police vessel speed away before the shark could get to it.

"What in the name of—how are you still alive?!" he exclaimed, as if speaking to the shark directly. He looked at his scattered supplies on the deck. Amongst them was his case for the harpoon rifle. He quickly started assembling it. He cursed when he found his harpoons. The explosives had been removed by the police inspectors. "Damn it! William, find the explosives and load up the harpoons!" He looked up to the wheel house. "Emi! Circle back! We've got a date with our friend!"

She saw the shark and turned the wheel. The large vessel steered to port, and its engine rumbled as it did so.

****

The Thresher felt the familiar vibration of the *Sea Martyr*. Instantly it swung its enormous body, ready to challenge its opponent. It thrust its caudal fin, closing the distance with haste.

Adam Wisk watched the huge dorsal fin slice through the water. He snapped more pictures of it, but stopped to lower his camera. He realized he was right in the path of the Thresher. The cone-shaped head emerged from the water, and the enormous black eye seemed to stare him in the face. The thrash of its tail came instantly afterward, hitting his boat so hard it sent it and him airborne. Wisk crashed down into the water, dazed and confused. He barely realized he was under water when the huge jaws chomped down on him. Air bubbles burst from his mouth as he attempted to scream. Teeth impaled through his chest plate, piercing his lungs and stomach. His body went into a spasm, causing his finger to continuously click the button on his camera. It continued to do so as the Thresher swallowed him, recording his own death on film.

The twelve-foot boat settled in the water, rolling until it was right side up. Water had filled the boat almost entirely, but it regained just enough buoyancy to remain afloat, with its sides barely over the surface.

Bronson saw the Thresher torpedo its way towards them. He saw the ravaged face of the fish, with teeth exposed even with the mouth shut. It swung its caudal fin so hard it bent its entire body. A tremor rippled through the boat as the tail hit the hull, blocked by the bull bars.

"You stupid fish! I might just have to take your other eye!" he taunted it. The Thresher circled and struck again with the same result. William appeared on deck with explosives in hand.

"Found 'em!" he said.

"Put them on the harpoons!" his father ordered. "I'll deal with this bitch in the meantime." As if on cue, Emi stepped through the open wheelhouse door and tossed down the Remington bolt action rifle. Bronson caught the loaded weapon, aimed it down and fired a shot.

****

Riker could see the disaster unfold in front of him as he raced his boat toward the other boats. As he arrived, the Thresher had moved away from the yachts to do battle with the Trio. It presented a perfect opportunity to start rescuing contestants from the water. He saw Crawford speeding his boat to shore with multiple victims loaded on deck, and Metzler had pulled up her cruiser near a large crowd of people clinging to each other to stay afloat. He reduced speed and pulled his vessel near them.

People swam over one another as they stroked their way to the police boats to pull themselves aboard. Riker reached down, hauling up one person after the other. He and Metzler made brief eye contact as she started doing the same thing. Her eyes expressed her gratefulness that he came back to help, despite everything being against him. Unfortunately, there wasn't time to express that in words. She refocused on hauling people into the safety of the boat. After he had his deck fully loaded, Riker started toward shore.

****

Blood squirted out of the fresh bullet wounds that entered near its right gill slits, received from Bronson's rifle. He shouldered the weapon for another shot, aiming the sights at the center of its head. The Thresher had clenched the side bull bar with its teeth, trying unsuccessfully to shake it free.

"Good night!" he said, starting to squeeze the trigger. The Thresher released its grip and submerged. As it dipped down, its tail swung upward and hooked over the deck. Bronson nearly fell to his side after being barely missed by the huge caudal fin. It slid back into the water like a tentacle. Bronson saw the shark's head once again, coming right toward the side of the boat. He aimed his sights again, but the shark made impact. The shaking of the vessel caused him to lose his center of aim when he fired. The bullet hit the shark in its empty eye socket, passing through downward and coming out the side of its meaty face. William saw the bullet hit the fish, and cheered when it dipped underneath. The Thresher disappeared from view and the surrounding water began to calm. Everything went quiet. After several quiet moments, William started to cheer.

"Ha ha!" he laughed. "I think that was the kill shot! I think you got it!" He jumped up and down like a member of a winning basketball team. He ran to the starboard side, still seeing no sign of the shark. He leaned over the side as far as he could and spat into the water. He started laughing hysterically again. "We got you! How do you like that, bitch!"

The water exploded upward with incredible force. Like a curtain in a stage play, it folded out of the way as the Thresher's enormous head broke the surface. Its devilish face stared straight up at William. In an instant, his laughter turned into a bloodcurdling scream. He felt frozen, with his eyes locked on the gruesome ravaged shark. It swung its tail at an upward angle, striking William directly on the neck. His head came clear off his shoulders and fell into the ocean, sinking straight to the bottom like an anchor.

Bronson turned around, just in time to see his son's decapitated body fall over the side. He ran over, seeing William's legs sticking out of the Thresher's mouth. It was swinging its head up and down, banging the dead body into the water, punishing him even after death. A flood of rage swelled Bronson's mind. He screamed like a madman and aimed the rifle. He squeezed the trigger, but the firearm simply clicked. It was empty. With his teeth bared, he threw the weapon down and picked up his harpoon rifle. William had loaded three harpoons with the explosives. He quickly loaded one into the barrel and pointed it toward the shark. The Thresher had already submerged when Bronson aimlessly fired a shot. He snatched up the remote detonator and pressed the button. A loud explosion kicked the side of the boat, sending large swells of water into the side.

Emi ran out of the wheelhouse. Seeing Bronson's enraged actions and no William on the deck, she instantly realized what happened. The mute warrior quickly felt the rage boil within her as well. She slid down the ladder and went right for the depth charge. She opened up the lid and removed a stick of dynamite. As she did so, the Thresher's tail hit the ballast, once again unable to get past the bull bars. Bronson went to the portside, loading up another explosive harpoon. He only saw the tail sink beneath the water about twenty feet away. Mad with rage, he fired the shot ruthlessly, and again detonated the charge immediately after. Another explosion kicked upward. Emi kept her balance as she grabbed a cigarette lighter from her pocket. The wick sparked after she lit it. She located the black shape in the water and chucked the stick. It splashed down about ten feet behind the shark, which had again submerged. Another explosion sent a shockwave through the water, overloading the fish's senses. It wasn't physically injured from the blast, but the force caused it to move forward at greater speed. It propelled right for the *Sea Martyr*.

Emi snatched up another stick of dynamite. She lit the wick and moved back to the side. As she did so, the shark breached, almost leaping out of the water. Its jaws came up over the edge, snapping inches away from Emi. She fell backward, losing the grip of the dynamite after hitting the deck. The shark slipped back into the water and began circling once again. Emi looked around for the stick, realizing it had landed right next to the depth charge barrel. She hurriedly crawled over to it, snatching it up. As she did, the wick burnt all the way down.

Bronson had moved to the stern to pick up the other harpoon when suddenly a huge fiery explosion consumed the boat. The dynamite had gone off, causing the depth charge to explode as well. Bits of wooden deck, metal, fiberglass, and Emi flew in all directions. Bronson was thrown down face first, dropping the remote device. The force of the blast detached the transom, which broke away along with the upper side of the deck. The superstructure collapsed and the bow completely broke away. The *Sea Martyr* was literally blown in half. The bow crumbled into unrecognizable bits, while the stern section began to lift at an upright angle as it started to sink.

****

Riker was on his way back to collect more passengers when he saw the blast. Metzler was just passing him when it happened. She stopped and turned around to see. The terrified passengers screamed when the fiery orange explosion consumed the horizon.

"Keep bringing them in!" Riker said to Metzler.

"What are you going to do?" she questioned. He gave a reluctant frown, and she realized he was going to attempt to rescue Bronson…the man who tried to kill him days ago.

"Get these people to safety," he said. He throttled his boat forward, and Metzler continued taking the passengers to shore.

****

Bronson was waist deep into the water when he was able to snap out of the daze he was in. He saw the wreckage of his ship sinking around him. As he looked upward, he could see through the back of the stern. The whole wall was gone. There was no trace of Emi anywhere, leaving him no doubt that she was gone with the blast. Looking behind him, he saw the huge black fin cutting through the water. It brushed past floating bits of boat, eventually turning to come straight at him. He weakly tried to pull himself upward on the floating stern, but the shark was coming too quickly. The cone shaped head was only about thirty feet away, and the teeth were baring.

"Choke on me!"

The sound of a boat engine drew his eyes to the west. Riker's police boat sped into view, on an intersecting course with the shark. Riker felt his whole body tense as he closed the distance between his boat and the fish. The bow crashed into the blind side of the shark, knocking it over to its left. The Thresher felt a powerful shock go through its body, and for a moment it was stunned in the water. The boat hopped over the surface after the hard hit, speeding past the wreckage.

Bronson saw the fish stunned, motionless on the surface. His hand felt the metal barb of the remaining harpoon. He snatched it up, holding it downward like a trench knife in his left hand. With his other hand, he removed the twelve-inch Bowie knife from its sheath. The blade glistened in the sun's reflection as he propped himself up to his feet, turning to face the shark in a crouched position. Riker circled the boat around and brought it close to the wreckage. He reached his hand out to Bronson.

"Captain, get on board!" he yelled.

As if waking up from a nightmare, the Thresher began thrashing its body as it overcame the shock of the hit. It arched and wildly lashed its tail, hitting the police boat from underneath. The hull was breached and water started flooding in. The engine began to fail just as the shark struck again. Riker fell backward, barely avoiding being hit in the face as the tail slashed down onto the deck and console.

Bronson leapt from the deck in a frog-like motion. He landed right beside the Thresher's dorsal fin, plunging his huge knife all the way into the back of the fish. It swung its tail and dove. Bronson clung to the shark, holding on by the handle of his knife. The water current lifted his body almost entirely off the Thresher, but he managed to stay attached. Snarling like a maniac, he lifted his harpoon over his head. With all his might, he pressed it into the thick flesh of the shark, successfully placing the barb.

The Thresher twisted upward, breaching the surface again. It twisted and turned madly, snapping its jaws in mid-air. Bronson was flung from its back, crashing down thirty feet away. He sunk until he was about ten feet under. Through the stinging water, he saw the black Thresher slowly circling him, keeping its remaining eye fixed on him. He watched it pass by, as if now taunting him. Then it finally pointed its bloody nose in at him. It took its position, and lashed its tail. His eyes bulged in pain after he was struck in the midsection. As the life fled from his eyes, he managed to look down at himself. The tail had severed his spine and muscular tissue, tearing his body completely in two. His vision faded to black as the Thresher took him in its jaws.

****

Metzler returned back to the water to collect more stragglers. She and Perry had just dropped off several, although there were still numerous people in the water. Several yachts had made their way to shore, and the beach became crowded with emergency personnel, people who needed medical treatment, and confused and curious bystanders. Metzler looked toward the *Sea Martyr's* wreckage, seeing Riker's boat slowly submerging.

"Oh no," she said. She looked around until she saw a vacant sailing yacht. She pulled the harbor patrol boat alongside it and hopped over. The engine was still running.

"What are you doing?" Perry asked.

"Just keep picking up people," she ordered him. She throttled the boat away toward Riker, leaving Perry behind to continue rescue operations.

****

Riker was able to get his boat to function enough to make his way to Bronson's last location. The Thresher emerged, and the last of the Trio's hand was sticking from the side of its mouth. The shark came straight for Riker's vessel. He drew his revolver and squeezed off three rounds. The hollow points formed a grouping on the right side of its upper jaw, drawing more blood from the ravaged face. He was about to fire off another round when the tail struck again. A large crease formed along the portside, and the vessel sank more rapidly. The Thresher's head was upon the boat with jaws wide open. Riker stepped onto the console and jumped as far as he could, leaping straight over the fish's head as it rammed the boat. He started paddling as soon as he hit the water. The Thresher bit onto the side of the sinking boat, chomping away as if attacking a whale. It spat out the inorganic parts and hooked its body around to look for Riker.

Every paddle was a struggle against the natural downward pull of gravity. He glanced back. The Thresher could feel his vibrations and had locked on to his location. He watched the dorsal fin angle in his direction.

Looking to his right, he saw the nearly submerged metal boat Wisk had been using. It was drifting about fifteen feet away. He paddled and kicked hard, cursing with each swift stroke. The Thresher was almost upon him as he climbed into the boat. Its jaws extended like a snake's. Seeing the several dagger-shaped teeth, Riker pulled on the side of the boat, turning its underside toward the shark. He clutched the seat, feeling the hard thud when the jaws bit down on the boat. The shark swam forward, kicking up speed with each swing of its caudal fin.

Riker tried hard not to swallow water. He realized he was in the shark's mouth, protected only by the metal hull of the boat. The jaws squeezed inward and the metal groaned from the pressure. The center of the boat started to buckle and the side slowly began folding in. Riker realized he didn't have any options. Fighting the current that sandwiched him to the boat, he crawled toward the bow. He gripped the tip of it and found himself looking directly at the corner of the Thresher's jaw. He pulled himself over with all his strength and somersaulted in midwater, just barely away from the shark's mouth. He swam downward a few strokes, and felt the large swish of the Thresher's tail as it passed overhead. He then swam upward.

He drew a much-needed breath after breaking the surface. He turned himself around and saw the dorsal fin still moving away. A moment later it stopped. The shark's Ampullae of Lorenzini detected Riker's rapid heartbeat. The beast turned around and moved toward him again. Exhaustion overtook Riker. He couldn't stay afloat for too long without a life vest, and there was nothing nearby to climb on. He struggled to keep his head above water while the shark moved in. Its head emerged, looking at him with its one big eye. It positioned its body and wound its tail for a strike. Riker took one last breath.

"RIKER!" Metzler's voice called out. The sailing yacht sped into view from his left, cruising right in front of him just as the Thresher lashed its tail. The side of the boat absorbed the impact. Metzler took a line with one end tied to the boat and tossed it to Riker, who snatched it up. "Hold on!" she yelled. She throttled the vessel to its top speed, dragging Riker behind it. He yelled and groaned as he skidded along the surface. The water felt like sandpaper grazing over his skin. Metzler stopped the boat and hurried to the side.

"Give me your hand!" she ordered. Riker was already reaching up. She grabbed onto him, pulling him up over the side. The feel of something solid beneath his feet was very welcome to him.

"Thanks," he said. He turned around to look for the Thresher, only to realize it was right behind them. He recognized its arched formation. "Shit! DUCK!" he yelled, pulling Metzler down to the floor. The whip-like tail crashed just over the top of them, hitting the wooden mast. Bits of wood exploded from the midsection, sending wooden shrapnel spitting downward. The mast collapsed down, pointing straight into the Thresher's open mouth. The tip of it impaled the back of the shark's throat, digging in over twelve inches. The beast twisted and turned violently to remove the foreign object. As it did, it slammed its side into the yacht and swam off. Metzler and Riker hit the water as the boat flipped. It floated upside down, and the two officers climbed onboard its underside. Riker took a few quick breaths, noticing blood on the fiberglass. He saw the red on Metzler's uniform. A piece of debris the size of a ruler was dug into her side, sunk in a few inches.

"Damn it," he said. "Don't take it out!" Metzler unbuttoned her uniform shirt, carefully removing it without bending the object. It stuck out from her left side, and blood soaked her black tank top. Riker took the shirt and pressed it around the shrapnel. He then started looking around for the shark. It was thrashing in the water about fifty yards out. "This bastard just won't die!" he said. At that moment, he saw the stern of the *Sea Martyr* drifting nearby. It was angled upward, kept afloat by an air pocket. On the very upper end of the deck was the remote detonator, safe from the water. Metzler saw it as well. The harpoon was embedded in the creature's back.

"Go! I'll cover you," she said. Riker didn't waste time. He dove into the water like an Olympic swimmer and paddled madly toward the floating stern. Metzler watched the shark as it fluttered in the water, trying to remove the mast that impaled it.

The shark lifted its head above the surface and slapped it down. The mast broke free, and blood sprayed from the back of its throat. The Thresher didn't register the pain and once again started moving toward its prey. It started slow and gradually picked up speed. Metzler clutched the grip of her Glock and put the beast in her sights.

"Come and get me," she said. She squeezed the trigger, sending nine-millimeter rounds to greet the leviathan.

Riker heard the shots and knew the shark was approaching Metzler. He was only a few feet away from the wreckage. He looked ahead, keeping his eye on the device. Suddenly a vibration in the water caught his attention, followed by a burst from some decking. The air pocket had ruptured, and the stern was now sinking downward. He stroked and kicked hard. He reached the vessel and clawed his way up the deck, trying to get the device before it would be disabled by the water. He held himself up on a board and reached for the remote. Before he could grab it, the board broke free. Riker slid downward, submerging under the water.

Metzler fired off the rounds in her seventeen-count magazine. Bullet holes exploded in red bursts on the Thresher's nose and chin. One round punched through one of its teeth, shattering it like glass. She fired her last round and the slide locked back.

"Shit." She reached for her spare mag pouches to reload. The Thresher was fifty feet away, and it reared its caudal fin, ready to strike.

The stern was sinking fast. The device was less than a foot above the surface. Riker grabbed whatever he could and pulled himself up. His hand reached above the waterline. He snatched the device and grabbed the edge of the stern with his other arm and pulled himself up, holding the device over his head. He turned and saw the Thresher closing in on Metzler, about thirty feet away from her with its head tilted and tail reared.

"You're soup!"

He squeezed the button. The charge detonated on the shark's back, erupting in a loud fiery blast. A fountain of red blood sprayed from the huge open wound. Flesh on its back and dorsal fin caught fire and the Thresher's momentum came to a dead stop. Metzler threw her arms over her face to protect herself from any projectiles that peppered the water surrounding her. The huge black shark was motionless in the water for several seconds, a gaping red hole centered in its back. Finally, its lifeless body sank under the bloody waves, disappearing into a watery grave. Metzler sighed in relief, and leaned back on the ballast.

Riker swam back over to the capsized boat. He pulled himself up next to her and did the same, exhausted. "How's the ribs?" Metzler chuckled painfully.

"Ow! Don't make me laugh," she said, clutching her injury. Riker couldn't help but start chuckling himself. Perhaps the first truly joyful laugh in what seemed like years.

The sound of helicopter blades whirling in the air made him lean back up. Several boats were coming in from the south, with several chopper units overhead.

"Hey look at that," he said. "They finally called the Coast Guard." Metzler leaned up to look. They made eye contact with each other, and again started to laugh.

"Ow! I said don't make me laugh," she said, laughing harder after saying so. They leaned back and patiently waited, chuckling the whole time until rescue came their way.

CHAPTER 29

It was early morning when Allison Metzler walked into the Cancer Center lobby at Saint Peter's Hospital. The nurse at the front desk was watching the early morning news. The T.V. screen showed Kathy Bloom ignoring reporters as she stepped into the back seat of her vehicle. News had spread quickly of her false reports to the public, and how she ignored warnings prior to the event. The nurse saw Metzler approach, and recognized her in her clean Merit PD uniform.

"Good to see you're doing better," she greeted her.

"Couple days off, I'm good as new," Metzler said. Under her clothing was a tight bandage over her left side. She'd be sore for a few days, but otherwise she was fit for duty. She held up a large binder of white forms. "I wanted to stop by before going to work." The nurse looked at the forms for Tammy.

"I'm sorry, these are for...?" She appeared confused.

"Uh, these are for initial payments for the treatment," Metzler said.

"Oh," the nurse said. She slid the forms back. "You didn't know? That's been taken care of." Metzler stared at her, completely baffled.

"I'm sorry?"

"There's already been a really big down payment," the nurse explained. "A hundred thousand dollars, on top of your insurance. You mean you didn't know?"

"No," Metzler said. She was in disbelief. "Are you sure? Who made the payment?" The nurse was surprised to be answering these questions.

"That guy you were with the other day came in," she said. "He said he wanted to put a payment down for costs up to that amount." Metzler's eyes welled up. She put the papers down on the desk, leaving them there for good and walked past the desk into Tammy's room. Her sister looked up at her with beaming eyes and a bright smile.

"Hey sis," she said. "I didn't know you were coming...why are you cry—" She stopped talking as Metzler embraced her with a tight hug. Metzler felt like a weight had been lifted from her. For the first time in a long time, she felt like things were going to be okay.

****

Metzler walked into the police station and went straight for the key vault. Midnight shift hadn't checked back in yet, but luckily a patrol car was still available. She snatched up the key and started back toward the door. As she turned around, she saw Crawford standing there. He had just entered, holding a cup of coffee.

"You're here a little early, Officer," he said. He noticed the glow in Metzler's eyes. "I see you're doing well."

"I've never felt better," she said. "I figured I'd pick up Leonard. God knows he's always late." Crawford sipped his coffee.

"I guess you'd better get to it," he said. They shared a smile and she went out the door. The chief felt a positive energy inside himself as well as he went to his office to start the day.

****

Riker had just finished gearing up in his uniform and stood in his freshly clean living room. He was clean shaven, showered, and feeling healthier than in a long time. The boxes had been finally unpacked and the beer bottles thrown away. He holstered his newly replaced revolver before taking a nice long look at the north wall. A small happy grin creased his face as he looked up at the beautiful wedding photo, which hung high over the living room.

"See you soon," he said.

He went outside, surprised to see Metzler standing in his driveway next to a patrol car. She looked at him with a glowing sense of gratitude, admiration, and affection. He shut the door behind him.

"Ready to go to work?" she asked.

"I thought I was the trainer," he said, and grinned. He strolled up to the vehicle. "Let's go. You drive this time."

"You got it," she said. They both sat into the car. Riker rolled the window down, enjoying the fresh morning air of the delightful sunny day. Metzler did the same. It seemed like a grand new beginning was in store for them as they drove off to patrol the streets.

EPILOGUE

As the ravaged Thresher's carcass sank, it became swept away in the ocean current. Warnings from the local PD and Dr. Stafford to retrieve the body were ignored by higher authorities, who wanted any evidence of the Bio-Nutriunt buried with the shark.

It drifted further out to sea, leaving a trail of blood behind it. After a while, small fish swam up to the large black carcass, taking nibbles of its flesh. Soon after, larger fish such as tuna came in with large groups. They dug into the open wounds and tore away shards of flesh. Many fish joined in on the feeding frenzy. Hammerhead sharks, blue sharks, and mako sharks darted into the fray.

Each of these creatures did not have the brain capacity to know of the product that tainted the flesh of which they ate. With each large bit taken, a tumor was ingested, secreting large amounts of experimental grown hormone. It would pass from the tissue into that of its new host once ingested.

The frenzy went wild, and the fish mainly targeted the large open wound along the Thresher's neck. Eventually the flesh was all eaten away, and the head became completely detached from the body. It sank into the deep black abyss, itself loaded with many tumors. As it descended downward, it was swept up within the many leathery tentacles of Architeuthis dux. With an undocumented mantle size of twenty feet, and arms stretching out to ten meters, it was hungry and in desperate need of sustenance. It ingested every bit of the enormous shark head. With its hunger temporarily satisfied, it rested. It waited.

CHECK OUT OTHER GREAT
DEEP SEA THRILLERS

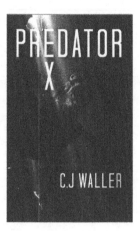

CHECK OUT OTHER GREAT DEEP SEA THRILLERS

MEGA
by Jake Bible

There is something in the deep. Something large. Something hungry. Something prehistoric.
And Team Grendel must find it, fight it, and kill it.
Kinsey Thorne, the first female US Navy SEAL candidate has hit rock bottom. Having washed out of the Navy, she turned to every drink and drug she could get her hands on. Until her father and cousins, all ex-Navy SEALS themselves, offer her a way back into the life: as part of a private, elite combat Team being put together to find and hunt down an impossible monster in the Indian Ocean. Kinsey has a second chance, but can she live through it?

THE BLACK
by Paul E Cooley

Under 30,000 feet of water, the exploration rig Leaguer has discovered an oil field larger than Saudi Arabia, with oil so sweet and pure, nations would go to war for the rights to it. But as the team starts drilling exploration well after exploration well in their race to claim the sweet crude, a deep rumbling beneath the ocean floor shakes them all to their core. Something has been living in the oil and it's about to give birth to the greatest threat humanity has ever seen.

"The Black" is a techno/horror-thriller that puts the horror and action of movies such as Leviathan and The Thing right into readers' hands. Ocean exploration will never be the same."

**SEVERED**PRESS

CHECK OUT OTHER GREAT
DEEP SEA THRILLERS

HELL'S TEETH
by Paul Mannering

In the cold South Pacific waters off the coast of New Zealand, a team of divers and scientists are preparing for three days in a specially designed habitat 1300 feet below the surface.

In this alien and savage world, the mysterious great white sharks gather to hunt and to breed.

When the dive team's only link to the surface is destroyed, they find themselves in a desperate battle for survival. With the air running out, and no hope of rescue, they must use their wits to survive against sharks, each other, and a terrifying nightmare of legend.

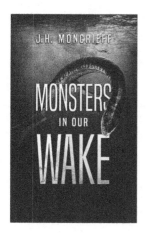

MONSTERS IN OUR WAKE
by J.H. Moncrieff

In the idyllic waters of the South Pacific lurks a dangerous and insatiable predator; a monster whose bloodlust and greed threatens the very survival of our planet...the oil industry. Thousands of miles from the nearest human settlement, deep on the ocean floor, ancient creatures have lived peacefully for millennia. But when an oil drill bursts through their lair, Nøkken attacks, damaging the drilling ship's engine and trapping the desperate crew. The longer the humans remain in Nøkken's territory, struggling to repair their ailing ship, the more confrontations occur between the two species. When the death toll rises, the crew turns on each other, and marine geologist Flora Duchovney realizes the scariest monsters aren't below the surface.

Made in the USA
Monee, IL
11 September 2024

65521696R00156